THE HEALER

The Gift of Suffering

A Novel

Book One of The Healer Saga

Terri Giles Exum

ISBN: 0692612181
ISBN 13: 9780692612187

For Makenna & Evan
You proved a smile can change the world.

Dedicated to Nicki, Melissa, and Cody. May the path that led you through the door to the other side be filled with peace and joy.
We miss you.

"The place I went inside myself to heal was the same place I found my books.
They had been waiting for me to find them."

–Terri Giles-Exum

Fall, southeast Georgia, 2002

He steps quietly through the trees, careful not to disturb the scattering of twigs or fallen leaves. For hours the hunter has stalked the six-pointer, and no matter how long it takes, he is going to bring him home. Too many times he has returned empty-handed, much to his chagrin. A modern Davy Crockett he's not, but audaciously flatters himself with the comparison, being truly mystified how the trophy bucks keep eluding him.

Reasoning if he purchased the best equipment, only the top makes and models, it would up his ante. But he has learned the hard way that experience and practice trump fancy, over-priced merchandise every time. Still, he wanted the odds stacked in his favor, like every other aspect of his hollow life.

He would love to spend more time in the woods or at the target range, but like so many others, the insatiable desire for bigger and better sank its lustful teeth deep into his psyche with a deadly grip.

Eventually there came a day when he realized he didn't own his possessions, they owned him. The pressure cooker of a job he toils in pays well enough, despite the fact it takes years off his life in exchange for every one he gives, a compromise he grudgingly accepts. A sour taste rises in his throat as he attempts to once again swallow away the bitterness.

He had good intentions this morning, he told himself. An open window inviting the glorious spring day indoors was to blame for his sudden change of plans. With the past two days a complete wash, courtesy of the monsoon rains falling from the sky, he deserved another day or three. With all the extra hours demanding his time, minus the extra pay of course, a particularly distasteful quirk of salaried life, he has earned these extra days. It wasn't his fault they don't provide more vacation days.

His lofty position afforded him the better things in life, a margin he convinces himself he's owed. To get where he is in life required cunning and manipulation, a craft he developed to near perfection. The quiet ability to maneuver around established lines of ethics was as natural to him as parking a car.

Most of society was comprised of weak-minded followers anyway, a bunch of sheep searching for a shepherd to guide them. He revels in the fact he is an important man, a free thinker, a leader with little patience for herd mentality. The reality he built for himself inside this carefully guarded façade sustains him in a world full of mediocrity.

Aunt Gayle, his mom's sister, became close friends with her doctor's receptionist. The two discovered a love of poetry and joined a local artist's group, hanging out on the weekends with other wannabes.

When Aunt Gayle discovered her new friend was unattached, her thoughts immediately drifted to her bachelor nephew.

Not fond of matchmaking, he tried to wiggle his way out of the situation but soon discovered why his aunt was such a successful businesswoman. He decided to go along with it to keep peace in the family, and besides, he reasoned it couldn't do much harm.

Walking into the restaurant that afternoon, he immediately recognized her from the picture his aunt sent to his phone. What surprised him was how much the photo failed to reveal.

Her body, or lack thereof, was strategically absent from the photos he'd received. There were no conceivable curves, no flowing legs beneath a tight skirt, just knobby knees attached to straight, boring calves that left nothing to the imagination. To top it off, there wasn't anything of interest to her upper body either, not even the suggestion of cleavage. This homely girl looked like puberty had passed her by entirely.

He also discovered she wasn't much of a talker. In fact, the conversation over dinner consisted almost exclusively from his end of the table, at least until she had a couple glasses of merlot. The wine apparently dislodged the proverbial cat, and suddenly volumes of pent-up dialogue the likes of which he had scarcely heard began to freely flow like a flood. Soon he was in a fight to just get a few words in. On and on she talked about her job at Dr. Williams' office, her family, pets, girlfriends, boyfriends—nothing was spared.

After her third glass, he could have sworn someone else had taken up residence inside her. She relayed accounts of questionable business dealings her boss had partaken in, shady tax shelters, and then the jaw-dropping revelation of his manipulation of Medicare funds. He let her continue to talk, cataloging the information. He certainly wasn't beneath using a little personal dirt on someone in order to turn a situation in his favor. Heck, everybody eventually used somebody along the way, so why shouldn't he?

If anyone questioned his sick days, he had her tucked away as a get-out-of-work-free card. When presented with the prospect of losing her job, or worse, the choice was clear: she would validate his time.

Although this was not the kind of girl he would normally seek out, she remained on his list of potential dates, until he met Tina. In two weeks his bachelor days would be behind him. Their appointment with the Justice of the Peace was set with a couple of witnesses present to make it official. No need to get wrangled into the money-making marriage machine when one hundred fifty bucks accomplishes the same thing without all the hassle and headaches.

Dry leaves crunched under his boot, bringing him out of his thoughts as he cursed himself for allowing himself to become distracted. The buck instinctively lifts its head in the air, nostrils flared, a heightened sense of awareness awakening within him. Both man and beast freeze as the chess match begins.

Although inexperienced, the man knows enough to stay downwind to avoid giving away his presence. Care was taken not to use soap or deodorant containing perfumes or fragrances. He considered using the female scent offered to him when he purchased his hunting gear, but couldn't get past the foul odor.

The hunter looks across the open meadow, carefully watching the big buck sniff the air again. The majestic animal doesn't appear to think he's been spotted, but nevertheless seems aware that something is not quite right and wisely stays within the shadows of the trees. There is safety in the forest, and the buck is old and wise enough to carefully use the terrain to mask his presence. He must trust his instincts if he is to live to father more of his kind. Just a few more steps and he will be close enough to the scattered corn he finds so irresistible.

Getting down on one knee, making sure no dry leaves and twigs are in the way, the hunter carefully prepares to take the shot. Slowly he raises the rifle and peers through the scope, making a few last minute adjustments to his scope. As the buck relinquishes his cover, overcome with the insatiable desire for the sweet golden nuggets, he commits a fatal error. The hunter readies himself to take the shot, the tension in his body mounting. A fraction of a second before the firing pin strikes the primer, he flinches, slightly altering the trajectory of the bullet. The piercing shot rings out, echoing loudly throughout the valley. However, instead of the mortal shot he envisioned, the bullet passes cleanly through soft tissue without disturbing anything vital.

He honestly expected the big buck to simply fall over, but much to his dismay, the terrified animal bolts straight ahead, carried away on wings of panic. Cursing as he gets to his feet, the hunter gives chase. His equipment was the best money could buy and he had aimed center mass, so he is baffled at how quickly the buck is moving. Surely he will keel over any minute now.

The buck crests a small ridge and gains speed going down the other side. The hunter had taken steps to keep fit, which enables him to make it to the ridge shortly after the buck. To his horror, he sees a road straight ahead, a fact that evaded him until now. In its panic, the deer is headed directly into the path of a truck, the only vehicle on this lonely stretch of highway. The two are directly on a collision course if something doesn't change. The hunter quickly ducks behind the crest, watching helplessly as the events unfold before him.

He sees a man in the driver's seat looking at something next to him, unaware of the imminent danger just ahead. The hunter raises his weapon and fires a round into the air, hoping to alert the driver, but his efforts are in vain. The man looks up just as the buck crosses directly in front of his speeding truck. With a sickening crunch of metal and bone, machine and beast collide. In that brief moment, the truck is relinquished to the forces of nature as it races uncontrollably off the road and onto the rugged landscape. A tire explodes as it smashes into a rock lodged at the base of an embankment, flipping the truck onto its side. Like a toy, it bounces and careens end over end, deep into a nearby ravine until it finally comes to rest on all fours at the muddy bottom.

Staring in disbelief at the devastation before him, the hunter timidly steps from his hiding place. Travelling down the ravine he abruptly stops at the sight of a pale, lifeless hand dangling out of the driver's window. He tries to look away, but a morbid desire pulled from the deepest of primal places commands him to indulge in the carnage.

Movement inside the vehicle startles the hunter as a shock of fiery red appears behind the broken glass. The driver's head wobbles helplessly before coming to rest against the steering wheel, causing the horn to blare out its deafening sound of danger. A battered face looks out of the window and directly at the hunter. Their eyes lock, and in that one horrific moment, the enormity of the situation descends on him like an avalanche.

The hunter is unable to move or even breathe; his mind a frozen jumble of frenzied thoughts rocketing inside his head, sending him into a cold panic.

Instinctively he reaches for the cell phone in his pocket and clumsily flips it open. Soft light bathes his hand in a warm glow as he stares at the screen in stunned disbelief at the enormity of what just happened.

As his trembling hand reaches for the keypad to dial 911, somewhere within his frazzled brain, a primal thought forces its way past the hysteria, awakening his will to survive. That's what this is all about, survival of the fittest. Only the smartest survive, that's what Darwin taught, he tells himself. As the shock of what has just occurred begins to subside, his mind begins a whirlwind of activity. He has to think his way out of this situation. He knows for certain he cannot be tied to this place, not today, not ever. Quickly he closes the phone, hands so slick with sweat he almost drops it, and puts it back into his pocket.

Frantically he looks to see if anyone else is around. To his relief, he sees no one. His entire time in the woods, he had never seen another living soul, except for the one lying dead in the truck. Oh God, he can't think about that.

The need to get out of here as quickly and quietly as possible takes over, putting an end to his erratic thoughts. Focusing all of his energy on the task at hand, everything falls away except one consuming thought: survival.

There are no witnesses to tie him to the scene; no one even knows he is here. If he runs back to his truck now and drives away, when the police investigate they will conclude that the entire scene was nothing more than a tragic accident caused by a deer running out in front of a vehicle. The papers are filled with stories like that every day.

Following the pattern of his contemptuous life, he flees the scene, hoping anonymity will be his only witness. Within a couple of minutes he descends over the ridge and is gone. All evidence of his part in the incident wisps away like steam trailing from a boiling pot of water. It was as if a ghost had appeared and disappeared without a trace.

CHAPTER ONE

One year later

Through a shadowy haze, I see myself walking through an elaborate maze of dusty corridors. I have no idea where I am, but the longer I walk, the more confused I become. Each new turn leads nowhere, and like the layers of this strange and desolate place, I find myself drawn deeper into despair. Anxiety, like a terrible suffocating vine, creeps into my every thought. I shuffle to a dusty wall and lean into its cold hardness. Closing my eyes, I cover my face with my hands and slide to the floor.

A measure of calmness settles in as I rest on the floor, causing me to open my eyes in the hope of seeing something other than the dreary sameness of the abandoned schoolhouse.

I must find my way out of here, I thought as I push myself back up. My feet feel like cement blocks, but I force them to move on.

I continue walking the long hallways in search of someone, anyone, but each new bend leads to another empty corridor. The lighting is poor, making it impossible to see very far. Goose bumps form on my neck and trail down my arms as I fight to stay calm. *Focus. You can do this.*

Doors line the hallway, but so far have yielded nothing. I stroll through the cafeteria and imagine what it must have been like before this place closed its doors.

The eerie silence and sheer emptiness overwhelms me. I continue on, hoping to see something I missed my last time through.

Another fork appears as I turn the corner. I am certain it was not here before. Did I take a different way this time?

Something rolls under my foot; I look down and see a broken pencil. Picking it up, I blow off the dust and hold it in front of me. Dropping it, I watch as it tinkles to the floor, dancing around like a lizard on a hot plate, before coming to rest. Its sharpened end points toward the left and I take this as a sign.

Starting down the dark corridor, I see a metal door on the far side that leads outside and push against it. Years of rust and decay summon their strength, but ultimately allow me passage.

My excitement at finding freedom is quickly diminished as I step out into an even darker and depressing courtyard. All color has drained away like that of a lifeless corpse siphoned of blood. Everything is so gray and desolate, I could just as easily be standing on the surface of the moon. There is no trace of life here either—no birds singing, rustling of leaves, not even the chirping of a cricket. No sound whatsoever. I never knew silence could be so deafening.

Wait, what was that? Something fluttered just beyond the wall and I bolt toward it.

Peering around the corner, a velvety wing comes into view. Stepping closer, I see the shape of a giant lunar moth. Its wings are enormous and the most incredible shade of blue I have ever seen. Woven into the wings are intricate patterns of lavender, green, and gold. In any other setting this creature would be spectacular, but here, in this hellish place, it is beyond imagination. I stand in awe of its beauty, afraid any movement will scare it away. It seems to detect my presence, but does not seem to be frightened. My chest grows warm as I feel an unmistakable bond form between us.

For the briefest of moments I look away to see if there are others I might have missed. Turning back, the moth is now inside of a small metal cage. Where did it come from and who put it here? Great waves of anger wash over me. Who would do such a thing? I look for a way to open the door, but find myself unable to free the latch.

To my horror, the moth begins fighting to escape, its wings slamming against the sides of the cage. Desperation sets in as I frantically search for a way to help my little friend. Sticking my stubby fingernail in the keyhole I try to pry it loose, but it refuses to give. I look on the ground to see if maybe a key fell out and is lying in the dirt somewhere.

As I crouch down, something stabs me in the leg. Quickly standing back up, I shove my hand into my pocket and feel sharp metal bump against my flesh. What is that? Pushing aside my confusion, I quickly pull it out and am shocked to see a key resting in my hand. I drop to my knees, stick the key into the lock, and feel the tumblers give way. Unhindered, the door springs open.

To my horror, the moth's beautiful wings are gone. Tattered stubs are all that remain. Every trace of the beauty they held just a moment ago is gone. Tears flow down my cheeks as I look down with pity at the poor helpless creature. Then for a reason I can't quite comprehend, I feel like I have lost a sacred part of myself.

Suddenly I am standing on the other side of the courtyard. From this vantage point I watch as my moth tries to fly, but it struggles to maintain even this lowly altitude. Soon it falls back to the dusty ground, exhausted and defeated.

With disturbing clarity, the reality of the situation becomes abundantly clear. A lifetime of regret and sorrow sweeps over me as the revelation finds its mark. I now understand that I am not observing another creature, I am looking at myself.

With a jerk, I sit up straight in bed. Shaking my head, I try to clear the haze and confusion. The familiar surroundings of my room slowly appear, causing me to realize I had lost myself inside of another dream. Intensely exotic dreams are nothing new to me and often the emotions of the place follow me back.

An uncomfortable bulge presses beneath my leg as I pull a twisted mess of sheets from under me. If I had a nickel for every time this happened, Mom would never have to work again. A sour knot grows in my stomach as I think about her search for a second job. I honestly don't know how she manages to hold it together. She claims if it weren't for God, she'd never make it. I wonder if she ever considered that God was the reason she's in this mess to begin with. If he hadn't let Dad die, life would be good again.

The morning sun is just beginning to break through the curtains, bathing the room in peach and golden hues. More awake now, I sit up and rub my face. I hear Mom making breakfast in the kitchen like she always does on the weekends. The mouthwatering smell of pancakes and bacon work their magic, helping me forget about where I have just been. I'm glad that twilight journey is over.

Reaching down, I feel the soft fur of my dog, Trixie, glide under my hand, reassuring me I'm in the right place. She looks at me with those big chestnut eyes, instinctively knowing I just had another grand adventure without her.

"Mornin,' ole girl, wish you had gone with me. Man, what a nightmare," I say as I ruffle her fur. She licks my hand and beats her tail against the floor. I swear she understands everything I say.

Climbing from under my crumpled sheets, I make my way to the door and let her out.

Turning to straighten my bed, I see a figure materialize from the shadows. As weird as this might sound, I've seen it so many times now that I hardly even raise an eyebrow.

This one is smaller than most, only a few inches tall. One thing about these visitors is they are always unique. One time they might be huge like a gorilla, and other times tiny as a bee.

This one looks at me intently, like I need to pay attention. To what, I have no idea. From down stairs I hear the familiar chime of the clock and turn to look down the hallway. When I look back, the angel, or whatever it is, has vanished.

Shaking my head, I walk into the bathroom as old memories of Dad follow me.

I see the two of us about two years ago, walking into a yard sale we spotted one morning on our way to the hardware store. While waiting for the light to turn green, our attention wandered to the tables piled high with all sorts of junk and decided to turn in. If Mom had been with us, she would have kept a tight leash on Dad, but she wasn't, and I didn't care. He was known for bringing home all kinds of Saturday morning specials. Mom learned right away not to even let them in the house. His treasures came from a garage, and in the garage they would stay.

Following behind Dad that morning, I recall how the sun reflected off his head, bringing out the deep copper and gold highlights of his auburn hair. I've seen people with red hair and others with orange hair, but never anyone with the color of his. It was unique and in a class all by itself. A mix of copper, auburn, and gold blended together in its own unique signature. No one else in his family had hair like his, so the joke was we needed to check out the mailman. The only one who didn't think it was funny was Grandpa.

Meandering around aisles of tables covered with old books, chipped bowls, and countless other relics of someone else's life, the usual gawking began. Heads always turned to look at the man with the unusual hair, so he was used to people staring longer than was generally considered polite. His even temperament and good looks didn't hurt either. He stayed lean and strong, even after most people his age started carrying around a spare tire or two. Staying active was important to him, so we were always busy fixing something or looking for our next big adventure.

On the next table, I spotted a big cast iron frying pan. Touching Dad's arm, I tell him it would be great for cooking the catfish over the fire instead of using palmetto sticks.

We walk around the table to get a better look and notice it had more than its share of battle scars. It was hard to find a spot that wasn't damaged. No telling how many tough noggins this thing has cracked.

Dad laughed and said, "You boys couldn't hurt it, that's for sure." Turning it over he saw they were asking only three dollars for it. He handed it to me and said, "I get to sample the first fish."

I start to protest, but he cuts me off with a punch in the arm and says, "Before you say anything, I've already cleaned enough fish to qualify for free samples for the rest of my life, boy. Besides, you're it!" and jumps to the other side of the table.

Ever since I was a little kid, tag has been our favorite game. It was the only one to hang on past the age when most kids thought it was dorky to play games with their parents. Something about being tagged last was far too appealing to pass up, even if it was only with your old man.

I try to move around the table, but he moves with me, just out of reach. Then Dad and I spot it at the same time and our stupid game is forgotten. There on the next table is a wall clock with a picture of a bare-chested Indian holding a spear defiantly over his head. A large gray wolf stands at his feet, looking up at the Indian. In the background, tall, snowcapped mountains complete the picture. It was way beyond awesome. By the look on our faces, you would've thought we had found a Rembrandt or Picasso. Dad set the clock to 9:00, and when he did, a short wind-flute melody chimed loud and clear. I knew at that moment we were about to be the new owners.

Like me, Dad was a big fan of any kind of Native American stuff, especially the Seminoles, since he spent time with them when he was about my age. His dad worked close to a reservation for several months of the year, so he and his brother and sister got to play with the Indian kids pretty often. He said they were very kind and generous people and treated them like family. After his dad found another job, they didn't see them very often, but remained close through phone calls and the internet.

The first time I met his Indian friends, I thought they would look like ones from the old movies. I figured they still wore moccasins, fancy vests, and maybe had a few feathers sticking out of their hair. When they walked in wearing jeans, t-shirts, and tennis shoes, I was surprised how ordinary they looked.

When I was younger, Dad and I scouted around Lake Okeechobee and found arrowheads and other artifacts, which he kept in an enormous display case. When he found stuff like this clock, he brought them home and hung them in our garage where his shop was.

Mom wasn't very big into gaudy things like this clock (in her opinion), messing up the décor of the house. Not that she didn't appreciate his affection for his Native American friends, she just didn't want that stuff cluttering up the house. I knew she wasn't going to like this thing one bit. Dad just smiled at me as we climbed back into the truck.

I reached over, smacked him on the arm and told him he was it, and all the ways Mom was going to kick his butt. He snorted a laugh and punched me back.

Sure enough, Mom hated it. When he hung it in the living room she tried to block him, but wasn't quick enough. He pointed out that it was the only thing that actually represented something he liked. All the rest of it was hers, and she should relax a little and let him have this one little thing. After a few more words jostled back and forth, a little kiss on the cheek, and a flash of that crooked smile she found so irresistible, the clock stayed.

For days afterward, when it delightfully announced the next hour, she cringed and threatened to throw the hideous thing out after he was gone, having no idea it would happen so soon. I'm sure if she could take back those words, she would. Now that he's gone, it's become her favorite piece of junk. She wouldn't part with it any more than she would with one of us. Twenty-four times a day now, we are reminded Dad is no longer here.

The clanging of plates from downstairs brings me out of my thoughts. Mom still wants us all to eat together at the table like we did before. She says it's important for us to stay close, especially now. The four of us had supper together when we were home, but as we got older, it didn't happen as often. Now Mom wants to make sure to keep it going for as long as she can. I'm fourteen, almost fifteen, and my younger sister, Mary, is nine, still just a kid.

There's always lots of work to get done on the weekends, so we need to get cracking right after breakfast if we want any free time later on. There's always something that needs fixing, like our lawn mower that was already over the hill when we got it. Heck, everything we own is old, but just like Dad, I can sweet-talk it into sticking around a lot longer than the manufacturer intended. That's what Dad always said.

My dad and grandpa taught me how to fix practically anything that has an engine. Ever since I was old enough to hold a wrench, I've helped them create "Metal Magic," as Grandpa says. His garage is where I learned most of it, a place we fix or create all kinds of engines, machines, and gadgets. He keeps it very organized and knows where every tool is. He's collected tools over the span of sixty years and has so many I could never count them all.

Looking into the mirror again with water dripping from my chin, I rake my hand through the mop on top of my head. Talk about bed head. Golden highlights mingle with the dark brown hair underneath as they cascade down onto my forehead. Girls at school tease me about having appointments at the beauty shop to get them so perfect. Nope, this is all Mother Nature.

Eyes the color of cinnamon, a little bloodshot around the edges, stare back at me. Mom tagged me with the name "honey bun" after they settled on this color when I was about a year old. It was cute when I was little, but now it's just embarrassing.

After drying my face, I amble down the hallway, straightening my wrinkled shirt. This one has a pattern of feathers scattered all over, most of them creased and mangled after following me on another midnight escapade. Mom knows how much I like outdoor-themed stuff, so when she comes across something like this, she buys it for me. Most of my things have animals or Native American pictures on them, my personal favorite. The toothbrush holder by my sink is a rowdy bunch of smiling raccoons holding hands, and silver baby opossums fasten my shower curtain to the rod with their wiry tails. We even found some towels with wolves howling at the moon on them. I can let my mind wander to these uncomplicated wild places and forget about everything else. They keep me in a good place.

My sister's door is shut, which is kind of unusual. We sleep with our doors open almost every night to let the air circulate better. Knocking on her door, I stick my head in to make sure she's awake.

We never really fought much before Dad died, but like any brother and sister, we had our moments. Now that he's gone, we watch out for each other more, kind of like Dad did when he was here. I guess we're missing him in our own way, not sure exactly how to deal with it.

Mary went to bed not feeling too great, like she ate some bad food or was coming down with a bug. I get the feeling in the pit of my gut this might be more serious. Maybe it's the different smell of her room or the way the light reflects off her damp hair; it's hard to say for sure. I know some mornings she wakes up a little sweaty, all of us do here in Florida where the humidity can be like walking through pea soup.

I take a few steps into her room and notice a wet ring on her pillow where her head had been resting. She looks up at me with those big brown eyes that remind me so much of Dad's. I feel my heart squeeze inside my chest at his memory for the second time this morning. "Stay focused," I silently remind myself, like I have to do often, as I gently pull back the blanket. She looks at me with a weak smile and tries to pull herself up. I tell her to lie still while I feel her forehead. It's hot enough to cook breakfast on. The vibrations from her body start to paint a picture inside my head.

"Hey little s-sis', you t-trying to get out of work t-today or s-somethin'," I say playfully. The only thing that flows from my mouth without a hitch is a whistle.

"My belly really hurts," she says, holding her arms over her stomach.

As soon as my hands made contact with her, I knew something bad was brewing. The vibrations are becoming more focused on the lower right side of her abdomen.

About three years ago, I began to detect things about other people by placing my hands on them. It scared me at first, thinking maybe I was going crazy or had a brain tumor or something. Whenever I get these vibrations, I see things that are happening inside their body. I imagine it's similar to the thing Grandpa uses to plug into a car when a warning light comes on. Information streams from the car's computer into the device that decodes it. That's as good as I can describe it.

Sometimes I get the sensation of being close to a waterfall and can actually feel the spray on my face. Other times I hear a voice call my name. It's not like the voice of someone standing next to me, but one inside my head, like a thought, but not my own. I really don't know how to explain the things I know.

No one knows about all this except my cousin Sam and our best friend Jake. They know everything about me, just like I know everything about them. I don't want anyone else to know my secret because I'm already marked as different. I'm one of "those" kids who need special help because of a learning disability (LD, short for "Loser Dude").

Reading is like a wicked game of chase, as the letters twist and change places. Speaking is just as entertaining as I stutter and sputter like a motor running on only half its cylinders. Like landmines, my words can be tripped at random, destroying anything intelligent I might have to say. When the teacher calls on me to answer a question, or worse, read out loud, my mind just locks up and suddenly I'm the Chief Executive Officer of Idiots Incorporated.

In elementary school, I went to Mrs. Prainer, the speech pathologist. She tried to help me, but I wasn't exactly her star student. Going to speech therapy was just one more way I was different. Besides, anything involving school was one giant waste of my time. After a while, the adults decided it was not going to work, so they dropped it. Mrs. Prainer is a nice lady and always tells me if I ever decide to get serious about losing the stutter to give her a call. She's easy enough to find since she goes to our church, but I'm pretty much a lost cause and don't want to waste any more of her time.

Did I mention Bryce, the guy who single-handedly makes my life a living nightmare? He's a kid from the rich section of town who has it all; looks, money, good grades, and the most popular girls in school following after him like some modern-day Casanova. Ever since the first week of middle school when I had a really bad stuttering fit, he's had me squarely in his sights. The stuttering, special-ed geek who can't even answer a simple question or read a page aloud from a kindergarten book without screwing it up. I might just as well have LOSER tattooed across my forehead. That's why I keep this "seeing" thing to myself. Heck, nobody would believe me, anyway.

I have to be careful what I tell Mom about Mary because she doesn't know either. I know I should tell her, but she's already got enough on her mind.

The vibrations tell me Mary's appendix is hot and inflamed. We can't wait long before she needs to get serious medical help. Now I understand why the angel was there this morning.

I tell Mary to lie back down while I get Mom, and to my surprise, she doesn't argue with me. This shows she really is in bad shape. I scurry down the stairs and find Mom setting the table, ready to serve breakfast.

"Morning, honey, where is your sister?" she asks, giving me a hug. I'm not a little boy anymore, but she still insists on hugging me every morning. I don't really mind as long as I don't have company over.

"S-she's upstairs in her b-bed, feeling r-really b-bad. I think sh-she's really sick M-mom and n-needs to see a d-doctor."

Mom takes a step back and looks at me a few seconds longer than I would like. She has a weird way of looking at me that makes me uncomfortable, one of those "mom" things.

"Why do you think she needs a doctor? I thought it was just a stomach bug."

This is where I have to be careful.

I scramble for an answer, and then all of a sudden something comes to mind. Several months ago a guest speaker came in, a nurse from one of the local hospitals, and showed us a video of how some medical conditions are not what they seem. I decided this sounded reasonable.

"In s-school we watched a v-video about how a k-kid had appendicitis, b-but everybody j-just thought it was a s-stomach bug, and the kid almost d-died. I d-don't want that t-to happen to M-Mary. C-could we p-please just t-take her to the walk-in clinic d-down the s-street?" I figured that sounded less stressful than asking to rush her to the emergency room, even though that was exactly what I wanted to do.

Mom steps around me and heads up the stairs to Mary's room, with me a couple of steps behind. Mom pulls up a chair next to her bed and sits down, gently folding back the blanket that Mary has pulled over her head. Her big brown eyes slowly open as Mom places a hand on her forehead.

"Good morning, young lady, I understand you're feeling a little under the weather."

I watch as Mary struggles to raise her head off the pillow.

"Easy there, hon, don't try to sit up."

Mary says, "My stomach really hurts Mom, like it's on fire or something. I think I'm going to die."

From the look on Mom's face, she realizes this is more than bad food or a stomach bug. "I think we'll take a little trip over to the clinic to see what the doctor has to say, okay, honey?"

Good, Mom is not going to "ride it out."

I help Mom get some clothes on Mary and then carry her down to the car. Even though I'm careful, every step hurts her. She tries to be brave, but a few tears trickle down her cheek.

As we leave the driveway, Mary starts screaming. I'm sitting beside her in the backseat and try to help her, but it's no use. I feel the car accelerate as we speed down the street toward the highway. We go right past the clinic and head straight to the hospital.

Arriving at the emergency room, paperwork is filled out, insurance cards are copied and verified, and finally Mary is taken to a room after waiting an hour.

A young male doctor walks in with a nonchalant look. With a plastered smile he says, "Good morning, my name is Dr. Ross. What seems to be the trouble today?" In a panic I jump right in before anyone else has a chance to speak.

"Her s-stomach is hurting d-down low on the r-right side, I think you sh-should check her ap-p-pendix."

An uncomfortable pause settles into the room as he looks at the floor instead of me. Then he clears his throat and says, "Well, I appreciate your input. I'm sure we can safely handle your sister's situation, whatever it may be. Now let's have a look see."

He crosses the room and stands next to Mary, who is even paler now and covered in sweat. His hands start at her throat, feeling the glands on either side of her neck. Satisfied, he gently inspects her abdomen. She moans softly and pushes his hands away.

"I think some blood work and an ultrasound are in order here. They'll give us a clearer picture of what is going on." Turning his head, he says over his shoulder, "Nurse, give her some morphine for the pain."

"Right away, doctor," she says as she enters the room.

"How long until the pain goes away?" Mary asks in a weak voice.

"Not long at all, so just relax, baby girl," he says gently. Maybe this guy will turn out all right after all.

The nurse gets an IV going into Mary's arm but she doesn't move a muscle, even though she hates needles. Within seconds after injecting morphine into the port, Mary starts to relax.

The nurse then takes some blood from her other arm. More vials are filled and set back into the tray. She gives Mary a gentle pat on the arm and tells her she will be just fine.

Next, a technician wheels her to another room where the ultrasound equipment is and they get to work right away. As the paddle moves around on Mary's belly, the lady carefully studies the image displayed on the screen. It looks like the Hindenburg has taken up residence in there. The young technician tries to hide her look of concern but doesn't do a very good job of it.

I ask as though I have no clue, "Wh-what do you see?"

With a practiced tone, she says, "Oh, I'm just checking a few things out. Her appendix looks a little inflamed but nothing to get too worked up about."

Yeah, right, and Albert Einstein was just a little smart.

"Okay, that about wraps it up," she says as she wheels the machine back into the corner. She gently wipes up the mess as Mary groggily looks at us.

"The doctor will get back with you as soon as he evaluates these images."

"How long b-before he s-sees those p-pictures?" I ask.

She gives me a look I despise, both pitiful and sympathetic, and says, "Don't worry, sweetie, we'll take good care of your sister." I simply nod my head.

As the tech walks out of the room, Mary looks at me with eyes filled with fear that asks the unspoken question.

"You're g-going to b-be fine, sis, these d-doctors and nurses are t-top notch and will h-have you w-r-restling alligators again in no t-time."

This is a private joke we share. A few years ago I brought home an alligator egg I found near the pond. Mary was fascinated with it and insisted on putting it in an incubation box we used for baby chicks. Several days later a baby gator emerged from the egg, hungry as a hog. Mary got on the internet and found out what to feed it.

Before long, it was following her around like the ugliest duckling you've ever seen. It even slipped into bed with her when Mom wasn't looking. Eventually it got big enough to release in the river. Mary cried for days until another critter came along to take its place.

After waiting for what seemed like an eternity, the doctor came back into the room with a look of concern.

"Mrs. Gil, we have the results from your daughter's ultrasound, and it looks like her appendix needs to come out right away. We're getting her prepped for surgery right now."

Mom looks stunned. I reach over and take hold of her hand and say, "M-Mary is g-going to be just f-fine, Mom, you'll s-see." She squeezes my hand hard and says, "I know, son, I know. I'm so glad you're here with me, honey bun." I hate it when she calls me that, but right now she can call me whatever she wants.

Mom and I are allowed to talk to Mary for a few minutes before she's taken away. Mom kisses her forehead and whispers something in her ear. Mary is almost unconscious but opens her eyes just enough to see us. She looks so small and frail lying on that big white bed.

I chuckle and say, "Hey, little s-sis, it's time for the d-doctors to change your oil and check your b-battery." A tiny smile crosses her lips as they wheel her away.

Mom and I retreat to the waiting area and sit down as an old *Happy Days* rerun plays on the TV in the corner of the room. Before long, a fat old man with a giant yellow hat is sitting on a horse next to a used car, spouting something about what a great deal he can make us.

I close my eyes and try to relax as the fat man's voice fades away. My mind searches for things to tell Mom that will ease her anxiety, but I find myself at a loss, so I just reach over and hold her hand. She leans over and rests her head on my shoulder. With each soft cry she tries to stifle, I feel like I'm losing Dad all over again.

Mom has worked so hard to provide for us since he passed away. I feel guilty not helping her more than I do. She works long hours at the drug store and has been looking for a second job, but hasn't found one yet. At least we manage to have enough to eat, between the garden and the eggs our chickens lay. Our grandparents help fill in the gaps when we run short.

Mom insists I finish school and get a decent education. She doesn't know that I plan to quit the first chance I get. There are plenty of good jobs I can get working on cars or as a handyman. Dad would not be happy about me quitting school. Oh well, it's my life and my decision. If we didn't have to read so much, I'd probably like school better. I have to concentrate so hard on forcing the words to make sense that I forget what I'm trying to read.

A grating snore brings me back to the hospital waiting room. I turn, expecting to see a chainsaw, but it's just an old lady snoozing on the other side of Mom. Next to her another woman is reading a magazine, oblivious to the racket. Tattooed across the top of her chest and just under her neck are the words, "God Bless America." Nice.

On the far side of the room, a giggling toddler runs around the lobby, deftly dodging chairs as he jostles a cupful of cereal that jumps onto the floor every few steps. A woman I assume is his mom runs behind him picking up the pieces of cereal as they fall.

In a distant corner, a couple is sitting together as the woman crochets something long and pink, while the man beside her is zoned out, staring at the television.

I don't want to be here. Too many bad memories are tied to this place. It was in a hospital just like this one that Dad was rushed to only a year ago. My insides feel like they are fighting for a way out as I recall that day.

He was returning home from a trip to South Carolina when we received the phone call that changed our lives forever. A deer apparently ran into the path of his truck and you can figure out the rest. An ambulance arrived after a woman on her way down to Miami found his smashed truck in a ravine, about twenty feet off the road. He was rushed to the hospital but had already lost too much blood. They got a pulse going at the scene, but he never regained consciousness. His heart stopped beating again before they even made it to the hospital. The police told us if dad had been found sooner, he might've survived. I can't let my mind go there. He's gone and no amount of pleading or bargaining will ever bring him back.

I feel Mom's hand squeeze mine, bringing me back to the present ... again. A doctor walks into the room and calls her name.

He tells us the surgery went well and we got her here just in time. Mary's appendix had burst just before they got to the operating room, but they were able to clean it up and she should be okay. My little sister is young and strong and I'd never forgive her if she died, too.

Two weeks later

My cousin Sam and I are spending our Saturday night camping on our grandparents' property, like we do almost every weekend. He and his family live on the far side of the property, so we've practically been raised together. The two of us are more like brothers than cousins.

We've been best friends before we could even crawl. Born on the same day and in the same hospital, our special bond started on the day we arrived. We made the local newspaper, two sisters giving birth to babies at nearly the same time, only forty-nine minutes apart to be exact (I am the oldest). The paper got us backward: I was Sam and he was me. That's okay; our souls are interchangeable, even though we look nothing alike.

He is the opposite of me in almost every way. Learning has always come easily for him, but for me it's like prying teeth from a bull. He is able to pass tests without even studying, while I have to work hard just to get a passing grade. Whole books are stored in his brain and he can just flip to whatever page he wants.

For the longest time he was withdrawn and shy, opening up only around his cousins. Spending time with Jake, our best friend, changed all that. Jake has a way with people like I've never seen.

Today, Sam and I are spending our Saturday morning helping our grandparents around their farm. Sam hasn't made it here yet since he has a little further to walk.

My mom's parents live just on the other side of an orange grove that Papa planted about forty years ago. During the early part of summer when the blossoms pop open, Mom opens all the windows and lets the sweet aroma fill up every room.

Standing in front of their house, looking at their small yard and patio, I'm amazed how many plants and knickknacks Grandma Nonnie can fit in here. It looks like a *Better Homes and Gardens* magazine on steroids.

My mom and her sisters inherited green thumbs from Nonnie, so our yard has lots of the same kinds of plants I see here, just not as many.

When I am alone, like now, is usually when I get a visit from the angels. I don't know what they really are but that's just what I call them. Sometimes they are dressed in clothes people wore a long time ago, and other times they look more like real angels with pretty wings that sparkle in the sun. One thing they have in common though, besides being translucent, is they kind of glow, like a light is burning inside them. That's how I know they are not human or even part of this world. At first it scared me, but I soon realized they didn't want to hurt me so I just let them be, a kind of live-and-let-live kind of thing. They seem to just be curious, nothing more.

I've only asked them one thing, and each time all I get is "everything will be okay." Great, but I would like a little more info than that, but each time I ask about my dad, that's the only answer I get. After a while, I just stopped asking.

The last one to come was a boy dressed in knickers and wearing a hat like golfers from the 1940s and 50s wore. He talked much more than the others and told me I was going to do great things with my life and lead many out of the darkness. Surely he has me mixed up with someone else. I can't even find my own way, much less lead anyone else.

If someone walks up, or my attention shifts elsewhere, they simply vanish. One minute they are here, and the next they are gone, like they were never here.

As I kneel down to check out an unusual bug, something reaches from between the corn stalks and pushes me over. Sitting back up, I hear feet hotfooting it away. I jump up and give chase, careful not to crunch any of the plants. Running between the rows, I sprint after him like a cheetah honing in on its prey. Making it to the open field behind the garden he zigs and zags, trying to throw me off.

One of his zigs cuts too close and I reach out and grab Sam's shirt, wrestling him to the ground. Both of us start laughing as we roll around in the dirt. Climbing back to our feet, we brush each other off.

We look at each other and laugh out loud. About the only thing we have in common physically is our small size. Dad always said we'd grow into ourselves, just like he did. What Sam lacks in size, he more than makes up for in brains. Hands down, he is the smartest dude I've ever known.

We walk to the grapevines Papa planted before we were born and pluck off a few ripe ones. They grow on an elevated trellis covering an area of about fifty feet square. Ducking under a low-hanging vine, we make it to an area where it's high enough for us to stand up straight without having to stoop. Here the vines are thick enough to block out most of the sunlight, scattering patches of light and shadow on the grass. Clusters hang every foot or so and most are already ripe. Further down, we see the muscadines still have a ways to go. They are much bigger and have a tougher skin. We snatch a few more grapes and munch as we walk back to the garden.

"Seen any Caspers lately?" he asks, bumping his shoulder into mine. Like I said, he knows everything.

"O-one was j-just here before you w-walked up."

Pushing me hard, he says, "Lucky dog, how do you do that? Maybe you're like a sea turtle or salmon that can find places a long ways away." He looks at me sideways and says with a chuckle, "Lay any eggs lately?"

"If I d-did they got f-flushed."

Laughing out loud, he says, "Maybe we should keep our eyes open for strange things climbing out of the sewer, stranger than usual anyway."

It's good to hear him laughing again. Sam's home life is not the best in the world, so he never misses the chance to do anything that takes him away from there, even if it means sweating in the hot sun.

Uncle Todd is as wide as a grizzly bear, with a personality to match. He's nothing like my dad was. It made Dad angry the way Uncle Todd treated his family, so every chance he could, he invited Sam and his sister Hope (before she left for college) to go along on our family vacations. We've been canoeing in the Alafia River, diving in the Keys, hiking in the Smoky Mountains, and fishing in the Gulf of Mexico. If something adventurous was around to do, my dad was the first to sign up.

I don't think Sam's dad is a "bad" man, but rather a very hard man to get to know, and even harder to live with. Unlike my dad, who never missed an opportunity to tell us how proud we made him, or how much he loved us, Uncle Todd is real stingy with his praise or compliments. On the other hand, he generously points out all the ways we don't measure up. He's not happy unless he griping about something.

He also thinks he is the only smart person on the planet. He's got several degrees from different places hanging all over the house, not just in his office, so whoever walks in knows how smart he is. Anybody who disagrees with him is a moron or an idiot; if you don't think so, just ask him.

Sam's brilliance should make his dad proud, but all he sees is competition. Allowing anyone, even his own son, to be smarter than he is would be more than he can handle, so he and Sam clash constantly. Sam's dad is so intimidated by him that he won't allow any kind of bond to form between them. I will never understand a man like this.

Aunt Lori, Sam's mom, is always more relaxed when Uncle Todd is away. She literally walks around on eggshells, nervous as a cricket at a blue jay convention when he's home. Sam checks his calendar religiously to see when his dad is going to be home so he can make plans to be anywhere but there.

His older sister, Hope, never regretted leaving home as soon as she could, but she still misses her little brother. They've managed to stay close over the years, even though she lives in another state. They talk almost every weekend, and keep up with each other on the Internet.

At our big family gatherings that were usually held at my grandparents' house, Dad tried to make conversation with Uncle Todd, which was not a pleasant task. It was always clear Uncle Todd didn't want to be there, but probably felt obligated because, for better or worse, he was a part of the family. Dad used to say getting close to Uncle Todd was like trying to hug a cactus. Things could get prickly real quick.

Eventually the subject of raising kids came up, and Dad would weave his way around the thorny places, reminding him that children are grown before we know it. Before long, Uncle Todd would bristle and tell Dad it was none of his business how he raised his kids and to keep his opinions to himself. Dad never seemed to get upset, which is more than I can say for me. I wanted to tell Uncle Todd what a jackass he was and how much his own kids hated his guts, but I never did. Keeping peace in the family was always important to our grandparents, so I did my part by staying as far from Uncle Todd as I could.

Most of our family get-togethers are fun, at least for us kids anyway. The events of one year in particular always make us laugh. All the adults were inside the house, eating and talking as they usually did and having a good time, all except Uncle Todd, of course. Sam and I were about eight or nine at the time and looking for something fun to do.

The neighbor across the road had one of the biggest, meanest bulls in our whole county, a fact everyone was aware of. The giant beast went by the lame name of "Big Black" because he was dark as night. He had a head so big and ugly there was no need for a guard dog.

Sam and I, along with our younger cousins, converged at the fence where Big Black was sleeping under a big oak tree. Being country kids, we learned to entertain ourselves.

On this particular day, we decided it would be totally cool for one of us to climb over the fence and take a ride on Big Black, like the rodeo guys on TV. It didn't look all that hard. The question was: who was it going to be?

Playing a game of rock, paper, scissors, I wound up on the losing end of the deal. Keeping an eye out for the adults, we got ready to rumble. All of us knew we would get in big trouble if we got caught, but it never occurred to us they would find out anyway after we got stomped into the ground.

When the coast was clear, my cousins hoisted me over the fence. Big Black was still asleep under the tree, completely oblivious to his part in our plans. Several cows were scattered here and there, but none close by. He was too grumpy for them to hang out with.

I decided the best strategy would be to sneak up quietly from behind and jump onto his back, nothing complicated. The sun was bright and hot that morning as I made my way to the tree. He was about thirty feet away, and with each step my heart beat faster. Somewhere inside a sensible voice begged to be heard, but I pushed it away. Finally I was right behind him. I was so close I could clearly hear him breathing and see his nostrils flaring.

I looked back at my cousins crowded around the fence, their faces pressed against the large mesh wiring. Whispering a silent prayer, I sprinted fast and launched as high as I could, landing squarely on his wide back.

At first nothing happened. Then all of the sudden, his head shot straight up and the most hideous sound exploded from his nostrils. I had no idea bulls could make a noise like that. I froze, too afraid to do anything but hang on. All at once he jumped to his feet, and before I knew what was happening, he started bucking. I somersaulted high into the air behind him then slammed hard into the ground. I thought for sure when I looked up, I would see a giant hoof hurling toward my face, but all I saw was dust. Apparently I scared him so thoroughly that all he wanted to do was get the heck out of Dodge.

I picked myself up off the ground, brushing the dirt off of my pants like I did this kind of thing all the time. Sauntering back to the fence, my cousins stood clapping and cheering as I climbed back over. It would be many years before we told our parents about that day.

CHAPTER TWO

Sam and I are gathering wood for our campfire tonight after finishing up a few chores at home. With acres and acres of trees at our disposal, we never have to worry about running out of firewood.

Since the weather is supposed to be clear tonight, we decide to leave the tent at home. Lying on the ground and looking up at the stars, they tell a story as ancient as the universe. For those willing to lend an ear and give them the respect they deserve, they will offer up their secrets.

Dad used to lie with us on a blanket in the backyard and tell us how the constellations got their names and the legends different civilizations came up with to tell their stories in the heavens. Then we would gaze in silence until we fell asleep.

One of the hazards we have to prepare for by staying outside instead of in a tent is not becoming a personal blood bank for the local mosquito population. Deep in the woods of central Florida they are big enough to carry off a small horse, so we keep the fire burning all night. To make sure the flame doesn't wander off, we built a huge pit lined with real bricks.

They came from one of Dad's friends who was building a house and had nearly a whole pallet left over. He gave them to us, and Dad hauled them down here in his truck, then helped us do some of the work.

Every time I look at the pit I see my dad placing the bricks. He had dirt stuck to his back and caked on his forearms but he loved it, laughing and joking as we worked. I can still smell his aftershave mingle with the pine and palmetto.

A nagging question interrupts my thoughts. Why doesn't he stop in for a visit like some of the others do? Has he forgotten about us already? Icy shards dig into my heart at the thought. Suddenly I jump as a smack on my back jerks me from my troubled thoughts.

"Hey, let's go swimming before it gets too late," Sam says, not bothering to slow down as he keeps walking, brushing dirt from his clothes. Blinking my eyes, I hesitate for a moment and say, "S-sure, cuz, let me j-just finish th-this."

We used to go skinny-dipping when we were younger, but once we hit puberty it was just way too weird. I actually had no idea what skinny-dipping was until my dad and I came across a bunch of teenagers a few years ago while canoeing down the Alafia River.

I'll never forget rounding the bend that afternoon. Dad was sitting behind me, keeping the canoe straight while I paddled up front. On the far bank sat a group of teenagers in shallow water. They were covered up to their shoulders, so we didn't think anything of sloshing up close as we passed by. People on the river are usually pretty friendly, so we drifted in.

As we got closer, I noticed there were no straps on the girl's shoulders. My dad picked up on that too because his tone suddenly changed. His carefree attitude abruptly disappeared as he told me to start paddling toward the middle of the river.

Being the ripe old age of ten, I had no idea people went swimming without any clothes on. Maybe they did this in their backyard or something, but not in public. When I asked why we weren't staying, all he said was "because I said so," with a finality that left no doubt this conversation was over.

My curiosity flew into high gear, but I knew not to disobey my dad. He was a great father, fun to be with and all, but I learned from an early age to do as I was told.

I paddled faster, but a little voice from somewhere in the back of my head, the place curious thoughts run rampant, got the better of me and I turned the oar a little sideways, letting the water pass over. At the same time, trying to act nonchalant, I glanced over at the teenagers, who by now were thoroughly enjoying the moment. The water was tea-colored, but plenty clear enough to see what was hovering just beneath the surface, and more importantly, what *wasn't.* My neck and cheeks burned as the girls started giggling. If Dad hadn't been sitting right behind me, I probably would've thought it was funny, too. Right then all I wanted to do was get out of there before he saw my face.

Sinking the oar deep into the water, I paddled with all of my might. I hear Dad mutter something about the depravity of youth as we headed downstream. Compared to the stories I've heard my aunts and uncles tell of when he was a kid, this was small potatoes, but I wasn't going to be the one to tell him that.

I stand up and follow Sam toward the spring. For a long time none of us knew it was there because it was so well hidden. My dad was the first to find it while hunting for wild hogs one afternoon when I was a baby. When I was old enough, the two of us would sneak down here together when he got off work and slide into the icy water. This was one of our favorite things to do—just sit back, relax and let the water's coolness wash away all the worries of the busy day.

I knew Dad's job was tough, but I don't ever remember him complaining. He was grateful for the mechanical job he had at the small airport in Tampa. The hours were sometimes long, but the pay was decent. He also made just about as much with his side job on the weekends, where I helped him fix whatever the neighbors managed to break. Going to the spring always reminded me of Dad.

Looking around at the surrounding woods, I wondered how much longer they will last. Nonnie and Papa are always getting offers from land developers offering to buy the property, but Papa just throws them in the trash can. He says as long as he's alive, he'll never let it go. He says a piece of him dies whenever the wilderness is destroyed to make room for more apartment complexes, shopping malls, and chain restaurants. I know how he feels; watching it disappear hurts a place deep inside my soul. I don't think they will stop until the whole of Florida is one big field of concrete from coast to coast. At least Dad's not here to see what's happening to all these beautiful places where he grew up.

Sam bumps his shoulder into mine and says, "We better cut some more palmetto sticks to roast the marshmallows with later. The last ones got old and we tossed into the fire."

"G-good idea," I say.

Sam is always full of good ideas. He is way smarter than me, but never reminds me of that fact. While he aces every subject in school, I barely manage to squeak by. He helps me with the worst subjects, like history and language arts, the stuff that requires so much reading.

My language arts teacher is a pretty black lady named Mrs. Langston. She goes out of her way to help me, which I appreciate, but she just doesn't understand. No one really does. I honestly try with everything I've got, but the words hide themselves from me, turning into a squirming, confusing jumble of symbols that don't make any sense. They are the single most profound source of frustration and embarrassment in my life. If I could find a place that didn't allow any kind of written words, that's where I would go. I've talked to Sam about quitting school a couple of times when I'm old enough, but he gets so mad that I don't bother mentioning it anymore. Like everybody else, he just doesn't understand. That's the only thing we don't share.

Sam and I head down the path through the woods that lead to the spring. Only a few people know about this place. Mom and Mary were here a couple of times, but they said the water was too cold and never bothered coming back.

We've found arrowheads and sometimes broken pieces of pottery around the spring and at the bottom, so it was probably used by Indian tribes that lived here long ago. According to Sam, the artifacts were probably left behind by the Tocobaga Indians. Unlike the Plains Indians, the Tocobagas lived in villages that had houses and a central meeting place in the middle of town. I like to hold the artifacts and imagine the hands that made them. Were they good men like my dad, or rotten ones like Uncle Todd? I wonder what kinds of things fathers taught their sons. Did their kids play in the spring? I wonder if they liked to dance around a fire, like I've seen on TV. I wonder ...

After a few minutes we reach the edge of the spring. Small flowers decorate the perimeter; we tiptoe around them being careful not to trample. Pulling off my shirt, I toss it onto a nearby branch.

We slowly descend into the frigid water, sucking in short breaths as it sprinkles tingly goose bumps all over. After a short time, our bodies adjust to the temperature like it was never even cold.

I look around at the surrounding woods and feel an intimate part of everything around us. This is my home; the place I can lose myself and find it all at the same time. Birds and bugs are the only sounds we hear besides the occasional rustling of leaves. I wish we could stay here forever. I feel so connected to my dad here, it seems like he never left.

Memories wrap around my heart like a comfortable old blanket on a cold winter day. Closing my eyes, I can still smell his favorite cologne and see that crooked smile that made me feel like I had warm honey swishing through my veins. I feel safe nestled inside these memories. I hold onto the hope that one day he will come by for a visit.

CHAPTER THREE

Without warning, brain cells from a different part of my mind come alive with a vengeance, driving away any sense of peace and calm I felt just a moment before. Like a switch turned on by an intruder, light suddenly floods into places reserved for only the shadowed, ugly, scarred, dangerous places. Without permission these thoughts are turned loose, sprung from their secret places to torment, ridicule, and humiliate.

I see myself walking home from school a few weeks ago. The straps on my backpack dig into my shoulders, making each step feel heavier than the one before. It felt like I had the entire school shoved in that thing. Letting the backpack fall to the ground, I plop down on top of it for a short break.

Normally Sam would have been with me, but he was out sick that day with strep throat. Tears form in my eyes, not from the sun or dust in the air, if I were so lucky. My ears ache from the words they allowed in that day that cut deeply. Why do they have to hear everything? Sometimes I wish I were deaf.

Mr. V, short for Volatile Vat of Vomit, or something like that, is unfortunately our science teacher. Always the charmer, he'd been in a particularly foul mood that day, a craft he has perfected into his own twisted art form. He came into the classroom with a snarl etched across his greasy face, daring anyone to cross him. I just wanted to get my hour over with. Some days were worse than others, and this was shaping up to be a real dandy. The kids who had him earlier that day gave us a heads up on the dragon that awaited us. Dread filled me from head to toe.

Science is my favorite subject, but he takes every bit of fun right out of it. Mr. V, a pudgy little man with oily black hair he combs way over to one side, what's left of it anyway. The crooked wire-rimmed glasses he constantly pushes back up his long, skinny nose makes his piercing eyes even more shifty and beady.

His shirts are always tucked into pants that are jacked up too high and held up by belts that are too tight, creating a pooch above and below. We noticed there's no wedding ring either, wondering how a prime catch like this could possibly get away. We also notice all the other teachers avoid him as much as we do. If they have to take the longer route to get to their classrooms, that's what they do. Apparently he is as popular with them as he is with us.

After the bell rang, we walked in and took our seats. The smell of burning sulfur hung thick in the air as he slithered to the front of the class. Death rays shot from his eyes as he looked across the class, sizing up his next adolescent victim. No one breathed at this point. Even if we wanted to, there's no air to breathe anyway. He opened his mouth and we all ducked, expecting to be incinerated. Instead, he said in a deceitfully pleasant tone, "People, open your books to page 176." He always calls us people, never anything like kids, guys, class, or boys and girls, like our other teachers do.

I remember the exact page number, along with the picture that was on it, the small crease across the top right-hand corner someone made, and the particular way it laid across my desk. Unfortunately, I can recall just about everything from that moment.

He looked across the class and everyone quickly buried their faces in their books or fumbled with something in their hands—anything to avoid direct eye contact. I held my breath as I felt his soulless eyes settle upon me. My face grew cold as the blood drained away, sensing the predator honing in on its prey. If only I could've been someplace more comfortable, like maybe a prison camp or firing squad.

Then I knew what was going to happen next as I felt the embalming fluid fill my veins and the nails drive into the lid of my casket, even before he bellowed another word.

With a look of great satisfaction, I hear, "Jason, why don't you read the first section for us today." I swallow hard as all eyes turn to me, feeling like a bug impaled on a piece of barbed wire. No other teacher asks me to read out loud because of my issues with words, but this diabolical fiend relishes in inflicting as much humiliation and misery as possible. Terrorists could learn a few things from this jerk.

I try to sit up straight and look at the words, these objects that have brought me so much anguish. My face feels both burning hot and icy cold all at the same time, as red blotches begin to form all over my face and neck. The pounding inside of my ears is roaring so loudly, I don't hear him as he walks up next to me. A "psst" comes from behind, and suddenly I realize the morbid beast is standing right in front of me. I expect to be burned alive right there in my seat as he stares at me with those terrible piercing eyes.

"I asked you to read the passage, right here," as he places a hooked finger on my page.

"I know M-Mr. V," I hear myself say.

Looking back down at the page, I try to make the letters stop going back and forth, but they just move faster.

"Are you mocking me, boy?"

"N-No sir, just give me a s-second, p-please."

I feel the heat building inside as his feral eyes bear down on me.

"Now, boy, we don't have all day. READ THAT PAGE!"

Everyone jumps as he yells the last three words.

Knowing there is no way I can possibly read this passage, I close my book and lay my head down on top of it, completely and utterly mortified.

I hear, "Get up, boy. Get up now."

Normally when an adult asks me to do something, I do it. The cornerstone of Southern breeding is pivotal in this regard, but for one of the rare times in my life, I refuse to comply. This jerk lives to humiliate those he has power over, taking full advantage of his position of authority, and is therefore unworthy of my respect.

All higher-order thinking disappears as my brain drops into the depths of Antarctica. Try as I might, not a single word can be snatched from inside the chaos that has turned my brain into an unmovable, solid chunk of ice. From somewhere deep in the recesses of my consciousness a primordial signal flares, causing my legs to pick me up and carry me out of the danger zone. Devoid of conscious thought, I stand and walk out of the classroom, and like a victim of prey, feel the eyes of everyone watch me as I go.

"Come back here now and take your seat," he bellows from somewhere behind me. I keep walking.

Opening the door, I step into the hallway and cover my face with shaky hands, sliding down the wall until my fanny smacks the floor.

I hear his footsteps echo toward the door, knowing he's headed my way and feel his shadow towering over me before I hear him speak.

"How dare you walk out of my classroom! Just who do you think you are? I have never been treated with such callous disregard in all my years of teaching!"

He moves in a little closer and I scoot closer to the wall. Indignant, he continues, "A third grader could read that book, and you can't do that one simple task. How on earth do you think you will survive in the real world, son? My job is to make a man out of you, not treat you like an infant. The problem is, you've been coddled and petted for so long that you can't do anything for yourself."

He paused to let that sink in. Then he carries on in a softer tone, but no less menacing. "You've been in school for ten years now, and for all of those years, you've not managed to learn one useful thing." He shifts his weight to the other foot, getting ready for the second round.

"Nothing we have taught you has stuck anywhere inside that brain of yours. As I see it, you are a waste of my time and everyone else's." Then with the most contemptuous tone he can muster, adds, "You'll never amount to anything."

I pick my head up for the first time and look into his weathered, angry face. His greasy skin glistens in the dull hallway light, illuminating deep pockmarks all over his chubby face. It's hard to imagine him being uglier than he is now, but I guess anything is possible. In that crazy moment, all I can think is: why would someone who hates kids so much ever want to become a teacher?

Then out of that thought, a zillion others dart around my brain as I try to mount a defense, but I find myself unable to lasso even one. So in my defense, I say absolutely nothing. Not a single word. I just stare at him, knowing even if I opened my mouth now, it would come out stuttering and sputtering, so I keep my words inside.

After a minute or so, satisfied his words have hit their mark, he slithers back inside his cave. I sit there in that hallway, thinking this day couldn't possibly get any worse, when Bryce comes waltzing up. Apparently, he saw the whole thing and wants to make sure to get his two cents in. Squatting down close to me he says, "Funny thing about the truth Jason, it really hurts, doesn't it?" I stare at him like the fool I feel and say nothing in my defense—again.

A devilish smile creeps across his face as he sees his words do their work. To make sure they are driven in good and deep, he tacks on, "W-what, n-nothing smart to s-say? No witty c-comeback? Oh, that's right, n-nothing in that b-brain but car g-grease," as he taps my forehead with his knuckle. I feel my hands clench as the volcano I keep pacified threatens to erupt. Then I jump as the bell rings loud and shrill. Shuffling sounds can be heard all around as kids prepare to move to their next class.

From around the corner, I hear the familiar sound of a power wheelchair and realize its Jake. To the rest of the world, it's just another kid in a wheelchair, but to his friends, it's a throne that holds a mighty king.

Hands down he is the most popular kid in school, and the gutsiest guy I've ever known. My heart sinks, realizing he's about to see me like a squashed bug under Bryce's heel. If only I could disappear beneath the floor.

Bryce and I turn to see him round the corner at the same time. I will never forget what happens next. With a look of unbridled fury, he pushes the control stick on his armrest as far as it will go and speeds toward us. The wide sturdy wheels carrying two hundred pounds of forged steel rockets forward as the distance between us quickly disappears. Jake thrusts his other arm into the air and thrashes it about wildly. Bryce and I jump at the same time as Jake starts screaming like a lunatic.

Bryce tries to get up and run but his feet get tangled as he falls face first to the floor. With the wheelchair bearing down on him, he rolls onto his back, a mixture of confusion and fear etched across his face. He tries to crab-crawl out of the way, but his hands slip and he falls hard on his butt.

Kids are coming out of the classrooms now as fingers point and giggles rise.

Flipping over, Bryce manages to find his footing and takes off down the hall with Jake right on his heels, still screaming and flailing his arm like something out of a sci-fi flick. He reminded me of Davros, the creator of the Daleks in *Doctor Who,* Mom's favorite move, going off on a tirade that struck fear into the heart of all who heard it.

Bryce darts around the corner, hair flying as he sprints away, nearly knocking over several kids. Jake finally eases off the throttle and comes to a stop. Then he turns his chair around and heads to where I am still sitting on the floor. He weaves his way through the cheering crowd, oblivious to the ruckus. His wheels are only inches away when I start to stand up, but he puts a shaky hand on my shoulder and I stop.

Before he says anything, I feel an uncontrollable giggle coming on. The thought of the biggest bully in the school being chased off by a little crippled kid is so hilarious, I can't help but laugh out loud.

"That was t-totally awesome, m-man," I say over the noise of the crowd. He allows a little smile, and then just as quickly, it disappears.

The next thing I know, he looks all the way into the depths of my soul and my breath catches in my throat. With tears in his eyes, he shows me in that compassionate look alone, he knows what it's like be crushed by the meanness and callousness of others. Jake knows that special kind of hurt and how painful those wounds can be. Then he spoke some of the kindest words I have ever heard anyone say; "Inside you are all kinds of smarts, Jason. They just haven't found their way out yet." Contained in those few little words was a gift I wouldn't trade for all of the world's treasures. I swallow hard and give him a weak smile.

Standing up, I smooth down my hair, trying to act cool as the kids start moving along to their next class. Jake sits up straight in his wheelchair, and with his best tough guy imitation says, "Yippee-K-Yay, cowboy, it's time to ride!" I salute him and say, "Yes sir," as we join the boisterous crowd.

So caught up in the details of this memory, I jump when Sam clears his throat.

"Penny for your thoughts, knucklehead."

"D-don't got no p-penny, so g-guess you're out of l-luck," I shoot back, kicking up a cloud of white sand that dances in the water around our feet.

His look tells me he knows what's going on inside that nameless place no one ever talks about. That delicate, hidden spot all of us have, deep in the recesses of our soul, where only the most profound moments of our lives are allowed to settle. The Bible refers to it as the chambers of our imagery. At least that's what Mom says, anyway, if you believe any of that stuff. Not able to look him in the eye, I focus on the soft white sand settling back to the bottom. I rub it between my toes, wishing it could scrub away the harshness and unfairness of life.

I wish we could stay out here in these woods for the rest of our lives. Out here there are no tests, no books with their despicable secret language, and especially no Mr. Vs or buttheads.

Bryce has been a boil on my butt for years. On the first day of fifth grade, our new teacher began calling out our entire name: first, middle, and last. Talk about stupid and embarrassing. She went straight down the line, oblivious to the lives she was ruining.

Bryce Hoyt Estralar is the next name she announced. More than just giggles escaped this time as catcalls and laughter bounced off the walls. Bryce was furious as he stomped his feet and yelled for us to shut up, his face scrunched up like a pug. She ignored him and kept on firing away. Maybe this lady was going to be all right after all. This was one of the few days at school that I actually enjoyed.

Jake was the one who came up with the name Butthead. BHE: Butt Head Extraordinaire. Perfect. Sam said Bryce should be a junior, since his dad is just like him. Most of us have never had any dealing with him, but the ones who have never want to again. I guess the sour apple didn't fall too far from the tree.

Tree. Yes, the tree! A smile forms on my face, as Sam's countenance takes on a curious smile. I simply say, "The t-tree house." He knows exactly what I'm talking about and his whole body begins to celebrate. Water goes everywhere as his arms beat an imaginary drum just below the surface. Then he yells, "Man, that was one sweet day."

Last year, Bryce's dad paid a company to build an enormous tree house for him. It was made of solid maple and was the most incredible thing any of us had ever seen. We'd all had tree forts at one time or another, but nothing like this. It had walls, a roof, windows, a bed, rugs, and even a real TV. We thought maybe he would want to play nice and invite some of us over to see his new place, but before the thought was even warm, he hung a sign on the door that said, "No idiots allowed." At school he made a big deal about how he and his rich friends were going to spend the weekend partying up there.

That same weekend, we were at my cousin Trey's house helping him fix the giant steel gate at the end of their long driveway. The tall posts extend about twenty feet into the air and strung between them was a fancy steel fixture in the shape of a number "3." A high wind caused it to come loose, so we got out the tall ladder to fix it. Sam and I were holding the ladder as Trey scaled the long rungs. When he reached the top and looked out across the landscape, he began laughing. Sam and I looked at each other, wondering what had gotten into him. Then Trey quickly came back down the ladder without fixing anything.

Sam said, "Uh, I thought the point of all this was to fix it."

Trey takes Sam's place and tells him to climb the ladder and then tell us what he sees. Sam just stands there, looking at Trey like he'd lost his mind. Trey points up the ladder and says, "Just go. Climb up there and look around."

Sam looks at me like Trey is up to something. I just shrug. I had no idea what was going on. He looked up at the ladder like he must've missed something and said, "Why?"

Trey just smiles and says, "You're going to love it." I push past Sam and start up the ladder. When I get close to the top, I look in all directions but don't see anything worth getting excited about. Going the last few rungs, I lift onto the highest point I can safely go, and there, dead ahead about three hundred yards away, is Bryce's posh tree house. I look at the angle of the steel rods and see all kinds of possibilities. I let out a laugh as Trey says, "I told you you'd love it!" Sam orders me off the ladder.

I giggle all the way down as Sam impatiently jumps on the ladder as soon as my feet hit the ground. He lets out a loud whoop when he gets to the top.

The three of us march back to the workshop in the back where some rescued bungee cords lay in a heap in the corner. Sam then goes behind the hen house where there are always a few old rotten eggs.

We head back to the gate and tie off the ends of the bungee cords to the top of the steel rods while Trey gets a pouch ready. Once everything is in place, we put one of the eggs into the pouch, then Sam climbs to the top of the ladder, guiding us as we pull back on the cords. This has got to be the biggest slingshot in the history of slingshots.

Trey and I move around, following Sam's directions. My arms were straining under the taut cords when Sam thrusts his arm downward and yells, "Fire!"

We let the cord go as the egg rockets from the pouch. I jump into the air, but it disappears beyond the trees and out of sight. Sam claps his hands one time really hard and says, "Too far, it went just over the top."

We load up another and let it fly. This one falls a little short. Finally, on the third try, we have the range and it finds its mark, splattering rotten goo all over the side of the tree house.

In all, we pelted fifteen eggs into the tree house that day. As soon as the eggs were gone, we removed all the evidence and finished fixing the gate like nothing ever happened. We were dead meat if Bryce ever found out it was us.

At school the next Monday, we found out that several of the eggs made their way into his tree house through an open window where they did their stinky magic. Bryce wasn't there at the time, but he had a big surprise waiting on him that afternoon. We heard he flew into a rage, kicking and tearing things up. I would've loved to have been one of the many flies on the wall that day and seen the look on his face. It took him weeks of cleaning to get rid of the odor, which you could smell from blocks away.

What we didn't know until later on was that some of the eggs that missed the tree house landed on his dad's Porsche convertible. And yeah, the top was down, of course. He was furious and demanded to know who was responsible. Heads were going to roll far and wide. We kept our mouths shut, and as far as we know, neither of them ever found out who conducted the aerial bombardment.

Sam and I smile at each other, enjoying the moment.

I would give anything to be more like Sam. It seems like there isn't anything he can't figure out. He'll probably wind up being an engineer, a scientist, or something else reserved for smart people.

Although the two of us are very different, we share the same soul. We understand each other like no one else, except for maybe Jake.

I've been hungry for knowledge all my life, curious how things work ever since my dad showed me an engine. I had no trouble learning while my dad and grandfather taught me how to fix things.

Even more fascinating was when they opened the belly of a fish to clean, and showed me how the organs were situated inside. Dad explained what each one was and what it did. If there is this much inside of a little fish, what must be inside of us?

Although we are supposed to learn these kinds of things in school, it is a different matter entirely. I've tried to learn the secret language of books, but the mystery remains hidden. That "seek and ye shall find" stuff our preacher talks about is a huge load of crapola. I've been seeking ever since I was old enough to know how, and the only things to show for it are barely passing grades and a whole lot of frustration.

I think when God, or whoever is out there, was handing out smarts, he gave Sam a double dip, and forgot to leave any for me. Then Jake's words reverberate in my head again, "the smarts just haven't found their way out." Nice words from a nice guy, but I know better. If there really is a God out there, he doesn't care about me. He doesn't care that I can't read, and speak like an idiot. God doesn't care that he took my dad from me and how hard Mom has to work now.

He doesn't care that kids like Jake are crippled and have to spend the rest of their lives in a wheelchair. No. Definitely not. I have no use for a God like that. Mom may be able to force my body to go to church, but my soul's not buying any of it. When my dad died, all faith in a merciful God died with him.

I realize Sam is looking at me, and like blood brothers, knows my thoughts like they are his own. I clear my throat and start to say something and then think better of it.

Without missing a beat, he picks up where my thoughts left off. "Hey, you had the coolest dad on the planet, man. I wished my dad was like him. I wouldn't wish my dad on anybody, except for maybe Butthead."

We both chuckle, then he continues. "I think about all the fun stuff he let me do with y'all. I don't know any other guy that would go out of his way to let another kid tag along, except maybe Uncle Wyatt. Hey, remember that time I told your dad I had never seen red clay like they have in Georgia?"

"Yeah," I say through a smile, "he c-called your m-mom to let h-her know we w-were taking a r-ride." None of us kids had seen red clay before, and without any reason other than that, we drove all the way to the state line. It was wintertime, so we got to see some snow, too. It wasn't much, but to us it was like we'd arrived in Alaska.

"How about that time we were headed to Key West, but the gas gauge was busted in your dad's old beater, so he pulled off the side of the road every now and again to poke a stick into the tank. How old was that car anyway? It was ancient before your dad ever bought it."

Dad could squeeze the last useful drop out of every machine we owned. He had a real knack for rigging things so their lifespan lasted far beyond what it should have been.

"I d-don't know, but I b-bet somebody hauled b-baby dinosaurs around in that thing b-before we got it."

"Probably so. I think I liked those trips to the Keys more than any of the other places we went. I mean, I loved going to the mountains and fishing, but those diving trips were the best."

"Remember the time we went to that island and found a little octopus hiding inside that rock just off the shore? He changed color to match the rock and we almost missed him. Then you reached your hand in."

"Yeah, and he r-reached out a t-tentacle. H-his suction c-cups kept t-trying to s-stick to m-my hand."

Sam laughs and says, "Then Tommy and Trey came over, making all kinds of racket and scared him away. That ink he spat out was awesome. I'd never seen one do that before. He sure was fast, huh?" Sam claps his hands together and shoots one out straight, then says, "He was gone in a flash."

I nod my head and let out a laugh.

Then he says, "Or how about the time we were heading back to shore in the dark and kept seeing flashes of something behind the boat. It took us a while to figure out what it was until we turned the spotlight on and saw flying fish sailing through the air. There must've been a hundred of them that night."

"Yeah, that w-was definitely a t-top ten moment. They were s-so close I th-thought some would l-land in the b-boat with us."

"I know, me too. Those were some killer times. If your dad hadn't taken me along, I would've missed it all."

The smile slowly drains from his face as he says, "Man, I wish I could go with you guys for Thanksgiving, but I can't get out of going to my grandparents' house."

Most people like their grandparents, and it's not like he doesn't try, it's just so much work to be around them. They argue, fuss, and fight so much you'd think they hate each other. Their house is immaculate and, heaven forbid, anyone touch anything. I feel for him, but at least he has Nonnie and Papa, and my dad's parents who treat him like they are one of their own.

"I know, m-man, but you can g-go with us the n-next time."

This year I am going with Trey and his family on a diving trip to the Keys instead of staying home for Thanksgiving. Mom doesn't want to go and has to work most of the time. Mary will be at Grandma and Grandpa's house so she'll be happy. That's always her favorite place to be anyway. It's like a party store, an adventure park, and ice cream shop all rolled into one. Every visit is like a celebration.

Sam's grandparents' house is more like a museum or china shop. You have to be quiet, not touch anything, and feel like you are not nearly as important as the precious treasures on display.

"I'll b-bring back a l-lobster tail for ya, cuz," I say, splashing water in his face.

Shaking the water from his hair he says, "You better, dork." Then his face grows serious. Oh crap, I hate that look and know where it's headed.

"Hey Jason." Here it comes. "I know you miss your dad, but things are going to be okay. I mean, I know times have been rough lately, but they will get better, you'll see."

I just stare into those hazel green eyes of his, as a lock of curly chestnut hair falls into his face. I do not want to go here, but at the same time, realize I need to. I'm sure Sam knows this too; he knows everything.

"I know," I say (even though I really don't). "With M-Mary getting s-sick and needing s-surgery, m-money is even t-tighter than it was b-before, so I don't know how l-long it will t-take b-before things start to get b-better. At l-least the house is p-paid off s-since Mom used the r-rest of the insurance m-money after the f-funeral for th-that. I'll be old enough to f-find a j-job s-soon, and can h-help p-pay some of the b-bills. I f-figure why w-waste anymore of my t-time in school."

I knew this would make him mad, but I just couldn't hold those words back any longer. They were like shards of glass in my belly that needed to escape before they tore up everything inside.

The smile has completely left his face, but his eyes remain soft and kind. "Jason, you are so much smarter than you realize. Just because you have a little trouble reading doesn't mean you're stupid. If you give up on school now, you have no future—none. Next year we'll be sophomores, then it won't be long until we graduate."

In a harsher tone than intended, I say, "In case you haven't n-noticed, I'm n-not exactly on the d-dean's list. I just barely p-pass every y-year by the sk-skin of my t-teeth. I hate that p-place and have n-no use for anything there, except for you and J-Jake. Guys like you that are so s-smart would n-never understand."

As soon as the words left my mouth I wished I could call them back. Sam has never been anything but understanding and kind. He has helped me every year, which is probably the only reason I have passed to begin with. He ignores my stuttering like it doesn't exist and treats me as his equal. Most everyone else looks at me and either suppresses a giggle at the stuttering fool or in sympathy for the poor sputtering idiot. I don't know which one I hate worse. I look at him and see him staring down at our feet.

"S-sorry man, I d-didn't m-mean it like that," I say softly.

"I know, it's just I worry about you sometimes. I wish you could see what we see. There's a whole world of brilliance inside of you fighting for a way out. You'll just have to find your own path, that's all."

Then very slowly, emphasizing each word, he looks at me hard and says, "You are not stupid." He breathes in deeply, tosses his head back, and lets the air out slowly. Then he looks at me and says, "One day you are going to do something phenomenal with your life, Jason, you wait and see. I know it and so does Jake."

Jake, now there's a guy who can't be conquered. Never in his life has he met a stranger. A natural gift of gab mixed with a gentle, easy-going way makes him everybody's best friend. He has them eating out of the palm of his hand, including the teachers. My mom says his ability in the art of persuasion is so refined he could talk a fencepost into buying a lifetime supply of toothpicks.

In the fearless department, nobody out-classes him. He just doesn't let things get to him like other people do. Everything is good, and if it's not right at the moment, it soon will be. "Just let go and let God," is what he likes to say. I might not agree with that last part, but he does, and that's all that matters. Hands down, he is the happiest person I know and one you would think least likely *should* be.

Jake can do a lot of things himself, but a lady at school helps him. Her name is Mrs. Wendell and she's been with Jake ever since first grade. She talks about her grandkids a lot and always shows us new pictures, which is kind of boring, but I guess that's what happens when people get old. They run out of fun things to do and spend all their time talking about their grandkids.

About once a month she makes us cookies and banana bread out of what she calls "good stuff, not the junk you kids eat." Sometimes she even mixes in pureed spinach to turn the cookies bright green, which are our favorites.

Some of the kids hide their donuts and cupcakes from her for fear of getting another lecture. She even grows stevia plants in her yard to use in place of sugar, which is kind of cool. I mean, if you could just go outside and pick a few leaves to sweeten your food that would be pretty neat. She's kind of a weirdo, but is nice enough, and so far hasn't hassled us too much, so for an adult, she's okay.

I know Sam mentioned Jake's name to put things into perspective. Jake's life certainly is not easy, but he makes the most of every single day. He may have a million bad things running rampant through his life and only one thing that's good; yet somehow he manages to focus on that one good thing and forgets all the rest. I don't know how he does it. He's always happy, which is the reason we became friends in the first place.

Since our first days together, I realized he was far more than he seemed on the outside. Even when some of the younger kids ask what was wrong with him, he never let it get to him. I don't know how he does it, 'cause it would bother me in a big way. I have nothing but respect for him because I know he has to work way harder than everyone else, including me, just to get by, which he does without a single complaint. That's more than I can say for me or just about anybody else I know.

Because of his condition, Jake has had multiple surgeries. I'll never forget when he had his hands worked on because they wouldn't work right, and after they healed up, he had to make his fingers move again. That's the only time I ever saw him cry. Sam and I did everything we could to take his mind off the pain. We told him stupid jokes and laughed about goofy stuff like spirit week at school that year.

We were supposed to dress up like one of our favorite sports teams, so that's just what we did. Together we came up with The Jake & Company Water-ski Dudes. I'm sure this wasn't what the teachers had in mind, but we didn't care. The three of us wore swim trunks and decorated his chair like a speedboat. We brought skateboards for me and Sam to ride the waves then attached two ropes to the back of his chair. He pulled us all over the school that day. The three of us cleared the hallways, the kids clapping and cheering as we whizzed past. Mr. Nucciol, our principal, came out of his office with a stern look, but once he saw it was Jake, he joined the crowd in cheering us on. It was, after all, sports day.

Hopefully one day he might be able to walk on his own, but for now he spends most of his time in a wheelchair, and a couple hours a day in a walker, plus therapy sessions two or three days a week. I can't imagine having to deal with all the things he's had to live with, but he just takes it all in stride.

As for me, I have been in and out of resource classes for the past five years because I can't read. I have what they call "dyslexia," which means you are dumb and can't read like everyone else. My parents put me on medication, but I stopped eating and began losing weight. I was angry and even more frustrated than before. My skin felt like it wanted to slither right off my bones. My grades came up a little bit while taking it, but not much. The letters still moved all over the page but I could keep a train of thought longer. The mood swings, insomnia, and lack of appetite were reason enough to take me off of it.

Mrs. Wendell, the lady at school who helps Jake, always tried to get me to eat something for lunch, but she didn't understand how hard it was to eat even just a little bit of food. I would usually give in and swallow a bite just to get her off my back. I know she meant well, but like everybody else, they just don't understand.

Jake is spending the night with Sam and me next weekend at our house. We usually spend at least one weekend a month together, either at his house or mine. Jake's mom taught mine how to do some basic stuff for him so he can feel comfortable spending the whole night with us. A hawk screeches overhead, and suddenly I realize I have disappeared inside my thoughts—again. I blink a few times and see Sam staring at me, a tight smile on his face.

I swallow hard and decide to tell him about last night. "I h-had another w-weird dream."

He grins and says, "You should write down all those nutty dreams of yours. One day they could make a movie about them and you'd be a millionaire! I don't know anyone who has crazier dreams than you, man."

I tell him about the moth nearly killing itself trying to get out of the cage. "That's exactly h-how I f-feel every day in s-school, Sam! I'm b-beating my w-wings inside a b-box I'm not m-meant to b-be in."

A serious look crosses his face and he's quiet for a moment then quietly says, "Jason, I know all the stuff you've had to deal with really bites, but you are so much smarter than that. I also know you are not a quitter."

Reluctantly I nod my head. I wish I had as much faith in me as he does.

Ready to change the subject, I say, "Hey, I w-wonder what T-Trey and Tommy are up to t-tonight. M-maybe they can c-camp with us after w-we hang some more s-stuff."

Halloween is only a week away and a major deal at their house. Their entire family goes all out making it THE place to be in Riverview.

Trey and Tommy are brothers and live close by. Trey is a year older than us, and Tommy is two years older. They are by far the coolest guys around, besides Sam and Jake. Trey already has a 4 x 4 he and his dad have fixed up for when he turns sixteen next year. His dad lets him drive it around the pasture, as long as he doesn't do donuts and burnouts where the cows graze. Papa gets upset if he tears up the grass his cows eat.

"That sounds like a first class idea, cuz," he says with a wide grin. "You're always full of good ideas."

Trey is the original wild man and loves to camp every chance he gets. Tommy is a bit more subdued, but cool in his own way. We spend a few more minutes in the spring and then head back.

As we make our way to the campsite, I think despite how different Sam and I are, how well we get along (except for our opinion of school). His green eyes and dark complexion compared to my sun-bleached hair, naturally pale skin and cinnamon eyes, it's hard to believe we are related. No one would ever guess how white my skin really is since I keep a year-round tan, courtesy of the land of perpetual sunshine. The only evidence is well hidden in places no one but me is allowed to see.

Sam is a little taller and leaner, but I still outweigh him by a few pounds, now that I don't take meds anymore. None of these differences matter, though; we are one on the inside.

He grew up frustrated, angry and shy, but around me, Sam is the captain of cool. His real self comes out around his cousins—a funny, intelligent, quirky genius able to figure anything out, except for making his home a happier place.

When Jake joined us in first grade, Sam and I took to him like fish to water. Over time, Sam learned to open up with more people than just me and our cousins. Before long, everyone knew the great guy that only a few of us saw. Jake has that kind of effect on people.

When we make it back to camp, I grab a bag of chips to share on our way to Trey's house. There's still plenty of daylight to get things arranged with the decorations. We'll be up all night having a blast anyway, especially if Trey and Tommy come along.

After rounding a bend in the road to their place, we notice the house that has been up for sale forever finally sold. The family is unloading their belongings from the moving van and carrying them inside. Sam and I stop to see what the new owners look like.

At first all we see is a woman carrying a bag of groceries inside. She is tall and thin with short brown hair, and looks to be around Mom's age. The defeated way she walks is not just from the exhaustion of a long day; this is something much deeper than that. It's like someone who has lost all purpose or hope. I've seen this before, and it scares me down to my bones.

Dark circles under her eyes only add to the misery carved into her sad face. Beneath it all, I think at one time she was a pretty lady, but now she just looks worn down to nothing.

From the rear of the moving van, a tall lean man walks out carrying a box labeled "kitchen" on it. He looks up at us as he makes his way down the sidewalk toward the house. I reach up and touch my hat. He nods back with a thin, stiff smile. Not exactly your friendly sort, but who cares. It's not like I plan on getting to know them anyway.

Just before we start to walk away, I take one last look and notice a girl about our age looking at us from one of the windows at the end of the house. She has dark hair pulled back in a ponytail, and even at this distance, I can see the blueness of her eyes. I nudge Sam and motion toward the window. We stop and stare back. Her face is like a blank page, totally unreadable. The girl turns away and disappears into the dark room. We take one last look at the house and keep on walking.

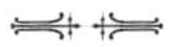

The moving van arrived two weeks late. *We should've been done with all this boring moving stuff by now,* Jesse thinks to herself. It's hard enough changing schools during the first year of high school, and then not getting the house they were hoping for. Their "new" house is tiny, and not even remotely close to anything civilized.

Her stepdad found this little paradise while surfing on the internet and decided it was too good to pass up. Who needs a mall within a day's drive, anyway? "I'm going to hate this place," she mutters to herself.

The only thing that makes this rat hole worthwhile is the fact she is only an hour away from Aunt Jean, her favorite person in the whole world. Living just a couple of blocks away in Georgia, she had a place to run to when life got crazy. Aunt Jean was never too busy or too tired when Jesse showed up on their doorstep, almost always unannounced. When Aunt Jean moved to Florida earlier this year, Jesse was devastated. Now they are only fifty miles apart. Her mom promised they would visit this weekend, and she's been counting the days ever since.

A loud noise rattles her door as she hears, "Jess, can you give me a hand with this table?"

"Be right there, Mom!" she yells through the closed door. *It's not like I have anything better to do, like arranging my busy social calendar.* Disgusted, she pulls another handful of clothes out of the box and shoves them into a drawer.

Just before turning around, movement outside the window catches her attention and she looks up to see two guys about her age staring at her. *Oh, great, a couple of local yokels gawking at the new kid on the block. This is probably the highlight of their entire week. Bet they're related, like everybody else out here. I hope we're not here long enough to get chummy with any of them.*

Turning away from the window, she heads toward the door. Peeking back over her shoulder, she sees the boys have lost interest and continue on down the road.

After helping her mom with the table, she returns to her room. Reaching into the pile of soft clothing on her bed, her hand bumps into something solid and realizes immediately what it is. Her heart skips a beat as hundreds of emotions bleed through the padding and straight into her heart. Pulling it out carefully, she removes the layers of paper and gazes into the two smiling faces that look so much alike, especially the piercing blue eyes. She was only twelve when this picture was taken, and notices right away how much she's changed. So many things have changed since then. Looking into the mirror, she notices her hair is a few shades darker and her cheeks a little more hollow. The smiling handsome soldier in his crisp uniform sends daggers through her heart.

Mom snapped this just before he boarded the plane for Iraq: Dad in his uniform, proudly standing with his little girl. Now that face is relegated to distant memories captured behind a lifeless piece of glass as cold as death itself.

She was daddy's special girl, a fact that she will never allow to fade. The sun rose and set on him as far as she was concerned. He was her number-one fan, her greatest hero. He taught her how to fight, survive in the wilderness, fish and camp, and most importantly, how to love. Why did he have to die? Why did that bomb have to go off under his Humvee? All these questions of hers and no one with answers. Carefully she takes the photo out of its packing and quietly places it on her dresser.

CHAPTER FOUR

As Sam and I walk down the long driveway to Trey's house, we see the giant five-foot ghosts and bats already hanging from the trees. After a few more days, this place will rock.

I can't help but grin as we pass under the towering entrance, the fancy "3" hanging proudly.

As we get closer, the gingerbread house comes into view. I call it the gingerbread house because back in elementary school, every December our art teacher let us make gingerbread houses for Christmas. An entire table would be covered with big bowls of candy—every color under the sun—along with sprinkles, chocolate chips and anything else she could think of.

Choosing our favorite candies, we glued them all over the outside with vanilla icing until every square inch was covered. I always tried to imagine how wonderful it would be to live in a house like that. Anytime you wanted something good to eat, all you had to do was just reach out and pluck a piece.

All day long I couldn't wait to get home and scarf down my beautiful creation, imagining how delicious it was going to taste.

No matter how good I thought it was going to be, it always tasted better. It made me feel all warm and squishy from my nose all the way to my toes. I get that same awesome feeling here.

Trey is out back under the hood of his truck with his hat turned backward, pulling on a wrench. His two beagles, George and Gracie, know us so well they don't even bother to bark as we walk into the yard. Trotting out to meet us in the driveway, we kneel down and scratch them behind ears that flop all over their heads. These two are as close to me as Trixie. She's at the vet today getting her shots; otherwise, she would be right here with us. The beagles look around for her since we are always together.

Trey doesn't see or hear us approach, so like any decent cousins, we take advantage of the situation.

Sam and I quietly sneak up as he strains against a wrench. I reach over and pull a long skinny stalk of grass with a "V" at the top, full of little seeds and black tassels. Carefully I inch forward, stretching out my arm so the end of the stalk touches his ear. He brings up a greasy hand, swatting at his ear. Sam suppresses a laugh as I continue tickling. Once again, his hand tries to shoo away the pest, sending drops of oil and sweat flying. His head turns slightly, suddenly realizing he's not alone. His head jerks up, banging into the roof of the raised hood.

"What the heck is wrong with you two dingbats?" he yells while rubbing his head. He snatches his hat off and swats me with it as we laugh.

"Man, you had me going there for a minute," he says, mopping sweat off his brow with a greasy rag he pulls from his pocket.

"It was the least we could do," says Sam, still laughing.

"What's wr-wrong with your tr-truck?" I ask.

"Just changing the belts and oil, regular maintenance stuff is all."

I nod my head, thinking I will be doing this same thing with Mom's car in a couple of weeks. Then before I can get the words out, I hear Sam say, "We're camping in the woods tonight and wanted to know if you and Tommy can come along."

Trey scratches the back of his head then adjusts his cap and replies, "Hey, sounds like fun. Tommy's working so he probably can't make it, but I'm free. Let me finish what I'm doing here and we'll get some more of the Halloween stuff ready," he says with a grin. "It shouldn't take too long, I'm almost done here."

"We have p-plenty of s-stuff to eat, so you d-don't need to b-bring any food, unless you j-just want to."

"How about we catch some fish, it's been a while since I've had any. The pond is stocked, but I ain't had the time to go. You guys put the johnboat in the back of my truck and I'll grab the tackle. You already got wood for a fire?"

"Yeah, w-we're all s-set."

Sam and I go into their barn to retrieve the johnboat. We've used this boat many times in the past. Dad borrowed it all the time so the two of us could go fishing on the weekends. My fingers tingle as they trail along the thin, scarred rail and wonder if this was where Dad touched it. Closing my eyes, I can almost feel him standing next to me. Tears begin to moisten my eyes, so I quickly grab the back of the boat before Sam notices.

After it's loaded, Trey puts his tools away and we spend the next hour preparing the woods around his house for the hordes of trick-or-treaters headed this way next week. After finishing up, we head back to their house just as Uncle Wyatt's truck pulls up the dusty driveway. He rolls the window down and waves at us.

Uncle Wyatt was in the Navy doing a short tour at MacDill Air Force Base in Tampa when he met Aunt Moe. They attended the same football game one night and met at the concession stand. The seat next to her was empty so he followed her back, and for the rest of the night neither of them heard or saw anything else but each other.

She almost didn't marry him because of his name, and what hers would become—Moe Hawk. Personally, I couldn't think of a cooler name, but women can be weird with that kind of stuff. Everyone they met never failed to make a comment. After discovering he was the kind of guy worth keeping, no matter the minor issue with his name, they decided to tie the knot. The day she agreed to marry him, he buzzed his hair into a Mohawk and threw a huge party.

Aunt Moe's real name is Maureen and she is Mom's older sister by three years. When Mom was born and began to speak, all she could manage to say was "Moe," and the name stuck. She and Uncle Wyatt are among my favorite people on earth. No matter how or when we show up, they are happy to see us.

Their two sons are world-class hunters, keeping a steady supply of all kinds of critters in the freezer. Aunt Moe has transformed scroungy varmints into delectable delights on more occasions than I can count. Anything that slithers on the ground or scurries under bushes is her specialty. She can turn the homeliest little possum into a world-class stew.

Last year for one of their parties, she made cakes out of a big rattler the guys found on the back part of their property. Aunt Moe rolled them out long and skinny like a snake and placed them on a platter labeled "snake cakes." Several of the guests thought they were cute and tried them, not realizing they were real snakes. It was a Kodak moment when Tommy told them how he acquired the main ingredient.

"Well, hey there, you two," Aunt Moe hollers from across the room as she walks into the kitchen, arms full of collard greens from her garden.

Putting them in the sink, she walks over and scoops us up in a big bear hug. Aunt Moe always hugs us, like women love to do. She smells like shampoo and some earthy smell I can't quite identify. She has all kinds of herbs, vegetables, and flowers growing out there, so it could be anything. "I guess you guys are camping tonight, huh?"

We nod our heads.

"Well, it's a beautiful night for it. You boys should have lots of fun. I guess Trey is going along with y'all."

"Yes m-ma'am, he is," I say.

"Too bad Tommy has to work tonight," Sam adds.

"Yeah, he would love to tag along. There's still enough boy left in him to enjoy sleeping in the dirt, but maybe next time. By the way Jason, I meant to call your mom. How is Mary doing?" she asks, her pretty smile fading a little.

"Oh s-she's still s-sore from surgery, but she's g-getting b-better every day."

"Wow, that's some scary stuff! Please tell her we send our best, and tell your mom if she needs anything, and I mean anything, to call me, okay?"

"Yes m-ma'am, I'll p-pass that along."

Aunt Moe is a nurse at St. Bart, short for Bartholomew. She's usually the one we call when anyone has a medical issue.

"Well, you boys be careful out there around that water and all. I realize y'all know those woods and pond like the back of your hand, but all those critters around that water makes me a little nervous, especially the slithering ones," she says with a little shiver. "You boys stay alert, okay, and make sure the dogs go with you, all right?"

"We're putting George in charge of security. Anything that can get through him has to deal with Gracie." With her, intruders run the risk of being promptly licked to death. She'd help carry a burglar's sack of stolen goods to his truck. Aunt Moe puts her hands on her hips and cocks her head to the side then says, "I'm serious, boys." I give her my best "we got it covered" nod, and pat her on the shoulder. She relaxes her stern look and puts her hand on my shoulder.

Something gets her attention from behind and suddenly her hand clamps down on my shoulder as she hollers at Trey.

"Mister, you put those potatoes right back. The last time y'all pulled out that potato gun, an entire ten-pound bag of potatoes disappeared. I can't afford to feed you and buy your ammunition at the same time. Food is too expensive to throw away like that."

Trey holds up several potatoes for his mom to see, green shoots sprouting in all directions.

"Look, Mom, I'm only taking the ones that are getting old. Besides, the varmints clean up what we splatter. None of it goes to waste."

The back door quietly swings open and everyone turns to look. Trey quickly shoves the rest of the potatoes into a grocery bag while his mom isn't looking and scurries out the door.

Aunt Moe starts to follow, not realizing Uncle Wyatt is still standing behind her, and runs right into him. She jumps like she's stepped on a smake. He laughs and says, "Hey Babe, good to see you too," grabbing her around the waist and winking at us over her shoulder. She pulls away and tries to be mad but can't. They stand eyeball to eyeball for a moment, like it's been years since they saw each other.

Aunt Moe returns his hug as he pulls her in hard and kisses her on the neck. She giggles like a little girl.

Whenever they go out together she tries to find low heels so he doesn't have to look up at her. Even when he does, it never seems to bother him. They might look a little funny as a couple, but all that disappears once people see how right they are together. I know that sounds corny, but it's true. Sparks fly, like their chemistry comes together at the perfect angle; separate from each other, they are incomplete. Trey, Tommy, and Vivian are lucky to have such a sweet family. I've never heard them fight like some of our other aunts and uncles do. In this gingerbread house there are sweet nuggets to pluck everywhere.

Uncle Wyatt's broad shoulders and slim hips have been passed down to their three kids. Each one of them have lettered in school sports, blessed with those Olympian genes. He looks tired and dirty, but is chipper, as usual.

Giving her a peck on the cheek, Uncle Wyatt turns to us and says, "Hey there, fellas," offering a hand for us to shake. Though his eyes are tired, they still sparkle like a kid's.

"How are you boys doing? I see y'all have made some good progress getting the haunted forest ready. I wonder if we'll have as many trick-or-treaters as we did last year. Seems like every year we get more," he says with a broad smile.

"Yeah, the kids at school are already talking about it," Sam says.

After telling him about our fishing and camping plans he rubs his taut belly, like he would love to join in. "How well I remember those long gone days of my youth, running around the pasture half the night like a pack of wild coyotes." He gets a far-off look in his eye and I wonder what he sees. We've heard stories over the years of all the trouble he got into with his friends as a teenager, like the time he threw some M80s into one of the boy's toilets at the high school and blew out a major section of piping. It had to be closed for a whole week. How awesome is that!

He shakes his head as the memories behind his eyes dissipate. "Those were definitely the days. You boys should stay kids as long as you can, 'cause growing up stinks like a yard full of hogs," he says, reaching for a glass of cold iced tea from the fridge. He offers us some, but we pass.

"Hey Jason, are you still on for Thanksgiving? You're going to the Keys with us, right?"

"M-most definitely, I have everything r-ready to g-go. I've got s-some c-cash saved up f-from helping P-papa and Mr. Adams," I say.

"Good man. We'll be leaving bright and early the Sunday before Thanksgiving." He looks at Sam's long face and adds, "Sam, sorry you can't make the trip with us this year, son. I'm sure you'll have a nice visit with your grandparents, though. You need to spend Thanksgiving with them 'cause there will always be more trips to the Keys, but you never know how long your grandparents will be around."

Without much cheer, he says, "Yeah I know, but I really wish I was going with y'all. They just don't understand me like you guys do."

Uncle Wyatt walks over and clamps him on the shoulder and says, "I know, son, but like I said before, there will be other years, okay? You are always welcome to tag along anytime you want." Sam just nods his head.

After saying goodbye, we head back outside to get things ready. Sam does his best to shake off the long face.

The three of us squeeze into the cab of Trey's truck. The boat and a few extra items are loaded in back, so he puts the truck into gear and heads toward the pond. We have to travel through our grandfather's pasture to get there. Trey is careful not to tear up the grass. He did that last year and got into big trouble with both Papa and his dad. He lost his driving privileges for a whole month.

After we clear the pasture, we have to navigate through some thick woods, but there's enough space between the trees for the truck to get through. It's kind of slow going and real bumpy, but before long the pond comes into view.

The pond is about the size of a pair of football fields and is filled with catfish, perch, brim, and bass, along with turtles, snakes, and water birds. Sand Hill cranes like to fly overhead and are so used to humans we can walk right up to them. They land in backyards all over town, and local traffic knows to look out for them when they walk their babies back and forth each morning and evening. Locals get out of their cars and block traffic for them to pass.

All around the back edge of the pond are water lilies. Most have white petals that are bright pink inside. One of our aunts bought them a couple of years ago and since then they have multiplied all over the place, forming a ring around the edge. On the other side where we swim, the white sand is wide and flat, so we call it the beach zone. Out here on the back side is where all the water plants and wild stuff likes to hang out.

The lilies keep the water pretty clean, but it's still pond water so a respectable amount of grunge is part of its charm.

As we pull to a stop, we open the doors and carefully step out, always acutely aware of water snakes, mainly moccasins. If we make plenty of noise, they usually get out of our way. None of us have ever been bitten, but Tommy had a close call once. Stomping around the thick grass at the edge of the pond last year, his foot landed on a moccasin's tail. In the span of time it takes to blink, the snake whipped around, sinking its fangs into the heel of Tommy's boot, missing his skin by the width of a gnat's eyelash. Aunt Moe's face turned white when Tommy went home bragging about it. He thought the whole thing was hilarious.

If we happen to spot a poisonous one, we chop its head off and carry it back to Aunt Moe's house for snake cakes. We leave the nonpoisonous ones alone. Black snakes actually keep rattlesnakes away, so they're like a good luck charm out here.

We stomp around the area a little longer and then head to the back of the truck to get the boat ready. Trey puts his beefy hand on the side and pulls it out one-handed as it plops to the ground. Then he slaps me on the back and says with a big toothy grin, "Hey, how 'bout we throw a little mud before we go fishing?" not waiting for an answer. This is his favorite part about owning a truck: mud-slinging.

Getting back into the truck we drive down to a lower section where it is never dry. The "bog" is a perpetual mud hole filled with thick, slimy black mud buried deep in the woods. In a clearing, the mud glistens in wide pools. Trey stops the truck, revs the engine and looks at us. I reach over and grab the "oh crap" handle mounted just above the door beside me. Sam leans forward and holds onto the dash as best he can just as Trey lets his foot off the brake.

The truck rockets forward, fishtailing in the deep mud as Sam and I hang on for dear life, hollering and yelling over the roar of the engine. Before we know it, we're bouncing in the air as the truck tears through the bog. Black mud rooster-tails off the rear tires, spraying in every direction. So much mud is flying onto the windshield and windows we can barely see outside. The three of us slam into each other, shoulders and hips bouncing all over the place. The rear tires continue to spin but we stop going forward. The truck is now spinning in circles as mud launches higher and higher into the air. There's so much noise inside the cab between our hollering and the roar of the engine that I give up trying to hold the handle and put my hands over my ears. I slide hard into Sam, who pushes me into the door. After a few minutes, Trey eases off the accelerator and slowly the truck stops spinning. He straightens out the steering wheel, but keeps yelling as we begin creeping to the other side, careful not to let the tires get bogged down. Once on solid ground again, we step out of the cab to survey the damage. Every square inch is slathered with such a thick layer of black mud, no one would ever guess the color.

Sam is the first to speak as we walk around to the other side. "That was by far the coolest ride I've ever had, man. This puts those monster trucks to shame." Trey beams at his truck like a proud papa.

"That was s-sweet m-man!" I manage to get out.

Trey looks around at the sky and says, "Daylight's a-burnin' boys, we better head back to the pond before it's all gone."

Once we get back to the boat, Sam and I carry it to the other side where the sand is thickest. Trey walks out into the pond up to his knees, bends over and dips his head into the water. He swirls it around a few times then slings his head back, shaking it like a dog. Water slings ten feet all around as he hollers "Yeah!" running his fingers through his wet hair. "I've been waiting all day to do that."

We flinch as dirty pond water splatters all over us. Sam pulls the bottom of his shirt up and wipes Trey's mess off his face. I just use the back of my hand and hear Sam holler, "You're worse than the dogs!"

"Everybody should have their head dunked in a dirty old pond every now and again. It'll put hair on your chest!" Trey hollers.

Sam says, "So that's your beauty secret." Trey looks at us, giggles and says, "Never a shortage of smart comebacks, huh, cuz."

Before Sam can say anything, Trey splashes water on us and says, "Let's go get some supper."

Carefully we step into the boat and take a seat. Dipping the oars into the inky water, we make our way to the back of the pond as the boat glides effortlessly over the quiet surface.

This is what I like best about this place, the quietness. A man can think out here and find himself again. All the hassles of life drown out the calm places inside, until I come out here. If I didn't have this place, I think I'd go stone-cold crazy.

The sun is just beginning to set, sending long, pink, and purple streaks across the surface of the pond. This is my favorite time of day.

Breathing in the musty, pungent smells traveling on the warm humid air taps into long-ago memories of family picnics and parties we've had out here. Just to the side of our camp is a shed covered with a tin roof and palmetto fronds. Underneath it is an old wooden table and benches. Dad, Papa, and some of our uncles helped build that shed when I was just a baby. So many great memories are tied up in this place; I can almost feel the juicy watermelon drip down my chin. The image of Cuban sandwiches and hot deviled crabs stacked high seem close enough for a bite.

A pole smacks the back of my hand as Trey passes them around the boat. Stowing the paddles inside the gunwale, I grab the fishing pole and bait the hook with a small piece of bacon.

About halfway out, close to the back where the reeds are thickest, is where the fish like to bite. I cast off the back of the boat toward the far corner where the reeds are spaced a little further apart, while the other two drop their lines on either side of the boat.

When I was a kid, our older cousins used to tell us a swamp monster lived out here in the pond under the lily pads. They said he had a secret cave tucked under the thickest part of the reeds. He was covered in green moss and liked to come out, roaming the woods when the moon was full in search of small children to take to his hideout. It was a long time before I would go fishing or swimming out here, especially at night.

"Hey Trey, we saw the house for sale down the street from yours finally sold," Sam said.

"Yeah, that place was up for sale since the turn of the century. I heard they got a really good deal on it," his hair still dripping onto his muscular shoulders.

"We saw them moving in on our way over tonight. I think they have a daughter about our age. She looked at us through one of the windows like we were something out of *Deliverance*."

"Is she cute?" Trey asks with a grin, disregarding the inbred remark. Besides fishing, sports and his truck, girls are his other passion.

"D-didn't get a g-good look at her," I say.

"Speaking of girls, I hear Vivian did a Zorro on you, bro," says Sam with a mischievous grin.

Trey's little sister is a force to be reckoned with. Having two older brothers toughened her into a ferocious little fireball, on top of what she came by naturally.

On more than one occasion Trey was the recipient of a black eye, bruised ribs, or shaved eyebrow. With a slight build and sweet, cherub face, only those closest to her know how deceptive those innocent looks can be. Talk about grabbing a tiger by the tail; I think she invented the phrase.

I look at Trey's hand and notice the slightest hint of red around his cuticles. "L-looks like you d-did a p-pretty good j-job of getting the n-nail polish off there, d-dude," I say with a laugh. He rubs his nails hard on his cutoff jeans shorts with a huff. The tops of his ears turn pink as he gives us a sheepish grin.

"Yeah, Vivian really got me good this time. She waited until I fell asleep Saturday night and painted my fingernails with the brightest red nail polish she could find. I was in such a hurry getting ready for church the next morning that I didn't even notice. It wasn't until we were praying that I looked down and saw my gorgeous new fashion design. Of course, there was no way of getting out of that place without somebody seeing, and if one person knows, 'then everybody knows'," he and Sam say together. There are no secrets in small towns.

"My guess is you'll be more careful the next time you borrow her stuff without asking, huh?" Sam says.

"She wasn't home, and I thought she'd never notice if I plugged one of her CD's into my player. I just forgot to put it back when I finished with it. She looked for it all over the place, thinking she'd left it at a friend's house. By then I had forgotten all about it."

"At l-least the nail p-polish can be t-taken off. Better than last t-time when she sh-shaved your eyebrow off!" I say, not even trying to stop laughing.

Sam joins in, "I'll never forget how hilarious you looked!"

Trey glares at us with mock disgust and says, "Yeah, very funny. We had class pictures that week, too. Mom had to paint one on me with her eyebrow pencil. I'll never live that one down. The captain of the football team wearing his *mom's* makeup."

By now Sam and I are laughing so hard I lose control of the south-bound express and cut the cheese so loud it vibrates off the sides of the boat.

Sam and Trey both move toward the front of the boat, fanning the air. Trey says, "Gross!" then in the next breath, "Good one," which makes us laugh even harder.

About that time, something starts nibbling on my line and our volume button suddenly gets turned off. I let a little more line out to give whatever is sampling it some running room. A second or two pass and I feel the line start to pull away. I give the line a good hard yank and watch as my pole bends nearly in half.

"Wow, that was fast, you lucky dog," Trey says.

I begin reeling in the fish as Trey grabs the net. As the line gets shorter, flashes of a white belly rolls and spins as the fish gets closer to the surface. He puts up a heck of a fight, and it doesn't take long before my muscles are burning. As I continue to haul him in, we see the outline of a big catfish.

"He's gotta weigh seven or eight pounds, easy," Sam yells behind me.

I try to pull him close enough to the boat so the net can scoop him up. Trey leans over the side, trying to outmaneuver him. Finally, he gets the net beneath the thrashing fish and hauls him into the boat. As the fish flops about, water flies all over the place. Trey dumps him on the bottom of the boat as we move our feet out of the way.

Pulling out his hunting knife, Trey quickly puts an end to all the ruckus. I've seen him do this many times and it never fails to impress me. He's done this his entire life and makes it look easy.

We determine this cat is big enough for all of us to feast on, so we paddle back to shore. Heading back in, Trey looks over his shoulder with a genuine look of concern.

"By the way, boys, while I was getting my gear together in my room, the radio was playing. They broke in with a message, something about a jailbreak over in Polk County, and the guy still hadn't been caught. So we need to be extra careful tonight, okay?"

Oh great, what good are a bunch of kids against a dangerous felon? Trey is pretty handy with that knife of his, but still. Maybe we should postpone our campout for another night. Noticing the look on my face, he says, "I'm sure they've got a dozen officers chasing him down even as we speak, so no need to get our shorts in a wad guys."

When we dig the front of the boat into the soft reeds at the shore, I hear all the usual night noises—crickets, cicadas, bullfrogs. A June bug clumsily flies by, bumping into the side of my head with a thump as I brush it away. Anxious thoughts run through my mind as all kinds of scenarios traipse through. Something sinister and dangerous is lurking out there in the darkness, I can feel it.

I jump when Trey says, "Hey Jason, go fetch the rope over by that tree," pointing to a small oak about twenty feet away. Not wanting to act like a wuss, I swallow hard and head for the tree. Looking over both shoulders, I continuously survey the area, looking for anything out of the ordinary. The only thing I see are a few scary-looking bushes, but they seem harmless enough. So far, so good.

The tree is only a couple more feet ahead, so I quickly take the last few steps, reaching down and picking up the rope all in one smooth motion. Just as I'm about to turn around and head back to the boat, a hand reaches from behind the tree and grabs hold of my wrist. Shocked, I look up and see a face emerge from behind the tree. Deep scars are scratched across the hideous face. I hear a scream and realize it is coming from me. Desperately I try to wrestle free, but he steps from behind the tree and drags me to the ground, pinning me on my stomach. I struggle with everything I've got, but he overpowers me. I scream for Trey and Sam, who seem to be nowhere in sight.

Suddenly, I hear laughter. Wait a minute, I know that laugh. I stop struggling and turn over. A hand reaches up and pulls the mask off, and there is my cousin Tommy, laughing his butt off.

"Man, you should've seen the look on your face!" he howls, just as Trey and Sam come running up. Trey is laughing so hard he can hardly stand up. Sam has a confused look on his face, obviously left in the dark about their little conspiracy.

It takes a minute or two for my breathing and heart rate to settle back down. I stand up and shove Tommy so hard he lands on the ground, where he continues to laugh. I can't stay mad at him for very long. Usually I'm the one that plays a stupid stunt like this, so I have no room to be angry.

I fall to the ground on my back next to Tommy, holding my chest and shaking my head. He reaches over and claps me on the shoulder, still in a laughing fit.

Trey and Sam sit down with us, laughing hysterically. Trey manages to tell me he called Tommy while we were loading up the boat and set up this whole stupid stunt. After a minute or two, the laughter dies down and all of us become silent, just listening to the twilight sounds surrounding us. The look on their faces mirrors my thoughts: how long will this wonderful place last? Will our children ever know it was even here? We see the bulldozers and land-clearing machinery hard at work every day as more and more of the wilderness disappears. We clear our throats and stand up, ready to get going.

Tommy asks, "Y'all catch anything out there?" Trey reaches behind him and holds up the catfish I caught.

"Wow, that's a nice one! We best get him cleaned up," adds Tommy. "Y'all watch out though, I heard there was a break at the jail tonight," he says with a chuckle. I punch him in the arm for good measure.

We hear barking in the distance and realize our dogs have finally caught up with us. They have free run over the entire four hundred acres, which they take full advantage of. They're not only good with the cattle, but great pets and love to camp as much as we do. They're just mutts somebody dumped off, like all of the pets we've ever had.

Sam's is a mixed breed named Smoky. He got that name from the soft, gray pattern of spots all over his body. He's stocky and strong, and not much more than a puppy. Sam has worked with him and trained him well, and besides me, is his best friend.

My dog is not as big or strong, but just as awesome. She's got some husky and cocker spaniel in her and the rest is anybody's guess. Her blonde hair and soft brown, intelligent eyes got my attention right away. I knew she was going to be a special girl. We named her Trixie, a name Mary picked out. We've had her ever since I was four years old, so she's getting up in years, but Smoky keeps her young at heart. The two of them are as close as Sam and me. Her muzzle is starting to show patches of white, and sometimes she coughs hard after a long run, but other than that, she still looks like a much younger dog. I know the day is coming when she won't be around, but I try not to think about that.

Trey and Tommy's beagles, George and Gracie, bring up the rear, running excitedly and wagging their tails.

The camp isn't far from the pond, so they trot over, knowing exactly where we're headed. Thick woods almost completely surround the pond except the part we swim in, which looks just like a beach after Papa had a truckload of white sand hauled in. Where the reeds begin is an enormous oak tree that holds our rope.

Trey reaches into his truck and takes the bag of potatoes he took from the pantry and throws them at Sam. At the last second, Sam realizes where they are headed and jerks his hands up. He manages to grab them just before they collide with his head and yells, "you knucklehead!"

Trey laughs and says, "Good catch. Just for that, I'll let you shoot first."

The big potato gun emerges from the bed of the truck in Tommy's hand. I'm amazed the thing hasn't blown up yet as many potatoes we've shot through it.

Sam pulls one of the larger potatoes from the bag and starts yanking out the sprouts. Trey hands him the gun as I get the long stick to shove the ammunition down into the barrel. He spots a large tree not far away and begins licking his lips. Tommy puts some hair spray into the hole at the bottom then pats Sam on the shoulder. We back up as Sam gets lined up with the tree. Another few seconds pass before he pushes the igniter button, then we hear "boom," as the potato flies from the barrel and smashes into the tree, splattering like a big white bug. We smack him on the back as he hands the gun to me. My turn to make a mess. Hash-browns, here we come.

I scan the area and find a larger tree further away. I get locked and loaded, and steady the gun against my hip. When I hear the hiss of hairspray stop, I press the button. The gun rocks hard in my hands, but I don't drop it like I did last time. The potato misses the tree I was aiming at, but manages to strike a smaller one next to it, making a respectable mess. That's all I really care about anyway. After all the potatoes are gone, we get ready for a dip.

A few years ago, we took a thick rope and tied it to one of the biggest, highest branches, then connected a bar to it. Not long afterwards, we found an old ladder and tied it to the tree. Above that, we made a deck to stand on, which makes it a lot easier to get a good take-off.

We watch as Trey shoves off from the deck. He sails easily through the air, hair flying in the wind, and after he can't go any higher he flings his feet way above his head and starts somersaulting end over end until he finally hits the water, head first. He always manages to enter with such a perfect dive you'd swear you were front and center at the Olympics.

He surfaces after a couple of seconds and slings his hair to the side, sending a spray of water behind him.

"A p-perfect 10," I yell.

Each of us takes turns until we're too tired to do anymore. On my last time up, I stand on the launching pad longer than usual and look around. From this vantage point, part of the countryside comes into view under the last fleeting moments of daylight. Turning around, I look to the south and spot my cousin Beth riding her horse with her little dog, Kinky, close behind. Kinky was another mutt that was dumped off. Wherever that horse goes, the dog goes. Somehow she has never managed to get stepped on.

Beth camps with us sometimes, but it doesn't look like she's headed this way tonight. Girls aren't allowed to camp with us anyway unless they're cousins. I know she sleeps at her friend Debbie's house when she's home. Debbie's parents are divorced, so she spends half her time here and the other half with her dad's family in North Florida. That seems to be the norm these days. More than half the kids I know at school live the same way.

Beth's dad is probably the meanest man I've ever known; not like Sam's dad that enjoys aggravating everybody or being obnoxious. No, Uncle Frank is way beyond any of that, especially when he's drinking. When he's not, he's a little mellower, but those times are few and far between.

We've seen Beth's mom, Aunt Barb, with bruises on her cheeks and nervous as a hen in a fox's den. I always feel sorry for Beth, but nobody knows what to do about it. I know Papa can't stand him, and he loves everybody.

He tried to get Aunt Barb to leave him, but she's still there. I think she has completely lost all sense of herself, afraid to stay and more afraid to leave. Sometimes the fear of the known is less dangerous in our minds than the unknown, even if the known is a living nightmare. I know how it feels to be in the chains of fear. If there's one thing I could change about myself that would be it.

Uncle Frank hardly ever comes to any of our family get-togethers. No one ever misses him, especially Beth and Aunt Barb. When his name came up around Dad, his jaw muscles got real tight. I don't know what kind of man I will be when I'm grown, but one thing I know for sure: I would rather be dead than turn out like Uncle Frank.

Beth's horse was just a filly when it was dropped off for boarding, but the owner decided it wasn't worth the time or expense to keep the little buckskin, so she was abandoned. The little horse was let loose in the pasture with Papa's cows and turned wild, and was becoming dangerous to the cows. Papa wanted to get rid of her, but no one wanted a wild, untamed horse. Beth needed something to occupy her mind and keep her out of the house, and that young filly was just the answer.

Since Beth is as crazy about animals as Mary is, she and the friend she's riding with tonight took it upon themselves to tame that wild filly and turn her into their nine-hundred-pound teddy bear. It took a lot of time and patience, but it really paid off. They debated on a name and finally settled on Stardust.

Finally the night we have been waiting for has arrived—Halloween. This year we lucked out because it falls on a Friday. At Trey and Tommy's house, this night is legendary. Folks from all over town come here, even if they only go one place to Trick-or-Treat.

I wanted to be Jason from the movie *Friday the 13th,* but Aunt Moe said, "Scary creepy is okay but scary evil is out, and Jason is just plain evil." When I tried to plead my case, I got "the look" and knew the argument was over. So instead of chasing people dressed like Jason, I dug a shallow grave about a foot deep then lined it with some plastic, covered it with a piece of Astroturf and climbed inside wearing a skeleton costume. A black strobe light hung above, catching the white of my costume, so that's all they see. The effect is totally awesome.

While staring at my skeleton rising from the grave, a pair of hairy arms reaches out from behind a tree and grabs the kids. This is Sam's favorite job, and his timing is perfect. So far he's only been punched twice. Since then, he's learned to duck.

When they make it to the porch, Uncle Wyatt emerges from a casket beside the door dressed like Dracula, holding a big bowl of candy. Each year we mix it up to keep things interesting.

In a large clearing on the side of the house, Aunt Moe, Vivian, Beth, and Mary have a big bonfire going. Aunt Moe is dressed up like the mom from *The Addams Family,* while Vivian is a witch, stirring a steaming cauldron filled with dry ice and water. Mary is the bride of Frankenstein with electric hair going straight up. Next to them is the dynamic duo. Trixie, the Caped Crusader is our four-legged Batman, while Smoky, the Boy Wonder is a way cooler Robin than the real thing.

George and Gracie are, well, George and Gracie Allen. George has large black-rimmed glasses attached to his head with a little black hat to match.

Gracie is wearing a skirt Aunt Moe made for her last year, along with some silly shoes tied to her feet she keeps pulling off.

Sitting beside Mary is Beth with a stuffed pumpkin under her arm, dressed like the headless horseman. Her friend, Debbie, is on the other side, made up like a female version of Paul Revere.

In a nearby cooler, there are hot dogs for anyone that wants to stay and roast one. I've seen folks try to give Aunt Moe money, but she never accepts it. All year long, when she finds hot dogs and buns on sale, she buys them and puts them in the freezer. By the time Halloween rolls around, she's got enough to feed the whole town.

There's always a big crowd around the fire, especially when Halloween falls on a Friday or Saturday. Neighbors bring their bowls of candy and a side of something to share. Kids go around the circle, collecting their candy from everyone.

When the trick-or-treaters are ready to leave, Beth and Debbie take turns leading them back down a lighted path to the road. This path is a "safe" zone for little ones too young to appreciate our Halloween spirit and for everyone to exit. Last year we had over 300 people come out here.

I peek out of my grave to see Trey and Tommy chasing each other through the trees with toy chainsaws that sound and look like the real thing. We've had so many trick-or-treaters come through already, it's hard to believe there could be anymore, but there are.

I see a couple of costumes approach but can't make out the faces in the dark. When they get a little closer, I realize it's my language arts teacher, Mrs. Langston, with her husband and son. They come out here every year, but have used the safe route since their little boy, Xander, was still a bit too young. She mentioned to me at school this week that he had been driving her crazy, claiming he wasn't a baby anymore and wanted to walk through the haunted forest like the other big kids. He's eight years old now and says nothing scares him.

Quietly, I peel back the Astroturf. At first they don't see me, and then all three spot me at the same time. I slowly rise from the grave as Xander's eyes grow big as saucers. He opens his mouth to scream but nothing comes out. About that time, Sam reaches over and grabs Mrs. Langston. She starts jumping up and down, screaming so loud it could literally wake the dead.

Mr. Langston starts laughing, slapping his legs and shaking his head. She sits down on the ground, covering her face with her hands like she can wish it all away. I sit down next to her, patting her on the back. Sam plops down on the other side, still laughing.

"Y-you okay, Mrs. L-Langston?" I say.

She slowly lifts her head and says, "I will be in a minute, Jason. You boys sure know how to do Halloween!"

Xander is holding onto his dad's arm, trying for all his life to smile, but he never quite makes it.

Sam and I each grab one of Mrs. Langston's arms and help her to her feet.

"Thanks, boys," she says a bit shaky. Mr. Langston walks over, still chuckling and takes her hand, while their son remains firmly attached to his side.

From over her shoulder she sees other trick-or-treaters coming along the path and decides her legs are strong enough to continue on.

"Y'all go get a hot dog and relax around the fire," Sam says.

This finally brings a real smile to Xander's face.

"Now that sounds like something I can handle. See you boys in a little while," she says. The three of them make their way to the front porch so Xander can collect his prize.

By ten o'clock, most of the trick-or-treaters are gone, so we close down the haunted forest and head to the fire. We're covered in grime and sweat, but nobody cares.

There are more people than I expected tonight, sitting around the fire, eating and talking. Mr. and Mrs. Davis are here talking to our neighbors, the Jacobics. Mr. and Mrs. Adams look like they always do, he in his overalls, the only thing I think he owns, and Mrs. Adams looks like she's headed to a party.

Uncle Wyatt is still in his Dracula garb, drinking a Bloody Mary with Mr. Langston and Mr. Littleton from down the street. Uncle Wyatt looks up and gives us a smile as we walk in. In the distance I hear the unmistakable sound of Jake's wheelchair closing in. He and Sam step out of the darkness as we reach the crowd, Jake jabbering on about this being the best night of his whole life. Every night is the best night of his whole life.

Looking out at all the people spread around the yard talking and laughing, I see Mrs. Langston and Xander sitting with another group that has young kids. The children are comparing the contents of their Halloween buckets while the adults chat. Walking in their direction, Xander spots me first then runs up with a big grin and says, "Hey, you scared me ta deaf tonight!"

"Good, then m-my job as the Halloween s-spook is d-done."

He stops smiling and says, "Hey, how come you talk funny?"

It occurred to me in that moment he never actually heard me speak before. I see his mom almost every day, but I've only waved to him from a distance.

His mom's head snaps up and she gets to her feet so fast she nearly trips over her chair. Making a beeline for us, she clamps her hand over his mouth, and then gets down on her knees so she is eye level with him. Gently, she removes her hand from his mouth, cupping his chin and says softly, "Son, we don't talk to people that way. That is rude and you need to apologize to Jason right now."

I hold up my hands and say, "Mrs. Langston, he d-didn't mean anything b-by it. He's j-just curious, that's all. It d-didn't hurt my f-feelings, honest." I feel bad for the poor kid. He just did what kids do. I learned a long time ago little kids have no filter and just blurt things out before they think. It happens to Jake all the time. You just can't let this kind of thing bother you.

Xander looks at me with a long face and says, "I'm sorry, I didn't mean to hurt your feelings."

Mrs. Langston doesn't look up at me right away.

I kneel down beside him and say, "Hey my m-man, no problem. I have what they c-call a stutter. M-my words don't w-want to come out r-right, that's why I s-sound funny." I hold out my fist for him to bump, letting him off the hook. Mrs. Langston finally looks at me and says, "Thank you, Jason, for not getting upset. You know how kids speak before they think."

"Yes m-ma'am, I do. D-don't worry about it, n-no harm done," I say with a smile.

She sends Xander off to play with his friends, then turns to me again and says, "You are such a sweet young man, Jason. One day you are going to do something incredible with your life, I can feel it in my bones." I just smile and say, "If you s-say so." She gives me a hug and walks back to where she was sitting.

From across the yard, Mrs. Thomason pulls out a guitar and starts playing a beautiful song she probably wrote herself. She writes almost all of her own stuff and sells them all over the country.

The delicate notes dance through the night air like golden drops of honey, filling the cool night with a sweet, delicious melody. Folks turn to see where the music is coming from, and begin swaying to the rhythm.

I feel a hand on my back and turn to see Mom, still in her work clothes. She gives me a look up and down with a smile and says, "So how did it go out there tonight honey b--, sorry. Old habits die hard."

I say, "It was great, Mom. Jake s-said it was the b-best night of his whole l-life."

She laughs and says, "He thinks every night is the best night of his whole life."

"Yeah, I know."

She smiles back, but it quickly loses its sparkle. "That's great, honey," she says, squeezing her lips together. Just before the smile disappears, she adds, "Glad you kids had fun." She stares at me for a moment longer than necessary, her eyes failing to hide the sadness they hold, then she heads toward Aunt Moe.

In that sliver of silence the pain comes through loud and clear. Yeah, Mom, I know, we all miss Dad. None of our days are going to be the same anymore. This is going to be the unspoken chapter of our lives from now on.

As I turn around to finish my food, I catch a fleeting look in Uncle Wyatt's eye. He reads my thoughts as clearly as if they were broadcast on a neon sign. He winks at me, and with an almost imperceptible nod of his head, acknowledges that it's okay. He is here. Tommy, Trey, Vivian, Sam, and our grandparents are here. We will help you through this. With that one simple gesture, I feel a multitude of shoulders lift this enormous burden from ours. Then he turns back to his companions and takes another sip of his Bloody Mary before finishing off his hotdog. I couldn't imagine my life without this wacky family of mine.

CHAPTER FIVE

The moon is bright and beautiful tonight, smiling down like a Cheshire cat. There must be a trillion stars scattered above, twinkling like polished diamonds on a black velvet canvas. This is the first time since her dad's death that she's ventured into any kind of wilderness.

Jesse realizes she needs to be careful out here, but staying in that cramped little house one more minute would've pushed her over the edge. Through the years, she's camped plenty of times with her dad, so she's familiar with the dangers that lurk all around.

Who this land belongs to is a mystery, but it's doubtful they would care about one girl just out for a little R&R.

Taking a deep breath, she lays back and whispers to herself how awesome the night sky looks out here. After living in the city for more than two years, she'd nearly forgotten what real stars look like. She is immediately able to pick out several constellations, allowing a tender smile to cross her face. Although she likes the conveniences and bustle of city life, she'd forgotten how much she missed the quiet solitude of the country.

Settling back on her blanket, memories of her father push their way past the barriers she has reinforced over the years, refusing to stay bound any longer. The incessant voice that began as a distant, muffled echo has escalated over the past few months into a deafening roar that demands to be reckoned with.

Now that she is alone in the hush of the wilderness, mental images like an old black-and-white movie begin traipsing through her consciousness, uninvited, as usual. This time her reluctance to allow these bittersweet memories to surface fades as she relaxes, allowing them to carry her away to a much happier time.

She's on her father's shoulders as they walk down a path through the mountains in southern Tennessee. It was the three of them—just Mom, Dad, and little Jesse. Mom was behind them, and every now and again, reaching up to rub her tanned little leg. Even from this height she could smell her special fragrance, a scent only children are aware of. From the moment she was placed on her mother's chest after being forced into this world, her essence was permanently infused into her consciousness.

That mom no longer exists. In her place is an empty shell wearing her mother's scent, serving as a haunting reminder of all that Jesse has lost. The happy, vibrant woman that once inhabited her mom's body is gone. Sometimes it feels as though both of her parents are dead.

At least she still has Aunt Jean, who always understands. She stayed several days there just last month, which saved her. Although Aunt Jean had moved to a new place in Florida, it had the same feel as the old one in Atlanta. Jesse liked her old house, but this new one is away from all the city noise. There's room for kids and animals to run around and relax and just *be.* Mom wasn't well enough to drive her, so Jeremy, her stepdad, dropped her off instead. Neither spoke much on the way, which suited her just fine.

Pushing through the pain, the memories continue to flow. Her family had spent the day hiking and picnicking in one of her favorite places along a small section of the Appalachian Trail. Her mom pulled squished sandwiches out of her backpack and passed them around. Peanut butter and jelly seemed to taste so much better out here than at home. Her dad was young and strong and Mom was still happy. This was before Dad's tour overseas in Iraq, before their whole world collapsed.

The air was crisp and chilly, heralding the first signs of fall. Each year they made the trip to visit his aunt and uncle. Dad spotted it one day as they passed Brasstown Bald, the highest natural point in Georgia. Dad said the Cherokee called this mountain Enotah, which means bald.

Her legs had grown weary from walking all day, so he reached down and hoisted her on his broad back and finished carrying her the rest of the way. He always had a way of making her feel safe and loved.

Being out here in these woods reminds her so much of him. He loved natural, unoccupied places like this. She didn't think she would ever enjoy being in the woods again without him, but amazingly, she can almost sense his presence out here.

Suddenly a loud noise rips through the night air, tearing her from her thoughts. Sitting bolt upright, careful to keep her head below the tall grass, she scans the area. Was someone hunting out here in the middle of the night? Strange sounds of laughter and shouts follow the blast.

Barking dogs join in. In the distance, through the dense layer of trees, she spots a fire. Intrigued, she begins making her way toward it, keeping low, out of sight. Within a few minutes, she is close enough to see a group of kids moving around. Bodies shuffle around the clearing, casting long, jagged shadows. The dogs seem to be more interested in playing than anything else, so maybe she can creep a little closer without them noticing.

One of the boys is holding a long white tube, while another sticks something inside it. They've got a potato gun! That's what the loud noise was. She and her dad made one before he was deployed, but it remains stowed away in the back of their garage with his other relics, still untouched. Too many memories rattle around inside.

So far, she's counted four figures. Something about being hidden and observing from a distance gives her a sense of power. Is this how her dad felt when he secretly watched his enemies on reconnaissance missions? Carefully, she pushes the thought away.

Moving to relieve a cramp forming in her leg, she snaps a twig and freezes, holding her breath. One of the dogs stops and looks in her direction. After a couple of seconds, he loses interest and goes back to playing with the other dogs.

She wonders if any of the guys noticed. They appear to be too preoccupied with the gun. Slowly she begins to move, with more stealth this time, until she finally reaches a point where voices can be heard. The words are patchy, not enough to piece together their conversation, but she tries anyway. She wishes she could read lips, but even if she could, the light from the fire isn't sufficient.

The boy with the potato gun turns and aims the barrel in her direction. A cold chill runs down her spine as she realizes she's in his direct line of fire. Did they spot her and decide to shoot first and ask questions later? A potato gun can do some serious damage if you're hit with enough force. Before she can move out of the way, the boy reaches back and presses the igniter. A loud boom echoes, and a split second later the tree next to her explodes into a cascade of white confetti. She covers her head as shredded potato pulp pelts all around, covering her in sticky goo. The boy's laughter brings her head back up again, wondering if round two is about to begin. Instead, he leans it against a nearby tree and sits down beside the fire as the others join him. One of the guys gets up and walks into the woods in the opposite direction, probably to take a whiz.

Her attention turns to the boy bringing a cooler closer to the fire. They place pieces of something into a large frying pan. Being so preoccupied watching their activity, she fails to notice someone standing right behind her. Not until dried leaves crunch under the heel of his boot does she realize he is there. In an instant she's up on her feet, potato pulp hanging from her hair, face to face with the one who walked away from the others. He's still as a statue, staring at her, not ten feet away. The look on his face turns her blood to ice water. Panic rises in her chest as she realizes just how big this guy is, and if he intends to—along with the others—and quickly slams that door.

Before she can form another thought, he quickly closes the distance between them and takes her by the arm, but she jerks away. He makes another attempt, but more deliberate this time. Feeling her handle on the situation slipping fast, she breaks his hold and instinctively twirls around in a roundhouse kick her father taught her, landing a boot solidly in the center of his chest. He tumbles backward, losing his footing and sprawling hard to the ground with a loud groan.

Hearing a commotion in the woods behind us, we look in that direction, but it's too dark to see anything. The dogs go ballistic, running towards the sound, so we put our sticks down and follow.

We trot into a small clearing and see a girl standing over Trey, who is lying on the ground, holding his chest and groaning. Slowly he gets up, a pained look on his face, and brushes off his backside.

The five of us stare at each other in awkward silence. All four dogs yap and bark until Trey yells at them to be quiet. Like obedient little soldiers, they sit down and stop barking, looking from us to the girl, back and forth, like spectators at a ping pong match.

Sam finally says, "Hey girl, you're trespassing, this is private property." She looks familiar, and then it occurs to me she's the one we saw moving into the house earlier today.

She holds her hands up in front of her and takes a step back. "Hey, I'm not looking for trouble. I didn't mean to trespass on anyone's property. All I was doing was getting a little fresh air," she says.

"We don't care what your excuse is. Like he said, this is private property, and you need to get the hell out of here now," Trey shouts, still rubbing his chest, keeping a respectable distance.

It just occurred to me how Trey wound up on the ground. This girl must've decked him.

Tommy walks over and brushes a few more leaves from Trey's back and says, "You okay?"

"Of course I'm okay, she's only a little girl for crying out loud," he shouts.

"A little girl that knocked you on your butt," Tommy laughs.

I thought for a second Trey was going to clobber him. He manages to pull himself together and walks a few feet away.

While Trey is blowing off steam, Sam asks her, "Aren't you the one we saw moving into that house today?"

She nods her head and says, "Unfortunately, yes."

They stare at her without moving, so she keeps talking. Maybe she can talk her way out of this without anyone dying tonight, especially her. "My stepdad found that house on the internet and decided to buy it. We were supposed to get one closer to Tampa, where his new job is, but this was a better deal."

Feeling calmer, she adds, "I'll just get my stuff and head back home," backing away slowly.

"Good, and don't think you can just walk onto anybody's property whenever you feel like it," Trey snarls.

As she turns around to leave, my chest burns to ask her something, anything, but before I can muster the courage, Sam says a little louder than necessary, "What's your name?"

She hesitates a moment, then seems to soften a little and says, "Jesse, Jesse Logan."

Tommy clears his throat, like he's the one in charge, since he's the oldest and will take over now, and asks, "Where are you from?"

Trey throws him a look that could kill and hollers, "Who cares what her name is or where she's from!"

I've never seen Trey like this before, and I'm beginning to regret asking him to camp tonight.

"Let it go, Trey, she didn't mean any harm," Tommy replies evenly.

"The heck she didn't! She whirled around like some psycho ninja and kicked me right in the chest and I hadn't done one thing to her," he says, jabbing his finger in her direction.

Jesse quickly turns around, looks at him sharply and said, "That's not true! You grabbed my arm and I didn't know what you were going to do." Then softer, she says, "Sorry if I hurt you," which makes Trey even madder.

Bristling, he snaps, "You didn't hurt me, girl, I play varsity football," like that explains it all. Then he adds, "Save your sorrys for somebody else."

"Hey Trey, she told you she was sorry. You probably would've done the same thing if you were in her shoes. She was probably scared and just acting out of reflex," Sam interjects.

Trey stops for a moment and thinks about what he said. If anyone can win an argument, it's Sam.

She looks less frightened now, but still seems way out of place here.

"Come on, Jesse, walk over to the fire with us," offers Tommy gently. She glances at Trey, but he ignores her.

"Do whatever you want, I don't care," he says with a tone of disdain, and walks back to camp without us.

Tommy smiles at her and says, "Don't worry, his bark is worse than his bite." She smiles and follows us back to the fire, brushing what's left of potato pulp off her shirt.

Trey is still nursing his wounded pride when we show up a few minutes later. The fire is dying down a little, so he gruffly throws a few more sticks of wood in without saying a word.

Sam clears his throat and says, "I'm Sam, and this is my cousin, Jason, and you already met Trey," he says with a chuckle.

"The tall guy next to him is his older brother, Tommy." She nods at us with a hint of a smile. She looks at me, and I realize I'm the only one who hasn't spoken yet. I swallow hard and say, "So Jesse, where d-did you m-move from," wishing I had kept my big mouth shut.

She looks at me a moment without a word, then says, "Atlanta. I've lived there most of my life. I've gotten used to the city, so living in the country is going to be different," keeping her gaze steady.

Without thinking, I reach over and pull a little piece of potato pulp out of her hair. A self-conscious smile forms on my lips as the guys stare at me. I quickly flick it into the fire and say, 'Lucky y-you d-didn't get walloped out th-there."

She shakes her ponytail around and says, "That's the truth. When I saw you guys aiming it in my direction, my whole life flashed before my eyes." She turned around to check out the gun and says, "Did you guys make it yourselves?"

Tommy says, "Yeah, me and Trey make all kinds of stuff in our dad's shop."

"That's cool, my dad made one when I was younger and we'd take it into the woods and shoot all kinds of stuff out of it."

"Like what?" Tommy asks.

"Apples, rubber balls, anything we could get to fit."

"Sounds like your dad's pretty neat," Sam says. The fire catches the highlights of her hair as smoke suddenly changes direction and obscures my view. She takes a deep breath like the answer will require a lot of effort and says, "Yeah, he was," then looks down at the dirt.

Was? I thought.

Tommy picks up on it too, and changes the subject. "Tampa has gotten to be huge, too. We get over there occasionally, and I can't wait to get back home. I like it out here where it's peaceful and quiet," his words laced with an air of sadness.

She looks into the woods and says, "Way too many people, that's for sure."

"Yep," Tommy says, as he pulls the catfish from the fire. I grab some plates and pass them around.

"Would you like a piece of catfish?" Sam offers.

"Uh, sure, where did you get it?" she asks.

"We caught it in our pond, right over there," Tommy says, pointing just over her shoulder.

"You guys caught this tonight?" she asks, like a kid listening to a fairy tale.

"Yeah, in our boat. We do this almost every weekend."

"Wow, that's really cool. I would love a piece, thank you," she says, reaching for a plate.

I scoop one of the bigger pieces and plop it on her plate. She samples a small piece, and then a much bigger one. "Wow, this is delicious!"

A hint of a smile forms on Trey's lips, but he says nothing. He just stares at the fire, continuing to act like none of us are here.

Sam finally asks what the rest of us are thinking. "Uh, what was that you said about your dad?"

I look at him, wondering if this is a good idea. After all, we just met her a few minutes ago. She picks up a stick and traces something in the dirt then after a moment says, "He was a sergeant in the Army and was sent to Iraq. He was killed by an IED a year and a half ago."

"Oh man, what a bum rap," says Sam. Jesse nods her head without looking up.

Tommy clears his throat and says, "Sorry about your dad." Trey looks at her for the first time, then at Tommy, whose face is somber in the pale light of the fire.

Sam says, "Who was that man helping y'all move in this afternoon?"

"That would be my stepdad, Jeremy," she said, as if the words left a bitter taste in her mouth.

I can't help but ask, "I-Is he a j-jerk?"

Shaking her head slowly, she says, "I wouldn't exactly call him a jerk, he's just all into himself. He pretty much leaves me alone and that's just fine by me. Kind of a 'live-and-let-live' kind of thing."

We nod our heads around the fire as Sam says, "There are definitely worse things." She just looks at him and smiles.

As if on cue, Gracie ambles over and nudges her hand. She strokes the dog's back and scratches behind her floppy ear.

"Traitor," mumbles Trey from the other side of the fire.

"Is he the one who taught you how to fight?" asks Sam, ignoring Trey as he breaks a twig and tosses it into the fire.

"Yeah, he was Special Forces and knew all kinds of combat stuff. Every weekend we spent a few hours working on Krav Maga, the kind of martial arts he learned in the military. He taught me how to defend myself in case I ever needed to use it," she says, casting a sideways glance at Trey.

Staring into the woods, Trey says just above a whisper, "He taught you one heck of a kick, girl." Those were the first civil words he spoke to her all night so far. It was good to see the old Trey coming back around.

Besides those intense pale blue eyes, she is easily one of the prettiest girls around. She's small but has long lean legs like a runner. I'll bet she was on the track team in Atlanta. I wonder what she thinks about us.

Trey breaks off a piece of fish and tosses it to Gracie and then Trixie. Both dogs catch the nugget before it hits the ground. The other two come running as he tosses each of them a piece.

We sit around the fire, telling stories of growing up together and life out here in the country. She enjoys our stories, laughing out loud and adding comments of her own. Before we know it, the night is nearly over and we haven't slept a wink. The eastern sky begins to lighten with streaks of pink and yellow as one of our roosters starts to crow.

"Wow, I can't believe I've spent the whole night out here with a bunch of guys! Mom would have a fit if she knew. I'd better get my stuff and head back home before they get up," she says, brushing herself off.

We offer to walk her home but she declines.

"We're out here just about every weekend, so come back if you want," says Trey. Once he got over himself, he discovered she was all right.

Within a few minutes we put out the fire and head back to our separate homes. Camping on Saturday night does not excuse us from Sunday services. I don't have much use for it, but Mom insists we go. No big deal, every now and again something cool happens.

A couple of months ago, Papa forgot to check his shoes before putting them on. He has severe arthritis and needs to wear shoes that are too big because his toes go in all different directions.

He and our grandma, Nonnie, keep their shoes outside. This started years ago after someone stepped in a cow biscuit and tracked it in. Living on a farm, there's no telling what you might step in, so from then on, all shoes were checked at the door.

Apparently, during the night an old frog was looking for a warm place for the night and found Papa's shoe. It must've been really old or sick because he crawled inside that shoe and croaked, literally. Several days later Papa slipped it on to go to church, not realizing he was bringing along company.

I guess since the shoes were so big, he couldn't feel the fat dead toad flopping around inside. When he settled into the pew, he slipped them off to get comfortable and the little "pew" suddenly became a great big P-E-E-Y-U-U! Everyone tried to ignore it, like when somebody cuts the cheese in public. One of the little kids asked really loud what stunk so bad before his mom could cover his mouth. His little sister, who always crawled around on the floor between everybody's legs each Sunday was the one who found it.

From under the pew we heard a loud squeaky voice. "Hey Papa, you brought a dead toad to church! You're not supposed to do that!"

Most Sundays are so boring I sleep right through them, at least until Mom jars me awake with her elbow.

Mary is finally well enough to attend. She still has a ways to go before wrestling alligators again, but every day she looks a little stronger. I walk over and give her a pat on the back and can tell quickly all is well.

Mom looks tired, but other than that is in good spirits. I don't know how she manages to keep from going crazy when she has so much to worry about. She's always talking about how God is helping her and how he sends his Holy Spirit to whisper things to make her feel better. If that's what she wants to believe, that's up to her. My dad is dead, Papa hurts all the time with arthritis, and my best friend is in a wheelchair. Why would anybody want a God who let those things happen?

When we walk into church, I spot Jake with his family and walk over. They have to use a pew on the far side to accommodate his wheelchair. Yeah, some great God we serve, putting kids in wheelchairs.

Jake's head is turned the other way, talking with someone from the pew just in front of him, so he doesn't see me approaching. As I get closer, I can't help but notice those thin legs of his that are much stronger than they appear. He goes to therapy twice a week because they give him a lot of pain. It's got to be awful, but he never complains. I think I would complain a lot.

I couldn't imagine a life like his, but he just takes it all in stride like it's no big deal. Despite all that stuff, he is the happiest person I know. The easiest way to describe him is simply joyful. Without a doubt, he is the most joyful person I've ever known.

I squat down next to him and gently rap him on the knee with my knuckles. He turns and smiles at me, blond wavy hair dangling on his forehead, still damp from his morning shower. His big blue eyes sparkle even in this low light.

"Hey bro, you guys go camping again last night?" he says with a big grin.

I nod my head and say, "Yep, w-we sure d-did," and tell him all about Jesse showing up out of the blue and Trey getting his butt kicked. He looks at me like I told him aliens flew out of the pond and says, "A girl beat up Trey? Our Trey? Muscle-bound, captain of the football team, all-pro wrestler Trey? Is that what you are telling me?"

"The one and o-only," I say with a laugh, looking around to make sure we don't have any Nosy Nellies listening in.

Realizing I'm serious, he says, "Holy cow!" so loud, several heads turn.

I hold a finger to my mouth, but can't help laughing.

In a low voice he says, "Does your mom know you had a girl at the camp?" he says looking around.

I shake my head.

He giggles and says, "Man, if your mom finds out, you're toast."

I shake my head and say, "Nothing happened, n-not like th-that anyway."

His smile loses some of its usual luster as he says, "Man, wish I had been there to see that."

"Me too, d-dude, m-me too. She t-turned out to be r-really nice and stayed m-most of the n-night with us, j-just talking and s-stuff. Her d-dad was k-killed in the w-war overseas. She's here with her m-mom and s-stepdad."

His smile fades even more as he says "Oh man, that bites."

"Yeah, t-tell me about it."

The music starts to play softly, so I turn to go, but he grabs my arm.

"Where is she from?"

"Atlanta."

"So you think she'll come back down there again, to the campsite I mean?"

"I th-think so. Her and Trey actually g-got along p-pretty good after they t-talked for a while. You should h-have seen him at f-first though, he was sooo m-mad. It was r-really funny."

"I'll bet. I gotta come camping with y'all one of these days, ya know?"

"Yeah, b-bro, I know. We'll s-see what we can d-do about that," I say, but none of our parents acted too excited about the idea whenever we brought the subject up. They didn't exactly say yes or no, but a lame "we'll see." I think every kid should have the chance to go camping with his buddies.

Jake asks, "Hey, we still going to your grandparents' house for lunch today?"

"Yeah, m-man." My grandparents think Jake is the coolest guy ever. "Right n-now I'm just l-lookin' to catch up on s-some sleep," I say with a wink.

"Right there with ya, bro. What's your grandma making for lunch? I'm already hungry."

"F-fried chicken and p-potato salad p-probably." Grandma is a great cook, but after pulling KP for three kids and a husband for forty years she's become a big fan of take out. She still makes homemade pickles and stuff like that, but the majority of their meals somebody else sweats over.

"Yum, wish we were there already," he says.

"I know, b-buddy, but we g-gotta get th-through this f-first," like some sentence handed down by a judge. "Nonnie's already ch-checked Papa's shoes for d-dead toads, so n-no luck th-there."

He snaps his fingers and says, "Rats."

"She ch-checked for th-them too."

He cracks a grin and says, "Crap."

"And th-that too."

A couple of old ladies give us a stern look as we laugh out loud. I say, "Later, dude," and walk back to our pew. I flop down between Mom and Mary, ready for this to be over with. The music is playing softer now and my mind begins to wander. Going without sleep for more than twenty-four hours makes it tough to stay awake, and this quiet music doesn't help. As it begins to fade, so do I.

From behind my eyes, I see images of Dad right before he died. We're at his parents' house, Grandma busy in the kitchen making pickles, and the rest of us in Grandpa's giant garage, salvaging what's left of an old bicycle he found dumped on the side of the road. It looks too old and beat up to fool with, but he's convinced the frame is still in good enough shape to be useful for some kid. I'm doubtful, but he's the expert.

I watch as he and Dad remove the handlebars, sprocket, chain, and pedals. Dad places the bike on the table, and then begins the process of straightening the frame into its original form. Grandpa has a tool for that, like it seems he does for everything else.

Before long, they've not only straightened it to near factory original, but have fixed the dents as well. They hand it off to me for sanding so we can apply a fresh coat of paint. It never ceases to amaze me what these two can do with seemingly worthless pieces of metal. I'm astounded at their ability to create something beautiful out of nothing.

We hang it outside after the sanding is finished so it can be spray-painted. Since it's a girl's bike, they decide on purple. We hook up the machine and watch as every nook and cranny turns satiny and glistens with a fresh coat of paint. We leave the bike to dry during lunch. Excellent! Grandma has made her famous hamburgers and French fries, my favorite! Nobody makes them like she does. I told her she could put every burger joint out of business. She just laughs and rubs my head.

A sharp pain in my ribs brings me back to reality and robs me of a big bowl of banana pudding. You'd think she could at least wait until after dessert. Opening my eyes, Mom is glaring at me, elbow ready to go again. Drat.

The music is playing again, but is now more upbeat. People are standing up and holding hands while singing the words to a song trailing across the front of the church, which means it's almost over and we can get out of here.

Pastor Jeff dismisses the congregation and reminds us about the evening service at 5:30; more power to ya, dude.

Looking to the left, I see Jake and his folks making their way out of the sanctuary. From behind, I hear someone call my name. I turn around and see Mr. Adams walking towards me.

Mr. Adams, a beefy, sturdy man with the disposition of a teddy bear, is waving at me excitedly. He and his wife own a big dairy farm just down the street from our house, and occasionally hire Sam and me to help.

He extends a wide hand for me to shake and says, "Hey there, Jason, glad to catch you here, son," he hollers like I'm across the room. After returning from Vietnam, he discovered the machine gun fire killed not only the enemy, but his hearing as well. Most of the time he forgets to put his hearing aids in, so he shouts at everyone when he speaks. It's made for some really interesting conversation over the years.

He thinks Max Lucado is Mashed Potato and Pastor Doyle down the street is Castor Oil. With all the hilarious stuff he says, I swear he could have his own comedy show on prime time.

Last week Sam and I went to help out with his cows. His wife, Mrs. Adams, answered the door when we knocked and invited us in. She called to her husband who was in the den that he had guests. As he walks to the door, he checks his shoes and says he took his Mylanta and she's probably smelling something he tracked in. Sam and I busted out laughing.

"Oh Herbert, I said guests, not gas. Where are your cotton-pickin' hearin' aides, for cryin' out loud? Why spend that kind of money and not even use them?"

She turns back to us and says, "If that don't beat all," throwing her dishtowel into the washroom. He looks at her like he has no idea why she's in such a huff. They are the funniest couple around and don't even know it.

He continues, "I was wondering if you aren't too busy tomorrow after school, if you and your dog could give me a hand rounding up some cows I need to sell. If your cousin Sam could come along, too, that would be great," he bellows.

"S-sure thing, Mr. Adams. I know T-trixie and I can c-come. I'll t-talk to Sam. You can at least c-count on m-me."

"Thanks Jason, you're a godsend, boy." He hesitates a moment, shuffling his feet uncomfortably for a moment and says, "How is your mom doing, you know, after your daddy and all. Is she making out okay? I think about her a lot, so young, and you kids and all."

I give him my practiced line because I have to repeat it so often. "Yes sir, sh-she is, j-just one d-day at time. Thanks f-for asking." I don't like talking about my dad, and he can tell. He clears his throat, his way of saying "I understand," then pats me on the shoulder.

"Okay, son, just tell her I asked about her, all right? If she ever needs anything, you'll tell me, right?"

"Yes s-sir, I will."

"Very good, we'll see you tomorrow after school then," he hollers.

Turning around, I see Jake doing wheelies in his chair while the little kids point and laugh, asking if they can take a ride. I walk over and he stops, disappointing the tots. They lose interest and skitter around, looking for something else to entertain them.

"Hey, dude, you r-remembered to b-bring your s-swim trunks, right?"

"Oh yeah," he says excitedly, "bring it on!"

We move from under the canopy of oak trees into the bright warm sunlight. That's one of the few things you can count on living in Florida; year-round sunshine even in places you'd rather not have it. If we're lucky, we get to wear long sleeves in December, and maybe January.

Lots of people walk around shaking hands and chatting as they mingle in the courtyard. Pastor Jeff stands at the door pretending to listen to everyone as they walk past, shaking hands and getting a bunch of hugs from everybody, mostly the women. Guys around here aren't too big into hugging other guys.

I find Trey, Tommy, and Vivian. Tommy is old enough to drive, so he is their chauffeur today since Aunt Moe and Uncle Wyatt both have to work. They are also coming to my grandparents' house for lunch. "The more the merrier" is Grandma's favorite phrase. It's so much fun at their house that I always have kids asking if they can come.

My grandpa has always been the coolest grandpa in the history of grandpas, except for my other grandpa, Papa. They're always in a tight running for the top spot.

Grandpa is full of energy and refuses to let a few years under his belt slow him down. He's more fit than most people half his age. Even in his sixties, he can still do one-armed pull-ups and run five miles a day. A retired Air Force Master Sergeant, the drive to remain physically and mentally fit refuses to go away.

Ever since I can remember, he's had an old VW van he calls a "hippie wagon," where he keeps a footlocker stuffed full of all kinds of treats like candy, puddings, and fruit snacks. We're allowed one dip a day, "So we don't grow fat and lazy," he says. Every kid in the vicinity knows about his goodie box, so he keeps the key hidden.

We make it back to our cars and drive the five blocks to my grandparents' house. Pulling into the driveway, we see through the window that the food is already here, piled high on the table. My mouth is already watering.

Jake is backing down the ramp of his specially designed van. Grandpa put a wooden ramp at his house when he found out I had a friend in a wheelchair. That's just the way he is.

Tommy, Trey, and Vivian drive up and park across the street, an enormous inner tube shoved into the bed of the truck.

"Hey knucklehead, where's the food?" Trey yells. Apparently he's fully recovered from his encounter with the psycho ninja last night. He looks to be his old, happy-go-lucky self again.

Vivian walks over and gives Jake a hug, and then his parents.

"Hi Vivian, how have you been?" asks Jake's mom as she grabs a gallon of tea from the backseat.

"I'm doing good, just trying to keep my GPA up so I can get into a decent college when I graduate." That sounds just like Vivian, always the scholar—until she gets mad, then all that goes right out the window. Only a few who have felt her fury lived to tell about it.

"Well good, honey, you keep up the hard work."

Everyone gathers inside my grandparents' cramped living room. They don't have much space, so we all squeeze around close to the walls. Everybody is laughing and joking as Grandma fills the glasses with ice. I zigzag my way over and give her a hug. Deep brown eyes that matched Dad's perfectly turn to me.

Even at her age she stands tall and proud, no stooped shoulders for this lady. If there were a picture of elegance and grace, it would be her.

She stands a full three inches taller than Grandpa, a fact he finds hilarious. Grandpa told me her love of life is what he first noticed about her. He didn't care if he had to reach up to kiss her, so long as she didn't mind bending down.

In my book, the greatest thing about Grandma is her homemade pickles, hamburgers, and French fries. I realize that sounds pretty shallow, even coming from a teenager, but there's no one in the world who can make them better.

She smiles at me as a reflection of Dad dances across her face, an unspoken air of sadness trailing behind it and says, "I'm so glad you kids haven't gotten too old to spend some time with your old grandma and grandpa."

"I'll never be too old for that," I say, and mean it.

We chat a few minutes, then I help her scoop more ice. As I'm shoveling it into a bowl, I glance at the pictures hanging on the walls. I've only seen them a thousand times but there's something fascinating about looking at old pictures, especially of those who have already passed on. One in particular always grabs my attention more than the rest. It's my grandpa's younger brother, Nolan. He took off twenty years ago, and hasn't been heard from since. No word of whether he's alive, dead, in jail, or otherwise. It's like he sailed to the edge of the earth and just fell off.

Kissing Grandma on the cheek, I place the bowl of ice on the table and move closer to the picture. Is there some subtle clue I might have overlooked the last hundred times I looked at it? My dad is standing next to Uncle Nolan with a fishing pole propped between them. He's not as old as me, maybe ten or eleven. I look so much like him, except for the hair anyway. Same high cheekbones, same almond-shaped eyes, and wide chin.

Grandma tells me stories of how Uncle Nolan and Dad were inseparable when Dad was just a boy. They spent lots of time fishing, their favorite pastime. It's hard to imagine my dad as a kid.

Then my eyes find the empty dog bed between the movement of bodies. Yogi Bear occupied that bed and everybody's hearts for almost twenty years. It tore my grandparents up to let him go, but the day finally came a couple of months ago when he couldn't get up anymore. Grandpa held him on his lap as the vet administered the secret cocktail. Their house is definitely missing something without him here. He loved parties like this and would be right in the thick of it.

We all eventually gather around the table, say grace and dig in. While filling our plates, Grandma asks Vivian about the incident at the movie theater Friday night. Like I said before, there are no secrets in small towns. Vivian's face turns red as her brothers start to giggle.

"Grandma (everyone calls her that, even if they aren't hers), I just don't put up with rude people. We took Trevor, the little boy I baby-sit, to see one of the kid movies, and this woman kept fussing and hollering at this poor little kid down front. He was just having fun, I mean it's a kid's movie, for crying out loud!

"Anyway, she was being way more obnoxious than that poor kid, and I could tell everybody was sick and tired of listening to her complain. After the movie was over and the lights came on, she stood up and yelled at the parents, 'Keep that kid home next time,' and that just did it."

"You go, girl!" Mary shouts, arms raised high in the air.

Vivian bumps fists with her and continues, "When I saw this ugly, big, fat woman shaking her finger at that little kid, I couldn't hold it inside anymore. Standing up, I yelled back, 'Hey fatso, why don't YOU stay home next time!' Everybody in the whole theater got to their feet and started clapping and cheering."

We hoot and holler around the table, but she shushes us. After we get quiet, she says, "Then do you know what she did? She turned around and shot me the bird! Sorry Grandma, I know I'm not supposed to say stuff like that, but that's what she did! And I know it's wrong to call people names, but she had it coming." Everybody, including Grandma, is laughing now.

"Well, I hope that scoundrel learned her lesson," Grandma says as she pats her on the shoulder.

"And that's not all, Grandma."

With a look of surprise, she says, "There's more?"

"Yeah, believe it or not. After we walked outside in the parking lot, she called me a bunch of four-letter words, right in front of the kids!"

With a look of disgust, Grandma says, "Some people!"

"Yeah, and then she tried to throw her drink on me, but guess what! I ducked and the police officer standing right behind me got it instead!" Everybody starts laughing again. Vivian says over the noise, "The cop was so mad, he arrested her for harassment. It was awesome!"

Tommy and Trey laughed the loudest, probably relieved someone besides them was the subject of her wrath.

"Sounds like the Vivian Show was the best ticket in town," said Grandpa. "I only wished I'd been there to see it."

After things settle back down, Tommy says, "Hey Grandpa, I hear you left a bunch of teenagers in the dust last week in that big bike race." Grandpa gives the mischievous grin he flashes when there's about to be a story.

"I tell ya what, those kids showed up thinking they had my number. They unloaded those fancy contraptions of theirs and strutted around in those silly biker shorts, ready to show everybody who was boss. When they saw me, they snickered, eyeballing my rescued twenty-year-old Schwinn and homemade seat.

"They had brand-new everything, all the way down to their water bottles. Well, these kids weren't used to riding outside like I do every day, no sir-ree. They spend most of their time riding in an air-conditioned gym, so when the Florida heat and humidity kicked in, they faded like pansies. I didn't finish first, but I crossed the line way before them," he says with a wink.

I don't know how Grandpa manages to stay so upbeat. I know he misses Dad, but he seems almost, I don't know, okay with it all. I don't mean that in a bad way. I know he misses him as much as we do; he just seems to be at peace with it, maybe because he saw more than his fair share of death during the war. Grandma tells me he has a whole box filled with all kinds of medals and awards. Grandpa is not the kind of man to brag about being brave though.

"Guess their trophy was a big helping of humble pie," says Sam. Grandpa pats him on the back and says, "Don't ya know it, son, and

I'll bet it was mighty hard to swallow, which is more than I can say for your grandma's banana pudding."

Just about that time, Grandma comes around the corner with a huge pan of our favorite dessert.

As she passes by, she whispers in my ear, "The only thing worth sweating over."

Big bowlfuls go around until every bit of it is gone. After clearing the table, Grandpa beats us all at a game of Chinese Checkers. He's the reigning champ around here. Afterward, we sit around and talk for a while, careful not to bring up the subject of Dad.

Mom gets up and heads to the back of the house, I assume to use the restroom. Guess she beat me to it, I was going to change into swim trunks but I can wait until she gets out. Meanwhile, I go to the truck and grab my bag and towel. Mom's still in there, so I wait in the hallway until she's done.

As I approach the bedroom door, I'm surprised to see it's open. Puzzled, I look around the corner and see her sitting on the edge of Grandma and Grandpa's bed in tears. I rush over to her, suddenly feeling very protective.

Then I see what has gotten her so upset. In her lap is a hairbrush. In the bristles are strands of hair that don't belong to Grandma or Grandpa. There is no mistaking the deep auburn, coppery color. This was my dad's hairbrush.

"Where d-did you f-find this, Mom?" I whisper, almost afraid to touch it.

She sniffles a little, wiping her face with her hands and says, "I opened one of the cabinets to get another roll of paper, and there on the side, toward the back, was this brush," tears roll down her cheeks. I pull her into my chest and feel her arms wrap around my waist. Hot tears burn my cheeks as I try to hide my embarrassment. I clear my throat, but this only makes matters worse. I decide to stop fighting and let them do as they wish.

Mom and I hold each other for a minute or two and then she pulls away, wiping her face with her hands again. She clutches the brush to her chest and closes her eyes. She looked so small and fragile in that moment, and somewhere in my heart a little piece of me died. Somehow we are going to make it through this, but I have no idea how.

Sitting there quietly, we don't say anything more. After a moment, she gets up and puts the brush back where she found it and says, "Jason, let's not mention this to anyone right now, okay?"

I wipe my face with my shirt and say, "Okay, Mom." That was about all I could manage. We look at each other with tears on our faces and unexpectedly giggle, of all things.

"We must look a sight," she says with a little grin.

"Yeah, we m-must."

She hugs me one more time before walking out.

My head is spinning as I push the memories back into a safer place. That will have to do for now, because I don't know what else to do with them.

By the time I get outside, Trey has the inner tube attached to the back of the boat with a long white rope.

Looking across the river, I take in the awesome beauty of this special place. The river is lined with thick woods so lush and green one might think they had yet to be discovered. Along the shore, tall grey birds peck at the water. One of them tosses a minnow into the air, catching it in its beak before it hits the water. From the narrow canal a mama duck appears with six babies following behind. They live in my grandparents' yard and get Grandma's scraps every afternoon. I've watched many a sunset from this very spot, and feel Dad everywhere.

When we first started taking the boat out a couple of years ago, we weren't sure if Jake's parents would let him tag along. He loves to do all the same stuff we do, but this can get a little rough. They agreed to let him try if he wanted to, so long as I went with him.

We slip into our stupid life preservers, a real pain, but it's the law. Nobody leaves the dock without them strapped on. Trey, Vivian,

Tommy, Jake, and I get on the boat. The adults gather around the dock to watch as we make our way to the middle of the river.

Grandpa taught all of us how to operate the outboard motor and navigate the river, something we've been doing since we were little kids. Since Tommy is the oldest, he drives the boat today.

Trey throws the inner tube into the water and climbs in. Tommy slowly moves the boat forward until the rope is taut. When Trey gives the thumbs up, Tommy guns the motor and the front of the boat rises. Approaching the 301 bridge, Tommy throttles down the engine as we loop back. He pours on the power again as we straighten out, sending Trey around so fast he careens off a wave, doing a complete somersault. He lands hard, bouncing high above the tube but manages to hang on.

We take turns riding behind the boat until only Jake and I remain. I get in first then Trey and Tommy help Jake down. Once we're secure in the middle, Tommy begins the whole process all over again.

As the rope grows tight, I shout over the roar of the engine, "Hey, man, you r-ready to rock and r-roll?" He yells back, "Like Twisted Sister!"

The tube starts bouncing and skipping over the surface so fast, it goes by in a blur. Jake yells at the top of his lungs as I tighten my grip on his life jacket.

We've reached the bridge now and get ready to head back. Just as we begin swinging wide, a big wave created from another boat appears directly in front of us. Our speed is high enough that I'm worried we'll flip over if we hit it at the wrong angle.

I grab hold of the tube and Jake a little tighter. The wave is getting closer and we're going even faster! I'd never forgive myself if anything happened to him out here.

The wave closes in fast, and suddenly we slam into it hard and launch high in the air. The tube rockets away as we careen through the air.

Jake continues to holler as we tumble end over end. A moment later we hit the water with a stiff jolt, and all goes instantly silent. Long shafts of light dance all around us as silvery bubbles escape upward. The life vests quickly spring to life and dutifully haul us to the surface.

When we break through, I hurriedly turn Jake around to make sure he's all right. His eyes are squeezed tight as water streams down his face in long rivulets.

I say, "Hey m-man, you okay?" He opens his eyes quickly as he gasps for air, looking around like he has no idea where we are. His eyes find me again as his fingers wrap around my life vest. At first I thought he was upset, but a smile creeps across his face as he says, "That was so rockin' cool, man! Can we do it again?"

Relieved, I throw my head back and holler. The adults back on shore are gathered at the end of the dock, staring intently in our direction, and none are smiling.

Tommy brings the boat back around and everyone leans over the side with a look of deep concern. Once they realize we're okay, they start laughing and clap each other on the back, as Tommy gives a thumps-up to shore. When they haul us into the boat, Vivian says to Jake, "Man, that was the coolest thing I've ever seen! How did you get to be so awesome?"

Jake nudges me and says, "It has a lot to do with the company I keep."

CHAPTER SIX

Early Sunday morning, Trixie announces the arrival of Trey's family. I peek through the curtain and see their van pulling into our driveway.

Mom walks from the kitchen table and gives me a hug before going outside. Trey and Tommy are just stepping out of their van when we come strolling out. I throw my gear into the open hatch while Mom talks with Aunt Moe and Uncle Wyatt through the passenger window.

"Hope you remembered to pack your underwear this time, Shark Bait," says Tommy with a snort. The dumb mistakes we make in life stay with us forever it seems. I picked up this stupid name after crashing a Moped face first, skinning my face and hands. I was riding with Trey and Tommy along the shore a couple of summers ago and hit a patch of rocky limestone. The front wheel jerked hard on a rock and down I went. The only water around to wash the blood off was the beach, so they helped me to the water's edge. The salty ocean water stung like crazy, but it cleaned up the bloody mess.

As I was scooping the water over my wounds, the three of us looked out and saw a large fin appear on the horizon. Even though it was a long way out and we were close to shore, we jumped up and ran onto the beach. When Tommy told the story later, it became a real fisherman's tale. Before long, I was Robert Shaw fighting off a King Kong shark trying to turn me into an hors d'oeuvre.

Five years ago I forgot to pack my underwear on a trip to the mountains and had to either keep wearing the same dirty pair or go without. I chose to go without, which taught me never to forget them again.

"W-what, d-don't have anything better to do than think about m-my underwear?"

"Very funny, dork. Just making sure so you don't ask to borrow mine."

"Uh, I'd g-go without for the rest of m-my life before I d-did that."

"Guys are so gross!" Vivian says, as she brushes by me on her way to see Mary before we take off.

Trixie is running around the truck, jumping up and down, about to blow a gasket waiting for George and Gracie to get out. They're staying here while we're gone.

"Keep your furry britches on, guys," Trey says, putting down an enormous bag of dog food.

He puts his face against the window and puffs his cheeks out like a blowfish, which makes them go even crazier.

"For the love of Pete, will you let the dogs out already? I can't even hear myself think," Aunt Moe hollers from the front seat. As soon as Trey opens the door, they bolt out. Trixie takes off for the pasture with them at her heels. They're probably headed straight for the mud pit, their favorite hangout.

Quiet settles in like an old friend as Mom and Aunt Moe continue their conversation. She places a hand on Mom's arm and tells her again that if she needs anything to call. I know Aunt Moe means well, but we don't like to ask for help. Between Mom and me, we've managed to handle most everything. As soon as I can get a job, nobody will have to worry about us anymore.

As they talk, light from the morning sun catches the highlights in Mom's hair as a few loose strands lilt softly around her face. She brushes them away, but they don't stay and float back again. She just pats Aunt Moe's hand and tells her she appreciates the offer.

Uncle Wyatt reaches over and takes Mom's hand, rubbing his thumb across her knuckles.

"Tom was like a brother to me. We miss him every day, and just want to be there for y'all. I know he would do the same for us if we were the ones, you know ..." Mom smiles softly and places her hand on his. Aunt Moe reaches up and kisses her on the cheek.

"Y'all have been such a source of strength. Just being here and including Jason in your vacation is a huge help. He loves being with Trey and Tommy. Don't worry about me. I'll be fine. This will give me a chance to catch up on a few things."

She steps to the side and the three of us climb into the back seat and fasten our seatbelts.

Mom reaches back inside and says, "You boys have fun and be careful. Jason, did you remember your sun block?"

"Yes, m-ma'am, I g-got it." At least she didn't ask about my underwear.

"Remember to bring me some mangoes, okay?"

"I'll make sure he doesn't forget," says Aunt Moe, as she pats Mom on the arm.

She stands in the driveway and waves as we make our way to the road. Looking back, my mom seems so small and frail, yet strong and determined all at the same time.

It will take us about eight hours to get to the Keys, so we'll arrive about suppertime.

The hours pass by quickly as we chat and snack along the way. The landscape slowly turns from oaks and pines to saw grass and mangrove swamps where mosquitoes the size of vultures live and can drain the blood from a man in about ten seconds. That's the last place on Earth you want to get stuck without bionic-strength insect repellent.

Around six o'clock, we pull into the dock where Uncle Wyatt keeps his sailboat *Second Act.* Stepping out of the car, we stretch and walk around, breathing in the warm salty air, ripe with seaweed and motor oil.

We'll stay on the boat tonight. It always feels so weird getting our sea legs, walking like a bunch of drunks on the listing boat, but after a couple of days, it comes effortlessly. When we get back on land, we have to go through it all over again.

Walking past the harbor to an area where I can see way out over the ocean, the surface of the Atlantic sparkles like a million diamonds scattered across the waves.

From the southernmost point of Key West, Cuba lies about 90 miles away. I wonder just how far I can see. The Atlantic seems to go on forever. A slap on my shoulder makes me jump.

"Hey Shark Bait, we gotta get the van unloaded so we can go over to the pier," says Tommy.

Following him back to the van, we reach inside and grab our gear and carry it on board.

Trey is already finished and is helping his mom carry the coolers of food into the galley. The kitchen is small but has everything Aunt Moe needs to whip up some of the finest meals on the seven seas.

Finally all of the unpacking is finished and the six of us head to the pier. No trip to the Keys is complete without paying it a visit. It has everything, and I mean everything: artists, belly dancers, magicians, fortune tellers, jugglers, people playing guitars, flutes, steel drums, and just about anything else you can imagine.

We dodge kids and wrinkly old geezers on roller skates as they weave their way around the pier. Getting closer now, the smell of cocoa butter, popcorn, hot dogs, cotton candy, and burgers all mingle together. We find our way to a hamburger stand and get one with everything. After finding a small grassy area, we sit down to devour our meal.

"Now this is how to start a vacation, kids," Uncle Wyatt says, a little mustard dribbling down his chin as he talks. Aunt Moe reaches over and wipes his face.

"I swear, Wyatt, you have worse table manners than the children."

He gives her a sideways glance and says, "For one, we've got no table, and two, I'm on vacation and etiquette doesn't apply here." He pauses a moment and says, "Do my lack of table manners offend any of you kids?"

We shake our heads and keep on eating. He says, "See," reaching over and giving her a kiss on the cheek, leaving a streak of mustard behind.

"For Pete's sake," she says as she wipes it off, smacking him on the arm.

Uncle Wyatt is by far the coolest guy I have ever known, besides my dad. They were good friends, and I know he misses him a lot too.

Uncle Wyatt is a Dive Master and certified each of us. He's held weekly classes in the basement of their house for years. His vacation time is usually spent taking his students and kids to all kinds of off-the-beaten path places to explore. One place in particular people really like is called "hospital hole," for reasons I don't like to think about. This is where most of us were certified.

Trey licks his fingers, looking around for his can of soda and almost knocks it over.

"The crowd's beginning to show up," says Tommy, as bodies shuffle by. Calypso music floats through the air as people dance and sway to the sultry beat.

Uncle Wyatt wipes his face with the empty wrapper as Aunt Moe rolls her eyes. You'd think she would've let it go by now. He reaches over and takes her hand as he stands up.

"My lady, may I have this dance?" he says with a really bad Jamaican accent, pulling her in close and kissing her on the neck.

"Dad, you're such a dork," says Trey.

"You're the dork, Trey, leave Dad alone," says Vivian, defender of her biggest fan. Anybody wanting to criticize her dad had better be ready for a fight.

"How do you think you boys got here?" he says to Trey, as Aunt Moe playfully pulls his hat down over his eyes before kissing him back.

"I think I'm gonna be sick," says Tommy.

"Boys are so dumb," says Vivian.

Trey gets to his feet, smacks me on the back of the head and says, "Let's go see what we can see, cuz."

Now we're talking. This is the mother of all weird, outrageous, strange, and downright raunchy places. In other words, the coolest place on earth.

"We're gonna walk around before the sun goes down. I can't handle any more of this," says Trey.

"I'm gonna see if I can find another girl to hang out with. The thought of having to spend the entire week surrounded by a bunch of sweaty, stinky guys makes me want to hurl," Vivian says.

I give my armpit a sniff.

As the four of us leave the lovebirds alone and head toward the far end of the pier, Uncle Wyatt calls from behind. "Hey boys, watch out for your baby sister, okay?"

With a roll of her eyes and hands on her hips, Vivian says, "I'm not a baby any more, Daddy. I'm almost a teenager, you know."

"You will always be my baby, no matter how old you are," he says back.

"We got it under control, Dad," Tommy hollers over his shoulder.

As we make our way to the pier, a guy swallowing a sword stands on a small grassy area and we stop to watch. My throat tightens and aches just thinking about it. When he pulls the sword out, minus the gore you'd expect, he takes a bow for the crowd. We clap and cheer as he motions toward a box sprinkled with loose change and a few bills. Tommy pulls out a crumpled dollar bill and tosses it in. The man thanks him with a nod of his head before getting ready to eat another sword.

Continuing on, we watch as a magician pulls a long line of handkerchiefs out of a girl's ear as her friends take pictures with their phones.

Up ahead, the crowd parts as an old fat guy blunders his way through, eagerly getting out of his way. In an attempt to cover up his bald head, he's done a comb-over with the few remaining hairs he has left. The bright red Speedo he's managed to squeeze into looks like it's harboring a stash of smuggled fruit fighting to escape.

Just above his fruit, a hairy flabby belly jiggles with every step he takes like a fuzzy sack of Jell-O. How can anybody look so utterly ridiculous and have no clue? The label inside his Speedo should read, "Fruit of the Loon." I need to get out of here before he spills X-rated fruit salad all over the deck.

Pushing my burger back down, we keep walking until our paths cross a pack of girls in tight bikinis. They are huddled together, talking and laughing excitedly. Like most guys, our babe radar is razor sharp and able to detect a good-looking girl from miles away. The three of us stop and stare, not caring in the least we have become gawking idiots. We stop so abruptly that Vivian doesn't notice and runs into Trey.

"What the ..." and before she can finish her sentence, she realizes what's going on.

"Should've known, guys are so gross," giving Trey's shoulder a shove. I don't think he even felt it. As we stare at the giggling girls, I absent-mindedly think about Jesse. I barely even know her, but in the short time we've spent together, I find her invading my thoughts more and more. I've never known anyone quite like her.

I push the thought away as Vivian walks past. I call out to her, but she ignores me. Now that's the kind of girl a guy will need special training to handle. Even a lion tamer would have his hands full with that one.

The crowd thickens as people start vying for the best place to watch the sunset. As the sun makes its descent, the music becomes more lively and intense. Deep crimson and lazy orange streaks paint the darkening sky. I've seen some amazing sunsets before, but none to rival anything down here. A hush falls over the crowd as the fiery canvas spreads wide and grows in intensity. As the colors bleed into the ocean, a lone pelican skims across the water just past the pier.

In a few moments the sun drops into the ocean, taking the last of the light with it. Darkness creeps in to take its place, and I notice Vivian has not returned.

The girls we were watching have walked on, as Trey and Tommy search for them. Somewhere in their browsing, it occurs to them their sister is nowhere in our vicinity. Both of them look at me, like I'm supposed to know.

"Vivian w-walked off a f-few minutes ago," I say quickly, feeling a little guilty.

"Well, let's start walking around until we find her. She probably didn't go too far," says Tommy. Always the calm one, just like his dad.

We fan out but keep each other in sight. There are so many people milling about, dancing and swaying to the music, it's hard to pick one person out in the crowd. Her cell phone got dropped into the toilet before we left, so we can't call her.

I make it to the edge of the water where the crowd is thinning and feel something rub against my bare leg. Looking down, I see a small brown and white sheltie staring up at me. Reaching down, I pat the dog on the head. She jumps in the air like her hind legs are made of springs. Looking around to see if anyone is with her, I hear someone calling "Lady" and see Vivian and another girl about her age running through the crowd toward me.

"There you are, bad girl," the girl says.

Vivian is grinning from ear to ear.

"Hey V-vivian, we were j-just looking for y-you."

The smile fades quickly as she says, "I told you guys I'm not a baby anymore, you don't need to follow me around."

"C-calm down, it was g-getting dark is all," I say in my defense.

The dog yips happily and suddenly Vivian forgets all about being mad. Getting down on her knees, she hugs the little sheltie. Lady licks her face and thumps her tail on the ground.

Vivian looks up at the girl standing next to her and says, "Oh Sandy, this is my cousin Jason. He came down with us from Riverview. He's a lot of fun but kind of weird, but you'll get used to him."

I feel my face flush as Sandy reaches out her hand. I shake it and say, "P-Pleased to m-meet you, Sandy."

"And always sooo polite," says Vivian with a grin.

Ignoring my stutter, Sandy says, "I think he's kind of cute."

I smile at her and say, "Thanks. W-Where are you f-from?"

"We live in Homestead, not very far away. My parents like to come down here every couple of months to snorkel around the reefs and do some fishing."

"We went by Homestead on the way down, just past Miami, right?" Vivian asks.

I nod my head.

"Yeah, Homestead is a n-nice little t-town," I say, brushing away a mosquito as I rub the dog's head. "Lady is r-real p-pretty," I continue, not sure what else to say.

From behind, Tommy's loud voice calls over the crowd, "There you are. We've been looking all over for you, little sis," he says out of breath.

I roll my eyes as she puts her hands on her hips and informs him of her grown-up status and to butt out of her business. Tommy throws his hand into the air and steps back.

"Chill, sis, we're on vacation, so how about taking a break from busting my chops already. Besides, Dad sent me out to round everybody up so we can head back to the boat."

He leans down and scratches Lady behind the ear. She leans into it like it's the best thing ever.

"Whose dog?"

Vivian says, "That's Lady, and she belongs to my new best friend, Sandy," motioning toward her.

Sandy shakes his hand and acts kind of shy. Just then Trey walks up and smacks Tommy on the back of the head.

"I thought you were rounding everybody up, bro, what's goin' on?" he says.

Sandy lays eyes on Trey and I know what's about to happen. I've seen it a million times. It doesn't matter how old or young the girls are, they respond the same way, gushing all over him to the point of embarrassment. All that sculpted muscle and tight olive skin turns them into silly schoolgirls, especially when he flashes those baby blues in their direction. He runs his hand through his short brown hair as Sandy turns a dark crimson and giggles.

"These are my two creepy brothers that follow me around and spy on me all the time," she says with disgust.

I don't think Sandy heard a thing. Lady begins to whine, breaking the spell.

Sandy blinks her eyes, as if just now realizing the rest of us are still here.

"Nice to meet you," she mumbles, reaching down to give Lady a rub.

"Oh, my mom and dad are probably wondering where I went. Vivian, I'll call you when we get home," holding up a little slip of white paper. The girls hug each other, like girls always do, then Vivian hugs Lady again before they leave.

We make our way to where Aunt Moe and Uncle Wyatt are sitting under a tree then pack up and head back to the boat, each talking about all the cool stuff we saw tonight.

The ocean is calm and beautiful the next morning. Sometimes there are white caps, but not today, so it's smooth sailing. There's just enough of a breeze to use the sails, and the sky is bright and clear, a perfect day for diving.

We set sail for an area past the coral reefs to a deeper area famous for big grouper and lobster. Uncle Wyatt found it a few years ago and has gone there every year since.

After motoring our way out of the harbor and into the open ocean, Tommy and Trey raise the sail. It waffles and flounders for a moment, then with a crisp WHOOSH, it catches a stiff breeze and fills fat and sure.

Our faces catch the mist from the spray as we cut through the waves, the taste of salt drying on our lips. Casting a look over the side, the ocean is so clear it looks like glass. The bottom is more than twenty feet below, but looks close enough to touch. I sit back and close my eyes, letting the soft mist caress my face. There's no sound except the gentle flapping of the sail and a couple of gulls cawing overhead. I breathe deep and let the warm salty air fill my lungs. I no longer smell seaweed or motor oil, just the pure, sweet breath of the ocean.

After a couple of hours, we reach our destination and secure the anchor. We pull the equipment out of the holding areas and get things ready. Aunt Moe makes sure everyone has sun block on as we sort out the gear.

Trey holds out a mask that belongs to his sister, but she ignores it as she searches for her flippers.

Getting impatient, he says, "If you don't want me to spit in your mask, you better take it now."

With a look of utter distain, she snatches the mask from his hands and says, "The first fiddler crab I find, I'm dropping down your shorts."

Trey laughs out loud, covering his crotch at the same time and says, "That sounds like the line from a country and western song."

Without missing a beat, she shoots back, "Yeah, it's called The Fiddler and the Fool take a trip down under!'"

Tommy cackles from the rear of the boat, "When are you going to learn you can't go toe to toe with her, Trey! She kicks your butt every time."

Finally, everybody has their gear strapped on and we're ready to go. Falling backwards off anything goes against every instinct I have, but I just suck it up and take the plunge.

Splashing down into the water is like entering another world, which in a way, I guess we are. Like alien visitors suddenly immersed in a foreign domain, I feel oddly out of place. All of the strange creatures here are so different than the world we just left; it's easy to imagine we've travelled to another planet.

As the warm water envelops me, I'm struck by the absolute silence until I draw my first breath through the regulator, and suddenly it sounds like Darth Vader has snuck up behind me. Unlike a reef where the constant scraping of fish chewing on the coral is everywhere, out here is totally without sound.

All five of us look at each other and give a thumbs-up before moving on. The bottom of the ocean in this area has none of the beautiful coral like the reefs do, but is covered with acre after acre of olive drab sea grass swaying back and forth. The current transforms these thin blades of slimy grass into a swaying dance floor. Nothing but the rhythmic movement of green goes on as far as we can see. The lack of anything interesting to look at keeps it from becoming a big tourist attraction like the coral reefs, so there aren't many boats around. Pretty things to look at are not the reason we are out here today. Our sole mission is to find lobsters, who love to hide in these grassy areas.

The only one not going in the water today is Aunt Moe. She says unless there is something pretty to look at it's a waste of her time. A stack of unread magazines and a frosty glass of sweet tea are her only companions today.

Our supply of air tanks allows us two days of diving before they have to be refilled. After that, it's strictly snorkeling.

Occasionally, there are interesting pieces of isolated brain coral or sponges with little fish living inside, or conch shells here and there, but other than that, it's the same old thing.

The five of us stay within sight of each other for safety reasons, since there is no such thing as calling for help. Since Uncle Wyatt trained and certified each of us, we had to prove to him we could handle the open ocean or we wouldn't be allowed to go to the Keys with him.

He and Vivian are dive buddies while Trey, Tommy, and me will be a threesome. Fanning out, we begin looking for signs of lobster. They like to walk in the tall grass along the ocean floor. They also like to burrow in holes left by something else and let a few inches of antennae poke out of the opening.

We catch them in a couple of different ways, depending on how we find them. Since they swim backwards, one of us gets behind the lobster while someone else approaches it from the front. When it tries to escape, it flicks its tail and the person in the rear snags it if they are quick enough.

If they are in a hole, we use a tickle stick to get them out into the open and then snatch them up.

Once they are caught, they thrash like Taz, twisting and jerking with their sharp spines, squealing and shrieking like a stuck pig.

We carry them to the boat, where Aunt Moe whacks them over the head with a hammer then tosses them into a cooler full of ice.

We've seen folks do some cruel, sadistic things to these little creatures, like twisting them apart while they are still alive and throwing the living heads back into the water. I remember being in the water near a boat once when some jerk did that and watched as the poor critter tried to use its skinny little front legs to get to the bottom. Of course, without a tail, it couldn't do a thing but sink down slowly and try to find a place to die.

My dad said we are supposed to be caretakers of the planet, not abusers. When we hunted, if a clean, one-shot kill couldn't be made, then we didn't take the shot.

About ten minutes pass as we glide over the bottom, when Uncle Wyatt signals us. Slowly, and without creating a stir, we circle around and spot several large lobsters walking one behind the other single file, just like we're supposed to do at school.

All at once they realize they are no longer alone and freeze, their feelers nervously jerking around.

Uncle Wyatt slowly approaches from the front, while the rest of us make a semi-circle around the sides and rear. He raises his arms out wide, like he's going to scoop them up in a gigantic hug. They become confused and don't know how to react. The one in the rear rockets toward us kids, headed right for Vivian, and for a moment I see a look of concern flicker across Tommy's face. If that lobster misses the net and hits his sister, she could get cut up pretty bad. She doesn't have as much experience with this as we do, but like a pro, she jerks her net to the side and it sails right in. The furious lobster thrashes about, shrieking like a banshee. Trey reaches over and pinches the net above the lobster and takes control. For once, she doesn't resist and gladly hands over the whole kit and caboodle.

As the others dart in different directions, Tommy and I lunge and each snag one. Our gloves are too thick for their jagged spines to penetrate when they go ballistic.

After a few minutes they relent and calm down, and become very docile. We manage to catch four of them, with only one making a great escape. Carefully we measure them to make sure they are of legal size. Once that's done, we haul them back to Aunt Moe.

She leans over the side with a bucket as we drop them in. All kind of ruckus breaks loose when she dumps them onto a thick piece of plywood on the deck. We hear a couple of loud thuds and all goes quiet.

The five of us pull our masks on the top of our heads and bob in the water while she takes care of business.

We don't see or hear anything after that, so Uncle Wyatt calls out, "Hey Babe, everything all right up there?" After a moment she leans over the side, a few strands of brown hair falling into her face and says, "There's my supper, where's yours?"

Uncle Wyatt lets out a loud laugh and says, "Kids, now that's a real woman."

Aunt Moe stands up, and with a quirky grin pulls up the shirt she's wearing, revealing a large fist stretching across the front of her bathing suit.

Uncle Wyatt says, "See what I mean?"

Shaking our heads, we stuff our regulators into our mouths and head back down to find the rest of dinner. Over the next two hours, we catch three lobsters for each of us, and five large grouper Aunt Moe managed to catch with her rod and reel. We're going to eat like kings tonight.

With supper in the boat, Trey, Tommy, and I decide to stay in the water a little longer while Aunt Moe and Vivian get the food ready. Uncle Wyatt decides he's had enough water for the day and changes into some dry clothes and cleans the fish.

Our tanks are flat, so we strip them off and snorkel around until it's time to eat. There aren't many sharks in this area, but one can be too many. I've seen a few over the years, and even the little ones are scary. Images of "Jaws" flash through my mind, hoping I don't have enough meat on my bones to look attractive. They never seem to pay me any attention; instead, they mostly just wander about, slowly cruising the reef.

Out of the corner of my eye, a small orange funnel-shaped sponge appears in the midst of the tall grass, only the top few inches showing. The current is flowing in that direction, so I let it carry me over.

Once I am directly above it, I take in a deep breath and dive down to have a peek inside. Little fish like to hide out in these things. Getting closer, I angle down and grab hold of a small rock.

There, floating in the middle of the sponge is a tiny seahorse. These are a rare find out here. I've only seen one in all my years of diving in the Keys. It looks up when I block the light, but doesn't seem to be upset about the rude intruder. I wonder if this is a pregnant daddy, since its stomach is so fat. A shiver tickles my spine when I think about a guy getting pregnant. That's just so *wrong*. Glad it only happens to seahorses.

My lungs begin to burn, so I push up and head for the surface. Trey and Tommy are on either side of me, looking at something off in the distance, eyes bulging behind their masks. I'm about to motion toward the seahorse, but Trey jerks my arm and points to where they are looking.

At first I don't see anything then several brownish gray figures appear. Whatever these things are, they are moving to beat the band. It occurs to me there is no way we could possibly get out of the water before they get here.

I lift my head a little higher and see about a dozen dorsal fins slicing through the water. Uh, sharks have dorsal fins, but so do lots of other big fish, I tell myself. I'm sure they occasionally get close enough to the surface to poke through. No reason to panic just yet. The little fish around us suddenly disappear into the grass or under rocks, and immediately I wish there was a rock big enough for me to squeeze under. Please don't let me live up to my nickname!

In a flash the creatures are upon us, rocketing inches away in what can only be described as unbridled joy. The attacking sharks aren't sharks at all, but a pod of dolphins. They are spinning, twirling, and jumping as they whiz by. Trey and Tommy squeal through their snorkels and I think I screamed.

One of the dolphins angles closer than the others so I extend my arm, fingers stretched out as far as they'll go, and feel the tips glance the underside of its belly as it speeds by. Soft, smooth skin over impossibly hard muscle caresses my fingertips as it sails by. I never dreamed anything could be this awesome. We watch as they zoom past, their wake jostling us back and forth, and then just as quickly as they appear, they vanish into the abyss.

All three of us stick our heads above the water, take off our masks, and yell at the top of our lungs. Aunt Moe and Uncle Wyatt jerk their heads in our direction but we give them a thumbs-up. They shake their heads and go back to whatever they were doing on the boat. We clap each other on the back and continue to hoot and holler. The ocean is about a cup deeper now, but that small piece of information I will keep to myself.

We climb in the boat a few minutes later, pumped up by what just happened. All of us start talking at once as we shed our gear, salt water dripping everywhere. Aunt Moe turns to look at us from under the canopy as she works on supper; smiling as we yammer on, not the least aggravated by all the ruckus. Vivian, who had been sitting on the bow letting her feet dangle in the water, turns around.

As we tell them about the dolphins, her smile disappears.

Then she says, "I knew if I got out of the water I'd miss something cool like that! It always happens that way," as if that were the sole reason the dolphins showed up. Looking across the waves, she strains to see if she can catch just a glimmer of their departure, but they are long gone. Frustrated, she ignores a passing boat that normally gets a friendly wave and sits down on a nearby seat to sulk.

The smell of boiling lobster and fish cooking on the stove brings everyone around the table.

Before the food arrives, the passing boat turns around and heads in our direction. Out here there aren't many boat patrols, so if something goes down, you're pretty much on your own. We've heard stories over the years of people being robbed and assaulted in all kinds of terrible ways.

Uncle Wyatt steps close to the compartment where he stores his pistol. All of us know what he is doing and what's behind that little door. Until we can ascertain the boater's intentions, he has no problem pulling it out and letting them know we will not be easy targets.

When he started carrying a weapon on board, Aunt Moe objected. Working in an emergency room, she sees all kinds of horrors people inflict on each other. Uncle Wyatt listened to her side of the story, and then asked her if she were isolated on a boat would she really want to be defenseless? What if the engine wouldn't start and you couldn't get away? If the bad guys had a weapon and we didn't, guess who is going to win. Eventually, she backed down.

All of us are required to know how to shoot and take firearms safety classes. Whatever scenario might take place, Uncle Wyatt wants us to be prepared.

He even managed to talk Aunt Moe into going to the range with him. She hates guns, but he needed to make sure she at least knew how to use one, just in case.

After teaching her the basics, he handed her the gun and stepped out of the way. She lifted the gun slowly toward the target, steadied it then squeezed the trigger. It jumped hard in her hands, but she held onto it, then laid it down quickly and said, "Ok, are you satisfied now?"

Uncle Wyatt hauled the target in, and as it made its way up, he thought she had missed it all together. Then he noticed a point of light in the last place he expected to see it and realized she had hit dead center bull's-eye. That was her last trip to the shooting range.

As the boat gets closer, a young girl and dog appear on the bow. The girl is frantically waving, calling Vivian's name. The dog is spinning around and around, barking wildly in the air. Vivian begins squealing, realizing who it is.

Tommy tells his dad what's going on. Uncle Wyatt walks to the gunwale as the boys throw out a couple of bumper guards.

"Hey cowboy, mind if we ride in?" a man we assume is Sandy's dad calls from the deck, putting his big hand on the dog's head so she won't knock him off the boat. He's wearing a baseball cap with a picture of a marlin on the front. From his weathered skin, it looks like he's been out in the sun most of his life. Deep wrinkles cover his body from head to toe, and his sleeveless shirt doesn't do a very good job of covering his paunch.

A woman peeks from behind the canopy as the men speak, a big floppy hat and sunglasses covering most of her face.

"Not at all, stranger," Uncle Wyatt calls back.

The girls are dancing around like they have to go to the bathroom, hands flapping in the air as they call to each other.

We haul *The Equine Devine* close enough for them to safely step over and secure the rope. Once everyone is aboard, the girls hug each other while Lady tries to squeeze her way in between.

The man extends his hand to Uncle Wyatt and says, "Daniel Trevine, you can call me Danny, and this is my wife, Cindy," he says, putting his arm around the woman's shoulder. "And the little filly over there entwined with yours is our daughter, Sandy. Apparently they became BFFs at the pier last night. Kids have a keen way of doing that, ya know."

"Yeah, they most certainly do, especially girls," Uncle Wyatt replies a little cautiously.

We shake hands all around as we introduce ourselves one by one. Aunt Moe takes Mrs. Trevine by the elbow and they go to the back of the boat where we have the table set up for dinner.

Mr. Trevine removes his hat, revealing a head as white as a cue ball, making his head look like an Easter egg that's been half dipped. The brightness of his blue eyes is a stark contrast to his dark, leathery skin.

When Mrs. Trevine takes her floppy hat off, I see a pretty face hiding beneath. It's heart-shaped like her daughter's and trimmed with short brown hair. Slightly slanted brown eyes set atop high cheekbones give me the impression she has some Oriental blood.

The Trevines were fishing in a channel not far from here when Sandy spotted Vivian through a pair of binoculars she was using to entertain herself. If Vivian had been diving with us they would've missed that opportunity. Guess she was luckier than she thought.

They haven't eaten supper, so Aunt Moe insists they stay. Heaven knows, we have plenty to go around. Even if we didn't, she'd find a way.

The women retreat inside the cabin, as pots and pans clang around. After a few minutes, the women bring supper platters heaping with lobster tails and fish.

"Wow, will you look at this! Y'all certainly were busy. I can see what you had these boys doing all day!"

Vivian turns around and announces, "Hey, I caught one of those lobsters, too, ya know!"

He chuckles and says, "Wow, I'm impressed! Those lobsters are nearly as big as you are, missy! Did it try to buck you off?"

"It tried," Vivian says, giving Trey a smack on the shoulder.

Mr. Trevine laughs as his belly flops up and down beneath his shirt. "That little filly of yours sure is a pistol."

"If only you knew," Uncle Wyatt says under his breath.

Once everyone is seated, we dig in. Mrs. Trevine brought over fresh fruit and rolls from their cooler, along with some wine, so the table is full.

Mrs. Trevine moans after every bite, leaning her head back and closing her eyes like this is the best thing she has ever tasted.

"I can't believe how good this food is! I don't think we've ever had it this fresh before."

Mr. Trevine shakes his head back and forth, making the same moaning sounds. "It's like a little piece of heaven jumped out of the ocean and landed right here on our plates," he says after a few bites.

"It's no secret recipe, just a good hammer and a big pot of boiling water," Aunt Moe says with a chuckle.

Uncle Wyatt reaches over and squeezes her shoulder and says, "You should see what she can do with possum."

"I can only imagine," says Mrs. Trevine.

"Would you be willing to swap a few recipes, Moe? I don't think I have one for road kill." Aunt Moe busts out laughing and says, "No problem, I'm sure I have one or two I can spare."

Conversation drops off as we finish the rest of our food. The splashing of waves against the side of the boat and the occasional call of seagulls overhead fills in for the lack of conversation.

The sun is still about an hour from setting as we finish the last of the seafood. All the kids pull KP, as Uncle Wyatt and Mr. Trevine sit around the table while the two women retreat to the back to finish up the last of the wine.

"So what is it you do in Homestead, Danny?" asks Uncle Wyatt.

"I'm a district manager for an aircraft parts and supply manufacturer. I've been there for twelve years now since retiring from the Air Force. What about you?"

Uncle Wyatt takes a swig of his drink and says, "I'm an electrician with a large outfit in Tampa. I've been with them for about twenty years, ever since I got out of the Navy. I also have a little shop behind my house where I do some freelance work. This boat," he says, motioning toward the sails, "I inherited from my dad after he passed about five years ago. He was a retired Navy man and loved to sail. He took my sister and me everywhere he went when we were kids. One year we sailed to Cuba and another the Virgin Islands. Almost every year we sailed somewhere exotic. We practically grew up on this boat."

"Wow, you certainly had an interesting childhood. I grew up in the panhandle of Florida on a ranch. We worked our childhoods away keeping that place running, but it taught us all about hard work. I wouldn't trade it for anything.

"Cindy and I have a small ranch in Homestead where we have a few horses and mules we use as therapy animals. We get busloads of special-needs kids from the local area twice a month. We've also got a couple of dogs we're training to be helpers. Cindy runs most of the affair. Without her, it never would've happened."

"What a great thing to do," says Uncle Wyatt, genuinely impressed.

"It's really something to see an autistic or handicapped kid responding to these animals. It opens a whole new door for them. It takes most of my retirement check to keep it running, but seeing the smiles it brings to those young faces is worth every penny."

"It takes someone with a big heart to do that kind of stuff," Uncle Wyatt says, rubbing his belly.

They grow silent for a moment as a warm breeze blows over the ocean. The sun is beginning to send long pink and purple streaks across the waves, and realize they are about to run out of daylight. Mr. Trevine stands up and stretches, and says, "Well Wyatt, it's been an absolute pleasure running into you folks out here! Guess we ought to start making our way back to the camper before it gets too dark."

About that time, Cindy and Aunt Moe appear from the bow with an empty bottle. Their cheeks are flushed as they giggle like teenagers.

Danny says, "Well Mom, we'd best round up the herd and start heading in. I know little missy isn't going to be too thrilled about leaving her friend, but maybe we can hook up tomorrow."

Aunt Moe pipes up and says, "Yeah, that would be wonderful! We're going to do some diving around Looe Key." She looks at Cindy and the two women smile at each other. I guess the ability to become fast friends inside of five minutes is just a woman thing. I don't know any guys who can do that.

Uncle Wyatt says, "We'd enjoy the company if y'all are able. I know the girls would love it."

"Sounds like a plan to me."

"I have the coordinates here in the Garmin if you need them," says Uncle Wyatt, as the two men head toward the captain's seat.

Mrs. Trevine walks down the stairs into the galley to get Sandy. If I know Vivian, she'll do her best to get Sandy to stay the night with us out here. We have one extra bed, but it holds all the clothes and extra stuff we use on the boat.

To my surprise, Vivian decides not to argue. After all, we don't really know these people and they don't know us. They may be just as nice as they appear, or a bunch of ax murderers.

The Trevines board their boat and get settled while the girls talk about all their big plans for tomorrow. Mr. Trevine cranks the engine as they wave a final goodbye. When he moves the throttle forward, the engine sputters and dies. He looks back at the engine with a look of surprise. He turns the key again; it catches after a couple of tries and runs without a hitch. An unsure smile crosses his face as he gently pushes the throttle forward. Even with a light hand, the engine sputters and dies once again.

Not even trying to hide his aggravation, he hollers, "Can you believe that bunch of nonsense! I just had this thing serviced a week ago and they told me everything was fine. Just can't trust nobody these days. I don't even have any tools out here."

Uncle Wyatt tosses the rope to Mrs. Trevine. Tommy comes out of the galley with a canvas bag filled with tools and hands it to his dad. Mrs. Trevine pulls the boats together as Uncle Wyatt starts to step onto *The Equine Devine.* Instead, he turns to me and says, "Jason, you know more about these engines than I do, why don't you see if you can figure out what's going on."

Then he turns to Mr. Trevine and says, "If that's all right with you, Danny."

I look at Uncle Wyatt with wide eyes, but he returns my stare with total confidence.

Mr. Trevine hesitates, the silence speaking volumes. Finally he says, "Uh, sure, yeah, that's fine. How old are you, son?"

"I'm fourteen," I say with a bit more attitude than necessary. If offense were taken, it doesn't show. At least I managed not to stutter in those two little words.

It's true I've had much more experience with outboard motors than Uncle Wyatt. With a sailboat, the engine doesn't get that much use. My grandpa had an old boat with an ancient motor that we kept running for years, but this is different. I've always had my dad nearby; now it's just me.

Swallowing hard, I step across and make my way to the back of the boat. The engine is an Evinrude V-6 engine that looks pretty new. Mr. Trevine raises the propeller out of the water with the flick of a switch. I take the cover off and look around with a small flashlight. No broken or burnt wires, nothing obvious so far.

I stop and think about how the engine behaved in the last few minutes. It could be a fuel problem, so I check the simplest things first, just like my dad taught me. I pull the fuel line out and give it a check. There in the filter screen is a chunk of rust along with some more trash that was probably sucked up from the tank. Carefully, I remove the trash and reattach the hose. Showing Mr. Trevine what I found, I ask him to prime the engine and give it another try. He does, and in just a moment, the engine roars to life.

"Now go in a l-little circle to see how sh-she does," I say.

He slowly moves the throttle forward, as the bow lifts up and forward. The engine purrs along without a hitch, steady and strong. We go out about a hundred yards and turn back around without a hint of sputter or hesitation, just pure raw power.

Everyone throws their arms up in the air and cheers as we come alongside.

Mr. Trevine comes up and claps me on the back and says, "Son, to be honest, I had my reservations about a kid so young working on my engine, but you obviously know more than those bozos at the shop, and they've gone to school to fix these things."

He continues, "Tell you what, son, when you finish high school, you give me a call. I can get you a job in one of our facilities, okay?"

I didn't bother to ask if I could get a job before I graduate.

I swallow hard and say, "Th-thank you sir, I appreciate th-that. Actually that t-trash probably got p-pulled from the t-tank after th-they checked it out," I say.

"That very well could be, but for all they charge, they should've been more thorough."

I simply nod my head, not knowing what to say.

He keeps his hand on my shoulder and says, "One more thing before you head back to your uncle's boat. Don't let that stuttering bother you. Some very smart people were stutterers at one point in their lives." I want to crawl under the boat, but he wouldn't let it go.

"Are you familiar with Winston Churchill or Thomas Jefferson? What about Bruce Willis or James Earl Jones?" I nod my head. I know all those names. "Did you know they once stuttered?" I raise my eyebrows in astonishment.

Squeezing my shoulder, he leans in closer, looking at me intently and says, "Don't you ever let anyone talk down to you, you hear me? The world is slap full of smart people that just haven't found themselves yet. You'll find a way to your words, son, I guarantee it."

I ask, "H-how do you know so m-much about this?"

"You're looking at the reason. I had one of the worst stutters in all of Florida. The day finally came when I decided to take control of it instead of letting it control me. I reached out to the right people for help and learned to put that stutter six feet under for good. Heck, if I can do it, anybody can." He gives me a firm smack on the shoulder and a wink.

I shake my head, smile, and step back. He grabs my hand and gives it a shake. "Trust me, son, you have a brilliant future ahead of you. Just don't you ever give up, ya hear me?" he says a little softer. "We'll see you in the morning, okay?"

"Okay, Mr. T-Trevine, th-thanks."

"No, thank you, son. I don't know the first thing about fixing outboard motors. We would've been stuck out here until somebody came to haul us back in if we hadn't run into you folks!"

I climb back aboard *Second Act,* where I'm greeted by a whole host of high fives. Uncle Wyatt stays in the back away from the crowd, an easy smile on his lips. After everyone had their say, he walks over to me and says, "I always knew you were your father's son," and pulls me into a hug and whispers, "He would be mighty proud of you today." His hug didn't make me feel like a little kid. Instead, it reminded me what it felt like to be appreciated and worthy. It also felt like my dad wasn't quite so far away.

Early the next morning we devour a breakfast of blueberry pancakes, oatmeal, and sausage. After cleaning up, we make preparations to head to Looe Key. Since no fishing or spearing is allowed there, the fish learn quickly they won't wind up on anyone's dinner plate, so they wander closer and are more relaxed than in other areas.

It takes us about an hour to get there, so we have time to finish getting our equipment ready and clean up the deck.

After arriving and securing the anchor, we look around at the handful of boats bobbing on the water, but don't recognize any of them. Guess we beat the Trevines here.

A man and woman on the sailboat closest to us wave when they see us look in their direction. We wave back as we get ready to jump in.

Trey, Tommy, and I begin diving around a shallow reef, watching and listening as the parrotfish chew nonstop on the coral. Sunlight dances on their brightly colored scales, making them glisten.

Vivian and Sandy are off to our right, watching a school of angelfish swim around a large head of brain coral. The Trevines arrive shortly after we dive in.

Looking around at all the natural beauty, I can't help but feel my dad's presence. He is everywhere.

I can almost see his deep auburn hair turning a hundred shades of crimson as the sunlight ignites each strand, setting it ablaze. I am both happy and sad all at the same time.

Moving on, I see Trey and Tommy huddled around a bright orange piece of coral. I know how ferocious that stuff burns and have no intention of getting anywhere near it. They've made a game out of seeing who can get closest without making contact. One touch is all that is necessary to make you a true believer. I hear Tommy laughing out of his regulator as Trey ventures just an inch or so away when a small wave delivers just enough force to graze an edge. Trey hollers and yanks back, rubbing his side. I shake my head and laugh.

Checking my air pressure gauge, I see I've got an hour or so of air left, so we're good until lunch.

Paddling over, I join them, and the three of us make our way deeper into the sanctuary. Scores of colorful reef fish meander around sponges and coral heads while lower down a shelf forms, extending over several feet of sandy bottom. This is a favorite hide-out for moray eels.

At the entrance, a few small crabs and urchins wander around the sandy floor, scrounging around for something to eat.

Dropping lower, I find myself just above Trey and watch his air bubbles rise. With a strong kick of my flippers, I angle my body directly into their path. Suddenly I find myself wrapped in a profusion of bubbles as they glide effortlessly over me. My whole body tingles with their playful kisses and then, just as quickly as the romance began, it is over.

Tipping my body downward again, I make my way to Trey and Tommy, who are just inches above the bottom. Dipping our heads under the shelf, we see an enormous grouper about six feet long snuggled into a deep recess. The grouper isn't the least disturbed. They see divers every day out here, and he doesn't bother to bat an eye, even if he could.

Sinking down a little lower a family of brightly colored snails appear. Their base color is pure ivory white, and sprinkled over the ivory are glittery golden spots, each etched with a thin blue ring, as though traced with fluorescent paint.

Watching them meander along the bottom, we grow bored, ready to see something else. I check my gauge again. It registers about forty feet, and I've still got about forty-five minutes of air if I don't breathe too deeply.

Dappled sunlight sends ripples along the sand, snaking thin streams of light, one chasing after the other. Shadows from the boats above cast eerie shadows, like lifeless tombstones across the bottom of the reef.

Deciding where we want to investigate next, another shadow emerges, smaller than the rest. Looking up, the figure of a woman hovers just below the surface. At first I think she is snorkeling, but then notice she isn't wearing any gear, not even a mask. Her arms and legs are motionless, and I realize something is very wrong.

I smack Trey and Tommy and point to the woman floating above us, her hair dancing lazily with the current. Our training kicks in as we yank the safety release latches and ditch our gear, taking a deep breath of compressed air just before the tanks fall to the bottom. Pushing off the floor of the reef, we rocket to the surface, a trail of bubbles flowing from our mouths. One thing Uncle Wyatt drove home over and over again during our training sessions was to never hold our breath while breathing compressed air. I can still feel the wooden handle of his baton poking me in the gut as we ascend.

Another person splashes into the water just above the woman and frantically swims toward her. He gets to the woman before we do, putting his arm under hers and desperately starts flailing toward the surface.

Trey and Tommy are the first to reach them, pushing the man away while grabbing her arms. He tries to grab the woman's legs, but I pull him away and try to maneuver him into a safe position so he doesn't drown us both. Saving a drowning person is incredibly dangerous because when they panic, they'll grab hold of anything, including you, and won't turn loose.

Eyes wide with terror, he watches helplessly as her limp body rises to the surface. His gaze turns back to me, a yearning so powerful it reaches all the way to my soul. He begins to sink, as if the life inside him just disappeared.

Grabbing him by the arm, I force my legs to drive us toward the surface that seems miles away. Small bubbles escape his mouth as his eyes begin to flutter, his movements growing small and lethargic. If we don't get to the surface soon, neither one of us is going to make it.

Sunlight taunts us as we draw closer, a stark reminder we are only visitors in this underwater wilderness and that our fragile existence can be snatched away in a single breath. The burning inside my lungs drives me, the man becoming a dead weight as he grows more and more subdued. Five more feet, three feet, one foot, and finally our heads break through the surface into the warm air.

Breathing deep, I look around and see Trey and Tommy climbing onto the loading platform of the nearby boat, straining under the lifeless weight of the woman. I hear a moan and realize the man is breathing on his own next to me, his eyes half slits as his lungs expand and exhale dramatically. He coughs a couple of times, then realizes we are no longer underwater and looks at me with great confusion. Regaining his strength quickly, his eyes grow wide as he begins screaming, "Karen! Karen! Where's my wife?" hysterically looking around for her.

I grab him by the shoulders and say, "She's okay, we pulled her out of the water," pointing in the direction of the boat.

He starts crying and says, "She fell overboard, and I jumped in after her!"

"It's okay, she's over there on your boat with my cousins," every word escaping without a single hitch. I can't remember a time when that happened. All at once I am a tumbled mixture of happy, upset, and confused emotions. Hoping my words continue to flow, I start to say something, but he shoves off of me and swims to the boat like a mad man, screaming her name.

I look around and see Aunt Moe and Mrs. Trevine poke their heads above the water. Pointing toward the boat where Trey and Tommy are lifting the unconscious woman I yell, "We found her f-floating in the w-water a few m-minutes ago," slapping the water in frustration. Aunt Moe makes a beeline for the boat with Mrs. Trevine trailing behind.

The man reaches the boat before any of us, and in one swift motion he is out of the water and on the back of the boat, still screaming her name. Trey jumps up to intercept him but the man pushes past him and disappears into the deck of the boat.

Following Aunt Moe, we make it to the loading platform at the same time. I look into the boat and see the woman lying on the deck with her head cradled in Tommy's lap. He is stroking her wet hair, but she's still unconscious. Her skin is sickly pale and her lips are turning blue. The man is on his knees beside her, crying like he's lost every last thing in the world. He reaches out to touch her but hesitates, holding his hand just above her arm. Then he draws his hand away, clinching it into a tight fist. This image will haunt me for years.

As soon as Aunt Moe's gear is off, she immediately takes charge. Tommy moves to the side so his mom can get through. She yells, "Get him out of the way," pointing to the crying man. Trey's eyes grow wide, but he doesn't protest. Trey gently takes the man's arm, but he quickly snatches it away, refusing to budge.

Trey looks at his mom, like "What now?" She snaps back, "Pick him up and carry him if you have to, just move him!"

This time Trey sets his jaw and forcefully grabs the sobbing man around the chest and drags him onto one of the nearby benches. Unless you have a yacht, there's no such thing as getting very far away on a boat. The man tries to get back, but Trey holds him firmly. Then, with a tenderness I'd never seen before, Trey starts talking reassuringly to him.

"Hey, it's okay, man, my mom is a nurse and knows what she's doing. Let her help your wife. She can't help if you're in the way."

The man seems to calm down a little as he looks at Trey for the first time. He wipes his face with his hands and says weakly, "Your mom is a nurse?"

Trey nods his head and says, "Yeah, one of the best. She's done this kind of stuff longer than I've been alive. Don't worry, she's got this, okay?"

Breathing easier now, the man slowly nods his head and stops struggling.

Aunt Moe feels for a pulse and puts an ear close to the woman's face. She turns around and asks the man if there is a first aid kit on board. He says the boat belongs to a friend of his and isn't sure what all it's got. She tells me to see if I can find one.

Moving as fast as I can on the rocking deck, I step over Aunt Moe's legs and duck into the cabin, looking for anything with a red cross on it. I see a couple of maps, some sonar equipment, a half-eaten apple, and then on the other side of the small room is a small white box attached to the wall with a big red cross on it.

Aunt Moe lifts the woman's chin, opens her mouth, and then places her mouth over hers and blows hard. The woman's chest rises then, when Aunt Moe pulls back, the woman's chest begins to fall. They do this a couple of times. Aunt Moe spots the first-aid box in my hands and without even looking at me, snatches it and lays it on the bench beside her. Rifling around the contents, she grabs a clear plastic bag that holds two short straw-looking things. She pulls one out, breaks it in half then waves it under the woman's nose. After a couple of seconds, the woman starts to moan and cough. Violent coughing brings up a little more water, as Aunt Moe gently rubs her back.

She looks at Tommy and says, "Swim back to the boat, get our first aid kit and bring it back here in the dinghy."

After a minute or so, the woman sits up, wipes her face, looks around at all of us, then notices her husband sitting beside Trey and starts crying. He jumps from the bench and is by her side in a flash, cradling her gently in his arms. She reaches her arms around his neck but draws back quickly, grabbing her wrist.

He pulls back slowly as his hands trail down her arms and come to rest on her elbows. She is holding her hands against her chest, her right one over the left.

In a shaky voice she says, "Paul, I think I broke my wrist."

He reaches for it but she turns away. Aunt Moe slides down beside her and gently touches her arm and says, "Honey, I need to look at your wrist. It's okay, I'll be as gentle as I can."

Hesitantly, she lowers her hand so Aunt Moe can see it. I ease behind the woman and watch over her shoulder. The boat bucks awkwardly with a big wave, and I reflexively place my hands on the woman's shoulder. When I do, I immediately feel the vibrations of her body. In that moment, I hear the voice clearly again, "Hello, Jason."

I've heard it many times, but it always surprises me with its clarity. Sometimes that's all it says while other times it keeps on going. Today it's more talkative.

"Pay close attention, Jason."

An image appears inside my mind like an X-ray, and I realize it's a picture of the woman's wrist. Each bone is clearly defined as I hear the voice say, "Take the woman's wrist in your hand, and I will direct you. Be bold and have no fear Jason. Her wrist is not broken, only partially dislocated, and I will guide you in repositioning it."

The woman turns to see who is touching her and I smile. She gives me a weak one in return. Shuffling beside Aunt Moe, I place my hands on the woman's arms and feel the vibrations even stronger. Aunt Moe looks at me like I've lost my mind but doesn't say anything, I guess trying to figure out what I'm doing. After a moment, she tries to elbow me out of the way but I refuse to budge.

She looks at me sternly and says, "Jason, what are you doing? Move back there with Trey." I hold my position, sure of what I am doing.

I have never disobeyed her before, and she is obviously perplexed when I don't move. I close my eyes, seeing the image of the woman's wrist more clearly, and slide my hands under Aunt Moe's and directly on top of the woman's.

Aunt Moe is beyond being merely annoyed, and with a tone she doesn't use very often, says, "Jason Thomas Gil, if you don't move this instant ..." and before she can finish, I hear myself say with authority, "Let us be, now move!"

No one has ever talked to Aunt Moe this way before, and everything grows dead quiet. I keep my eyes closed, focusing all of my energy on the woman's wrist, listening as the voice directs my hands. Amazingly, the woman remains still and does not resist. I feel Aunt Moe's eyes on me. I keep my eyes closed, since her look alone would probably kill me.

From behind, Trey says, "It's all right, Mom, Jason knows ... things. He's done stuff like this at school before."

I didn't know Trey knew.

I feel Aunt Moe slowly move away as I get better positioned. Placing both hands on either side of her wrist, I hear the voice say, "Good Jason, you are doing fine. Now place your thumbs on top of her wrist and you will feel a small bump. That is the dislodged bone."

Moving my thumbs, I feel a ridge and see the image get sharper. The voice said, "Push down with your thumbs as you pull down on her wrists sharply." Scooting back, I extend her wrist, and carefully push just where the voice directs me, giving her wrist a quick jerk, and feel the bone slide back into place. She squeals a little and tries to pull her hand free, but I hold it snuggly and feel to make sure it is right.

I hear Aunt Moe call my name, but ignore it. The voice says, "Very good Jason, you did well, son. The woman and the child she is carrying are both fine."

The child she's carrying? She's pregnant? Wow, it must be a new thing, because she sure doesn't look like it.

Opening my eyes, I look into her startled expression, then down at our hands. Slowly I remove mine from hers, and say, "How does that f-feel?"

She rubs her wrist, flexing her fingers. Holding it out for all to see, she rolls it around, her smile growing wider with each roll. I move out of the way as her husband and Aunt Moe step in to take my place. Aunt Moe looks at me hard before turning her attention back to the woman. She examines her wrist carefully, her face registering a mixture of shock and disbelief. I look at Trey, who shrugs his shoulders then pats me on the back.

The woman's husband looks at me with gratitude and says, "I don't know how you did it, but thank you for what you did." I just nod my head then look at the deck.

The woman stands up for the first time and gingerly sits down on the bench across from us, looking at me intently. Her husband sits down beside her, putting his arm protectively around her shoulders, kissing her softly on the top of the head. He stopped crying a little while ago and is much calmer now.

She looks at us and says, "I can't believe I caused all of this fuss," shaking her head. "One minute I was standing on the deck, looking at the water and then everything went black. I don't know what happened."

Aunt Moe said, "Most likely you passed out and landed on your wrist before you fell overboard."

Her husband said, "I heard something as I was getting our gear together, then I turned around and she was gone. I went to the side, looked into the water and saw her …" and stops talking, looking down at the deck. After a moment he says, "It was a good thing you boys were where you were. I can't imagine what would've happened if you hadn't been," shaking his head.

The woman reaches her hand to Aunt Moe. "I'm Karen Franks, and this is my husband Paul. Sorry to meet you this way," she says with a little laugh.

Aunt Moe takes her hand gently and says, "Working in a hospital, I've met people in worse ways than this, believe me."

The rest of us introduce ourselves, and when I say my name, everyone looks at me. She says, "Jason, how did you do that? How did you know what to do? You're way too young to be a chiropractor."

I feel Aunt Moe's eyes bore into me as I say, "I d-don't really know, I j-just did, that's all." I expect to see her flinch, but all she does is take my hand and say, "Thank you so much." She looks at all of us and says, "Thank you all so much," and starts crying again.

Paul holds her tighter, laying his cheek on the top of her head.

Trey and Tommy look at the deck, moving their hands around, unsure where to put them, reaching for pockets that aren't there.

Mrs. Trevine finally steps into the boat from the loading platform and sits down next to Aunt Moe and says, "It was meant to be that they were here." She looks us and says, "We know all about that, don't we, boys!"

Trey says, "You got that right." Tommy gives her a thumbs-up, and I just nod my head.

The adults start talking, exchanging names and numbers. I sit and listen to it all, amazed how everything came together like it did. If we hadn't been at the shelf when we were ...

My attention drifts to Aunt Moe and I wonder how much trouble I'm in. I've never disobeyed or even spoken a harsh word to her. She's deliberately not made eye contact with me for a while now. I wish she could understand the things I know. Heck, *I* don't even understand, so how could I possibly expect someone else to?

Mrs. Franks gets up, holding her husband's hand, and stands in front of us. We stand up as she reaches out, each one of us getting a big hug. I am the last one in line, and turning to me, she looks at me intently, shaking her head. She whispers to me, "I probably won't ever understand how you did it, but thanks again for what you did. I'll never forget this day as long as I live."

I whisper back, "No p-problem, glad we were able t-to help. B-Both of y'all will b-be j-just fine."

She steps back and says with a confused look, "Both of us? You mean Paul and me?"

I feel my ears turn pink. Is it possible she doesn't know? How could a woman be pregnant and not know it?

She looks down and places her hands over her belly, then looks back at me, asking the unspoken question. I simply nod my head.

Cocking her head to the side, she says, "How on earth do you know that? I just found out, like yesterday, with one of those test strips."

I shrug my shoulders and say, "I d-don't really know, I j-just do."

Everyone is looking at me again. Paul looks more confused than ever.

She takes his hand and says, "Paul, remember what we were talking about last night, about—you know? How we might be parents?"

He nods his head slowly, still confused, and says, "Yeah, so."

Excitedly she says, "Well, I think it's for real!"

His eyes grow wide as he touches her belly and says with a laugh, "You mean it's really happening?"

She nods her head and hugs him tightly. He's so shocked he almost forgets to hug her back.

The others look at me like I'm supposed to say something. Mrs. Franks takes the burden from me and announces to everyone what's going on. Trey and Tommy start giggling while Mrs. Trevine and Aunt Moe look shell shocked.

Aunt Moe cuts her eyes at me so sharply it hurts. I just look down and shuffle my feet.

After leaving the Franks' boat, I know Aunt Moe will be all over me like white on rice. Sure enough, it doesn't take long before she's cornered me alone after the rest of the crowd takes one last dive for the day.

I hold my hands out in surrender and say, "Aunt Moe, I d-didn't mean any d-disrespect b-back there this afternoon, b-but it was important th-that I d-did what n-needed to b-be done."

She stares at me hard without saying a word for a long time. Then she said in tone far less hostile than I anticipated, "Jason, what happened back there? Where did you learn how to do that? You could have hurt that poor woman."

I shake my head and tell her everything—from the very first time it happened, all the way up to now.

Stunned, she says, "Honey, does your mom know about this?"

I look down at my feet then shake my head and say, "No, ma'am."

She places her hand under my chin, bringing my face up to meet hers and says, "This is something she definitely needs to know about." She shakes her head and says incredulously, "How on earth? You even knew she was pregnant?"

I just nod.

Then she does something that takes me completely by surprise; she gives me a hug then kisses me on the forehead. She pulls back and says, "Jason, boy, you never cease to amaze me. If I hadn't seen it with my own eyes, I never would've believed it."

I say, "Me, too." This makes her chuckle.

Then she gets serious again and says, "Promise me you will tell your mom about this, okay?"

"I will. P-please let me t-tell her. She w-would be upset if it c-came from someone else, e-even you."

"Okay, honey, I'll let you tell her."

The next evening, the Trevines join us for supper again, our last night on the ocean. They contribute a few cans of green beans and a loaf of Hawaiian bread they picked up in Key West.

The girls go downstairs to help Aunt Moe with the food while the rest of us clean up and sort the gear.

When Uncle Wyatt was a teenager, he learned the hard way to keep the deck neat and orderly. On a trip to the Virgin Islands one year, his older sister Nancy tripped over a flipper and landed on her arm, breaking it in two places. They had to get to land in a hurry and find a hospital in an unfamiliar place. It turned out to be a major ordeal, so ever since then he's adamant about keeping the walking space uncluttered.

After dinner, we clear the dishes while the Trevines gather their stuff to head back inland. Vivian and Sandy are still side by side, like they've been ever since they got on the boat. Sandy reaches into her purse and brings out a pink journal with a buckle the shape of a horse on it, the kind of stuff girls love.

As she's handing it to Vivian she says, "I want you to have this. I got it in my stocking for Christmas last year, but I never used it. Guess I was waiting for a special friend to give it to. It has our address, phone number, and email in it."

With a sad face, Vivian takes it from her and holds it in her lap. Lady sits in front of them, watching every move they make, like it's the most interesting thing she has ever seen.

"I'll email you as soon as I get home. Make sure you friend me, okay? You'll get home before we do."

The girls embrace like they'll never see each other again.

Sandy's mom calls for her as they climb aboard *Equine Devine.* Sandy's lip starts trembling as they share one last hug. Lady jumps across first, her paws skidding as her nails scrape across the hard slick surface of the deck.

Finally Sandy crosses over and scoops Lady into her lap.

Mr. Trevine hollers over the engine, "Thanks for everything, y'all. The company was as good as the food. Maybe we can hook up again next year if we get the chance. I'm sure our girls have about a half dozen ways to get hold of each other!"

We yell our good-byes and after the chatter dies down, he adds, "Jason, remember that offer, son. If you need a job after you finish school, you call me!"

"Yes s-sir. T-thanks again."

Mrs. Trevine looks at me like I'm holding the secret to the universe in my pocket, but says nothing. Instead, she simply waves as she finds a seat near her daughter.

Vivian finally stops waving after they are out of sight then slides her hand into her pocket, wrapping it around the pink journal.

"Well, boys and girls, as much as I would love to sit here and chat the night away, we gotta get our booties back to port, so let's get things cleaned up and ready to sail first thing in the morning," says Uncle Wyatt, finishing off the last roll.

By the time we get everything done, the sun is just starting to paint the sky again. A few lightning clouds nudge their way across the horizon, silently erupting into brilliant orange and yellow profusions of light. The only sound is the sail softly flapping in the breeze as the water gently laps against the sides of the boat.

I bring my gaze up from the darkening ocean, now the color of ink, to Aunt Moe, who is manning the helm, guiding us to our last night's stay on the ocean. Trey and Tommy are playing a game of checkers made with Velcro. Vivian is busy writing in her newly acquired journal, hunched over her treasure as the last of daylight slips away.

Uncle Wyatt comes up from the galley, looking around to make sure the deck is clear and things are in their proper places. Satisfied with what he sees, he quietly steps behind Aunt Moe, and without a word, places his hands on her hips and gently moves them around just below her bellybutton. For a long time, they stand like this. He reaches around and kisses the side of her neck as she nuzzles his cheek with hers.

I used to see Dad hold Mom like this and I thought it was kind of gross, but now I understand. Without a word, their love will transcend whatever trouble life throws their way, a love they can count on when everything else fails. If you fall, I will catch you. If I falter, you will catch me.

Watching them, I am both happy and sad. I hope Dad knew how much we loved him, because in the end, it's the only thing that really matters.

Arriving at our new location, we anchor and get ready for the night.

Not much chitchat tonight as we settle bone-tired onto our cots, ready to be rocked to sleep for the last time this year. It will feel strange sleeping on a bed that stays still all night and walking on land that doesn't move.

Finally Aunt Moe and Uncle Wyatt crawl into bed and turn off the lights. Wood creaks inside the hull as the boat lists slowly from side to side. It's not long before Trey is snoring quietly from across the cabin. My eyelids grow heavy as the waves rock me to sleep.

From the darkness, the afternoon emerges bright and clear. I'm sitting by the Alafia River with my dad after finishing up some work at Grandma and Grandpa's house. I feel his hand on my back as he claps me on the shoulder, an unspoken debt of gratitude. He turns and looks at me like he's never been more proud.

Joy and pride beam from his eyes as a peaceful and warm fuzzy feeling grows inside my belly. The warm fuzzy begins to cool as I realize something is not quite right. The peace is replaced by confusion, as anxiety tingles uncomfortably inside. Dad's face reflects none of what I am feeling.

Suddenly the harsh reality of the situation settles in. My father is dead; he can't be sitting here next to me. His smiling face begins to drift away as I rise into the air, yanked away by the stinging pull of consciousness. His face gets further and further away, as I drift away. Desperately I call his name, but the distance between us continues to widen.

Sharp hands dig into my arms as I scream his name. A woman's voice calls to me. My eyes adjust to the darkness and I see Aunt Moe's face only inches from mine. Loose hair falls into her face, but she doesn't bother to brush it away.

"Jason, honey, it's Aunt Moe. You were having a bad dream. You're with us on the boat, sweetheart, remember?"

Looking around in the darkness, I see four pairs of eyes staring back at me. Self-consciously I pull the covers over my bare chest. All at once I feel out of place, like I don't belong here.

How could anyone possibly understand how I feel? It was my dad who's dead, not theirs. Aunt Moe reads my thoughts like an open book, a momentary pang of hurt cutting across the empty space between us. They might not understand, but they love me just the same. These people have been an anchor throughout my whole life, and I can't imagine my life without them.

A soft, knowing smile tugs at the corners of her mouth as she squeezes my hand tight, and whispers that it was only a dream. I hear Tommy talking to me from his bunk, "Nothing to worry about, man, happens to me all the time." Trey is already back to sleep, sawing logs. All I see of Vivian is her eyes peeking out from beneath her covers.

Aunt Moe kisses me on the cheek then gives my hand a squeeze before heading back to her bunk. Uncle Wyatt gives me a smile and thumbs up.

Aunt Moe pads quietly across the floor, nearly falling back into bed. When all is quiet again, Vivian's covers move. Gingerly she heads in my direction with something tucked under her arm. When she gets closer, I see it's her cherished stuffed unicorn. One eye is missing and its tail is frayed to only a couple of ratty strings. She's never slept without it that I know of.

She kneels down beside me, and without a word, hands me her beloved, bedraggled pet. I just stare at her a moment, not sure what to say. Then she whispers, "It keeps the bad dreams away," and pushes it into my chest. Silently, she zigzags back to her bunk and dives under the covers. Her head pokes from beneath her thick blanket as she smiles at me. I feel surrounded by love as I tuck the tattered little horse close to me. I don't recall a thing for the rest of the night.

We arrive home the next afternoon, having found a fruit stand with mangoes, pineapples, and coconuts. I bought plenty for Mom and Mary with my own money. Aunt Moe tried to pay for them, but I wanted to do this.

Before I get out of their van, I quietly slip the unicorn under Vivian's arm with a wink. Her face flushes for a brief moment as she tucks it quickly under her shirt.

CHAPTER SEVEN

Monday morning comes way too soon and jolts me back to reality. The thought of all that awaits me at school fills my entire body with dread from the top of my head all the way down to my toes. Without Jake and Sam to keep me afloat, I'd sail right down the poop chute, straight into the sewer, never even slowing down. Closing my eyes, I roll back over in bed and bury my head beneath the covers.

Later that morning I walk into homeroom and see Jake waiting for me. Mrs. Wendell is busy getting his computer and other equipment set up for the day. She's scanning workbook pages and writing down some notes. Sam and I help when we can throughout the day, just like we've done ever since first grade.

"Well, well, looks like Shark Bait has returned to the scene of the crime," Jake calls as I walk through the door. "How was your diving trip? Leave any body parts behind?" he asks, looking me over.

No matter what kind of mood I find myself in, Jake has the uncanny ability to cut through all the garbage and make me feel good again. I can't help but laugh, "It's all where I l-left it the l-last time I checked," I say with a crooked smile, pulling up a chair.

I feel a pat on my shoulder and turn to see Mrs. Wendell smiling at me. "I heard all about the fun weekend you two had at your grandparents' house. He hasn't stopped talking about it since he came in this morning."

"Yes ma'am, we g-got drug b-behind my grandpa's boat like a couple r-river rats."

She lets out a silly laugh and says, "Wish I had been there to see that." Then she puts her hands on her hips and says, "When are you fellas going to invite me?"

She's always joking around with us, which is cool, and gets upset when Bryce gives me a hard time. I've seen her talking to him in the hallway, and I feel like such a wuss all over again. In my dreams I'm brave and bold, afraid of nothing, squashing him like a bug under my heel.

I sit down at my desk and open the book to the page written on the board. I stare at the jumble of letters and begin the process of making sense out of all this nonsense. It takes so much concentration that I'm mentally exhausted by the end of the day.

In a few minutes the bell mercifully rings. Jake and I bump fists as he fires up his wheelchair.

"S-see ya in a c-couple of hours, kn-nucklehead," I say as he leaves. "It takes one to know one," he shouts back.

Watching him go, I recall the time a few years ago when we were in fourth grade. Mrs. Avery gave us a writing assignment about someone we thought of as a hero. Mrs. Wendell suggested he write about Wilma Rudolph, since she thinks nobody is cooler than her. She talks about her almost as much as she does her grandkids.

Jake chose to write about God. He worked all by himself, typing on his laptop forever, getting it just right. Looking over his shoulder as he sweated over it, I read things like, "He protects me and my family, and keeps us safe. He gave me life and helps me to be happy every day." When he was finished, Mrs. Avery and Mrs. Wendell read it together and cried right there in the middle of class.

I collect my books and head to History for first period. Mr. Collins is one of our better teachers, always mixing it up to keep things interesting. The girls think he's hot since he could win a Matt Damon look-alike contest, and like some of Matt's characters, Mr. Collins can convince you he's stone-cold crazy. When he dresses up like the people he's teaching about (props and all) and dramatically performs in front of the class, talking with some goofy foreign accent, nobody falls asleep. Other times he jumps onto his desk and sings (even though he can't carry a tune in a bucket), as we laugh and clap along. With him, we never know what to expect.

Last week he came in dressed like a nurse, carrying his guitar, a big red cross painted on his white hat. When he began to sing, we laughed and cut up until we heard what the song was about. He sang about a Polish lady named Irena Sendler. Through the lyrics of the song, he told us how she saved about 2,500 Jewish kids during the Holocaust, and all the ways she snuck them out to safe places. Even after the Nazis captured and tortured her, she kept going back to save more. After he finished, he sat the guitar down quietly as we stared in silence. Somberly, he said we'd probably never hear about her again, and wanted to make sure we remembered her and what she did. It worked.

Then there are the times he can pulverize you into bone meal with just a look alone.

When his cool blue-gray eyes bear down on somebody who's starting some kind of crapola, that's all it usually takes for them to chill. Even Butthead can't stand up to that kind of scrutiny. He's tried on a few occasions, but Mr. Collins doesn't back down. Other teachers have total meltdowns with that moron, but not him.

From what we hear, Mr. Collins served in Afghanistan for a few years when he was in the army. I guess after the real thing, dealing with a bunch of teenagers is a walk in the park.

After settling into my seat and writing down homework, I take out the textbook and turn to the page he's assigned.

From behind I hear, "Hey J-J-J-Jason, w-w-what are you d-d-d-doing? Th-th-th-t book's got no p-p-p-pictures in it." Not wasting any time this morning.

I turn around and glare at Bryce. Tall, blond, perfectly tanned, built like a tight end. And oh, did I mention his father is filthy rich? Yeah, ain't life grand.

Back in elementary school, we were sort of friends, but not real chummy, just not enemies. After we reached fifth grade, for some reason he became hostile and mean. I don't know what triggered the change, but he's been a boil on my butt ever since.

Mr. Collins lifts his head and looks in our direction, then goes back to writing something down. After glaring at Bryce a second longer, I turn around and continue flipping through my book.

Bryce's family owns lots of land and businesses around town, so he pretty much feels he can do as he pleases. On more than one occasion his dad has visited the school and had a little "chat" with our principal, Mr. Nucciol. Everyone noticed how his detention time dwindled after that.

A minute or two passes, and I feel something whack me on the back of the head. I look down and see a fat eraser lying on the floor next to me.

I spin around, knowing exactly where it came from. Bryce is eyeing me like the cat that ate the canary.

"W-w-w-hat are you l-l-l-looking at?" he says with a sneer.

I open my mouth to say something, but the only thing I can manage is "k-n-nock it off, B-Bryce." Oh great, now let me shoot the other foot.

"Oh m-m-man, wh-what a c-c-comeback," he laughs.

"At least he got hit where it can't do any damage," says Jeremy Jones, otherwise known as JJ, another snotty rich kid. They play tennis and golf together on the weekends. JJ usually totally ignores me if Bryce isn't around.

"Hey, good one, JJ," he says, holding his hand up for a hi-five.

Mr. Collins walks over and asks what's going on. I look down at my book and mumble something incoherent. He stares at the eraser lying on the floor then looks at me. My face burns as I feel my ears getting hot and tingly. Dampness settles into my shirt as I try to control my breathing. With great effort, I fight the urge to run out of the room. I realize there's no place to crawl under or hide, so like I've done my whole life, I just suck it up and hope it passes quickly.

Bryce sits smugly in his seat, knowing full well whatever Mr. Collins does won't stick. His dad will be knocking on Mr. Nucciol's door to make sure of it.

"You three boys, in the hallway—now," he says with a finality that leaves no room for argument.

"But we didn't do anything!" Bryce and JJ protest in unison. I keep my mouth shut and do as I'm told. Turning to walk down the aisle, I see Jesse sitting in the back of the class. I was so busy in my own little world I didn't even consider she might be in here. She has a sad look on her face as I walk by. I just nod.

I hear Mr. Collins say, "Outside now, and no more lip out of you two," looking directly at Bryce and JJ. For a minute they sit still, defiantly staring him down. JJ waits for Bryce to make the first move. Once Butthead stands up, JJ dramatically shoves his seat back and stomps across the room with him.

My back is already to the wall when they arrive. I hear some of the other kids inside snickering as the two idiots march out the door like they're royalty forced to mingle with the masses.

The three of us stand against the walk, avoiding eye contact and just stare at the floor.

"Okay, what's going on this morning?" Mr. Collins says. Bryce looks at him arrogantly and says, "I was just sitting there minding my own business, and if you want to ask me anything else you can call my dad." He pulls a business card out of his pocket and flicks it at Mr. Collins. It bounces off his chest and lands on the floor at his feet. JJ snorts a laugh. I cut my eyes at the card lying upside down on the floor next to a broken pencil.

Mr. Collins is quiet for a minute and then says softly, "I know all about your dad, Bryce. You can drop the attitude. When are you going to finally grow up and be a man for once?"

Bryce's smirk turns ugly. I thought for a minute he was going to take a swing at him. That happened one year in third grade. The kid, Gene something or other, had been held back a couple of years, and was as big as the teacher, Mr. Spendez. It took everything he had to wrestle Gene to the floor. We were hoping Gene would win because Mr. Spendez was mean as a rattler.

"I'm not afraid of you Bryce, or your father," he said in an even tone.

JJ grows pale as the blood drains from his face when Mr. Collins turns his attention to him. With a look as cold and hard as steel, his eyes bare down on JJ like lasers.

"What about you, JJ, what did you see?" he asks with calm ferocity. JJ looks down at his feet and shoves his hands deep into his pockets.

"I didn't see anything. That eraser was already on the floor when we came in."

"Uh-huh," says Mr. Collins, never taking his eyes off of him.

Then the dreaded moment arrives. Mr. Collins walks in front of me and looks in my face with soft, understanding eyes.

He says, "Jason, I know these two have made your life miserable for a while now. They will continue to do so as long as you put up with it. I know you are far smarter than you let on. I know it, and so do they." I see Bryce and JJ shuffling their feet and fidgeting with their hands. I've never been talked to like this by a teacher before and I'm not sure what to say.

In some ways, he actually reminds me of my dad.

"M-Mr. Collins, I d-didn't see who th-threw the eraser (which is the truth, but everyone knew it was Bryce). I-I'm fine though, it d-didn't really hurt."

Mr. Collins has always treated me well, and I have no reason to not trust him, other than he's an adult, which puts him in a whole different category. There's an unspoken code, a line that is rarely crossed. No matter how bad things might be I would rather be skinned alive than fink to an adult about another kid. He looks at me for a long, uncomfortable moment until my armpits begin to itch.

He rubs his chin thoughtfully a moment then says, "Fine, back into class, all three of you."

Hanging my head in shame, I walk past Jesse. We take our seats and continue where we left off. The rest of class went by in a blur.

Right after lunch, I see Jesse at her locker, about ten feet from mine. I thought she would never want to have anything more to do with a loser like me, but to my surprise, she smiles and walks over. "Hey Jason, some school you have here," she says.

"Yeah, n-n-ever a d-d-ull moment."

Without beating around the bush, she asks, "So, what's the deal with those idiots in first period, anyway?"

I shrug my shoulders and say, "That would be B-Bryce Estralar, AKA B-Butthead, and his s-sidekick J-Jeremy 'the Jackass' Jones. They apparently d-don't have anything b-better to do than g-give me a hard time."

She lets out a chuckle and says, "Good names, very fitting. Why don't you kick their butts and get it over with already?"

"E-easy for you to s-say, Miss Psycho Ninja. They are way b-bigger than me, in case you haven't n-noticed. Besides," I say sarcastically, "I can't t-talk right. I-I morph into a m-moronic t-tongue-tied idiot. S-See what I mean."

With a dismissive way of her hand she says, "So what if you stutter every now and again, big deal. You're making it way worse by getting all worked up about it. Don't let them push you around. Once you get tired enough of it, you'll find a way to make it stop."

Annoyed with her casual attitude towards something that has been so painful for me, I say, "Easy f-for you to say, g-girl." Boy, I let *her* have it!

About that time, Butthead waltzes around the corner and spots me talking to Jesse. I try to act cool, but know this is going to go from bad to way worse in a nanosecond.

He walks over, shoves me out of the way and says, "Well, well, well, a new girl in town. Let me introduce you to the real men around here." He cuts his eyes at me and says, "You've already met the class dunce."

Jesse steps a little closer to him and says with a cute little smile, "Actually, I think it's the other way around, Bryce. What kind of a real man childishly throws erasers and then doesn't even have the guts to admit it?"

This is definitely not what he expected. The smile vanishes as he opens his mouth to speak, but she stops him.

Pretending to pull a phone from her pocket, she holds it to her ear and says, "Uh, Bryce, I have bad news. It's your village calling.

Seems they're missing their idiot, so you better scoot along now." Wow, this girl is good.

He abruptly pushes himself off the lockers and towers over her. I thought about warning him about the psycho ninja thing, but nah, I'll let him find out on his own.

She remains relaxed and calm, like they're talking about the weather. He bores a hole in her with his eyes, but she doesn't back down even a little. Finally, he gives me a look that could kill, then mutters something under his breath and stomps off down the hall. Darn, I was hoping she'd waste him.

She turns to look at me, not the least flustered, and says, "He's just a big spoiled brat, Jason. The sooner you deal with him, the better off you'll be. We had way worse than him in Atlanta, trust me."

The bell rings, so I tell her bye, not sure what else to say, and head down the hall.

Math is next, so I'll be with both Sam and Jake, excellent. Hey, Mrs. Wendell brought some banana bread today. Good, I was getting hungry.

Sam, Jake, and the entire class have already heard about the incident in first period. Good news travels fast, bad even faster.

"Do you think Mr. Collins will get in trouble?" they ask, as I wolf down the banana bread Mrs. Wendell hands me.

I swallow the last of it and say, "Well, I've n-never heard anybody t-talk to B-butthead like th-that and g-get away with it. We'll s-see."

The three of us finish a couple of worksheets and chitchat some more since the teacher doesn't care, as long as we don't get too loud. Before we know it, the bell rings and it's time to go our separate ways again.

The last class of the day is gym. The three of us are there together again and no Bryce or JJ, which is always good.

Jake has a special walker he uses for this kind of stuff. Normally he's in an electric wheelchair, but he parks it for a while so he can get some exercise.

We assemble in the gym like we're supposed to and Mrs. Oliver, the gym coach, announces we're playing softball this week. After a few warm ups we divide into two groups.

Our team is up first, so Jake shuffles out, the picture of confidence. I don't know how he does it.

Jake walks to home plate, me on one side and Sam on the other. The pitcher is a cute redhead named Claire Duncan, and like almost everyone here, I've known her my entire life. Her dad owns one of the grocery stores in town and her mom cuts hair.

Claire steps to the mound as Jake taps the plate with his bat like he's ready to knock it out of the park.

Right before Claire pitches the ball, she blows Jake a kiss. He catches it and slides it in his pocket, giving her a wink. Then he pats his pocket and says, "I'm saving that one for later, now bring it on, baby!" This gets both teams going, especially the boys.

A few years ago he thought all this attention was ridiculous, but now he loves it. It's a good thing, because it's like this all the time.

As the noise dies down, Claire pitches the first ball, but it goes wide.

Jake yells, "I know ya love me, Miss E-Claire, now dish it up right over this here plate, sweet cakes."

Her face blushes a little as everybody laughs. Jake's the only one who can say something like that and live to tell about it. She throws another pitch, and this time it sails right over home plate. He swings for all he's worth, and smacks it right through the third baseman's legs, and into left field.

The three of us take off for first base, Jake hollering at the top of his lungs. His walker rocks hard from side to side as we fight to keep him steady. A cloud of dust trails behind us as we round first base and sprint for second. Jake hustles like it's the last game of the

World Series, bottom of the ninth, and he's holding the winning run.

His wheels get caught on something, but we manage to keep from toppling over. He crashed a couple of years ago, but didn't get hurt. All the girls screamed, and some of the guys did too, but the only casualty was a button that got ripped off his shirt. I thought Mrs. Wendell was going to set a world record in the hundred-yard dash getting to him. I never knew old ladies could move so fast.

Rounding second base, we make it all the way to third before the ball is thrown in. Jake dances all over the base, yelling for someone to bring him home.

The next batter is Brian Fipps, but he goes by JD, for reasons nobody knows. He's one of the smallest guys in the entire school, including some of the girls.

JD steps up to the plate and everybody in the outfield relaxes, thinking a shrimp like him can't hit it very far. The first pitch is called a little low. Claire looks perturbed with the call, but doesn't say anything. JD looks down the line and gives Jake a thumbs-up.

The second pitch is high, but JD swings like his life depended on it. He and the bat spin completely around like a teeny little baseball ballerina. To everyone's surprise, the ball sails over the second baseman's head and into the outfield. Elated, he drops the bat and takes off for first base like his britches are on fire. After all the dramatics, the ball rolls about midfield before anyone catches up with it.

As soon as Jake sees the ball leave JD's bat, he takes off for home plate. His walker zigzags all over the place as we try to keep up, his skinny legs scrambling down the baseline so fast they look like a cartoon.

As we hotfoot it down the base line, Sam hollers, "It's gonna be close!" I look over my shoulder and see the second baseman about to throw the ball. Just as we cross home plate, the catcher scoops it up. Mrs. Oliver dramatically waves us safe as everybody on both sides cheer. You'd think he just clinched the World Series by all the fanfare. Sweat drips off his hair and down his cheeks as he yells, "This is the best day of my whole life!"

Every day is the best day of his whole life.

⟹ ⟸

That afternoon as I start to walk home, I see Mr. Estralar pull into the school parking lot. There is no mistaking that beautiful dark blue Porsche. Bryce must've called him already. I hope Mr. Collins doesn't get into too much trouble. I've never heard a teacher talk to Bryce like he did, but the jerk had it coming. Sam will probably hear about what happened before me, since he's staying late for drama practice.

I look back over my shoulder as I cross the parking lot and see Mr. Estralar walking up the steps to the front door with his characteristic scowl. Moving quickly for such a shrimpy little guy, he takes the steps two at a time, checking his phone as he goes. He's smaller than most every man I know, but from what they say, he's ferocious as a caged badger. I've never met the man, and have no desire to. I watch him walk into the front door before turning around and heading home.

Mom wants me to pick up a loaf of bread at the store on the way home. My shirt is wet around my backpack by the time I walk through the big glass doors, so I gladly welcome the air conditioning, something we don't take for granted here in central Florida.

I navigate my way to the bread aisle looking for the kind she likes with her coffee in the morning. A woman with a little boy, maybe three years old, is in the aisle beside me. His blond curls bounce up and down over big blue eyes that remind me of someone I know, but can't quite place. I've never seen this little guy before, so they might be new in town, a common occurrence these days.

Turning my attention to the bread again, I've forgotten how many varieties there are; Mom usually does the shopping. Then out of nowhere, the kid reaches over and grabs my arm. Instantly I get such an intense reaction, I almost knock over a display stand. In my mind I see images of his throat and bronchial tubes swelling, but this doesn't match his happy, carefree attitude. When he releases my arm, the sensation vanishes. The boy's mom looks embarrassed and apologizes.

Taking his face in her hands she says in a syrupy voice, "Oh no, Kyle, we don't bother other people in the store, sweetheart."

She looks at me and says, "Sorry, he's kind of hyper since we just left the doctor's office. He had to sit still for two hours and now he's just dying to get home and play!"

"No p-problem, ma'am. Is h-he okay?" I ask.

She gives me that 'poor kid' look I hate so much, then blinks her eyes deliberately and says, "Yes, he has an ear infection, his first ever. His older brother used to get them all the time when he was little. We got the prescription filled and he just had a dose. They flavor it here, so it tastes good. I didn't have to bribe him or anything." She's way more talkative and friendly than I expected.

With more confidence, I say, "What k-kind of m-medicine did he t-take?"

She looks at me curiously before answering, then says; "Amoxicillin, a type of antibiotic. Why?"

I reach over and rub his head, and this time the urgency is even greater. Fighting to keep a steady tone, I say, "Ma'am, I r-realize you don't know me, b-but the medicine you j-just gave him is about to c-cause an allergic reaction, a r-really b-bad one. You n-need to get him to a h-hospital r-right away."

She looks at me as if I have lost my mind, and I can't blame her. Her son looks perfectly fine. It's coming soon though, the rash, shortness of breath, wheezing, and then …

"Who are you and where are you from?" she says, all of the friendliness gone.

"That's n-not important. Your s-son is going to s-stop breathing if you d-don't ...."

As the words are coming out of my mouth, tiny red splotches appear on his face. He gives a hoarse cough and starts to cry, but the high-pitched squeal abruptly becomes pinched and strained. His eyes begin to bulge as he struggles to draw a breath.

The woman looks at her son, then back at me with terror in her eyes, as she grabs him from the cart. Frantically, she runs out the door clutching him to her chest, as people stop what they are doing to stare. She runs into the parking lot and pushes a button, then slings the door open to a white Yukon, and gets in with him on her lap. I'm right behind them.

"The h-hospital is only two m-miles away, to the r-right." She doesn't even look at me. By now he is having great difficulty breathing and is in a full-blown panic. His lips are turning blue, and he's losing consciousness. She slams the car door, speeds past me, and I am left standing there alone, hoping they make it in time.

I walk back inside as a few people gather around the window, watching her tear out of the parking lot.

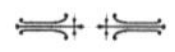

The next day at school I don't know what to expect in History class. I wonder if Mr. Estralar succeeded in getting Mr. Collins fired. My mind is also preoccupied with the boy from yesterday. Did he make it to the ER in time? I didn't even know his name. The woman thought I was crazy, of that I'm certain. Oh well, if it saved that kid's life then I don't care.

Walking into homeroom, Jake and Sam are working on an assignment together. Mrs. Wendell is at a county meeting this morning, which happens every so often. Mrs. Timmons is down the hallway if he needs anything, but we've got this.

They look up at me as I walk in a little late.

"Hey, about time you decided to show up," Jake hollers.

Before I can say anything, Sam says, "Hey, did you hear about Bryce's little brother? He almost died yesterday while his mom was buying groceries. He had a bad reaction to some medicine he took. When they got him to the ER he wasn't breathing. If they had been only a minute or two later he might not have made it."

I mumble to myself, but loud enough for them to hear, "So th-that was B-Bryce's little b-brother."

"I didn't realize Bryce had a little brother," Jake says.

Sam looks at me and says, "When did you find out?"

I put my hands on my chest and say, "I w-was with him at the st-store when it h-happened. He t-touched my arm and I f-felt his b-body g-going haywire inside."

Their eyes fly open wide and say, "Wow," at the same time.

"T-Tell me about it. S-So is he okay?"

Sam nods his head and says, "Yeah, I think so. That's what I heard, anyway."

That's a relief. What a weird coincidence.

I wonder if they know what happened to Mr. Collins. Chances are they've heard something by now. Before I ask the question, Sam says, "While that was going on, Mr. Estralar was in Mr. Nucciol's office reading him the riot act. All of a sudden he gets a frantic phone call from his wife and tears out of the office. I guess the deal with Bryce suddenly seemed like small potatoes."

Just then the bell rings, ending our conversation. No big deal, we'll finish the rest at lunch. Bumping fists, we gather our stuff and head out the door. I'm just about to turn down the hallway to Language Arts when someone shouts my name. Turning around, I almost don't recognize Bryce.

His hair is matted against his head and his clothes look like they've been slept in. Walking directly toward me with a strange unsettling look in his eye, he hollers my name even louder. I'm not sure what to do, so I turn around and keep walking. He screams my name and breaks into a run.

Now things are getting serious. Darting around the corner, I turn into the empty art room, hoping he didn't see me. No one will be in here for at least another hour, so it's a good place to hide. Immediately I look around for anything I can use to defend myself, but all I see are empty plastic bottles of paint and some paper. Just my luck.

He rounds the corner and sees me as I duck behind some chairs in the back of the room and stops. Without wasting a second, he sprints over and suddenly he's staring down at me. Realizing I cannot hide from him, I stand up and face him. He reeks of body odor and foul breath as he glares at me through bloodshot eyes.

He grabs my shirt, effortlessly lifting me off my feet, then pins me to the wall with his forearms against my chest. My head bangs hard against the cold, hard wall as I feel the air leave my lungs.

"What do you know about my little brother?" he snarls.

Oh crap.

"My stepmom made me get out the yearbook last night 'cause some stuttering kid at the store knew Patrick was getting sick. I knew who it was before she found your picture." His eyes narrow as his face moves in so close our noses almost touch. Then he whispers, "How did you know?"

His breath smells like something crawled inside his throat and died.

Looking around to make sure we truly are alone, he slowly turns his attention back to me and says, "Nobody to save your pathetic sorry ass today, pal. No white-knight retard riding in on his shiny steel chariot to bail you out." A satisfied smile slithers across his sneering face as he adds, "His day is coming soon enough though, after I deal with you."

Something indescribable happens to me in that moment. To insult and harass me is one thing, but to bring Jake into this is an entirely different matter. Time seems to stand still as all the taunting, humiliation, and tormenting tear something loose inside. Like looking into a mirror for the first time, I see with undeniable clarity the pathetic, sniveling coward I had become. How could I have allowed myself to fall so low? Wasn't I more of a man than this? Surely there was something bigger and better inside of me. In that frozen moment, I decided then and there I will find that bigger, stronger man I have kept buried beneath all the layers of denial and shame. No longer was I going to live like I was spawned from a bunch of spineless amoebas. My father was a strong man and so are my grandfathers. It is high time I allow those courageous genes to take their rightful place.

Way deep down, a wave begins to form. It gains strength quickly, moving up with such ferocity it nearly burst through my ribs. Without warning, it suddenly unleashes with a thunderous explosion of pure, raw power. My arms fly up, breaking his hold. Before he can recover, I launch into him with such force he flies backward, sprawling onto the floor. I run over before he can get up and jump onto his chest. He stares at me wide-eyed, but makes no effort to get up. The prey has turned the tables on the predator. Putting my face within inches of his, I dare him to move.

Then in a clear, even tone, without the suggestion of a stutter, I say, "Listen, and listen good, you filthy pig. I don't care how stinking rich you are or how your daddy thinks he owns everybody in town. You are nothing but a pathetic, overgrown spoiled brat."

Adjusting my position a little, I grab the front of his shirt and continue. "You had better, NEVER, mention Jake's name again, or I'll make sure you have a front seat on the first train to hell, got that? He has more class, guts, and character than you ever will."

Nothing comes from him except shallow breaths and blinking. With a look of profound disgust, I say, "There is nothing about you that's worth saving, you miserable jerk! You're more worthless than the garbage in the street."

I hear the words spilling from my mouth but can't believe I'm actually saying them. All the years of pent-up frustration and anger came to a head, and he was the one who popped it. If he hadn't brought Jake into this, I would probably still be the sniveling coward in the corner.

The look on his face is beyond astonishment or shock. I don't really know how to describe it. He neither resists nor tries to get up. He just lies there staring at me as I hurl insult after insult. Finally I guess all the poison finds its way out, and we just sit there staring at each other, me sitting on his chest, him like a slab of meat on the cold, hard floor. Reality begins to settle in as he stirs. I roll off of him and crawl to the far wall, physically and emotionally spent.

It takes me a second or two to realize what's happened. As the adrenaline rush leaves, I feel weak and shaky. Sitting up, Bryce stares at me, and I know this fight is far from over.

This was definitely not how he planned things to go. With the back of his hand, he brushes a trickle of blood from his nose. Our eyes lock, and for a moment I swear I am looking at Satan himself. He is blind with rage, and I know if he gets hold of me, I'm a dead man for sure. Looking from left to right, I see my only escape is blocked by a tall stack of chairs the custodians left after cleaning the floors last night.

Bryce is on his knees now, a fresh flow of blood falling in large drops from his nose. They splash onto his chest, making his appearance even more frightening. I brace myself for an all-out assault.

Without removing his eyes from me, he climbs to his feet and grabs a chair that has fallen over next to him then hurls it across the room with such force it smashes into a cabinet, knocking it over. One of the doors flies open and all kinds of art supplies spill out onto the floor.

Eyes wide with terror, I search again for any possible way out. Before I can even move, he is in a full run, sprinting straight for me, nostrils flaring as blood streaks down the sides of his face. His eyes are no longer Bryce's, but those of a monster.

I open my mouth to yell but nothing comes out. He launches into a dive and like a rabbit cornered by a wolf, I manage to slide sideways under the desk next to me just enough to avoid the full impact of his assault. He hits with such impact, the entire row of desks moves back several feet. An iron fist grabs my shirt, tearing the sleeve and sending buttons flying.

All I can think is this is how my life will end, on the floor of a dirty art room in some Podunk high school in the middle of a Podunk town, ripped limb from limb by an insane madman. Memories of a life I never lived flash before my eyes. I see my family crying over my grave, which is right beside Dad's. Sam and Jake will be there too with their folks, and they'll cry some too, I'm sure, but other than that, I'm just another faceless name in a long list of those whose end came way too soon.

Suddenly the lights flicker on and a booming voice rings out.

"Who's in here!" calls the familiar voice of Mr. Kearns, our assistant principal. I look over to a mirror across the room and see a reflection of his shoes in the doorway. We've landed in a corner blocked from where he's standing, so he can't see either of us. If we get caught fighting, we are both royally screwed. It won't make any difference who your daddy is or who he knows or how well connected he is. You get caught in a fist fight in high school these days, cops are called, paperwork is filled out, charges are filed, orange suits with your name are printed on them, and your life is over, period, end of story. They don't care who started the fight or what it was about. By the time it's over with, you'll wish the guillotines were still around.

Bryce and I freeze. We are lying on the floor, our faces only inches apart. His stench overwhelms my nostrils, but I don't dare move a muscle, not even a blink. Bryce's jaw is clenched so tight his cheeks are quivering. We are nose-to-nose, closer to each other than we have ever been before. Truth be told, I would rather be curled up with an angry rattler.

Our eyes are locked onto one another, every muscle fiber pulled tight as piano wire, both aware any movement will give us away. We are like fallen statues.

"I know someone is in here, and I am going to find out who it is," Mr. Kearns angrily yells across the room. His shoes scuff the floor as he moves around, and for the first time since all of this started, Bryce takes his eyes off of me and glances at the mirror. His grip on my shirt loosens just a little as his attention is taken elsewhere.

In the hallway outside, a loud crashing sound breaks the silence as girls start screaming.

Mr. Kearns yells, "What in tarnation now!" as we watch the reflection of his shoes move across the room as he disappears into the hallway. Neither of us breathes for a moment, then realize we are alone again.

He turns to face me with eyes cold and dead as a shark's. Silently he lifts himself above me, pressing my back into the floor.

"You think you can talk to me like that, you worthless piece of crap! There won't be enough of you to fit inside a shoebox by the time I finish with you."

I stare at him and wonder what events in his life could have occurred to produce such a beast. Pure hatred oozes from his pores and fills the room with its putrid stench.

For the first time since I was very small, my mind begins to clear itself of the damnable fog that has held it captive for most of my life. Maybe the rush of adrenaline and the very real threat of physical bodily harm are the keys to the chains that have kept it bound for so long. I look into his face and decide in that moment I am sick and tired of being afraid. Sick and tired of not standing up for myself. Sick and tired of the secret language of books revealed to everyone but me. Sick and tired of sounding like a fool every time I open my mouth. I may get pounded to a pulp in here, but I will not go without a fight. Recalling some of the courage from a moment ago, I make up my mind right then and there I am done acting like prey.

His fist rises above my face, elbow cocked, ready to deliver a deathblow. As soon as his shoulder begins to rotate, I quickly roll my head to the side as his fist rushes past my face and slams into the tile floor. His eyes fly open wide as he screams in agony, grabbing his hand. I squirm from under his weight and skitter like a spider toward the door. Before I can clear the desks, a hand wraps around my ankle and yanks. With my other leg, I kick like a mule that stepped on a snake. Something under my heel crunches, and the vice grip on my ankle gives way.

The door is a few feet away now and I stumble to it as quickly as I can, but my legs are shaking so badly they almost fail me. Turning around, I see Bryce laying on his side, blood profusely running from his nose as he cradles his mangled hand in the other. The pulse in my ears roars so loudly that's all I can hear. He lifts his head and looks at me. What I see is not even human. Tortured, deranged eyes, stare back at me. I close my eyes and turn away.

Falling to the floor on my knees, I put my head in my hands and stifle a cry. Then, from deep within, a small voice reminds me I need to get out of here, and right now. Mr. Kearns will be back soon, and I cannot be here when that happens.

Crawling to the doorway, I peek around the corner and see Mr. Kearns hunched over something on the floor. There is chaos everywhere, kids wall to wall, and a couple of girls holding their hands over their mouths hugging each other. Then I see him as the crowd shifts, opening just enough. Jake is sprawled on the floor in a sickening heap. Mr. Kearns is trying to get him untangled and help him back into his chair.

My first reaction is to run over and lift him out of harm's way, but he sees me sticking my head out of the doorway and does something I will never forget. Our eyes lock as a tiny smile forms on his lips. Just as I'm about to dash over, he gives me a wink. It is only then I realize what is happening. All I can do is shake my head in amazement.

With all eyes on Jake, quietly as possible, I get to my feet and make my way into the hallway holding the front of my shirt together. No one ever pays me one bit of attention anyway; I am just one more kid in the crowded hallway. Quickly I head in the opposite direction as all the fuss stays buried behind me.

I half expect to hear Mr. Kearns yell for me to stop or Bryce to come flying down the hallway and tackle me, but neither happens. I round the corner to the gym, where I know I can find some fresh clothes. I swear I could have qualified for an Indianapolis 500 pit crew with the speed I changed that shirt.

With the torn one lying on the floor, I need to get rid of it quickly. My eyes dart around until I spot a small space under the lockers that no one ever checks. I get down on my knees and shove it deep inside.

With the evidence safely hidden away, I walk out of the gym just as the first kids arrive for class. I give every appearance of being exactly where I am supposed to be. My troubles aren't over yet, though; I still have to explain to Mr. Collins why I skipped his class, and the even bigger problem of running into Bryce again. No way he's going to let this one go. Well, I have news for him. That scared little stuttering coward he chased into the art room is gone. If he wants to tangle with me again, he'd better be up for a fight.

As fate would have it, that was Bryce's last day at our school. His father withdrew him that afternoon and enrolled him in an exclusive private school. It would be years before we meet again.

I have an important phone call to make when I get home. As soon as I walked through the door that afternoon, I pick up the phone and dial. It's answered on the second ring.

"Hi, Mrs. P-prainer? This is J-jason Gil. Have you g-got just a m-minute?"

CHAPTER EIGHT

Seven months later

Summer is finally here, which is better than Christmas and every birthday I've ever had. A whole two-and-a-half months' worth of not hammering my square head into a round hole is the greatest part of summer vacation.

Despite all the bad memories involving school, a few decent ones managed to come along. I can't help but smile when I think of Mrs. Langston and all the ways she finds to make us laugh. It's not only that, she looks out for us like we're her own kids or something. She never talks down to us like others have done. Not once in all the time I've known her has she ever treated me like I always felt—*different.* I hope she knows how much that means to me. Maybe one day I'll get the nerve up to tell her.

Over the years there have been a few good teachers like her that took the time to help me learn in other ways. To most teachers I just feel like a liability, a burden they are forced to carry.

Then my thoughts drift to Mr. Collins, our History teacher. I recall the day he summoned me to his desk to ask why I had skipped his class the day Bryce and I had our little scuffle. He didn't seem particularly upset, just curious.

As best I could, without giving too much away, I told him I had to take care of something personal that came up and apologized for not letting him know about it beforehand. I didn't lie, but I didn't tell him the whole truth either, which I'm pretty sure he knew. He stared intently at me for a long time but said nothing. I told him it wouldn't happen again, and he told me that would be wise. He could have been a jerk, but was cool about it.

I plan to spend most of the summer helping Mr. Adams with his dairy farm to make some extra money. I'll have enough to make a down payment on a car if I keep up this pace. Before long I'll be old enough to drive, and the only way I'm going to have any wheels is if I buy one myself.

I won't be spending the whole summer working though. Uncle Wyatt is taking Sam and me, along with Trey and Tommy, to Juniper Springs for a whole two weeks. He does this every year and we always have a blast.

I'm meeting with Mrs. Prainer this morning, like I've done every Saturday for the past few months, so she can help me not sound like an idiot anymore.

When I first called her to get all of this started, she said she had been waiting for the day when I would call. One of the things on her bucket list was to help make my words flow.

For the longest time, I really thought there wasn't any hope for me, but realize now I was wrong. Guess I just wasn't desperate enough to make the effort. Like they say, "You can lead a horse to water, but you can't make him drink." Well, this horse was finally parched.

When I make it to her house, she's carrying a big bag of laundry to her car. She told me her washing machine was broken but had to wait to call a repairman until she got paid next. Her husband passed away last year of a heart attack, and she's working only on a part-time basis at the elementary school. Mrs. Prainer is not the kind of lady who likes to ask for help, so I offer to look at her washing machine since I was there anyway. She's helping me with my speech and not charging me anything, so I think it's a fair trade. I would have looked at it regardless if I had known it was acting up.

A big smile crosses her face as she leads me into the laundry room. After giving it a once over, I spot the problem right away since I've helped Dad fix these things dozens of times. She gets on the phone and orders the part, and when it comes in, I'll replace it.

She tries to hug me, but I tell her I'm all sweaty from riding my bike over, which is true, but she hugs me anyway. Then she tells me I'm an answer to prayer. If I'm the answer to anybody's prayer, then God, or whoever is in charge, must be scraping the bottom of the barrel.

After my hour with Mrs. Prainer is up, a few chores need to be knocked down and then Sam, Jake, and I will have the whole night to ourselves. Sometimes we spend the night at Jake's house, but his parents have a meeting in Lakeland early this afternoon, so we're having our sleepover at my house. Sam will meet me at Nonnie and Papa's, then help with the chores, which makes the day go by a lot faster.

Papa has a couple dozen new calves he's taking to market later today. Every year he takes a fresh bunch to the cattle auction in Plant City. Sam and I have Smoky and Trixie trained to herd the cows with us to make the job a lot easier.

Papa's big bull is penned up in another area, so we don't have his cranky attitude to deal with. It's bad enough ticking off the mama cows, but that's the way life is on a farm.

Cows are normally very peaceful, easy-going animals, as long as they don't have babies to protect. We have to be careful, because if this is done wrong somebody could get hurt.

That happened on a farm not far from here a couple of years ago. Their young son, probably five or six years old, was playing with a calf, like kids do, when suddenly its mama got bent out of shape about something and charged the little boy. One of her horns caught him in his face below his right eye and the other got him on top of his head. He healed up okay, but was left with a permanent scar the shape of a smiley face on his cheek.

Since we're getting calves that are already weaned, it won't be as traumatic on either the mamas or their babies, so hopefully everything will go okay.

Sam and I strip out of our shirts since the temperature is already well into the nineties, even though it's only ten o'clock in the morning. The herd is still lounging around under the giant oak trees they slept under last night, so we head their way. We whistle for the dogs and they stop playing and follow us.

The dogs know what's about to happen and get ready. They like this part. Their soft coats ripple in the sunshine and I think back to how they came to be ours.

About two years ago, Sam and I were out messing around playing ball when we heard a high-pitched whining in the ditch in front of my house. We put the football down and walked to the road where we found a half-starved puppy covered in ticks and fleas. That's how Smoky started life, like a dirty old rag that nobody wanted. Strays are the only pets we've ever owned, and I wouldn't want it any other way.

Dad found Trixie around the old phosphate ponds almost eight years ago and brought her home. She was pregnant, scared, and skinny as a rail. At the time, our cat Pretzel was also pregnant. After Pretzel got over the trauma of a dog in her midst, they got along really well. The two had their babies the same week, so we had furry little critters everywhere. When it came time to eat, the puppies and kittens nursed from both moms. Nobody seemed to mind, so we had kittens that thought they were puppies and puppies that thought they were kittens.

The cows pick up their heads and know we're up to something. Many of them have done this before with calves from previous years, so they know the routine. They don't like it any more than we do, but that's just the way it is. It happens every year, whether we like it or not.

The dogs go on either side of the herd and start running, biting at their heels and barking to get them up and going. It's not long before all of the cattle are on their feet and moving toward the pens.

Fortunately, we don't have very far to go. Once we get them inside the holding pens, we feed them, separate the moms from the babies then turn the adults loose into the pasture again.

The babies are nervous and scared, so we get into the pen with them, rub their backs and talk to them. We give them some more food and water and let them get used to their new surroundings. By the time we're finished, they are calmed down and settle in.

Sam and I climb out of the pens, run cool water from the hose over our heads, then towel off and put our shirts back on. It's noon and time for lunch.

We take off our shoes and leave them beside a dusty old doggie bed their little Chihuahua used when she was here. I was just a kid when Aunt Lori and Nonnie found her behind the grocery store. Nonnie heard something whimpering as they walked through the parking lot one morning, and when they couldn't find the source, they called the manager. He sent one of the bag boys outside to help and when he opened the lid to a dumpster, he saw two little black eyes shining in the darkness. The boy reached in and got her out then wrapped her in a paper bag because she was so filthy. Nonnie and Aunt Lori cleaned her up as best they could before taking her to the vet. The poor dog was so eaten up with mange the vet didn't think she'd survive. Nonnie and Papa thought otherwise.

They brought her home, bathed her every day, treated her with some homemade concoction they used on their sick cows, and before long she was covered with soft brown hair. They named her Chiquita, like the banana. She lived a long life and died a happy old senorita, but nobody has had the heart to get rid of her old bed.

When we walk in, Papa is sitting in his chair watching something on the Nature Channel while Nonnie is busy making our lunch in the kitchen. When they see us, they stop what they are doing and greet us like they haven't seen us in years.

We give them each a hug, a tradition our family takes very seriously. If you walk into a relative's house, you must give said relative a hug before doing anything else. I think it's written in a book of conduct somewhere.

"Well, look at these two fine strappin' young fellas," Papa says with a wide grin. His weathered face reflects a lifetime of hard work under the hot Florida sun, but he seems to not have a care in the world. Honestly, I don't know how he does it. I would be miserable if I were in his shoes. In all the years he's been my grandpa, I don't have a single memory of him being grumpy or discouraged. He sees each new day as an adventure, especially if his grandchildren are involved.

Papa's skin looks so thin over his fragile bones, it's hard to imagine him as the big strong man from the stories we hear. The pictures hanging all around their house are of a man I hardly recognize.

One in particular is of him and Nonnie taken right before they got married. The two are standing outside the fairgrounds, along with Nonnie's sister, Jenny, who must've been about thirteen. I never got to know her because she died of typhoid a year after the picture was taken. Nonnie still gets sad when she talks about that.

Nonnie is sitting between the two of them beaming with pride. Even in the black-and-white picture, I see a lot Nonnie's good looks in my mom and her sisters. She was quite "the looker like no other," as Papa likes to say.

This photo is one of my favorites, even though it causes my heart to ache seeing how much my grandfather has changed. His facial features are recognizable enough, but the body attached to it is what troubles me. The frail little old man next to me was once the dynamic young guy in the photograph.

Mom tells me Papa worked from sun up to sun down taking care of his family. He and Nonnie bought this land we've grown up on before she was even born. The life he traded to make ours so much better causes an unsettling feeling inside me I can't quite identify. Will I grow up to be so dedicated? I'd like to think so. This picture definitely gives me a lot to think about.

I wonder if Nonnie had other men she thought about marrying. How different would my life be? What if Mom had married a man like Uncle Frank or Uncle Todd? Maybe I wouldn't even miss him. My head hurts thinking about all the possibilities. Fate is a funny thing.

Papa has rheumatoid arthritis and it is so advanced, about the only joints he can move are the ones he's had replaced.

Sam and I get on either side and lift him to his feet. My hands always react to his condition, but I have no idea what to do about it. His gnarled fingers do their best to hold my arm as we help him to the table.

After settling into our seats, I feel my stomach rumble. Everything looks so good. Sam smiles at me over the table then looks at Papa and says, "Hey Papa, those calves look real healthy this year."

Papa is proud of his cows. He says with a wink, "Our cows are always the best, just like our grandkids."

Nonnie puts her hands on her hips and says, "Otha, I declare."

We can't help but laugh.

Even after all these years her blue eyes still sparkle. I know some of their times together were really hard from the stories we hear, but they seem to only remember the good ones. I hope I inherited those same genes.

Everything smells delicious, but we have to say grace first. We bow our heads and join hands. I hold Nonnie's left hand and Papa's right. His fingers feel more like knotted tree branches than fingers. He always says grace, like it's his duty or something, but one he really likes. You can tell by the way he speaks it's not just a quick mouth service. I don't know if I could pray to a God who let people he's supposed to love suffer so much. Papa never complains, but the pain must be terrible. I wonder if he thinks about these things. It must have occurred to him if God were all-powerful, then he could heal him and other people who are sick. I bow my head like I'm supposed to, but my heart isn't in it.

When the food starts moving around the table I say, "What were you w-watching on TV?"

"Oh, something about lovebirds I think. It reminds me of your grandma and me when we were young and carefree," he says with a wry smile. She shakes her head and rolls her eyes.

Nonnie hands me a bowl of rice and says, "I hear you boys are having a sleepover at your house tonight, Jason."

"Yes, ma'am, Sam and Jake are c-coming over, so we won't be camping. It's too hard for Jake to walk through the w-woods since he can't take his walker or wheelchair out there," I say.

"We've got lots of fun things to do, so no chance we'll get bored," Sam adds.

"Do you know what happened that caused him to be crippled?" Papa asks between bites of pork chop.

"S-something happened while he was being born," I say. We've talked about it before, but Papa forgets sometimes.

Sam pipes up, "Yeah, when he was born the placenta tore away too early and his brain didn't get enough oxygen. Brain cells die after just a few minutes and they never grow back. Most people with cerebral palsy get it when they are being born, like Jake did."

"He's such a sweet boy, I'm glad you three have stayed friends all these years. I know he enjoys doing fun things with kids his own age," Nonnie says.

"Yeah, he's a r-really cool guy, and tough, too," I say. I tell them about the two of us sailing off the inner tube after hitting a wave in the river. Papa laughed out loud and wanted to hear it again. He loves to laugh and hear our stories.

"Hey," he says with a mischievous grin, "Did you hear about Mrs. Conyer's latest prank?" Oh man, there's no telling what she's done now.

Mrs. Conyer has been a friend of my grandparents since they were in high school and is the craziest old lady I've ever known. She loves to play pranks on the younger crowd for entertainment. For her, anyone under sixty is fair game.

We never know when or where she's going to strike. She loves to wear long skirts that have large pockets to hide her tools of the trade. In those pockets she carries whoopee cushions, fake cockroaches, plastic barf, rubber doggy doo, plastic spiders and snakes, and who knows what else. Those are just the things we know about.

Since everyone in town knows her and the stunts she pulls, she thinks nothing of traveling to another town where no one knows her. They just see a little old lady and pay her no attention.

One of her favorite tricks is to place her remote control whoopee cushion beside a register in an inconspicuous spot. Then she slips away and takes a seat close by until a customer comes up to the counter. Nobody suspects a little old lady is behind those embarrassing baked bean moments.

Dad thought she'd slipped off her noodle, but I think she's cool.

"No, we didn't hear about it, what did she do this time?" asks Sam.

"Well, you know that big gray wig she likes to wear around town?" Sam and I nod. That wig is legendary. Inside that big honeycomb is a fake rat. She has him arranged so he's peeking out the front of one of the curls, like he's taking a nap on her head. It's the same color as the wig, so nobody notices it at first. She can be carrying on a conversation with somebody and they suddenly spot it. The shocked look on their face is what she lives for.

Papa swallows another bite of cornbread and says, "Well, she decided to go one step further and spring load the thing. When she pushes a button inside her shirt, the rat flies straight out of her hair," almost choking on his sweet tea as he laughs again.

"Anyway, she puts that crazy wig on and goes over to the store to see who she can get. Most everyone avoids her, knowin' she's probably up to no good. It doesn't take long before she spots a new checkout girl.

"After grabbing a few things, she gets in line and patiently waits. Finally, when she gets ready to pay for her stuff, she innocently looks at the girl and smiles. The young clerk smiles back and just before lookin' away, spots the rat.

"When Mrs. Conyer saw the look on her face, she pushed the button. Like a hairy dart, that rat flew out of her wig and landed in the girl's long blonde hair. It got all tangled up, and the poor girl goes to jumpin' around, screamin' and hollerin', and slingin' her head from side to side. Half the store stopped what they were doing to see what all the ruckus was about. It was one of the funniest things I've ever seen!"

"You were there when all this happened?" I ask incredulously.

"Yeah, your grandma left me in the front of the store on the bench, like she usually does while she does her shoppin', and I watched the whole thing."

Papa is notorious for his funny stories, but this one seems a little too good to be true. Nonnie is giggling with the rest of us, so I ask, "Is that t-true, Nonnie, did that really happen?"

"I was in the next line over, watching her scare that poor gal half to death," she said, shaking her head, but still laughing. "And actually, once the shock wore off and everything calmed down, she laughed a little, too. Nobody can stay mad at that dear little lady for very long."

I give Sam a disgusted look and say, "See all the fun stuff we miss while we're in school!" He just shrugs his shoulders and says, "Maybe somebody got it on their phone and put it on the internet."

After lunch, Sam and I head back outside to mow the lawn. He gets the mower going while I grab the edger and start knocking down weeds. Before long, we're done with the yard work and have everything cleaned and put away. We tell Nonnie and Papa bye, but before we go, Papa pulls me to the side.

"Son, I didn't want to say nothin' at the table with everybody around, but I noticed your words sound … less encumbered," he says, looking at me expectantly.

I feel my chest swell with pride and say, "Guess I finally got tired of sounding like a motor running on only half its cylinders."

He smiles and says, "I'm so proud of you, boy. Wish everybody had grandsons as fine as ours."

Wow, I don't know what to say to that. Nonnie and Papa are always big on compliments, but I've never heard him say anything like this, so I say the only thing that comes to mind. "Thanks, Papa, I wish they did, too."

He laughs and gives me another hug before we go, then whispers in my ear, "Your grandma and I have prayed about this day for a long time. We always knew it would happen."

When he finally lets me go, I pull my arms gently away and look into his eyes, surprised to see them brimming with tears. He looks like he has something else to say, but instead, gives me a strong pat on the shoulder and says in a voice loud enough for everyone to hear, "You boys have fun tonight, and tell Jake we said to come and see us, okay?"

Sam yells back, "We will, Papa."

I wonder if all grandparents like spending time with their grandkids like ours do. Actually I know the answer to that since

I've been around Sam's other grandparents, and have seen how cold and distant they are. What a bummer to have grandparents like that.

Sam and I wave goodbye as we walk down the driveway, like we've done a million times before.

It's about three o'clock, so there's time to go to the store before Jake gets here.

As we head down the hallway to my room, Mary's door is wide open so we peek inside and see her holding a baby mockingbird in her hand, rubbing its tiny gray back. She has a way with critters like I've never seen. Even the meanest ones that would bite anybody else turn into sweet, cuddly bundles of joy in her hands.

Sylvester, our black-and-white tabby, was only a few days old when she found him under a bush. We thought he was a goner, but she brought him home and nursed him back to health. Looking at him now, you'd never know he was once at death's door.

Mary holds out her hand, showing us her new friend and says, "I went into the backyard to check on Thumper," one of her rabbits, "and saw Sylvester with something in his mouth. I made him drop it and out fell this baby mockingbird. I named him Marley. He wasn't hurt, just really scared, so I took him inside and made him a little home in the old fish tank. See, he's fine and happy now," she says with a smile.

"Sure looks like it," Sam says. "I don't know how many lives a bird has, but I think he just used at least a couple."

"What time is Jake coming over tonight?" Mary loves Jake; in fact, I think she sees him as another one of her pets. Jake doesn't seem to mind, so if it doesn't bother him, it doesn't bother me.

"About six, but Sam and I are walking to the store to get some stuff for tonight."

We walk out of the house and head down the road. After reaching the store, we go to the produce section to get Mary's rabbits some carrots and lettuce. After grabbing a box of cookies, a six-pack of soda, some candy, and a bag of popcorn, we're ready to go.

Papa paid us thirty dollars apiece for our work this morning, so we have more than enough. He says, "If a man works, he needs to get paid." No argument here.

After we pay for the stuff, we start the long walk back home. Along the way, we see a familiar sight—a big gray tortoise we call a gopher. When I was younger, we used to carry them around from place to place. They didn't seem to mind and just went along for the ride.

All of a sudden, Sam grabs my arm and points to something on the other side of the marsh. I pull my hand up to shade the sun and squint in that direction.

There, on the other side, is an enormous white bird digging its long beak into the soft mud. It abruptly stands up straight and looks around, like he can feel our eyes on him. That's when I see how tall this white bird really is. It looks like some sort of crane, but much bigger than the sand hills we normally see. This beautiful bird is so elegant and majestic it looks like it belongs in a palace.

Sam whispers, "Do you know what that is?"

I shake my head. I've never seen anything like it before.

"That, my kooky cuz, is a whooping crane."

Shocked, I say, "You're kidding, I thought they were like extinct or something."

"They just about were, but they've bred enough of them in captivity to put some back into the wild again. They put a few here in Florida, and some way out in Idaho. Can you believe we would be lucky enough to spot one?" he says, giving my shoulder a hard shove.

Still shaking my head I say, "Wow, I *never* thought I would see one; not here, anyway. Maybe in a zoo."

I heard our grandparents talk about how they were hunted like crazy, almost to extinction. Why would anybody want to kill something so beautiful?

We stare at it a few more minutes and watch in amazement as it suddenly leaps into the air, spreading its enormous black-tipped wings like it's about to take off. Then it begins dancing to some mysterious music only it can hear. Sam and I feel like we've stumbled upon our own private show as it boogies down in tropical paradise. Then, just as quickly as it began, it stops and stands still as a statue. He looks around intently in our direction and we stare back. Maybe he's expecting us to applaud, or something. No one moves for several minutes and then the spell is broken. It turns around, jumps into the air one last time, and struts over the ridge to another marshy area out of sight.

Sam elbows me and says, "How cool was that?"

"Icebergs wish they were that cool," I say, as we turn to head home.

Sam grins and says, "I'll bet he's got a lady on the other side who wants to teach him a thing or two about the birds and the bees," moving his hips around like some Prince wannabe.

With a snort, I shake my head and say, "I wonder if cranes have their babies delivered by storks, too."

He smacks me on the back of the head and says, "Good one, dork."

We make it back to my house just about the same time Mom gets home and meet her in the driveway. She gives us both a hug and asks how our morning went herding the cows. She looks tired, but manages to stay chipper. I guess happy genes just run in the family.

"Everything went fine, Mom. Jake should be here soon."

"Sounds good, honey," she says as she pulls a couple bags of groceries out of the car and hands them to us. We carry them inside and set them on the table.

About that time I hear Trixie barking. Jake must be here. I look out the window and see his van pulling into the driveway. When they stop under the big oak tree, the driver's door opens as his mom steps out. Sam and I walk out to meet them.

"Hey, boys, have a big night planned?"

"Oh yeah, we're gonna swipe Aunt Trish's car and hit the bars all over town using our fake ID's we got from Uncle Vince," Sam says with a stupid grin. Without missing a beat, she says, "Oh good, I was worried you boys might not have any fun."

Uncle Vince is a private detective in Georgia and has lots of cop friends, so he has access to way more super-cool stuff than your average uncle. He tells us stories involving fake ID's, forged checks, confiscated goods, and all kinds of awesome stuff he's seen. He also makes sure to tell us all the trouble the culprits got into, just in case the thought ever crossed our minds.

She opens the side door so Jake can get out. "Hey knucklehead, how's it going?" I say as I unbuckle him. Sam climbs in beside me as we lift him out.

"Doing good, man, where's the pizza?"

"You sure don't waste any time, do ya?" says Sam.

Most people would not realize how strong Jake is since he's in a wheelchair most of the time. He can walk a long way, if he can keep from falling over. That's where things get tricky.

His mom has his walker waiting for us and he glides into it like he's done a thousand times before. This has been the story of his life, but he's still the happiest guy I know.

"You boys have a fun time tonight, and try not to get into too much trouble," his mom says as she closes the door, giving Sam's shoulder a pat.

Mom walks out and gives her a hug like she hasn't seen her in years. What is it with women and all these hugs, anyway?

As we head inside, they stay outside and chat on the porch. I elbow Jake and say, "Hey, Evel Knievel, you ought to work with a net. A guy can get his skull cracked flying out of a chair like that."

He laughs and says, "No worries, man, I do that kind of stuff all the time," like it wasn't any big deal at all. The heck it wasn't, and the three of us know it.

Sam shakes his head and says, "They'd be doing nine to life if you hadn't dumped the chair, dude."

Jake laughs and says, "No problem, man, I just wish they'd caught Butthead. I wouldn't break a nail to save his sorry hide."

I pat him on the shoulder and say, "I appreciate the stunt, man."

He smiles up at me and says cheerfully, "Hey, what are brothers for? I know you'd do the same for me."

"Yeah, of course I would."

Both Sam and Jake look at me smiling, but say nothing for several seconds. Then feeling like a bug under a microscope I say louder than necessary, "What?!"

Jake looks at Sam then back at me and says, "Mrs. Prainer's got your number, dude."

I can't help but smile. I never thought I would sound normal, much less intelligent, but Mrs. Prainer is making both of them happen. They take turns smacking their affection into my shoulder.

Feeling a little self-conscious, I smack them back a couple of times as we head back to my room.

We get Jake out of his walker and let him flop into a big beanbag that fits him perfectly. Sam gets the controller and puts it in his hands and the three of us start playing.

"Hey," Jake says after a few minutes, "You think the other guys are going to be camping tonight?"

Sam says, "Imagine so. They do just about every weekend if the weather is good."

Jake says, "I've never been camping, what's it like?"

He's asked us this before, but it's like describing what ice cream tastes like to someone who's never eaten any. His thoughts seem to leave the game, but his eyes never drift from the TV. In a moment he looks at me, then at Sam, then back at me again.

"What?" I say.

"Do you think maybe we could try it, like after it gets dark?" he asks with puppy dog eyes. Sam's face mirrors my thoughts—not a good idea.

"Well, Jake, we have to walk through some pretty serious woods to get there and your walker can't handle all the stuff we have to cross," I say as gently as I can.

"I could walk out there if you guys helped me a little," he says. "I know I could."

Sam and I stop playing the game and look at each other. If our moms knew we were even having this conversation our butts would be toast. Jake looks back and forth between us with a hopeful expression. I'm beginning to feel like we're in some kind of reality TV show.

I can't imagine never having the chance to camp, something everybody should get to do. Imagine how much better the world would be if everybody camped at least once or twice a month. Forget all your troubles and just live in the moment. If he gets to go just one time, how much harm could there be in that?

"What do you think, Sam?" I ask, already knowing the answer.

Sam ignores me and says, "You've never been camping with your parents before, Jake?"

"No, we don't even own a tent. I've heard you guys talk about it and seen it on TV, but have never been. I've wanted to forever," he says with a pout. He knows just how to play us.

Sam ponders it a moment then finally says, "I'll leave it up to you guys. We'd have to wait until Aunt Trish falls asleep though."

I feel their eyes on me as I think the situation over. If I say no, Jake might never get the opportunity to go again. If I say yes, then we risk getting in big trouble with both sets of folks. Man, there's no easy answer.

Knowing what the answer was going to be all along, I whisper quietly, "Like Sam said, we'll have to wait until Mom is asleep."

Jake's face lights up like a Christmas tree and he begins to hoot and holler.

"Hey dude, keep your voice down," I say, putting a hand over his big mouth. He peels my hand away and whispers, "This is going to be the best night of my whole life. Thanks, guys," then places a finger across his smiling lips. Every night is the best night of his whole life.

Mom knocks on the door, letting us know the pizza is here.

Sam and I follow her into the kitchen, grab the whole box, and carry it back to the room.

Around nine o'clock, we plug in a movie just before Mom sticks her head in the door to tell us good night. She reminds us even if we stay up all night, that we still have church in the morning. We tell her that's fine, we'll be ready.

We let the movie play long enough to make sure she's asleep. Our backpacks are waiting for us by the door as Sam and I check the hallway; all clear.

We pick Jake up and place him between us, each holding an arm. We walk quietly down the hallway sideways, careful not to touch the walls. As we make our way through the kitchen, my elbow bumps into the stand that holds Mom's potted plants. It starts to wobble but I quickly grab it with my free hand. Sam's face clouds over as I sheepishly flash him a smile. Carefully, we continue our way to the door.

Once outside, Jake says, "Wow, that was close."

"No kidding, man," I say. Sam just shakes his head. For a couple of minutes we take a breather and admire ourselves for having made it this far.

We are just stepping out of the garage when a voice slices through the night air, "Where are you guys going?" All three of us nearly jump out of our skin, grabbing Jake just before he hits the floor. We turn around and see Mary sitting at the picnic table. Trixie is curled up at her feet, Sylvester a bundle of fur on her lap, and Marley perched on her index finger. It would appear she's talked them all into being friends.

Just above a whisper I say, "Girl, you scared us to death!" She just giggles and strokes Sylvester's fur as he purrs loudly on her lap.

"Sorry, didn't mean to. Where are you going, camping? "

I get all panicky and say, "Mary, Jake has never been before." She scratches Sylvester behind the ear as he lifts his head to see what's going on. He decides this isn't worth his time and goes back to sleep.

Sam gives me a worried look, but I just shake my head a little like this is no problem, even though it very well could be.

She looks at us for a minute as a smile slowly crosses her face. It gets bigger the longer she stares, and I feel a cold sweat break out down my back. Then she says, "I knew you guys were going to do this."

The three of us look at each other, then Sam says with a furrowed brow, "How did you know, did you hear us talking?"

"No, guys are just so predictable is all." She turns to face the woods and says, "I can see the fire from here between the trees and knew one day y'all would do this."

I wonder what else she knows about us.

Sam gives her a long look and says, "Mary, are you going to say anything about this to your mom?"

With a wounded look she says, "Why would I do that? It's all for one and one for all, right?" quoting a game we used to play.

Smiling, Sam says, "Right."

Although Jake is several years older than Mary, they are just about the same size. She's adored him ever since the first day they met.

"Thanks for not blabbing," Jake says.

"No problem, y'all have fun."

I ask Mary if she wants to tag along but she declines, like I knew she would. Camping involves way too much dirt and effort. Trixie on the other hand is more than happy to go along. She jumps up, turning in circles as we get ready to go.

With Trixie in the lead chasing away all the monsters, we step out into the night. Walking through the thickest part of the trail, we nearly topple over a couple of times, but manage to stay on our feet. The moon is exceptionally bright and clear tonight so our path is easy to see. I can tell the effort is taking a toll on Jake, but as usual, he offers no complaint.

As we finally step into the clearing near the pond, several familiar faces appear, including Jesse's. She's been a regular ever since that first night.

Our cousins Beth, Ricky, and Brad have joined Trey and Tommy.

"Hey guys, it's just us," Sam says.

"Cool, is that Jake with y'all?" asks Trey, his surprise obvious.

"Yeah, it's me, I wanted to camp with y'all and see what the big deal's all about," he says with a huge grin.

"Wow, come on over and have a seat, big man, we've got a place right here for ya," Trey says, clearing a spot on the blanket next to him.

Beth comes over with a can of Sprite and hands it to Jake, sweat pouring down his face and dripping onto his shirt.

"Thanks," he says before gulping it down.

"Anytime, and there's more where that came from."

He wipes his mouth with his sleeve just as a fat beetle clumsily flies in and lands on Beth's forehead. He laughs as she lets out a startled squeal before quickly brushing it away.

Stardust appears from the shadows to see what all the commotion is about. We hear her before she makes her entrance as loud farts echo with each step.

I look at Beth and say, "Got into the dog food again?" Every time she does, it gases her up. Beth used to get mad about it, but now just lets it go.

"I forgot to put the bag up high enough and she cleaned it out, so we should be entertained for hours."

Jake raises his eyebrows and says, "Even horses camp with y'all?"

Beth replies, "Only this one. She's mine and goes with me everywhere I go out here." Pointing toward the dogs playing at the edge of the light she says, "And right there is my dog, the black one with the curly hair. Her name is Kinky. Real creative name, but it works. She goes everywhere the horse goes."

Jake nods his head and says, "Cool … dogs, horses, water, fire, food, this is like heaven."

She nods and says with a short giggle, "That's right, Jake, it feels like it sometimes."

I sit down next to Jesse who smiles at me sheepishly. She leans into me playfully and I catch a whiff of the softness of her scent. Light from the fire dances on her face, reflecting the brightness of her eyes, making them even more intense.

"Fancy meeting you here," she says.

"Yeah, imagine that. Drop anybody lately?"

Without missing a beat she says, "No, but the night is still young, so who knows."

"I'll keep that in mind."

She laughs, "This a friend of yours?" motioning toward Jake.

That's right, they've never met. The three of us don't share any of the same classes, so I guess I just overlooked it.

"Yeah, this is my best friend Jake. We've been buddies since first grade."

She gets up from her spot next to me and walks around the outside of our little circle and sits down next to him. The fire pops loudly, sending bright orange sparks into the air between us. It quickly rises into the damp night air and disappears.

Like all the girls, she's smitten in under thirty seconds. Casanova has nothing on this guy. They talk for a few minutes, and then she reaches over and hugs him. Romeo could take notes.

"Hey, where's the spud gun?" I call to Tommy.

He puts his hands together like he's going to say a prayer then says "bang," opening them quickly.

I raise my eyebrows and say, "Anybody hurt?"

"Nope, just the gun. We're building a new one out of stronger PVC this time."

Jesse sits down next to me, still staring at Jake and says, "Wow, he's amazing! He has some powerful energy."

Giving a little laugh, I say, "I know, he's been like this for as long as I've known him."

She turns her head and looks at me deliberately for an uncomfortable moment as I squirm like a worm on a hook. Casually she says, "What happened to your voice, I mean, you sound ... different."

I say a little self-consciously, "Guess I finally got tired of sounding like a moron and did something about it."

"You never sounded like a moron. Don't say things like that about yourself," she says with a sad smile.

"Thanks, but that's how it sounded to me. I guess unless you have to deal with something like that, you wouldn't understand."

She nods her head and says, "That 'somebody else's shoes thing', I get it."

I nod my head.

"Well, I think you sound awesome."

Awesome? Wow, this is big. All that comes to mind is, "Thanks."

She gives me a playful smack on the arm, then looks back at Jake with soulful eyes and asks, "Where does he live?"

"Only a couple of miles from my house. We usually spend at least one Saturday night a month together, either at his house or mine. His parents had a meeting this afternoon in Lakeland, so he's sleeping over at my house this time."

"His parents don't mind him coming out here?" she asks, surprised.

I get quiet for a minute and then whisper, "They don't exactly know we're here. He begged us to bring him down, so we snuck out after Mom fell asleep."

She looks at me with wide eyes and says, "You guys could get into a lot of trouble."

Defensively I say, "We're not doing anything that bad. All he wanted to do was see what it was like out here. He's never camped before, and we're going back real early so nobody will even know."

A little softer she says, "I understand, I just don't want you all to get into any trouble, that's all."

Interrupting our conversation, Trey yells, "Man, you should've seen the size of the catfish we caught tonight," holding his hands far apart.

"Is there any left?" asks Jake.

"Heck yeah, man, right here," he says, reaching for the frying pan.

Jake says, "I've never had catfish cooked over a fire before."

Sam grabs a plate and hands him a piece. Jake eats it quickly, like it's going to disappear in the next thirty seconds, then says, "Man, that's good. Y'all are so lucky to do this all the time."

An uneasy giggle floats above the fire.

Jesse says, "Just wait until you have a s'mores!"

Tommy yells across the fire, "Now you're talkin.'"

We have to make Jake stop after three. He licks his fingers as the fire casts long lazy shadows over our faces.

"Hey, check this out," Trey yells from across the fire. He jumps up and heads toward the tree. Grabbing the rope, he's swinging over the pond like Tarzan. In one smooth motion, he releases the handle and sails high into the air, somersaulting over and over, then just before hitting the water, straightens out and goes in head first. Everybody around the fire claps and cheers.

Tommy climbs up next, a look of determination on his face. He swings out higher than Trey, and as soon as he releases the rope, starts twisting and turning in all directions, and all I can do is stand amazed when he enters headfirst.

Climbing the ladder, I'm a little nervous since all eyes are on me. Reaching the deck, I'm surprised how far I can see by the light of the full moon.

Taking the bar in my hands, I jump off, slicing through the night air already wet with dew. When I can't go any higher, I let go and vault head over heels, landing in the pond butt first, rocketing deep into the warm water. I remove my hands from my burning rear and pull upward. When I reach the surface to a cheering crowd, I see Jake up on his knees clapping wildly.

The next thing I know, Jesse makes a big splash right beside me, followed by Sam. They swim over and we paddle to shore together. Once on the beach, Sam and I try not to notice the wet clothes clinging to her body. We walk back to the fire and plop down on old towels.

Jake is the only one not wet. He looks at us and then at himself. We look at each other, realizing all at once what he sees.

"Hey, you think I could do that?" he finally asks.

I hadn't planned on him wanting to swing off the rope, but then again, I hadn't really planned any of this. The only ones out here strong enough to help him would be Tommy or Trey. We're quiet for a minute as we look at each other uncomfortably over the fire, not sure what to say.

"You ever swing off a rope before, Jake?" Tommy finally asks.

"No, but if one of you goes with me, I'm sure I could do it," he says confidently.

"I'll go with him," says Trey matter-of-factly. Jake is so excited he bounces up and down on his knees, yelling out loud.

"Easy, man," I say, not at all comfortable with any of this. Things are moving way too fast. The smile vanishes from Sam's face. Trey and Tommy walk to the truck talking to each other.

Trey carries all kinds of extra stuff in his truck, including some rigging for mountain climbing. He digs around until he finds a harness. He straps it on and cinches it up until it's snug, then Tommy lifts Jake onto Trey's wide back as we secure them together. Jake chatters away, happy as a clam, but I'm too nervous to even smile. Tommy gives it one last go over to make sure everything is right.

Trey has let some of our younger cousins piggyback with him before, but this is different. Jake is not very big or heavy, but still ...

They scale the ladder quickly as Tommy helps them up. Trey catches his breath at the top and turns his head to say something to Jake we can't hear.

I hold my breath and try to close my eyes, but I can't. Jake is holding onto Trey's neck and shoulders like he's having the time of his life. With a deliberate step, they launch off the deck toward the pond. The tree limb creaks loudly as it sways, the leaves rustling in unison.

Trey's muscles ripple and bunch under the heavy load as they sail through the night sky. At that moment, seeing them dangle from that rope, I think this is about the dumbest idea we've ever come up with. Fear snares me in its grasp as I watch helplessly from the shore. All at once, I want to snatch Jake off that rope and get him over here with me where he's safe.

With a loud holler, Trey releases the handle and they launch confidently into the warm air. Time stands still as the two bodies glide as one through this tiny space in time. They sail high, Jake's arms outstretched wide and free as the two boys arch into a slow, perfect somersault. We watch in awe as they float above the water like a beautiful gravity-defying dance.

Suddenly, images of the dancing whooping crane flash across my mind, and I finally get it. The reality of the moment becomes abundantly clear as I watch in wonder the scene before us. Free and unencumbered by the natural laws that govern the rest of us, they simply rejoice in the moment. Jake hollers with delight, concerned only with squeezing every last drop out of the life he's been given. They don't need a reason to be joyful, they just are.

Finally the two splash down about twenty feet from shore. Sam and I dive in, swimming as fast as we can and wait impatiently for them to surface.

Oh God, if you are really out there, please let them be okay.

Bubbles break the surface a few feet away. Both come up spitting a little water then begin laughing. I'm so relieved I almost cry.

"Wow, did you see that?" Jake shouts. "We must've been a hundred feet in the air. That's the coolest thing I've ever done in my whole life!" He's talking so fast he has to stop suddenly to draw in air.

We remove the harness and pull Jake free from Trey's back. Sam and I drag him back to shore and wrap him in a towel. In a few minutes, all of us are by the fire again, Jake and Trey bumping fists.

Before long, we're passing hot dogs and s'mores around, telling stories. We toss the dogs a few bites when they meander close, then they go back to playing.

When the scary stories start, it's funny to watch heads turn to look into the dark woods behind us. Tommy is the Stephen King of scary stories out here. His favorite is the true story of a stalker they caught in our woods one night. It happened about ten years ago, but nothing big ever came of it. When Tommy gets going with it though, it becomes a real fisherman's tale. By the time he's done, you'd think this had been Dr. Hannibal Lecter's old stomping grounds.

The air seems heavy and suspiciously still tonight. Something sounds different out there in those dark woods, or maybe it's just my imagination.

Suddenly the sound of large limbs breaking gets everybody's attention. The dogs stop playing and bark loudly. Jake looks nervously around as the rest of us jump to our feet. I swear I see images of Lecter's masked face lurking just beyond the darkness.

Stardust dances nervously about as the dogs continue barking. Tommy hollers for them to be quiet, but they keep barking even more frantically. Twigs snap close by as the tiny hairs on the back of my neck stand on end.

Trey searches around for his flashlight, while Tommy reaches for the knife he keeps in a leather pouch on his hip. I check to make sure everyone is still here and not playing some stupid trick. Can't be any one of us, we are all here and accounted for.

Finally Trey finds his camouflaged flashlight and sends a tight beam into the darkness just as a huge black figure bursts through the thicket. Trey's light catches something huge, reflecting the enormous eyes of a monster. We holler and yell as it bears down on us, dirt and dust flying in every direction. Then we hear our cousin Greg calling from the darkness. His big black cow, White Socks, has gotten out again, and storms into the clearing with a loud bellow.

The dogs run to her like they've found their long-lost pal. She lets them run around her feet, delighted to be the center of attention.

Stardust blows an exaggerated snort like all of this excitement is just too much, and resumes munching grass again.

No lock invented yet has been able to keep this Houdini heifer from breaking out of her stall. Ever since she was a baby, this has been the story of her life. Wherever people are, that's where she wants to be.

White Socks was raised by our cousin Greg from the time she was just a tiny little calf. Her mother died birthing her and Greg raised her as a pet. It didn't take long before she was strong and healthy, but White Socks had no idea she was a cow. In her mind, she was people, never mind the physical differences. With absolutely no fear of humans, she cannot be intimidated, so her thousand pounds pushes around until she gets what she wants.

Everybody is relieved and mad all at once, first yelling, and then laughing.

Sam grabs a bun lying on the ground and throws it in her direction. Before it even hits the ground, she snatches it with her long tongue and scarfs it down, looking around for more.

Tommy finds her a few more unclaimed buns, which satisfies her momentarily. Greg grabs a bag of marshmallows and lets her eat all she wants. Finally she flops down just outside our circle, and with a loud snort begins chewing her cud. Sam laughs and says, "Jake and Jesse, meet White Socks, our furry four-legged cousin."

Greg finds an open space around the fire and sits down with a huff. Sam pats him on the back and says, "Never a dull moment, huh, cuz."

"Not with that crazy cow," replies Greg, shaking his head.

It must be about midnight now and the fire is starting to die down. Tommy adds a few more logs, sending orange and gold sparks into the air. We know we have to get up early, but want to stay up and talk all night. My watch is set to go off at five o'clock; plenty of time for us to make our way back home, shower off the smoky smell and get dressed. I look across the fire at Jake having the time of his life and know for sure we did the right thing.

Finally, at some wee hour of the morning, all conversation dwindles off as we fall asleep.

The next thing I know all kinds of ruckus is breaking loose. Hollering and yelling, bright sunshine blinding me, people moving and scurrying all around. What the heck is going on?

All of a sudden it hits me. My blood turns to ice water as I realize we've overslept. My alarm clock failed to wake us and our moms have tracked us down. I never even heard it go off.

Only a few times have I seen Mom this angry. She's in my face, demanding to know why we are out here and how we could have done such a terrible thing to her. She didn't know where we were when Jake's mom stopped by this morning to drop off his shoes for church.

"Mom!" I jump up from the ground, praying I'm just in the middle of a nightmare. My brain is so totally lost in a fog, I honestly don't know if I'm awake or asleep. If this is just a dream, I still have the rest of my life to live. If not, I can hear the hammer smacking the nails down into my casket now.

Mom is a great mom, don't get me wrong, but man, there is major heck to pay if you make her mad. Grizzly bears turn tail and run whenever she's on a rampage. We found out a long time ago it was better to tick off Dad than her.

Jake pipes up, and in a voice loud enough for everyone to hear says, "Mom, this was my idea. Mrs. Gil, please don't be mad at Jason or Sam, we came out here because I begged them to. It's all my fault, not theirs," he says again, his splotchy face covered with grime. He wisely leaves out the part about dangling from the end of a rope. When he turns his head, I see part of a s'mores stuck to the side of his face. If the situation were different, it would be hilarious.

Hearing Jake's voice must've jostled something loose inside my brain, and I manage to say, "Mom, I know we should've told you, but we didn't want you to worry."

Stepping abruptly into my face again, she hisses, "Well it's a little late for that, mister."

The mister bit means she's ready to call in the firing squad. I haven't heard her use that word since I accidently caught the woods on fire behind our house when I was eight. Good-bye, cruel world.

I look where Jesse was sleeping and see only an empty spot where she had been. She must've headed out before the sun came up. If Mom is this mad now, I can only imagine what it could have been if she had found Jesse. Girls are strictly forbidden out here, which we always followed until Jesse came around. Beth doesn't count because she's family. Besides, it's not like we're having wild orgies or playing strip poker. It's just a cool place to hang out and be kids.

Stardust is curled up a few feet away, looking anxious. Beth reaches back and strokes her mane, talking calmly to her. The horse looks ready to bolt, but after a little more talking and soothing, she settles down.

For a moment all is quiet as we just stare at each other, waiting to see what happens next. So far, Jake's mom hasn't said a word. I see her looking intently at him, like she hasn't decided what to do yet.

He smiles at her and says with a soft, husky voice, "This was the best night of my whole life, Mom. Nobody got hurt; all we did was camp. It was great, Mom, really." The look on his face would be enough to break even the hardest of hearts.

Now everyone stares at her. A strange look crosses her face like what she is seeing in her mind is too painful for words. Then out of the corner of her eye a tear starts to form and quietly trickles down her cheek.

Oh crap, now I know we're dead meat. We've made the sweetest lady in the whole world cry. Nobody makes a sound.

Quietly she says, "All we ever wanted was for you to have a happy life, Jake." More tears flow. Now Mom is crying too. They hug each other tight and stay that way for a long time.

We look at each other, not sure what to do or say. Finally our moms let go of each other, wiping their faces with their hands and let out a little giggle. Trixie ambles up slowly and nudges Mom's hand. She kneels down and gives her a scratch behind the ear.

Sam slowly walks over to Mom and says, "Aunt Trish, I'm sorry we didn't tell you about this ahead of time, that was a bad decision on our part." I nod my head in agreement. He continues, "We made sure everyone was safe, though. All we did wrong was not tell you beforehand."

She stares at him for a long time and finally says, "Sam, you have always been one of my favorite nephews, but today you are really pushing it. You boys had better swear you will never, ever, pull another stupid stunt like this again," without taking her eyes off him.

"I promise Aunt Trish, this will never happen again," he says without blinking. She reaches over and gives him a hug. He hugs her back just as hard. Normally when an adult hugs you, a conciliatory pat on the shoulders is all they usually get in return. To actually return a real hug means you are really in deep stuff.

She waves me over and all three of us have a group hug, the big wraparound kind. First, she's ready to shoot us at sunrise and now we're getting hugs. Who can figure women?

Jake's mom walks over to him and ruffles his hair.

Mom turns her attention to the rest of the crowd as they deliberately avoid looking at her. She tells them they aren't in trouble; we were the delinquents, not them. Tommy nods a thanks and clears his throat as the rest move nervously about, straightening things up—anything to keep from looking at her. White Socks gives a snort and goes back to munching grass again.

Stardust gets to her feet, stretches long and hard then cuts loose with the loudest, biggest fart I've ever heard. Normally we would roll with laugher, but we act like nobody heard it.

Mom lets out a snort and says, "That's the most intelligent remark I've heard all morning."

CHAPTER NINE

We make it back to my house with just enough time to have a quick breakfast and change clothes. Hmmm ... the house looks cleaner today, tidied up and organized. Then I remember Uncle Vince and his new wife, Jillian are arriving this afternoon to stay for a couple of days. I met his new wife once during Thanksgiving and she seemed like a nice enough lady. Just about anything would be an improvement over the one he had before, Aunt Roseland. If dictionaries came with illustrations, hers would be found alongside obnoxious, manipulative, and bossy. Everyone celebrated with him when he finally let her go.

Uncle Vince lives in Georgia and comes to visit once every so often. They'll stay in Mary's room, since she will be spending the night with Grandma and Grandpa.

Uncle Vince is my dad's older brother, a nice guy, but kind of loud. They didn't look much alike, but everybody could tell they were brothers.

As I round the corner to go upstairs, I spot Mary before she sees me. She lifts her head and our eyes meet. A startled look sweeps over her face and immediately she looks down again. A hand runs through her hair, just like Mom does when she's stressed.

She's the one who spilled the beans to Mom and Mrs. Maloy after they cornered her. If I had been in her shoes, I would've done the same thing.

"Mary, you did the right thing. No harm, no foul, okay?"

First surprise, then relief washes over her as she realizes there won't be a fight after all. Then she says, "I wasn't going to say anything, honest, but they were both freaking out," her voice trailing off as she stuffs her hands into her pockets.

"You did good, little sister. Mom decided to let us live another day, so no big deal."

From an open window near the kitchen the chirping of a bird fills the room. Mary looks out the window and says, "Hey, Marley."

"Sounds like your little bird is feeling better."

"He ought to, as much as he eats. Take a look."

We walk outside together and Marley is in the last cage snuggled in a pile of hay. He looks at us and immediately starts begging for food, the little moocher.

Opening the cage, she fills a dropper with some milky stuff from the fridge and lets a few drops fall into its gaping mouth. The chirping is interrupted only as long as it takes for him to swallow, then it cranks right back up again, even louder than before.

"He thinks I'm his mom."

I nod my head and say, "He's set up like a king in here. He'll never want to leave this life of luxury. You two might be together for life."

I feel Mary's arm on my sleeve and turn to see her smiling at me. Confused, I say "What?"

"Do you hear yourself?"

I feel pride swell in my chest again, but don't let too much of it show and say, "How 'bout that."

From the doorway Mom hollers for us. Mary gently closes the cage door as Marley continues begging for more.

Mary and I pile into the backseat of the car as Mom slips in behind the wheel. Looking at her reflection in the mirror, I notice the lines on her thin face seem to have deepened, and faint dark circles under her eyes bleed through her makeup. I feel my jaw set hard as I realize I'm watching her age in hyper speed.

Walking into church, we take our usual place in the back and watch as other folks mingle in. A few minutes later, I spot Jake and his family rolling in. He waves at me with a thumbs-up, like all is right with the world.

After a couple of sappy songs and a few announcements, Pastor Jeff comes to the pulpit and starts his usual spiel. I take that as my cue to catch a few z's. I close my eyes, but before I fade too far something he says catches my attention. He's quoting from the Bible about that "do unto others" thing. Then he goes on about how an act of kindness shown to "even the least of these," is like doing it for God Himself. I'm still not buying all this God stuff, but something about those words digs deep.

Mom squeezes my hand and right before trying to pull away, I feel a small, almost undetectable vibration make its way up my arm. I've never felt this before and wonder what's up. Maybe she's coming down with a cold or something and let it go.

She smiles at me, and the softness of her stare catches me off guard. A couple hours ago she was ready to send me to the firing squad, and now I'm allowed back in the fold again.

I return the smile and look at her with newfound awareness, seeing those lines on her face a little differently. They add character and strength, telling a story of a lifetime of love, laughter, and some heartbreak too. I think of all the times she's been there for Mary and me, and how hard she's had to work. I hope I find a woman as good as her when I'm grown. She gives me a wink and turns back around, completely unaware of my thoughts.

After church, we flow into the courtyard for everyone to gab. Old folks really like this part, and can stay out here talking until next spring. I walk to the big-ear tree behind the sanctuary and wait for Sam and Jake to show up, kicking around a few of the ear-shaped pods littering the ground. We're usually the only ones back here, so this has become our favorite place to hang out.

I feel a shove on my arm and expect to see Sam or Jake, but instead, it's my annoying younger cousin Gordon, grinning like a mule chewing briars. My dad's brother, Vince, and his first wife are the ones responsible for creating this walking disaster.

Not quite a teenager yet, he already has enough cockiness and sarcasm to make two of us. His laziness is world renowned, and he already has a Michelin around his middle from playing video games and scarfing junk food all day. Zits have a heyday on his face, taking up residence like urban sprawl.

After his parents divorced, he and his mom moved to the other side of town, so fortunately I don't see him very often. He hates to camp, "too dirty and no video games," so we never really spend much time together, which suits me just fine. Once every two or three months they attend church, so when he's here, he never misses the opportunity to catch up where he left off.

True to form, he says, "Hey, c-cuz, w-what's been g-goin' on?"

Because he makes good grades, he thinks he's so much smarter than me and loves to throw it in my face every chance he gets.

Smiling, I realize he has no idea the stuttering idiot is gone. Standing up straight, I casually look down at him and say, "Actually, life's been exceptionally busy. I've been working, making decent money this summer, so it's good. How about you, cuz?"

In an instant, the arrogant smile vaporizes into thin air. His jaw drops down so low, I get an up close and personal exhibition of the latest color in orthodontics. Behind those beady eyes, I can almost see the wheels turning in that pea brain of his as he scrambles for something to say.

With great satisfaction I watch him struggle. Finally he says with genuine surprise, "Wow, what happened to you? I mean, what happened to the stuttering stuff?"

An inch or two taller than him, I stretch it up just a bit more and say, "Guess I got tired of guys like you reminding me how stupid I sounded. Suppose you'll have to find someone else to pick on now."

His face drops a little like he's hurt, but I know better.

He holds his palms up while taking a step back and says, "Hey man, all I was doing was poking a little fun, that's all. Didn't know you were so *sensitive*," with an irritating smirk.

That's when I do something I've never done before in my whole life: I make fun of this gross little fat guy. Some of my good friends are overweight. The best one I have is handicapped, and if anyone talked to him like I'm about to do with Gordon, I'd deck 'em. Being fat, skinny, short, tall, whatever, makes no difference to me, but a point needs to be made, and this is the first thing that pops into my brain. There were probably better ways to handle this, but at the age of fourteen, impulsiveness is our specialty.

I look at him through narrowed slits and say, "*Sensitive*? You little jerk! Listen Porky, did you ever wonder why the guy taking our pictures at school has to stop and change his lens when he gets to you? It's because he has to use a wide angle just to get your megaton ass into the frame. That thing's so huge it could be declared its own country.

"Or, how about I ask you if you ever tried connecting all those zits and see if they spell the word 'idiot.' Feeling *sensitive* yet, chubbo?"

Like a slap across the face, he winces and takes a step back. He seems to have lost control of his hands, as they dangle limply around his jiggling middle, while the top of his ears grows bright red.

Spitting on the ground, he yells, "You jerk, that's none of your friggin' business. You have no right to talk to me like that, you friggin' retard." He jumps at me like he wants to take a swing, but both of us know he's too much of a coward. Instead, he struts back and forth like a chicken, head bobbing back and forth. All that's missing is the clucking sound.

Something breaks loose inside and I begin to laugh. Not just a little snicker, we're talking great big, rippling laughter, the kind where you lose your breath. If I had to go to the bathroom, I'd be in trouble.

This makes him even madder, so he stops pacing and walks straight up to me and says, "Hey, you big moron! Yeah, you might not stutter anymore, but you're still a moron, probably can't even write the alphabet without tracing the dotted lines. And I'll bet your mommy still has to read books to you like a baby."

I'm not laughing quite so hard now.

A rainbow of angry hardware dances around on his grimy teeth as he gets ready for a second round, but then he suddenly stops. His face loses the prune, as a satisfied look takes over, which makes me very uncomfortable. With syrupy rottenness, he says, "I was going to tell you the real reason my dad and stepmom are coming to your house tomorrow, since he found out what really happened to your dad, but now I'm not gonna," and turns to walk away.

Now I'm the one who's been slapped. His words punch me in the gut like an iron fist. My vision tunnels as blackness swallows everything except him. Forcing air back into my lungs, I order my feet to move and sprint after him. Grabbing the first thing my hands touch, I spin him around so hard he nearly falls over. Nose to nose, I grab as much of the front of his shirt as my hands can hold, and pull his face so close to mine, I can smell the cupcake he wolfed down earlier. I hear a couple of stitches let loose as my hold tightens.

Our breath mingles together as one, the pupils of his eyes enlarging so quickly they almost eclipse the blue of his iris.

Slowly and deliberately I say, "What did you just say, Gordon? What do you know about my dad?"

His breathing is now shallow and irregular, the surly attitude gone. Standing on his tiptoes, he does his best to balance, leaning this way and that, then manages to squeak, "Jason, you're hurting me!" I grab ahold tighter as he tries to wriggle free.

Spittle flying onto his face, I hiss, "Tell me right now what you know about my dad!" giving his collar a hard jerk.

Looking around the best he can, he realizes there is no one coming to his rescue. His chin begins to quiver as his cheeks turn splotchy.

I lean closer and say with a nasty tone that elicits fear, "Tell me."

Panicking, he jerks backward with such force, both of us topple to the ground. I land on top of him, not turning loose of his shirt. Rolling around, my hands never leave his shirt collar as the two of us wrestle on the ground. He tries over and over to push me off, but becomes exhausted and finally stops resisting.

Getting to my knees without letting go of his shirt, I pull him up with me. The two of us are back up on our feet again, just like we were a moment ago, only now covered with dirt and grass clippings.

"Okay, okay," he says with a deep sob, "I'll tell you, just don't hurt me, all right?"

Letting my hands relax a little, his shirt slips from my fingers just enough for him to quickly reach up and push my hands away, pulling his shirt back down over his bulging belly.

Wiping his face with the back of his hand he says, "Last week when I was at their house for the weekend, I listened in on my dad's phone when he thought I was outside playing. I heard him talking to somebody about your dad, a friend of his that works for the GBI."

Gordon has always been sneaky, manipulative and nosy, just like his mom, so this sounds about right.

I impatiently ask, "The who?"

"The Georgia Bureau of Investigation."

"Yeah, okay, and what did they say?"

He sniffles once more and says, "His friend found some video from a pole cam that he said had something he should see."

"What the heck is a pole cam?"

"It's a camera up high on a pole, like in the middle of the woods or something, I don't know," his hands unsure what to do.

"Anyway, from what the man said, it shows the day that deer ran into the road in front of your dad's truck and someone was there when it happened."

My eyes grow wide, but I suddenly grow suspicious.

"If that's true, why didn't he tell us about it?"

"Dad didn't want to tell anybody until he talked to a friend of his here. The cops in Georgia said they couldn't do anything about it—something about hunting deer not illegal. It's the truth, I swear, he didn't want to upset your mom, honest."

Relaxing a little, I guess that makes sense, so I say, "Okay, what else do you know?"

"My dad started poking around and found some more stuff, taken from a different camera at another place, with that same man on it. I think he found out who he was." He begins to shuffle from one foot to the other and says, "I'm not supposed to know anything. If he finds out, he'll kill me," and starts crying.

Desperate to keep him talking, I say soothingly, "Gordon, it's okay, man, I'm not going to say anything, I promise, just tell me everything, okay?"

More relaxed, neither one of us on the defensive, we both remember that despite our vast differences, we're still blood kin.

"Promise?" he says through watery eyes.

Holding my hand up, thumb over pinky, I say, "Scout's honor."

Nodding his head slightly, he reaches up then wipes his face with his chubby hand and says, "He's coming to town tomorrow to talk to his friend because the man in the video ran away. He didn't even try to help your dad. He's got it all on his laptop."

Raking my hands through my hair, I force myself to stay calm. Gordon says, "Promise you won't tell?"

Nodding my head, I mumble, "I won't say a word." Suddenly I feel the need to thank him, even though I had to nearly hammer it out of him.

Looking him in the eye, I say, "Thanks, man."

He doesn't say anything, just sniffles a little more and wipes his face with his shirtsleeve, then waddles back to the crowd of people gathered in the front of the church.

Sitting down on the ground hard, I feel my whole world slipping away. Head in my hands, I try to wrap my brain around everything I just heard. My head pounds to the beat of my heart as it thunders away.

Somebody was there that day and watched my dad die. Why wouldn't he try to help? Why would he turn and run away? These are the questions I need answers to, and I need them now. I can't ask Uncle Vince anything, so I'll have to find another way.

I know with absolute certainty I've got to get into his laptop. How I'm going to do that, I have no idea.

Off in the distance, I hear my name and ignore it, but it persists. Annoyed, I jerk my head up and see Sam standing a few feet away, looking totally perplexed.

He walks closer and says, "Hey, man, what's going on? You okay? Jake and I got held up by a couple of old ladies."

Ignoring his question, I ask, "What's a pole cam?"

Confused, he says, "A what?"

More impatient than intended, I brusquely say, "Do you know what a pole cam is?"

He looks at me unblinking for a moment, a fleeting look of hurt passing between us. He sits down next to me, studying my face.

His eyes stir old memories captured by a locket in time. Venturing inside, I see a terrified little kid clinging to his self-made prison. Inside those imaginary walls he is safe, the rest of the world locked securely out. Not until he met Jake did he realize it wasn't the bars that had locked the world out, but him. Sam learned to cope with his fear and anxiety, and before long, the bars fell away. I can't help but smile.

"Sorry, man, didn't mean to snap at you like that. I'm just kind of stressed is all." He smiles back with a nod and says, "No problem, bro." He shuffles around to get comfortable and says, "Why do you want to know about pole cams?"

"I heard somebody talking about them and was curious, that's all" which is the truth, just not all of it. I'll share the rest of it with him later, but not right now.

Realizing I won't stop until I get an answer, he says, "Pole cams are hidden cameras mounted on top of utility poles that police use to catch bad guys making drugs or growing pot out in the middle of nowhere. They're usually along old country roads." He pauses a moment, then says, "This is a weird subject; you sure you're okay?"

For the first time in my life, I don't tell him the truth. I've never lied to him or held anything back, but right now, I must.

Looking away, unable to face him, I say, "Yeah, I'm okay. It's just been a really long week. Thanks, man."

Realizing that's about all the conversation he's going to get out of me, he pats my knee and says, "Hey, your mom was looking for you, I think she's ready to head home. We'll get together soon though, okay?"

Feeling like a schmuck, I simply nod my head. We stand up together and walk back to the crowd.

At home later that afternoon, after getting a bite to eat, I notice Mom is acting kind of funny. She keeps following me with her eyes, but not saying anything. Something is up, I just know it. Could she have found out about our conversation behind the church?

I don't have long to wonder, as she walks across the kitchen and takes my face in her hands. Again I feel the faint vibrations.

I am now an inch or so taller than Mom, so she has to reach up a little. Her eyes lock onto mine and she just stares at me for a moment. I take in her smell and the softness of her breath, which reminds me of when I was a little boy.

Her eyes become more focused as she draws a little closer then says, "Jason, I appreciate the fact you don't give me much trouble. I guess you got most of it out of your system when you were younger. For a teenager, you haven't given me too hard a time, this morning not included," she says with a lightness she doesn't own.

I can feel a "but" working its way in here.

"I get the feeling you are holding something back from me. Something I can't quite put my finger on. Moms just get these feelings sometimes."

I try to look elsewhere, but she moves my face around until I am looking at her again. "Jason, please, trust me, I love you and just want to help, that's all."

"Mom, it's not a matter of trust. You know I trust you."

"Then share with me what's going on, son."

"Honeyb ... ," she catches herself. "I mean, honey, there's something you're not telling me about Mary, how you knew she was so sick, and I heard something about that Estralar boy," she says with an uncertain look.

Oh, that secret. Looking down at my feet, I let out a sigh. Feeling bad for not sharing this with her already, I rub my face hard. I honestly half expected Aunt Moe to tell her about the woman in the Keys, but to her credit, I guess she didn't. I was planning on telling Mom at some point about this stuff but the time just never seemed right. I wonder if it ever would be.

Taking a deep breath, I say, "Mom, I don't know how to describe it exactly, but I'll try. When someone touches me, or I touch them, I can somehow feel if they are getting sick. I get a mental image of what is going on inside of them." I leave out about hearing the voice. If you really want to freak out your mom, just tell her you're hearing voices in your head.

"It started about three years ago. That's how I knew Mary was sick. I'm sorry, I guess I should've told you sooner, but I was afraid you would worry about me more than you already do."

Everything grows quiet as she processes what I just said.

Finally she says, "Jason, I knew something was special about you from the time you were born. I just didn't know what it was. Something about your sensitivity maybe, I don't know, made me feel you had something great stored up inside you. I knew one day we would all find out. I'm glad you finally shared this with me, son."

"You're not mad at me for not telling you before?"

Smiling, she shakes her head, and I watch her silky hair slide over her shoulders, catching some of the afternoon sun, highlighting the blonde streaks. She says, "I'm not mad, maybe a little disappointed is all. I hope you feel you can trust me enough to share these things with me."

"It was never about trust, Mom, I completely trust you. I just didn't want you to worry."

"Come here, you big silly boy, moms were made for that kind of stuff," and wraps me in a warm hug.

Pulling away, she kisses me on the cheek and says, "Jason, I am so proud of you and the kind of man you are growing into, and ..." she says with a big grin, "I am so happy you finally let Mrs. Prainer help you. Your speech is just amazing!"

Nodding my head, I say, "Yeah, she's great. I just wish I had listened to her when I was younger. Oh well, like they say, better late than never, right?"

She laughs and says, "That's right, son."

She yawns and moves her head around, loosening her shoulders and neck. "Right now, I'm exhausted and need a couple hours of sleep. What are you going to do this afternoon?"

"I'm not sure yet. Maybe I'll get together with Sam, or do something in the garage."

"Sure, honey," she says with a soft smile, "Just be home before dark. You boys be careful if you decide to get together, okay?"

I just nod my head and give her shoulder a pat as I walk past. Right now all I can think about is figuring out a way to get into Uncle Vince's laptop.

I make my way toward Sam's house, deep in thought. I can't tell him everything yet, but just being with him makes me feel better.

On my way to his house, I see Jesse in front of her house digging in a flowerbed. Debating on whether or not to keep going, I stop.

Careful to stay where she can't see me, I quietly tip toe behind her and say, "Hey, girl."

Her whole body reacts, and in one quick motion she whirls around as a small squeal escapes her lips. I jump back and duck, making her laugh. When I stand back up, she looks at me with those incredible eyes, then playfully smacks me on the shoulder and says, "You little dork, I nearly jumped out of my skin."

I say with a grin, "Now that would be a sight worth sticking around for."

She blushes a little then looks down at the ground.

Looking over her shoulder, I say, "Is this how you spend your Sunday afternoons? I thought you city girls had better things to do."

She laughs and says, "Mom wanted to put some flowers here next week, so I'm getting the place ready. She hasn't been feeling very good lately. I needed to get out of the house anyway, too cooped up in there."

About that time, I hear a screen door open and see her mom walk onto the porch, looking even worse than before.

Jesse looks at her and says, "Mom, glad you're feeling better. This is Jason, the friend from school I told you about." Shocked to hear Jesse told her mom about me, I give her a little wave.

"Hi Jason, I'm Mrs. Hylitt, nice to meet you. I'm glad she's met some nice kids already."

"Yes, ma'am, good to meet you, too."

I see the window curtain move and a face appears. Her stepdad is sitting in a recliner with a newspaper on his lap. He never seems to take much interest in what we do, which is just fine by me. If we leave him alone, he leaves us alone.

"How do you like living out here in the sticks?" I say with a smile.

"Oh, it's not too bad. It's sure quiet. I sometimes miss all the activity of a big city, though."

"Yeah, well out here we make our own activity. It'll grow on you after a while."

A few strands of brown hair dance around her face as a gentle breeze flutters through the yard. For a fleeting moment, I can almost see the young woman that used to be there. I try not to let my thoughts show. She smiles at me and says, "Jason, would you care for something to drink?"

"No thank you, ma'am, I'm fine."

"You country boys are so polite, 'yes ma'am and no ma'am,' which is more than I can say for most of the young folks we run across in big cities."

I feel the tops of my ears turn warm and say, "We were raised that way, ma'am. If nothing else, we better be polite."

She laughs a little and says, "It certainly makes a difference. Simple respect is fast becoming a lost art these days. It's good to know it's still important to some people."

"Yes, ma'am" is all I can think to say.

She looks around at the ground her daughter has been working with no particular interest and says, "Well, I'll leave you two alone and finish what I was doing inside. Nice again to meet you, Jason," she says, turning around.

As she walks away, her steps remind me of an old woman, worn out and beaten down. I hear Jesse stir beside me and quickly look away.

Awkwardly, I clear my throat and say the first thing that comes to mind. "So how much more weeding are you gonna do out here today?"

"I'm done with this. My knees are tired and I'd like to think I have a life other than digging in the dirt on a Sunday afternoon," she says with a smirk.

Off the top of my head, without giving it much thought, I say, "Would you like to go swimming with me and Sam this afternoon?"

Placing her hands on her hips, she turns to look at me with those incredible eyes. Instantly I feel sweat forming on my upper lip, as my hand flies up to wipe it off. So much for being macho.

"Where are you going, to the pond?"

"No actually, this is a quieter place. We can show you if you'd like to come along. It's not too far from the pond."

She looks inside for a minute while making up her mind.

"Sounds like fun, just the three of us, huh?"

I nod my head.

She tosses her gloves on the ground, brushes some dirt off her shirt and yells toward the house that she will be back later. The curtains move as her mom's face fills the small space in between. Jesse waves at her as we walk away. Her mom watches us leave then gives us a little wave as she disappears behind the curtain again.

Walking the short distance to Sam's house, we find him laying outside, getting some sun. In Florida, that's something you never have to work at. He looks surprised to see Jesse with me.

"Hey, you two, hot enough for ya?" he says as he swings his feet around and stands up. For some reason, I always expect him to be taller, but he never is. I guess neither one of us have a growth spurt coming anytime in the near future. Loose curls dangle around his face as he brushes them away. One of them stays behind, like it always does.

He looks at me intently, still confused about what happened earlier today no doubt, but without a word spoken, assures me all is good. An easy smile crosses his lips and all is right with the world again, at least between us. Like I said, we share the same soul.

He looks between the two of us like we've been up to no good, and chuckles to himself. I let him have his moment of fun. He clears his throat and says, "Where are you two going?"

I stretch out my arm and rest it against the side of his house and say, "I thought we'd go to the spring."

Sam and I have never taken anyone to the spring before, and at first he just looks at me then at her. If she's offended, it doesn't show. He fights the rebellious curl again, which makes more of them join in, then says with a shrug, "Sure, why not. Nothing else is going on around here. Let's get something to drink first."

We step inside Sam's house and say hello to his mom while trying to avoid his dad. Most of the time he has us beat, ignoring us before we get the chance to ignore him.

As we walk past the living room, Uncle Todd has his nose buried in a newspaper. Hearing the door open, he briefly peeks above the top, and without a word, continues reading. We keep walking into the kitchen where Aunt Lori is peeling potatoes. She stops what she's doing when she sees us. Her blonde hair looks thinner than it did the last time I saw her, and the dark circles under her eyes are a deeper shade. Everything about her resonates tired and lonely. I wonder how much longer she'll put up with Prince Charming. That's what Dad used to call Uncle Todd.

Sam opens the fridge and pours each of us a glass of tea, then introduces Jesse before walking to his room for something.

"Jesse," Aunt Lori says as she sits down at the kitchen table, "What a pretty name. Where are you from, honey?"

Jesse stops looking around the room at all the fruit and flower patterns that fill the kitchen wallpaper and smiles at Aunt Lori. I imagine in another house it would be warm and inviting, but here it loses all of its appeal. Uncle Todd can drain the last bit of joy and happiness from even the wallpaper.

"I'm from Atlanta, lived there my whole life. My stepdad got a job in Tampa, so we moved here a couple of months ago." Aunt Lori's eye twitches when she hears "step" in front of dad. She has a stepdaughter in college from Uncle Todd's first marriage. I don't have enough time to stop her before she asks the obvious question.

"Oh, where does your dad live?" as I close my eyes tight. To my surprise, Jesse acts like she hears that question every day, which she just might for all I know. Without missing a beat, she says, "My dad was killed overseas in Iraq two years ago. He was in the Army Special Forces. It's okay though, I get asked that a lot." Guess I was right.

Aunt Lori covers her mouth with one hand and puts the other on her chest and says, "Jesse, I am so sorry! I had no idea!"

"Don't worry about it, lots of people don't know. I mean, how would you know if no one told you?"

Aunt Lori shakes her head as a cascade of blonde hair falls into her face. Reaching up with a free hand, she rakes her hand over her head, pulling the loose flowing hair through her fingers. She looks a lot like Mom, more so than her other sisters. The lines on her face tell a much different story than Mom's. Years of being ridiculed, put down, and chided have taken their toll, running rampant across the landscape of her tired face. I've never heard Uncle Todd speak to her like she has any worth. One would think their wedding vows must have included, "Loathe, humiliate, and rebuke."

Dad hated the way he spoke to her but couldn't do much about it, not from a lack of effort though. He tried on several occasions to talk to him, but all of their little talks ended the same way: Uncle Todd telling Dad to mind his own damn business.

I always wondered why Aunt Lori stays with him. Maybe one day she'll finally get enough. As far as I know, he has never hit her, but sometimes words can sting worse than a balled fist.

"Really, it's okay," Jesse says in a reassuring tone. "There's no way you could have known," she says with lightness that betrays the pain beneath.

Aunt Lori walks over and places her hands on Jesse's shoulders and says, "How is your mom doing? Is there anything I can do to help?"

Aunt Lori is good at helping everybody but herself. I think in her mind, if she focuses all of her attention on other people's lives, she won't have time to see what's going on in her own. Sam's older half-sister, Hope, got out as soon as she could, and never comes back home to visit, even though she's married and has a baby. She calls Sam and talks to him pretty regularly. They've stayed close, which is how they survived living here together. Sam is waiting for the day he can be gone for good as well.

"No, ma'am, we're doing okay. It's been a real long two years, but she's hanging in there."

Sam comes back into the room and tells everyone goodbye. He can't stand to spend one more moment in his house than necessary. From the corner of the room, Uncle Todd continues to bury his nose in the paper, pretending to read like we weren't even here, eyeing us suspiciously over the top of the paper when he thinks we're not looking. I know he's listening to our conversation, analyzing what we're saying to use against us later. At least he's predictable.

His favorite tactic to use with Aunt Lori is arrogance. He makes the money around here, so his position in the family is more important than hers, at least so he thinks. All she does is wash laundry, cook, and clean like women are supposed to.

He loves to flash his degree in her face and never lets her forget she's only a high school graduate. Mom tells us stories of when they were kids, Aunt Lori was outspoken, fun, and adventurous—always the life of the party. I wonder what happened to that girl.

Sam comes into the kitchen, and without a word turns to walk out the back door. Jesse and I look at each other, then give Aunt Lori an apologetic wave and follow Sam out the door.

Once we're outside and out of earshot, Jesse whispers, "Nice." I just shrug my shoulders and cock my head. If there are words to explain that wacko family, I sure don't know them.

We catch up with Sam as the three of us find the path that leads to the spring. It's overgrown and hard to see at first, since it's not well traveled. We have to enter some pretty dense woods but hear no complaint. Once we make it to the spring, Sam and I plop in quickly, the best way to get over the biting cold. Jesse sticks a toe in and wraps her arms around herself, a little "brrr" escaping her lips. We look at her expectantly. Not wanting to be outdone by a couple of guys, she eases into the water, holding her breath until she is up to her armpits. After she starts breathing again, her head turns in every direction, taking in the place and forgetting all about the cold. Finally she says, "When you said a spring I had something else entirely in mind. This is a sacred, almost holy place. Can you feel it?"

Sam and I look at each other. For a long time we've felt the same way, but didn't know anyone else did.

"Yeah, it's a special place," Sam says after a second or two. "We're the only ones who know about it, except for Jason's mom and sister, but it's too cold for them. It's buried so far in the woods no one else bothers to look."

"We've found arrowheads and broken pottery buried under the sand, so it was probably used by Native Americans before white people got here."

The smile on her face fades as the reality of what happened centuries ago sinks in.

"What a raw deal," she says. "I'll bet they had a whole village right here where we're sitting!" looking around like one might be hiding behind a tree somewhere. She turns back to me and says, "Do you still have some of the stuff you found? I'd love to see it."

"Yeah, we have a whole box of things at home," I say. "My sister's made some neat jewelry with the prettier pieces."

We are definitely speaking her language.

All grows quiet as we relax and let the cool water works its magic. We breathe easy and lean back against the soft sides, looking up at the thick canopy of trees overhead. Flowering vines have woven themselves so well amongst the massive limbs they look like part of the tree. Bright orange, blue, and yellow flowers are so profuse they seem to be decorated Christmas trees. A small circular opening just above is the only place the sky peeks in. I feel Jesse stir next to me and shift my gaze to her.

"Hey, Jason, what happened to your dad, if you don't mind talking about it," she says quietly.

I didn't see that one coming. I swallow hard, and she quickly adds, "But not if it makes you uncomfortable. I went through that too with my dad, but once I talked about it, I felt better."

"No, it's okay, I just wasn't expecting it, that's all." I run my hands through my wet hair and close my eyes for a minute and see Uncle Vince and his laptop. I shove that thought to the side and say, "Dad was returning home from a trip to South Carolina when we think a deer ran into the path of his truck. An ambulance arrived after a lady found his truck in a ravine about twenty feet off the road. He was rushed to the hospital but had lost too much blood and died in the operating room. The police told us if he had been found sooner he might've survived, but I can't let my mind go there."

Her face grew sad and long as I spoke. "I know how you feel, Jason. I felt the same way after my dad was killed." She pauses for a minute and then asks, "Was he a good dad?"

I open my mouth, but Sam jumps in before I can say a word. "He was one of the best dads ever. He always spent time with his kids and talked to them like they were more important than anything else. He taught them all kinds of great things and wasn't afraid to let them know he loved them. Anytime they went on vacation, he always took me along, too."

He gives me a sad smile and says, "Those are some of the best times of my whole life," looking a little embarrassed. Then he adds, "Sorry, Jason, didn't mean to jump in there like that. I just wished so many times my dad was like your dad."

My foot bumps into his and I say, "That's okay, man."

We all get quiet for a minute just listening to the birds while the wind gently rustles through the leaves. From a distance, we hear bullfrogs croaking. Finally I break the silence and ask the question I've wanted to ask ever since Jesse and her family arrived here.

"Jess, your mom seems like she doesn't feel very good. Is she okay? She seems kind of … sad."

The sparkle in her eyes loses some of its luster as she looks at me. Turning her attention to our feet, she digs her toes into the soft sand like the answer lies down there somewhere. "Mom used to be happy before Dad died, full of energy, funny ... "

Suddenly becoming aware that she's wandered off, Jesse shakes her head. "Sorry," like we need an explanation.

Then she clears her throat and continues. "When we got the news, she lived in denial for a long time and refused to believe he was dead. She thought maybe the Army made a mistake since we didn't get his body back for a long time. Something about him being in the Special Forces with all their secret missions I guess, I really don't know. Anyway, once the reality sank in, she just kind of disappeared inside herself. Sometimes it feels like both my parents are gone."

She wipes away a tear and takes a deep breath then says kind of wispy, "She met my stepdad, Jeremy, about a year ago, and they've been married about six months now. He's kind of weird, not in a mean way, just weird. I don't know him very well, and don't really want to. I just want my dad back."

We look at each other a long time, understanding each other's pain all too well.

She clears her throat and says, "This afternoon we're going to see a new doctor my aunt knows. We're driving to my aunt's house in Orlando this afternoon. She's real worried about Mom, too. We'll spend the night, then see the doctor in the morning, so I won't be at school tomorrow."

Sam and I nod. The three of us quietly lie back and let the magic of this place penetrate deep into our bones, cleansing and healing everywhere we allow it to flow. That afternoon, our souls mingled in that frigid water, and we became at peace with each other and ourselves. I wish there was some way to carry some of this feeling back to Sam's house.

After a while, Jesse says, "I could stay out here for the rest of my life."

Sam says, "Right there with ya."

Uncle Vince's laptop taps me on the shoulder, and I know we need to get going. I rub my arms and agree, "Yeah, this place is awesome."

Jesse gets quiet for a minute then says, "Thanks for inviting me to come out here with you guys. I had no idea a place like this even existed." She looks at the flowers hanging in the trees and the lush greenness all around. I catch myself thinking how terrible it would be if all of this were bulldozed over, like so many of the pretty places around here. It feels like our whole world is changing and we're helpless to stop it.

Jesse breaks my morbid thoughts. "You guys feel like … family to me, and I appreciate that. I thought I would hate it out here in the sticks, but you guys have made it fun," she says with a smile.

Sam grins wide and says, "Hey, no charge. Not all of us out here are a bunch of backward inbred crackers, ya know." He looks at me and says, "Most of us, anyway." I splash him with water just as he dunks below the surface.

Standing up slowly, we pull ourselves out of the spring and feel the air swirl around us as goose bumps cover us.

After walking Jesse home, Sam and I head back to his place. He looks at me and says, "I guess one day you'll tell me what we talked about earlier, huh?"

I stare at him a long moment without saying a word. Finally, I say, "Yeah, I just can't right now."

With a little shrug of his shoulders, he says, "I trust ya, bro." Then a serious look crosses his face and adds, "You be careful with whatever's going on, promise?"

"Promise," I say as we bump fists, feeling like a schmuck all over again.

Sam turns and walks through the gate, waving over his shoulder without looking back. I swallow hard and feel lonelier than I have ever been.

Later in the afternoon, Jesse and her mom make a brief stop at a diner for an early supper. Jesse hopes the food gets here quickly so they can get back on the road. She can't wait to see Aunt Jean.

When their order arrives, her mom busies herself by pushing the food around her plate, nibbling around the edges. Jesse tries to make conversation, but as usual, all she gets is a shrug.

This doctor had better be good, because nothing short of a miracle is going to get her mom back. Somewhere inside this sad stranger there must be some remnant of her.

Jesse is scared. No, she's terrified. She can't lose another parent. When her dad died, a piece of both of them perished. The adaptability of youth helped bring her back to ground level again under the careful guidance of Aunt Jean.

Her aunt had always been a big part of her life, providing a solid source of strength to lean on. All of their holidays were spent together, but Aunt Jean also had a way of making regular, everyday moments feel special. Somehow, she managed to squeeze every last drop out of life.

Aunt Jean and Uncle Bryon moved from Atlanta to Orlando about a year ago. They had lived in the same neighborhood as Jesse in Atlanta for as long as she could remember. Just two streets were all that separated them, so nearly every day she found an excuse to be there. When they moved to Florida, Jesse cried for days, begging her mom to move there to be with them again. Later, when she found out they were moving to Florida, she hoped they would be in the same neighborhood again. While that didn't happen, at least they were within an hour's drive, which would have to do for now.

After getting back onto the road, her mom gets behind the wheel without saying another word. Jesse notices that the dark patches under her mom's eyes seem to be even deeper than before. Turning her attention to the landscape whizzing by only adds to her loneliness.

No teenager would ever admit they loved their parents, at least not in public, anyway, but if it meant having both her parents back whole again, she would shout "I love you" from the mountaintops.

About thirty minutes later they turn down Aunt Jean's familiar tree-lined street. A couple of turns later, her big white house with black shutters appears. As they turn into the driveway, an old golden retriever hobbles over, wagging his tail, ecstatic to have visitors. She recognizes Hank as soon as she sees him, her heart aching as she realizes how much the sweet dog has aged.

The side door of the house opens and Aunt Jean's smiling face appears from the doorway, as usual. It seems no matter how bad a situation might be, she always finds a bright side. Jesse doesn't realize how much she missed Aunt Jean until that moment. The car isn't even stopped before she bolts from the door and runs into her aunt's open arms, soaking up the rich aroma of cocoa butter and lavender. Memories flood back of happier times spent at their house, baking cookies and playing games, feeling a part of something special and important. Even though she saw her a couple of months ago, it seems like years since their last visit.

Stepping back to get a better look, Aunt Jean said, "My gracious, sweetie, just look at you! You're nearly as tall as me, you beautiful thing," shaking her head as her short blond hair gently sweeps over her strong shoulders.

Aunt Jean takes Jesse's face into her hands and plants a big kiss right in the middle of her forehead. Jesse feels her face flush as Aunt Jeans says, "AHTP, Aunts Have Their Privileges." Jesse smiles and hopes this never changes.

The soft brush of fur on her legs reminds her she is neglecting her other favorite relative. Getting down on her knees, she hugs the gentle dog as his tail swishes back and forth on the grass. She hears Aunt Jean laugh as they get to know each other again. Jesse buries her face in Hank's warm, soft fur and knows he understands the pain in her soul. After a moment, she realizes her mom is still in the car and stands back up.

The driver's door slowly opens and they both turn to see her mom cautiously step out of the car. Jesse hears Aunt Jean draw in a sharp breath. Her smile starts to fade, but forces herself to reclaim it. Giving Jesse a quick glance, she says with forced enthusiasm, "Hey, sis, long time no see!"

The distance closes quickly as the two sisters fall together, holding each other tight.

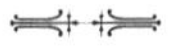

By the time I make it to my place, the sky is growing dark as a thunderstorm moves in. I run upstairs to my room and hear Dad's clock announce the next hour. Looking into the hallway, I see it is now 6:00. The crunch of gravel drifts into the open window. I look outside and see Uncle Vince and his wife, Jillian, step out of his Ford pickup truck as a strange ripple runs through it. For a split second, it appeared to be on the other side of a fire, distorting the image. I blink my eyes rapidly, momentarily perplexed. When I look out through the window again, all appears normal. That's weird. Uncle Vince's loud voice breaks my trance as he hollers a loud hello to Mom. He has a small suitcase in one hand and his laptop case in the other. All of my attention focuses on that case, the strange distortion all but forgotten.

The screen door opens as Mom walks out to greet them. Am I supposed to call her Aunt Jillian, like I call his ex-wife Aunt Roseland? I've not had to deal with any of this before, so I'm not sure what to say.

As they walk inside, I step from my room, and meet them in the kitchen.

Before I can say anything, Uncle Vince hollers from across the room, "Well, look here if it ain't my favorite nephew!" I'm his only nephew. He walks over and holds out his hand for me to shake. When I take it, he pulls me into a hard, rough hug.

He steps back for a moment then looks at me from head to toe and says, "Good grief, Trish, whatcha been feedin' this boy, Miracle Grow?" as he smacks me on the shoulder. Uncle Vince does everything with an exclamation point.

His wife stands by Mom, smiling at the two of us. Uncle Vince and Mom realize at the same time she's waiting to say hello. This is only our second time meeting, so it's a little awkward. She helps me out by extending her hand and says, "Hi Jason, Aunt Jillian, in case you forgot my name. It's been a while since Thanksgiving."

I smile and say, "Good to see you again, Aunt Jillian, glad you all could make it down. How was your drive?"

She gives me a half smile and says softly, "Actually, I slept through most of it. Your Uncle Vince drove while I dozed, so it went pretty fast for me." She seems like a nice lady. He deserves one for a change.

Uncle Vince stops dead in his tracks and looks at me with dramatically raised eyebrows. Then he cocks his head, digs his finger into his ear and says, "Wait just a dad-gum minute there, sport. Was that you talkin'? I don't mean to put you on the spot, but wow, what happened?"

I chuckle a little and say, "I finally got all my cylinders firing at the same time."

His mouth hangs open a moment, then blinks a couple of times and says, "Well, if that don't beat all. I'm really proud of you, boy. I know that must've been some piece of determination to make that happen."

I smile and say, "You could say that." Mom beams with pride as she rubs my back.

They make some small talk as I fight the urge not to stare at his case. Looking around, holding up his computer case he says, "Trish, where can I plug this thing in to give it a charge? I need to check the weather."

"Right over here," as she leads them into the living room, clearing a space on one of the end tables. Her face flushes pink when a sheen of dust floats into the air. He doesn't even notice as he plugs it in and cranks it up.

He navigates around a few places here and there, as I do my best to act nonchalant. Peeking over his shoulder, I study the icons on his desktop, wondering which one holds the secrets.

Aunt Jillian steps into the restroom to freshen up before they go out for dinner. Mom asks if I want to go along, but I say there's something I need to take care of here. She nods her head and says they'll bring me back some pizza. I say that would be great, ready for them to leave.

Before they go, Uncle Vince claps me on the back and says, "Sorry you can't come with us tonight, I'd like to talk to you about the things your dad and I did when we were about your age, but maybe another time."

I look at him and say, "I'd like that. I heard you two got in trouble everywhere you went."

He throws his head back and laughs then looks at me and says, "I sure do miss that ole boy, but I bet he's having the time of his life about now."

Not sure what to say, I just nod my head and say, "I hope so."

"Well, we'll see you when we get back. I'll make sure the girls don't scarf down all the pizza," he says as he elbows me in the ribs.

"I'd appreciate that," grabbing my side.

Mom gives me a hug before they go and says, "Make sure to lock the door behind us. See you later."

"Will do, Mom, y'all have fun."

As soon as the screen door shuts, I watch them drive off, lock the door and run to the computer and jiggle the mouse pad, praying it hasn't gone into sleep mode. I have no idea what the password is, so my only chance is to make sure I'm in before it's too late.

A rush of relief sweeps over me as his waterfall screen saver pops up.

Looking over my shoulder to make sure they are really gone, I start decoding the icons on the screen. This shouldn't take too long since I don't need to decipher long pages of text, only a few words at a time.

None of the icons volunteer any hint of holding anything useful. Bringing up "My Documents," a long list appears on the screen. Scanning them I see "accounts," "payables," "monthly bills" and then one that says "Tom's deer." Clicking on the file, the screen fills with a jumble of words.

Trying to remain calm, I whisper to myself, "Just look for keywords, no big deal, you can do this." I hold a piece of paper under the line I'm reading to help steady the words.

In the text, I pick out "gun, Blaser R93 .300 mag." The words "rare" and "expensive" accompany it. The next sentence stands out, "not likely two of these guns in the same woods."

I know a few things about guns, having picked up a lot of knowledge hanging around my dad and grandpas. They were all hunters and always owned rifles and shotguns. In the country, guns are just a way of life, but I had never seen one like this before.

Scrolling down, I see a video attached and click on it. A miniature hourglass appears on the screen, turning over several times until an image appears. I press another button and a picture of a road and surrounding countryside materialize. I lean in a little closer so I don't miss anything.

All is still for a moment, just another day out in the country. Suddenly a deer emerges from the woods. On the road ahead, Dad's truck appears over a small hill. I watch in horror as the deer is on a collision course with Dad's truck. On the bottom left-hand corner of the screen, a man with a rifle appears, but his cap blocks the view of his face. It doesn't look like any gun I have ever seen. The man points it straight up in the air and fires.

Suddenly the deer and truck collide, and I hear myself scream. The deer rolls onto the windshield as Dad jerks the wheel, trying to keep his truck under control, but it veers off the side of the road and starts flipping end over end, for what seems like an eternity. Finally the battered truck lands in a ravine about fifty feet from the road. I jump back from the screen, falling out of my chair. Waves of pain shoot through my stomach as I stumble back to the chair. Tears spring to my eyes, but I defiantly brush them away.

Forcing my attention back to the screen, I see the man with the gun pull out a cell phone from his pocket. He looks at it for a moment, and then with seeming indifference, casually slides it back in his pocket. He stares at Dad's truck again, like he's confused. Then he does something I will never forget: he turns around and runs back into the woods. The screen suddenly goes black, as the video is over.

My mind is as empty and devoid of thought as the screen. Shock waves shoot through every part of my body as I relive the nightmare of what happened to Dad over and over again. Scenes of the hospital, the doctor with Dad's blood on his gown as he utters those terrible words, telling us our life will never be the same again, Mom screaming … .

Burning coals fill my chest as the image plays over and over in my head. No matter how long or whatever it takes, I will track down this man. I will find out why he left my dad to die alone in those woods, not doing one thing to help him.

Closing the screen, I go back to the original document and scan through the text. I see notes Uncle Vince made. "Light from phone = good battery. Confirmation of active c. towers in vicinity. No call placed (???). No record of call to 911 center until pm by woman who found him."

Looking further, I notice something about a license plate, with "(see photo)" beside it. My hand reaches for the case, bringing it up to my lap. Feeling around in the open compartment, I find nothing but a cord and a pack of old breath mints.

Turning the case around, I see another long zipper and pull it open. Inside is a large manila folder. I gently pull it out, ensuring nothing is disturbed.

Carrying the folder to the couch, I open it and see several 8 x 10 photos. One is of a pickup truck at a park or someplace similar. The Georgia license plate is clearly visible, the numbers easy to read.

The next photo is of the same truck, but this time a man is getting into the driver's side door, holding the same rifle as in the video. Pulling the picture closer, I notice he's wearing the same kind of hat and clothes too. It appears to be the same guy. Only a portion of his face is visible, but not enough to identify him. I stare at the picture, wondering if this is the guy. Quickly, I remind myself I don't have all night and grab the next picture.

In no way am I prepared for what I see. Surely a mistake has been made. The face staring back at me in the picture is Jessie's stepdad, Jeremy Hylitt! Under his picture, written in black marker, is his name, and the same tag number that was on the truck. Like a thunderbolt, the reality overwhelms me with such force it knocks me to the floor. I put both hands into my hair then drag them to my mouth to suppress the scream that is coming. Jesse's stepdad is the reason my dad is dead.

A loud clap of thunder echoes through the house. A major storm is brewing outside, but it is nothing compared to the full-blown hurricane that has been unleashed inside of me.

Leaving the scattered pictures on the couch and the laptop open on the nightstand, the only thought that comes into my ravaged mind is the overwhelming need to get to Jesse's house. Darting out the door, I nearly knock the screen door from its hinges.

Heavy rain is falling but it goes undetected on my skin. All sensation has gone numb, as if my entire body has been stripped of nerve endings. The only primal thought that registers is getting to Jesse's house. As I round the bend, somewhere in the frenzied mess of my brain, I'm reminded that Jesse won't be there. Good thing, because all hell is about to break loose as my rage intensifies with each passing step.

My legs are rubbery by the time I reach her house, so I lean against a tall tree for a brief moment to catch my breath. Moving around the trunk, I see an aluminum baseball bat leaning against the other side, beckoning me. Without a clear reason, I pick it up and feel its weight in my hands. It feels smooth and natural, like it belongs here. Then something strange happens. A glowing wave of static electricity silently emerges from the slick metal and begins flowing over my hands. The glowing traverses along the length of the bat several times in a macabre dance and then dissipates into the moist air in the blink of an eye. For a brief moment, I remove my attention from Mr. Hylitt and focus on the bat. I turn it over a couple of times, but notice nothing unusual or out of the ordinary. Blinking my eyes, I steel my resolve and force myself back to the situation at hand, forgetting everything else.

Up above, the sky has grown darker as the storm increases in intensity. I am now at the murderer's house. Peeking through the window, I see the soft flickering light of the television dance across the room. He appears oblivious to the carnage he caused our family, but will soon know it all too well. Placing my back against the brick wall, I silently make my way to the door. Grabbing the knob, I try it and it obediently turns in my hand, inviting me in. Slowly I push the door open and creep into the kitchen. Before I know it, I find myself standing behind Mr. Hylitt as he watches TV, unaware his judgment day has just arrived.

For a moment, I consider just charging in and smashing him over the head without any warning, but then I decide that would be far too kind, for he would have no idea how or why this happened to him. No! I want him to see my face when I confront him. I want to see his reaction when I ask him why he left my dad to die alone. I want to know why he didn't call for help. I want him to feel my rage and experience the pain my dad felt as he lay there dying alone in the woods.

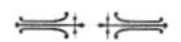

Alone for the weekend, Jeremy Hylitt decides to pour himself a scotch and try to relax. With both his wife and stepdaughter gone, the house is unusually quiet and empty. A movie he's been waiting to watch, but never made time for, is in the DVD player waiting patiently for him to start it up.

Before that horrible day, the one he still refuses to acknowledge, a night alone would be welcome and inviting. But now, the quiet that settles in brings no peace and calm, instead it only strengthens and empowers the will of the demons who seek to devour him in their unrelenting fury. If he keeps his mind occupied, never allowing an idle thought to enter in, he can outmaneuver their deadly grasp. The dreams are bad enough, but the sleeping pills help keep most of them at bay. It's these unoccupied moments of relaxation where idle thoughts manifest themselves that he fears the most.

Tonight he will let the scotch work its magic, keeping the monsters at bay. A steak sizzles on the patio grill as he drains the last of his drink.

A fresh bottle sits on the counter, his best and only friend for the night. As he settles onto the couch with his charred steak and second glass, a memory pushes its way past the barriers he's so carefully constructed in his mind, sidestepping the scotch. It beats on the door of his subconscious, dragging him back to those awful woods and the terrible secret they hold. He's never spoken of that day to anyone.

He should have been at work that day. Silently, he curses himself yet again for fraudulently taking those sick days.

Reliving those horrific events, he feels the rifle rock against his shoulder as he sees the deer lurch away. The "what if's" are now doing their relentless work on his meager thoughts. Had he not flinched, that deer would have fallen right where it stood. He found out later someone in a truck died on that road. Although he couldn't say for sure it was the same guy, he knew. He knew he was the one solely responsible for that man's death. He saw the look and smell of death in the cab of that truck before he turned tail and ran. Not a single day goes by that he doesn't see that bloody face staring back at him, crying out with a moaning sound, *Why? Why didn't you stay and help me?* He would give twenty years of his life to go back and change the way things went down that day.

Stricken with the reality of a life devoid of any true meaning, he hangs his head in utter shame. He feels weak, emasculated, and worthlessness. How could anyone ever love him if they knew what lived inside?

In an attempt to assuage the guilt, he reasons that maybe the man was a deadbeat who did nothing but cause pain and suffering wherever he went. Maybe he actually did the world a favor by taking him out. But deep in the recesses of his soul, he knew better. He knew he took out a good man that day, a family man. Deep down, he knew.

Jeremy shakes his head violently, knocking the demons loose from their perch and forcing them back down into the pit. Realizing his glass is empty, he's sure that's the problem.

Pouring another drink, he settles onto the couch and clicks the play button. A thick slice of steak mingles with the bitterness of the scotch, bringing a sense of satisfaction. His secret is safe, he tells himself reassuringly. There were no witnesses, no one around for miles. No chance of anyone knowing about that horrible day. He'll just have to find a way to live with the demons it left behind.

Draining the last of his second or third scotch, he's not quite sure, he scoots back and feels something hard poke into his leg. Reaching down, he pulls a small hairbrush that had fallen between the cushions of the couch. It must belong to either Jesse or Tina. His thoughts drift to his bride of nearly a year now.

They met one afternoon shortly after her husband was killed. She liked to walk in the same park where he ate his lunch every afternoon. It was the only part of his weekday that gave him even the slightest degree of solace. His job at the federal building was filled with tension and stress. Anyone who knew what he did for a living avoided him, and the people he worked with weren't much better. He felt shunned and unappreciated on all sides, realizing what a miserable place in life he had found. He thought surely there's got to be more to life than this.

The only real friend he had was a guy named Fred, who worked with him several years ago. Fred had a way of making people feel special, relaxed, and *centered.* Nervous taxpayers, struggling with complicated tax matters came into the office frustrated and angry.

After a few minutes with Fred, they soon discovered a friendly man who was willing to help them iron out their problems.

He'd known a few others like Fred over the years, but not many.

Fred lived in Ohio now, and they occasionally contacted each other by phone or email. At one time they entertained the idea of starting a computer software company together, but neither was in a position to branch out into something that risky with such a volatile economy.

When he met Tina, he saw in her a kindred spirit. Reserved and quiet, with eyes that held mystery, he was intrigued.

A pretty woman of only thirty-five with elegantly high cheekbones in a heart-shaped face, she was a natural beauty. Petite and attractive, he was surprised to find her without a mate. He never saw her walking with anyone or a ring on her finger. He sensed fresh emotional wounds resonating from her, sure she had lost a soul mate. He figured time would do its magic and eventually bring the smile back to her pretty face.

It had been five years since his divorce and he'd become lonely for the company of a woman. Day after day, he and Tina waved to each other as she passed by the picnic bench where he sat alone with his meal. One day, she came over and sat across from him, and thus began a friendship. This became a part of their daily routine, and before long she was bringing him home to meet her teenage daughter.

Although he was married before, they never got around to having children. That was one thing he always felt was missing from his life. He wasn't sure what kind of a father he would make, but decided he would very much like the chance to find out, maybe. Images of his father's violent temper were never very far away. If he ever had a child, he had a front row example of how not to be.

Tina's daughter turned out to be a stunningly beautiful girl. Her most prominent feature was her incredibly piercing pale blue eyes. They were the color of the sea, set against olive skin and dark hair that hung just past her shoulders. She had a sweet way about her, too, not the usual mouthy adolescent typical of her age.

The second thing he noticed was her extremely protective nature. Early on, he realized the girl was more in charge of the home than the mother. Following the news of her husband's death, Tina fell into a deep depression, like what she was experiencing again. His insides cringed when he saw the vacant look in her eyes, feeling once again like the helpless little boy at his father's mercy. She had been such a pretty thing when they married and his head spun thinking how much her physical appearance had changed. Her skin hung on her bones, as if she had morphed directly into old age overnight. Maybe this new doctor would be of some help.

He also knew that he had to keep his demons corralled, or they would destroy them both.

All of these thoughts came together in his mind while holding the brush. It felt unusually warm in his hand and seemed to change slightly in color. Taking his attention away from the screen as it flickered a couple of times, he notices his hand begins to change color with the brush. Sitting forward, his full attention is now on the brush as a warm wave of electrical current wraps around it. Startled, he jumps and drops the brush to the floor. Blinking, he tries to make sense of what he just saw. Staring at the brush as though it were a snake curled at his feet, he pulls his legs quickly up onto the couch.

Staring at it a moment longer, he carefully reaches down and gives the brush a nudge with the remote control. Nothing. Slowly, he carefully picks it back up again, looking at it from all angles.

"What the …" he says, turning it over in his hand again, unable to see anything out of the ordinary.

Shaking his head, he tosses it to the other side of the couch, making a mental note to never purchase this particular brand of scotch again.

Grabbing the remote, he sees the movie going through the opening credits and slices off another bite of steak, forcing the strange incident from his mind. Just as he's about to put the juicy bite into his mouth, a floorboard creaks behind him. He hits the pause button on the DVD player and draws his attention to the reflection in the glass cabinet door directly in front of him.

With each step, the rage builds. So many thoughts are racing through my mind, but all of them come to a screeching halt when my foot finds a loose board. The noise from the TV goes silent and both of us see my reflection in the glass at the same time. Slowly he turns around, a look of confusion or anger washes over him, I'm not sure which. Then his complexion goes pale as the blood drains from his face. After a moment of staring at each other in the darkness, he seems to realize the intruder is not an adult.

With a shaky voice, he says with visible relief, "Hey, kid, you just scared me to death! I think you must have the wrong house, son." When I don't move or back down the look of concern returns.

Slowly he stands up, holding his hands out in front of him. Showing me his palms, he says very deliberately, "Hey, kid, just take whatever you want. There's no need for anybody to get hurt."

Suddenly a look of recognition crosses his face. An uncertain smile forms as he says, "You're one of Jesse's friends, right? I saw you this afternoon on the porch." When he sees no reaction from me, the somber look returns and he says, "We don't have anything of value, if that's what you're thinking."

My chest is heaving so hard I feel like I might black out. I've got to get a hold of myself, but the little bit I've managed to hang onto is quickly slipping away.

"I'm not here to rob you!" I scream. I must look totally insane by the terrified look on his face. I don't care, all I want are answers. "You killed my father, you bastard!"

He's standing in front of me with his hands up, not having moved since he stood up. With a look of confusion and terror, he says, "Son, I think you have me confused with someone else. I've never killed anyone in my life. Just calm down and I'm sure we can work this out."

"You shot a deer that smashed into my dad's truck, then he wrecked. You didn't even bother to help him," I yell, pulling the bat across my chest like a rifle. I grip it tightly and feel my fingers dig into the cold aluminum.

Time stands still as we stare at each other. It feels as if all the air has been sucked out of the room. The walls and furniture disappear into the background, the light from the TV fades away, and the only thing left in the world is just the two of us, alone. His face loses what color it had as he starts to stutter something, but it sounds like gibberish. His eyes blink rapidly, and without warning, he vomits on the floor. He wipes his chin and staggers to the table. I follow him, the bat still across my chest.

He's talking incoherently then out of his delirium, he says, "How did you know? Oh God, what have I done?"

"You killed my father," I say again, a little quieter this time.

He looks at me with wild, tormented eyes, tears streaming down his face as he sobs, "I thought that buck was going down!" shaking his fist in the empty air between us. "I didn't realize there was a road! I tried to warn your father but it was too late." His eyes grow wide as he says, "After he lost control of his truck and crashed into that ravine, I just panicked and didn't know what to do," dropping his head to his chest, covering his face with his hands.

Suddenly, like a crouched lion, he reaches out and grabs my shirt. Startled, I try to pull away but he yanks harder. Pulling my face close to his, he says in a panicked tirade as vomit drips from his stubbly chin, "Son, you've got to believe me, I didn't mean to kill your dad. It was a freak accident! I didn't know there was a road!"

Disgusted, I shove him off of me. He loses his hold and falls to the floor in a crumpled heap.

"Don't you dare call me son. The one who is supposed to call me that is dead because of you!"

He rolls onto his back and looks up at me. Smeared with his own vomit, reeking of alcohol and sweat, tears streaming down his face, he's a pathetic sight. For an instant I almost feel sorry for the poor slob, except for the fact he's the reason my dad is dead. That one terrible thought drives away any kind of compassion I might otherwise feel.

Lightning flashes across the sky so violently it rattles the windows, but the storm's fury is no match for mine. I raise the bat over my head and prepare to bring it down. Then I look into his face and see … resignation. He doesn't even put up an arm to block the blow or try to talk me out of it. I think he really wants me to end it all.

The bat comes down towards this pathetic wretch of a human being with all the force I can muster. The chair beside him explodes across the room and comes to rest upside down next to the couch. He covers his head and stifles a sniveling cry. Lifting the bat over my head again, a sudden memory springs forth from a time long ago. In the image, my dad is holding my hand and looking down at me as we walk together to the boat behind my grandparents' house. The day is bright and clear, a perfect day for fishing.

As we come to the side of the boat, my dad kneels down and says to me, "Jason, I'm glad God gave you to me and your mom. You make us proud every day." Dad told me things like that all the time. He always wanted me to believe in myself even if the world didn't.

I stop dead in my tracks as a thought begins shouting in my head. Would this be something that would make him proud? Is this the way he would want his son to avenge his death? I blink my eyes, struggling as these tortured thoughts fight each other for control. Am I really in this man's house, ready to pulverize him? Is this how the rest of my life will play out, angry and vengeful, hating myself and everyone around me?

An unexpected calmness settles in, and suddenly the reality of the situation falls on me with the force of an avalanche. Here I am, standing over a man with a baseball bat, ready to crush his skull. Blinking my eyes rapidly, I suddenly find myself overcome with a greater torrent of emotions than I ever knew existed.

Quickly I throw the bat as hard I can and watch it fly end over end across the room. A muffled thunk reports from the other side as it lodges deep inside the wall. Without warning or permission, I begin to cry.

Jeremy slowly lowers his arms from his head and turns to look at the bat poking out of the far wall, then at me. Slowly he stands up, the two of us facing each other, neither having any idea what to say or do next. Then suddenly he's grabbing my shirt again.

Stumbling backward, all I want to do is get out of here and forget this night ever happened. Twisting and turning I try to break free, but he holds on to me like a gator. I lean over and wiggle out of my shirt as he continues to yank, tearing my shirt completely off.

Suddenly free, I smash into the table and tumble over it and fall off the other side. The window is open, and the nearest exit I can see. I get back on my feet and dive blindly through the screen, landing hard on my back, thinking of nothing but getting away.

I jump to my feet, and in one quick motion I start running as fast as I can. I don't hear the lightning crashing all around me or feel the rain pelting against my skin. Nothing registers except my desperate need to get as far away as fast as I can.

I turn down the path that leads to the woods just over the ridge. I look over my shoulder to see if he is chasing me and see no one. Running deeper into the woods, the area around the spring comes into view. I turn to head home but stumble over a clump of tall grass, which causes me to crash hard to the ground and start sliding down a steep embankment. I hit a patch of thick grass and try to grab hold, but it slips through my wet hands. I manage to slow my descent by digging in my heels, but it doesn't last long, and I quickly pick up speed. Feet first, I continue down the slippery path, saplings and saw grass whipping past me as I rocket down the incline. At any moment I expect to collide full force into a tree or rock.

To my collective horror, I see an end to the embankment and nothing past it. How could this be? Have I reached the bottom of the world? With no way to stop, I brace myself to plunge into the abyss.

Suddenly the slope disappears and I find myself freefalling. I want desperately to close my eyes, but I'm too terrified.

Below me, I see something taking shape. Forcing myself to look down I see an indistinct form becoming more organized and defined. The outer edges solidify as an enormous hole expands directly below me.

My arms and legs flail helplessly as I fall closer to the hole. Suddenly I find myself inside, and am shocked to discover it is cool and dark. As I rocket downward, the tunnel twists and turns but somehow I manage to stay in the center, never coming close to the edge. I'm riding on a cushion of cool air, bringing the hair on my body alive with static electricity.

Beyond the transparent tunnel walls, deep space fills the growing void. As I continue to gain speed, colors appear all around the walls. Disorganized fragments move in and out, pulled by some mysterious force. Shapes emerge as large pieces turn, guided by a mysterious invisible hand. After a while, clear images appear from the arranged pieces.

I see soldiers wearing uniforms from hundreds of years ago, like we see in our history books. They are fighting and killing one another in terrible ways. Children are screaming in the background as they flee from the fighting with their mothers.

As this image fades away another takes its place. This time I see giant walls being built by people wearing strange clothing. Their hair is long and stringy, faces gaunt and rugged. Many wagons filled with wood and rocks are being pulled by donkeys and mules. Women carrying large jars of water on their head and wearing long colorful dresses mingle with the wagons.

Eventually these images also fade away as others take their place. A man's face appears; he's standing in front of a large crowd. He's talking into huge microphones like politicians do, but I can't understand any of his words.

People in the crowd are silently cheering and shaking their fists into the air. The man remains calm, looking confident and self-assured. The people are waving flags of a design I don't recognize.

As the tunnel continues to spiral, the images disappear completely. I begin to smell flowers and hear birds singing, and sense the presence of water close by. My speed has slowed down over the last few minutes, how or why, I don't know. For the first time, light filters through the translucent tunnel walls, bathing me in a soft glow. Looking down, I find myself falling into a blanket of fine mist. Like sailing through a cloud, I am enveloped by cool wet air as I speed downward. As the mist begins to dissipate, I see a small opening and then a canopy of trees appear directly below me. To my great relief, I see the most beautiful thing I could imagine, a big body of water. I'm directly above a giant lake!

Off in the distance, I see an enormous waterfall surrounded by mountains. Everywhere I look, the ground is covered with all kinds of flowers.

Rocketing toward that small opening, I did something I haven't done in a long time—I prayed. I prayed for deep water. I prayed for no floating objects hovering below the surface. Oh God, I'm too young to die!

I angle my legs downward and hold my arms close to my body. The tree's outstretched branches pass harmlessly by as I fall helplessly through them. Large animals look up and see me falling from the sky and launch from the edge of the water in a full gallop, dirt and grass flying from their pounding hooves. At the last possible moment, I close my eyes and hold my breath, preparing as best I can for impact.

With an enormous rush, I slam hard into the water, jarring every bone in my body. I rocket down, piercing deep into the water, until I can descend no further. My feet touch the soft bottom as I feel loose sand mingle between my toes. It is only then I realize I have finally stopped falling.

Carefully, I open my eyes to see the crystal clear underwater world I've landed in. Fuzzy outlines of brightly colored fish circle the perimeter, completely unfazed by my presence. Before I can form another thought, the coldness and need for oxygen direct my thoughts toward the surface.

I'm unable to move very fast at first, but I push aside the pain and shove off the bottom. Sunlight filters through the trees from above, streaming its way down into the water all around me.

I pull myself harder toward the surface, watching the bubbles trail just above my face. As sunlight dances all around, it reminds me of our dives in the Keys. I wish Dad or Uncle Wyatt were here, they would know what to do. *Just a few more feet,* I keep telling myself.

With a rush, I break through, feeling fresh cool air greet me. After coughing and spewing a little, I take my first real breath. Air has never tasted so good. Guess I managed to survive after all, but where am I? Treading water for a couple of minutes, I try to get my bearings.

Looking at the world around me, I realize this is not a lake, but an enormous spring. It must be a hundred feet across. Looking down, it figures to be a good forty feet deep and crystal clear. The bottom is covered with white sand that glistens and ripples as the sun's rays touch it.

The whole place is surrounded by a very dense forest. Looking up at the canopy I just passed through, I feel my heart catch in my throat. I know that canopy. This is the same one that hangs over the spring back home! The flowers are all in the same places, the same colors, like Christmas trees decorated with lights. How can this be?

Totally confused, I look around for anything else familiar. Flowers of every variety are everywhere, each one like they just opened, still fresh and moist. Hummingbirds and butterflies of the most unusual colors and patterns flitter from flower to flower, completely oblivious to my presence.

All around a strange, creeping ivy covers every square inch of the ground. I swim to the nearest side and feel the familiar grit of sand between my toes. I walk on shaky legs to the edge of the ivy.

Getting a better look, I notice it is nothing like the stuff at home. Its dark-green leaves are shaped like four-leaf clovers and etched in thin lines of gold. Reaching over, I pluck one and gently roll it around in my fingers. It feels like an ordinary leaf, soft and supple, but the colors are just incredible.

Peering across the spring, I spot a place far in the back where the water churns in a familiar circular pattern. Several streams flow into the woods, probably leading to a river.

Lying flat on my back on the soft ivy, I breathe deep, filling my lungs with the rich aroma. A faint tickle in the back of my brain raises the warning of touching plants I don't recognize. I got into poison ivy once, a lesson I will never forget. So far nothing feels weird or itchy, so maybe I'll get lucky.

The plants actually remind me of my grandma's garden during the spring, only more so. Then I notice something is missing: bugs, mosquitoes primarily. I should be surrounded by now, but have yet to see or feel a single one. Checking out my legs and arms, I brush around looking for ticks or fleas, another critter that keeps the great outdoors interesting, but find none.

Looking at the canopy of trees again, I see no trace of the tunnel that brought me here, just a great big blue sky above.

The cuts on my back and legs are beginning to burn as my skin dries. Grimacing, I stand up slowly, my legs still weak from the shock of the long drop. I reach around to examine the scratches on my shoulders, but they don't appear to be anything to be concerned about. To a country kid, scratches and scrapes are as much a part of the life as green grass and fresh air.

In the distance, I spot the waterfall I saw right before hitting the water. Reaching up, I rub the back of my head. It's still sore after hitting the water so hard, and I expect to find a giant goose egg but discover only a small knot.

Walking to a nearby clearing, a soft flutter draws my attention to the dense forest just beyond. From behind a wide magnolia covered with snowy-white blossoms, an enormous butterfly emerges. The wings are so large they could cover an entire dinner plate. It's the most brilliant shade of blue I have ever seen. The edges are traced with a deeper blue, highlighted with tiny white diamonds. After this one appears, another floats down, and another, and another.

Then different kinds of butterflies—some as big as crows, others as small as yellow jackets—appear in every size and color. Suddenly, the space above me is a gigantic fluttering rainbow, surrounding me on all sides. They move as one, like a living magic carpet. I stand in awe as they hover all around, flittering joyously. Only inches away now, they dance effortlessly, enveloping me in their delightful dance.

Slowly I bring my hand up and reach carefully toward the wall of wings in front of me. They swirl around my hand until a pretty little auburn one separates from the crowd and lights on my finger. I pull my hand closer for a better look as it turns round and round, flexing its wings, revealing an elaborate maze of white and gold patchwork underneath. I hold my breath, not believing any of this is actually happening. It crawls up my hand and comes to rest on my forearm, where it looks at me with an intelligence I never knew existed in such a small creature. We stare at each other for several moments before it lifts into the air, brushing across my cheek as it joins the others.

The butterflies stay with me a few more minutes and then spiral upward toward the trees, dissipating into the sky, each going their own separate way. I watch in amazement as the sky above me returns to powder blue again.

Then, from somewhere deep inside the forest, someone calls my name.

CHAPTER TEN

Frantically, I look around but see no one. Wait a minute … I know that voice. Jumping to my feet I look carefully into the forest, peering through the trees. Someone has got to be out there.

My body shivers as a cool breeze rustles through the forest, bringing the quiet leaves to life. A million different thoughts race through my mind, each one demanding an answer, but the one screaming above them all is, *Am I dead*?

I hit the water so hard, what if I cracked my skull? I mean, how do we know when we're actually dead? I've heard stories of people who had died and walked around like they always did, but nobody could see or hear them. What if that's what happened to me?

The old familiar anxiety weaves its way into my thoughts, chasing off any kind of peace that was here just a moment ago. Icy fingers of dread tighten around my chest as breathing becomes shallow and ragged. I hunch over to catch my breath as fear, like a tidal wave, washes over me.

Once again, the voice calls my name, this time more urgently. Forcing myself to calm down, I close my eyes, imagining Jake and

Sam here with me. A degree of calmness settles in as I see their faces in my mind. Jake would no doubt have something clever to say and Sam would probably smack me on the back of the head for acting like such a dork. Slowly the panic and anxiety slither away as I concentrate on familiar things instead of the fear.

Images of heaven dance through my mind as I try to recall what they taught us in Sunday School when I was a kid. What if this really is heaven? Then where are the angels, God, The Pearly Gates, and St. Peter? Is that who is calling my name?

Wait a minute, if this is heaven, maybe Dad is here!

I run around to the other side of the spring, darting into the trees beyond and see a ... plateau? How did I not notice this before? We're definitely not in Florida anymore.

Finding a foothold, I begin climbing, and within a half hour, reach the flat surface at the top and gasp at the scene before me.

I see a tall mountain range, the tops silvery white with snow, surrounding everything as far as I can see. Below, a deep valley is split by a river that branches off like a giant's fingers. In between, open meadows are covered in a blanket of flowers and soft green grass, spreading all the way to the foot of the mountains. Roaming in great herds, hundreds or maybe thousands of animals frolic and graze on the meadows. None seem to be wary or on guard; instead, they play together perfectly at peace. It's like something out of a storybook.

The enormity of this place is beyond anything I knew existed. In every direction the scene expands dramatically from horizon to horizon. I ask myself again, *Where have I landed*?

Standing close to the edge, I listen for the voice, but all is quiet. Maybe it's waiting for me to answer back, so I take a deep breath and holler, "Helloooo." I wait, but hear nothing. Again I call, but this time more direct. "Dad, I'm here!" Silence is my only response.

There have been times in my life when I've felt lonely, especially after Dad died, but there have always been other people around I could go to. Here, no one is around except the mysterious voice that has since grown silent.

That same creepy feeling comes back from my dream when I was trapped inside that old school. Is this another one of my crazy dreams? It feels too real to be a dream, too concrete. Reaching down, I run my hand over the rocky surface and feel the small pebbles roll under my fingers.

Dejected, I climb back down the plateau and walk to where I was lying just a moment before, the impression of my body still fresh. Images of Mom and Mary wandering the woods, searching for me drift through my mind. Sam, Trey, and Tommy are probably there too, poking and prodding every nook and cranny for any sign of me. Mom has already lost her husband, and now her son, too? What kind of God allows that kind of misery?

Overwhelmed, I collapse to the ground. My knees buckle under the reality that has crashed down on top of me. Burying my face in my hands, I try in vain to hold back the tears.

"Jason."

I jerk my head up quickly. Slowly I wipe my face, feeling the dampness on my hands. Pushing myself up, I sit upright on the soft ivy and look around more carefully this time, but see no one. It is only then I notice several openings in the woods that I missed before.

A swirl of something soft and fluid, like a dewy early morning mist, flows from a thick shrub. The mist becomes denser until it takes on a life of its own, vibrating and shimmering in a hypnotic, seductive dance.

Within the mist, small bundles of light emerge and slowly begin to separate. The bright colorful marbles break apart and hover around the opening of one of the paths. Intrigued, I creep forward for a better look, my desperate situation all but forgotten.

As I move toward the bush, the mist quietly dissipates into the air. The twinkling balls of light hang suspended in the cool air, free of the shroud of fog, revealing giant fireflies the size of golf balls. They swarm and dive, emanating elaborate patterns of light that blend together like a stirred rainbow.

I watch the colorful serenade, feeling more peaceful than I've ever felt in my life. The soft light summons a primordial yearning to become a part of it.

The swarm starts moving into the forest and I follow. They lead me into the woods through a thick forest of pines, oaks, and hickories. Every so often, enormous flowering dogwood and orchid trees dangle their foliage over the narrow passage, each flower a different color. I've never seen anything like this.

I keep following the flow of light and discover a well-worn path that cuts through the dense undergrowth. Birds call and chirp above in the tall canopy as I make my way deeper into the forest.

A rustling of leaves from behind gets my attention, the trance momentarily broken. I turn to see what it might be. A flash of something darts behind a bush, quiet as a mouse. I stare at the bush for a moment, but the leaves are too thick to see anything. Waiting a moment longer, I decide it must have been my imagination and continue on.

The bugs patiently hover in the same position since I stopped and are now making a soft humming sound. Forgetting about the bush, I walk into the rainbow as we continue on our journey.

As we wind along the path, a rustling of leaves stops me again. This time I just stand still.

Carefully and methodically, I turn my head ever so slowly then let the rest of me follow. At first I don't see anything and then a figure begins to materialize from the pattern of leaves. Something furry and orange with a long bushy tail stands about twenty feet away. A small fox stands so still it could be stuffed. If not for the movement of its long whiskers, I would probably never have seen it at all. Crouched down low, it looks ready to run. Neither of us makes a move or a sound as we check each other out. Realizing this little guy is probably just curious, I take a step toward him but he darts into the forest. So much for that. Disappointed, I turn back to the fireflies.

As we continue on our journey, the path suddenly makes a sharp ascent as we move up the side of a mountain. I always considered myself to be in pretty decent shape, but before long I'm winded and begin lagging behind. The fireflies slow in response, keeping the same short distance between us.

From the side, I hear the leaves moving once again and can't help but smile as I catch the little fox out of the corner of my eye. This time I don't bother stopping.

As my legs grow weary, I ignore the need to rest and keep trudging along, anxious to get to where they are taking me.

After we hike for what must have been over an hour, I finally see an opening in the side of the mountain appear just above the path. Flickering shadows of light dance around the entrance of a cave as the sweet smell of a hickory fire drifts by. The fireflies settle onto a nearby tree and go no further. I guess we've reached our destination.

With trepidation I approach, not sure what to expect. After a few more steps, I am finally able to peek inside. My eyes spring open wide at what I see. Inside this insignificant little opening spreads a cave so enormous I can scarcely comprehend its size. An entire football stadium could easily fit inside.

The light from the fire extends much further than it should, bathing the cave in a soft, mellow glow so warm and inviting that I almost miss the music coming from somewhere deep inside. Instruments of every description come together as one in a massive symphony. It sounds like dozens of different songs playing at the same time, but instead of chaos, it's the most beautiful thing I have ever heard. Soft melodies and loud choruses mingle like they were born to be soul mates.

From above, a twinkle gets my attention, and that's when I notice them. Millions and millions of stones embedded everywhere. Huge deposits of fluorite, rubies, emerald, celestite, amethyst, sapphire, calcite, and diamonds are scattered all over the ceiling and sides of the cave. I learned to identify these stones when I was in the fifth grade and they made such an impression that I never forgot them, or our teacher.

Mrs. Lovensby was an awesome lady who made our science lessons come alive. Every week we did hands-on experiments that opened a whole new world for me.

She never wore a stitch of makeup, not even lipstick, and talked to us like we were real people, not a bunch of dumb kids she was stuck with all day. I rank her right up there with Mr. Collins and Mrs. Langston because she made it clear we were her priority. Each of us was special to her, even me and Jake, but not in the way we were used to.

Mom referred to her as pleasantly plump, or full-figured. We didn't care what she looked like; she was just cool. We worked extra hard in her class, not because we had to, but because she made us want to. That was one of the few bright spots in all my years in school.

As the jewels twinkle and shine by the light of the fire, I'm so overwhelmed I almost forget that I am most likely dead.

Deep shivers rock me back to reality as the word *dead* sinks in like a lead weight. Dread seeps into my bones, sapping the last remnants of my strength.

Right in the middle of my pity party, I hear the voice call my name again, close by this time, and nearly jump out of my skin. Right there in front of me sits an old Indian resting by the fire. He looks up at me and smiles. So caught up in the splendor of this place, I almost stepped on him.

Long gray braids decorated with small ribbons hang over his shoulders. He's wearing a tan leather vest and pants, like the kind they wore in old Westerns. His vest is covered with all kinds of small, colorful jewels that sparkle in the firelight, like the ones embedded in the rock. Maybe that's where they came from. His dark brown eyes emanate warmth and kindness.

Behind him, I become aware of something else I didn't notice until now—books, so many I could never count, sitting on heavy wooden shelves. The wood is so highly polished it shines like a mirror.

Meticulous designs along the front and sides of the bookshelves carved into the grain are detailed beyond anything I've ever seen. I can't imagine the amount of work required to create these. They extend back as far as I can see. It figures a dude like me that can't even read gets dropped into some cosmic library. Somebody out there sure has a wacky sense of humor.

"Hello there, Jason, come on in, sit by the fire and get warm," he says like an old friend, as the music quietly fades into the background.

Not even attempting to hide my astonishment, I say, "You! You are the voice I've heard my whole life!" Smiling, he nods his head. We stare at each other a long moment, then, in a tone that betrays my fear, I ask, "Who are you, and how do you know my name?"

He smiles softly and says, "I go by many names, but you can call me Egahi. Please don't be frightened, I am here to help."

I creep a little closer, my feet having a mind of their own.

He continues talking like he does this kind of thing every day. "You have a sister that is nine years old named Mary, who loves animals. She just rescued a little mockingbird from your cat Sylvester, and named him Marley. Good name," he says with an approving nod.

"You and your cousin Sam like to think you share not only the same birthday, but the same soul as well." He winks and says, "I really like that one."

He sits up a little straighter and continues picking apart my life, sparing no details. "Your best friend Jake has cerebral palsy and is the bravest guy you know. He carries his considerable burden with unusual grace. Throughout your entire life, he will remain one of your most positive influences."

"Your mom is a widow and works long hours as a pharmacy tech since your dad died a year ago. She is looking for a second job to help cover the many expenses. Your grandparents help out financially as well as emotionally to keep your little family afloat." He hesitates a moment, looking at me with kind, soft eyes and says, "Need I continue?"

He pats the blanket next to him and looks at me expectantly. Taking deliberate steps, I make my way around the fire and slowly sit down next to him. After a moment, I find my voice and say, "Did I die? Is this heaven?"

He doesn't answer right away. Instead, he says, "First things first. You must be thirsty after that long hike." He reaches beside him and hands me a large wooden mug. I take the cup slowly from his hand and give it a sniff, then a tiny swig. It tastes like water all right. Feeling the raw pull of thirst deep inside my throat, I guzzle the rest.

A smile crosses his weathered face as he says, "Would you like some more?" Satisfied, I shake my head, hand the mug back and say, "No thanks."

"Good, then let's get on with your questions. First of all, do not worry, you are not dead. Indeed, you are very much alive." He looks around at the cave and reverently says, "And this wonderful place, this beautiful paradise, is about as close to heaven as one can get."

Blinking rapidly as my brain absorbs this revelation, I close my eyes, trying to keep my breathing under control.

Okay, so I'm not dead, but not far from heaven, either. Seems the more I learn, the less I understand, which up to this point has been my life story.

Frustrated, I ask, "How do you know so much about me?"

He extends his hand, and reluctantly I take it. He feels real enough. His skin is warm, like real flesh, muscle, and bone. I don't think a ghost would feel this way. The ones I've seen I've never actually touched, but they never looked this solid.

With a thoughtful, mellow voice he says, "I am your guide, sent by God to help you along your journey. I know you have heard me speak to you from time to time while feeling the vibrations of those in need of healing." He slowly rubs his hands together then gently folds them onto his lap again. I feel my face flush as he taps into even the most carefully guarded places of my deep secrets.

Like plucking the words from my brain, he says, "It's all right, Jason, I understand how you feel. It's actually quite normal to feel the way you do. The others who share this gift also felt the same way at some point in their lives."

I sit up straighter, pushing all other thoughts away. "You mean there are others who can … do what I do?"

"Yes, Jason, there are many others. Some have already completed their mission on Earth and have moved on. Others are fulfilling their time right now, while others have yet to be born. You will eventually find each other at the appointed time.

"Together, you will help many to heal. Over time, you will understand that the crux of human affliction is a manifestation of several things. The most prevalent is the unfortunate matter of unresolved anger and bitterness. Holding onto old hurts and grievances is a continual battle inside the human heart. The root of what ails most of mankind is an unforgiving heart." He shakes his head sadly, like it's painful to say the words.

"Another reason people fall ill is because the human body was created to be a holy temple, a sacred place. It must be cared for and treated with respect. Many have silenced the inner voice that guides them, but with your special gift, you will help those who wander aimlessly to find their path again."

Confused, I feel my eyes grow wide. "Me? I'm supposed to show people how to do all that stuff? How am I supposed to do that when I don't even know myself?" I ask, exasperated.

"That's why you are here, Jason. I will help teach you these things."

A little calmer now, I try to relax and let it sink in. A soft glow from the entrance of the cave gets my attention as one of the lightning bugs hovers low. I point to it and say, "What are those things that brought me here?"

He looks to the entrance of the cave and says, "Ah, those are heart-songs, Jason. If you recall, there were several paths you could have chosen, but the heart-songs led you to the right one. Their sole purpose is to illuminate the path to help you find your destiny. You were wise to follow.

"With the right perspective, you can find them in your world as well, but they cannot be seen with the human eye," he says, wagging a finger between us. He places a hand on his stomach and says, "They are felt deep inside. When you are on the right path, your soul joyfully sings in peaceful delight, no matter your circumstance."

He closes his eyes and breathes deeply of the rich fragrance from the fire. He looks at me again and says, "Did you notice how they enticed and delighted you?"

I nod my head.

Then he turns toward me, his face taking on a more serious countenance and says, "Jason, you have been brought here so we can have the chance to talk face to face, man to man, if you will."

"Okay, that works," I say, when nothing else comes to mind.

He continues, "You were selected before birth to become a healer. You have already used some of your ability to help your little sister and the little brother of the one you call Butthead," he says with a chuckle.

Lifting my eyebrows I say, "You know about that, too?"

"Yes, I do. Like I said, there is nothing about you I don't know." He repositions slightly and says, "Son, we realize you are struggling with the loss of your father and the difficulties you have in school."

Looking around, thinking I missed something, I say, "We? I don't see anyone here but you and me. Wait, do you mean those ghosts that I see sometimes?"

Nodding his head, he says, "Yes, that's who I'm talking about."

"Who are they? Are they angels, ghosts or what?"

"As for the beings you have encountered on Earth, most are angels, God's personal messengers. Others are spirits of those who have already crossed over into Heaven, free to move about where ever they wish, like the angels do."

"The beings you have encountered so far have been peaceful and benevolent, and their mission is to assist humans on their journey. But you will occasionally be visited by others, who are not kind. They are interested only in creating confusion, chaos, inflicting pain and suffering—anything they can do to detract humans from their path and sabotage their mission, which causes frustration and anger. These negative feelings produce dark energy, which they feed on. The more they can generate, the more they consume, becoming stronger, creating a vicious cycle that is difficult to break. You will recognize these beings by their unique vibrations; they are much different from the ones you have encountered so far."

I interrupt and say with a smirk, "Yeah, I haven't seen any red suits, pointy horns, or pitchforks."

He laughs and says, "I would expect not, except maybe on Halloween. They are seldom that direct. Instead, they cleverly hide inside the things humans desire most. Many healers like you have learned to identify them already. The feeling of impending danger, eternal darkness, confusion, anxiety, and fear are their trademarks, and can be felt no matter how they may appear. Others come with very subtle vibrations, which require deeper insight to identify. These are the most dangerous, for they burrow in slowly, digging deep roots that are nearly impossible to uproot. They usually begin with small things, slipping in here and there. Before long, little things lead to bigger ones, and the line between right and wrong becomes so obscured, it is no longer even recognized. That is why it is important to identify them before they have a chance to take hold."

"So we always have to be on guard against these punks," I say with a bit of attitude.

A sad smile creases his face as he says, "Temptation and freedom of choice are an integral part in the development of character on your Earthly walk."

Without a trace of humor, I say, "Wonderful." This makes him chuckle.

More questions arise in my mind. "Why am I the only one who can see them, and why do they disappear when other people show up?"

"They do not disappear Jason, they are still there. Your attention just shifts back to your Earthly realm when someone else enters that space. When you are alone with your thoughts, your mind naturally drifts to other realms, since that is where it feels most comfortable."

Sitting up straighter, I say with surprise, "Other realms, you mean like other dimensions?"

"Yes, realms are very similar to dimensions, and the universe has many of them. Certain individuals have the gift of seeing beyond. They have sight into other dimensions."

Shaking my head, I say slowly, "So I have this ability to see things that belong in other places."

"Yes, exactly," he says enthusiastically, like I finally get it.

"Any other questions?"

I have at least a million, but I decide to pick one of the more bizarre ones, and ask, "What about those weird pictures I saw on the way here?"

He takes another deep breath and says, "What you saw were images of what has transpired on Earth, and others that have yet to take place. You entered a space in time that stands still, where all things take place at once, so time, as you know it, simply ceased to exist."

Hmmm, I remember Sam talking something about that once. My head hurts trying to keep up.

Getting back to the issue at hand, he continues, "One of your tasks as a healer is to not allow the evil ones to fulfill their purpose, much like you did with Bryce."

Raising my eyebrows, I say, "You know about that, too?"

"Like I said before, Jason, I know everything about you. On that day you decided to overcome your fear and claim victory over the forces that have kept you shackled. That was a very brave and liberating moment, my son." His eye catches a twinkle from the fire as he adds, "Just listen to how well your words flow now."

I feel pride swell in my chest. My face grows warm as a smile tugs at the corner of my mouth. After a moment, I ask, "So if I'm supposed to be so 'blessed' with this other dimensional, x-ray vision stuff, then why can't I do simple things, like read?"

He smiles at me like my dad used to and says, "Jason, your mind is brilliant, it just learns differently. I will teach you ways that are more agreeable with your unique design and channel your energy in a more positive way instead of working against it. Up until now, anxiety has greatly interfered with the processes necessary for you to filter information properly. It gets disorganized and lost, which then creates more anxiety."

That sounds exactly like what I have been going through and it angers me to think there was a way to have avoided all of the grief and humiliation. All the frustration and anger I've kept carefully controlled and locked away in the deep recesses of my mind pound at the door, demanding to be reckoned with.

Like everything else, he seems to know my angry thoughts and says with a small frown, "Jason, I know these are troubling subjects for you right now, and I will help you to understand why they have been necessary. It is important for you to move on, so your mission on Earth will be fulfilled."

With a smirk, I say, "I have a mission, like *Mission Impossible*?" I say sarcastically.

He finds this funny and laughs. I didn't mean it to be funny. This dude, or whatever he is, needs to get this over with already. Tell me what I need to know and let me get back home.

On the other hand, this might be another insane dream I'm swept away in. This *Twilight Zone* guru might be concocted from one of my nighttime escapades. There's no way anyone could know all the stuff he knows. If he really does know everything about me, then he's aware that I'm no scholar. Even working hard, I barely pass any of my classes. Why would he want someone like me to do something important and brainy like heal people? Why not choose somebody smart, like Sam?

Finally, I say louder than necessary, "I can't even read the books we have at school. I concentrate so hard on trying to make out the words that I forget what the sentences mean. How am I supposed to be a healer if I *can't even read*," putting extra emphasis on the last three words.

"You can read if you look at the words in a different way," he says casually, running his hand across some of the larger stones hanging from his vest. "When you were by the spring shortly after arriving here, you didn't even see the other pathways until you fell to your knees, right?"

I think about it for a second and say, "Yeah, so?"

"Well, until you changed your perspective, they were obscured from sight, correct?"

"That's right."

"Sometimes we must change our point of view in order to see what is right before us. Concentrating on the problem will never fix anything. We must focus on the solution, not what blocks it."

He picks up a book from the other side of him and places it on my lap.

Things were going pretty well up until then. I travel into a whole different dimension, maybe millions of miles from home, only to have a stupid book dropped in my lap. If it weren't for bad luck, I wouldn't have any at all.

Reluctantly, I look down at the object of my deepest source of frustration, and for once in my life, feel a strange connection to it. This particular book appears to be very old; its pages worn thin from many hands. The title says *Huckleberry Finn* by Mark Twain. This is a book we have at school! I recall Mrs. Langston reading a portion of it to us as I sat mesmerized. The way she made the words come to life inside my mind was like magic. A whole movie traipsed behind my eyes as she read. I would give anything to read like that.

He gently places a hand on my shoulder and says, "Open the book, son." Taking a deep breath, I place my hand on the cover and feel a tingling beneath my palms. My fingers settle somewhere in the middle and I open it. Looking down, I expect to see the familiar gibberish, but that's not what happens at all. I can't believe what I am seeing! The words are just words. The letters don't dance around, trade places or turn upside down! I look up at him in astonishment and say, "Are you some kind of magician or wizard? What have you done with this book? Why can't I see it like this at home?"

"Jason, you are in the place of Enlightenment and Understanding," he says reverently. "Some of the greatest thinkers, philosophers, poets, and leaders of all time have come here for their inspiration and guidance."

I think back to all the struggles I've faced; not able to read, stuttering, the incessant fog that shrouds my brain, bullied for years by idiots like Bryce, and worst of all, the death of my dad.

Like a tornado that blasts through without warning, I become furious. Furious at all the rotten deals in my life, and knowing this guy has known about them all along but did nothing to stop them. I feel my face grow red as blistering anger surges through my veins. Roughly putting the book down, I stand up quickly without taking my eyes off him.

With biting rage, I say, "Okay, if you're so smart and know all this stuff about me, then why didn't God make me better? Why do I have to work so hard in school just to barely squeak by while idiots like Bryce have it so good?"

Pointing to where I think Earth might be, I say, "And why does my grandfather have to suffer so much with arthritis, and how come my best friend is crippled? What did they ever do to deserve that?" Disdainfully, I spit, "What kind of God puts kids in wheelchairs?"

Wiping the hot tears from my face with the back of my hand I kneel down, and only inches from his face, yell, "Why did my dad have to die?"

His peaceful expression remains the same as he looks into my eyes with deep compassion. Not once did he say a word or attempt to defend himself during my rampage. In fact, he never appeared the least bit flustered. He just sat silently while I pitched my little fit, like we were talking about the weather or something.

After venting all that pent-up anger and hostility, exhaustion overwhelms me as I struggle to stay on my feet. Giving into its effect, I flop back down on the mat, angry at the tears that will not stop. Burying my face in my hands, tears course down my chin and onto my lap. He places his hand on my back like he completely understands. After a minute or two, I pull myself together enough to sit back up. I wipe my face with my hands, sniffle a couple of times, and then look up at him with watery eyes.

He offers me a cup of something warm to drink from a tray next to him. It smells like hot chocolate, but I'm too upset to eat or drink anything right now.

He rubs my back and says, "Son, you haven't had anything to eat in quite some time. You need to relax and take some sustenance. Please, try some," as he brings it closer.

Without a word, I take it. Then he brings out a plate of sliced fruit and cheese and places it on my lap. I pick up an apple wedge and bite into it. I can't recall a time when an apple tasted so good. The cheese is soft and white, but not like the kind Mom buys. I carefully lift the hot chocolate close to my face; it's still steaming in the cup and I take a whiff. The smell alone brings to mind happier times. Allowing a little to trickle down my throat, I feel the last vestiges of anger float away with the steam. It feels like it not only nourishes my body, but my soul as well.

Self-consciously, I thank him for the snack and stare at the fire. Suddenly feeling guilty about all the things I just said, I start to say something, but a shuffling sound outside the mouth of the cave draws our attention away. We both look at the opening and see a small black nose appear. It sniffs the air then the rest of the face emerges. It looks like the little fox that followed me here!

Before I can say anything, Egahi says, "Well, hello there, Chester, I was beginning to wonder if you were coming by today."

He reaches down and pats his soft blanket and the little critter bounds inside. He prances in, nimbly leaping over a stack of logs and lands right beside Egahi. His short fuzzy ears go up and down quickly as his bright pink tongue peeks out and licks Egahi's hand.

Egahi reaches over and strokes its soft fur as the fox wags its tail excitedly back and forth.

Egahi seems amused with my expression and says, "Chester, this is my good friend Jason." The fox seems to know what he is saying and looks at me with intelligent, golden eyes. Egahi picks up a big piece of cheese from my plate and holds it between his forefinger and thumb. Chester very gently takes it and quickly devours it then sniffs around on the blanket to make sure he didn't drop any.

I say with excitement, "He followed me here through the woods!"

Egahi laughs and says, "He's a very curious little fellow, but a bit shy at first. Every new arrival gets the same treatment. Once you get to know him, he's really quite friendly."

I start to hold my hand out, but withdraw it, feeling unsure.

Egahi says softly, "Go ahead, Jason, Chester would love to get to know you. It's okay, he won't bite, will you, boy?"

Chester swishes his bushy tail on the rug and nuzzles closer to Egahi. I extend my hand again and watch as he leans across Egahi's lap and gives my hand a careful sniff, just like Trixie does when she meets a stranger. His soft, warm tongue reaches out and licks my fingers. I've never been kissed by a fox before.

Chester gets up and steps over Egahi's lap with the agility of a cat and sits down next to me. I look at Egahi with surprised wonder. Gently, I stroke the soft fur of his back, amazed how incredibly thick and silky it is. Chester yawns, his tongue slipping out of his mouth then lies down next to me, placing his head on my leg. I feel a huge smile cover my face as he settles in. He closes his eyes and opens his mouth just enough for a satisfied lick of his chops.

I've never been this close to a living wild animal before, at least not grown ones anyway. The baby ones we sometimes find in the pasture don't know to be afraid of humans yet, but Chester is plenty old enough. Once again I am in awe of this incredible place. As the three of us enjoy the warmth of the fire, Egahi picks up the conversation where we left off.

"Jason, those are all very good questions, and they deserve an answer. Believe me, you are not the first one to ask. Many before have come demanding them, and many more.

Let's talk about your so-called learning disabilities," he says.

Immediately my anger roars to the surface. "What do you mean 'so called,'" I say defiantly. Chester looks up at me with big eyes. I stroke his head softly, reminding myself to chill. He lays his head back down and snuggles in a little closer.

"Just hear me out before you jump to any conclusions, okay, son?" he says gently, holding his hands up defensively.

I nod my head, letting Chester's calming presence settle inside me. He continues, "I say so-called, because you have been trying to learn in a way that is not compatible with the way your brain is designed. You simply learn in a different way. You learn differently," he says with emphasis.

"Don't worry, though, I am going to teach you how to gain knowledge and understanding in your world. But first, you had to experience what it's like to struggle and feel alienated, to experience pain, frustration, and worthlessness. All of these qualities are an important part of the process in forming the kind of man you are to become. It is known as the gift of suffering, and anyone who wishes to gain wisdom must cross this path."

This stuff sounds heavy, but I keep quiet and let him continue.

"Nothing about you is random or by accident. You are fearfully and wonderfully made, whether you realize it or not." Pointing a finger at me, he says emphatically, "Let me make one thing clear: God makes no mistakes. Every part of you, down to the smallest detail, was specifically designed. You are of great value, a treasure created by God Himself. Even the very hairs of your head are numbered." He clears his throat, places his hands back in his lap and says, "By the way, do you remember how you got your name?"

I think for a minute and say, "Yeah, Mom told me. When I was born, her and Dad had a few names in mind but couldn't decide. She said a little old black cleaning lady came every day to tidy up Mom's room, and afterwards always stayed to talk, which made her feel a lot less lonely. She asked what my name was, and when Mom told her they hadn't quite figured it out yet, a big smile crossed the lady's face. She said, "Ya know, I've always been partial to the name Jason, what do you think about that one?" Mom talked with Dad about it later, and even though it wasn't a name either had considered, they liked the sound of it."

"That's right, Jason, that's just how it happened."

"You mean ... that lady was like an angel or something?"

"Or something, yes. She was very much human, spending her days cheering up those poor lonely and hurting souls in that hospital. Every day she prayed God would place her where she could make a difference in someone's life. She didn't care about titles or status, just about making a difference wherever she could. The treasures she's built up in heaven far outweigh anything she could have acquired on Earth. As a result of her willingness to serve a greater purpose than herself, she helped change many lives.

"Very few things in life are by chance, son. Your name, just like everything else about you, was planned. It was chosen before you were born."

"Wow, that's pretty cool. Why Jason? Does it have some kind of special meaning?"

"It most certainly does. It means 'healer'."

I sit there just staring at him as he speaks, feeling myself pulled away to a different place. His words traverse all space and time, with a meaning so rich I can't possibly absorb it all. I think he knows this, just like he seems to know everything else about me.

"Don't worry about understanding all of this right now, son. Just listen. The older you get, the more you will comprehend."

He pats me on the back and says, "Jason, your gift of suffering will open the way for you to help others. You have been given this amazing opportunity to change many lives. Like all of mankind's gifts, they are meant to be shared and shine like a beacon in the darkness, showing the way for others."

"Your grandpa, the one you call Papa, suffers from rheumatoid arthritis, which has robbed him of his youthfulness and causes great suffering. Tell me, how often do you hear him complain about the rotten hand he was dealt or the pain he has to endure?"

I shake my head and say, "That's the weird thing, Egahi, he never complains. I don't get it. If I were him, I think I would complain a lot. He's never even in a bad mood. I see him at some point every day, and he's always smiling and happy."

"You and your cousins have been blessed with wonderful grandparents."

I nod my head and say, "That's for sure. Papa and Nonnie have lots of grandkids, but they treat each of us like we're the only one they have. My other grandparents are the same way."

Egahi nods in agreement. "What else do you notice about your Papa?"

I never really thought about it like that and feel ashamed. Pushing that away, I say, "People like to be with him and listen to his stories. After a while, I think they forget about their own problems and just concentrate on how good he makes them feel."

Egahi's warm eyes become moist as he says, "Your grandfather's deep and abiding faith was forged through his suffering. To be sure, he has had much adversity in his life, but it has only served to strengthen his resolve. Your grandfather realizes the strong young man of his youth is gone, at least for now. He accepts that fact and moves on. His body has become weaker, especially as the arthritis continues to advance, but he knows in his brokenness, he is allowing God's grace to fully manifest itself. His earthly body will eventually fall away, but his spirit will live on forever. The grandfather you know is not the physical body you see falling apart, but the powerful light he carries within. He will always be remembered for maintaining his faith in the face of great adversity, allowing God's strength and wisdom to shine through.

"Your friend Jake is not so different from your grandfather. He also has had many trials and challenges in his young life."

I nod my head and say, "I noticed that. They both have so much to deal with, but never complain. Jake is always happy and positive, even when I know he's in pain."

As I think about what I have just heard, it starts to make sense in a strange sort of way. Papa and Jake seem strangely content with their situations, almost as if they've made peace with it and decided to let the rest go.

"My grandfather had a normal childhood, but Jake never did. Ever since he was an infant, his body has been broken. Why does God make little kids suffer like that?"

His smile fades a little as he says, "I get asked that a lot. The best way for me to answer that is to ask you something first. What do you notice about the people who are around Jake?"

That's an easy one and I say, "Everybody loves him. He's the most popular guy in our class every year. All the girls want to be near him, and the guys want to be his pal. He has this energy about him I think people are just drawn to."

Egahi nods his head and says, "Before he was born, he made an agreement with God, which involved sacrificing a significant part of himself in order to strengthen others. Jake, and others like him, will lead many to their true calling. Those like Jake help people view life through a different lens."

"Wait a minute," I say, confused. "If Jake made this agreement thing before he came, why didn't he ever tell me about it? We tell each other everything, and I know for sure he never mentioned anything about this."

He nods his head and says, "That's because he has no memory of it in his conscious mind. It remains buried deep down inside his subconscious, where it was placed before he arrived."

"Oh, okay, I guess that makes sense," I say, even though I really have no idea what he is talking about.

Continuing, he says, "Nothing about Jake, or anyone else for that matter, is by accident son. Jake knows deep inside his time on Earth will be used to help others find their way. Like your grandfather, Jake's weakness is a pathway for God's strength. After his journey is complete, all will be restored." He pauses as he looks at me, making sure I understand.

"Jake and your grandfather are the salt shakers of earth. Wherever they go, they leave a little bit of themselves in other people that draws out the goodness inside."

I nod my head as he continues to talk. "The light they carry inside will remain forever, as do all who follow the path God sets before them. Their time on Earth is a short one, which they knew before they were formed."

With a sudden sense of dread, I stammer, "Do you mean they are going to die soon?"

"No, I'm not saying that, son," he says with a reassuring pat on my knee. "They will go at their allotted time. Compared to eternity, their time on Earth is but a vapor."

Nodding my head, I move onto the next question on my long list and ask, "Egahi, why don't I get any weird vibrations when my hands are on Jake? His body is crippled and bent, so why don't I feel anything wrong, like I can with other people?"

"That's because he was destined to walk this path. Therefore, he has no need of healing. This is his destiny."

Confused, I say, "What about Papa? My hands go crazy when I touch him. What's different about him?"

"Papa's situation came about much differently than Jake's. His illness did not manifest itself until he was thirty-eight years old. Because of this, his body remembers the vibrancy of good health, but is unable to restore balance again. His soul knew it was necessary for him to develop this disease in order to complete his mission. He knew someone close to you had to become ill and suffer for your training as a doctor to be complete. God uses all things, *all* things for good for those who love Him, according to His good purpose."

Wait just a minute, now I'm really confused. I blink rapidly and say, "Did I hear you right, that Papa knew I was going to be a doctor?!"

Nodding his head, he looks up at the ceiling for a moment then says, "Yes, that is exactly what I am saying."

My mouth opens, but no words come out.

"Your grandfather 'knew' the moment he saw your grandmother that he was going to marry her. He 'knew' the land he bought was set aside for him and Nonnie to raise their children, and their children's children.

"When your grandfather saw you, he 'knew' you were destined for greatness. He understood the tiny little blip in time that made up his life would be used for the betterment of the world, but would involve tremendous personal sacrifice."

Finding my voice again, I say, "But why wouldn't he at least tell me about it?"

"Actually he was planning on having that conversation with you soon," he says with a smile. "When you and Sam were at their house last Saturday, he almost said something but 'knew' it was not the right time because," I interrupt and say, "Because I was supposed to find out now, today."

Egahi looks at me with pride and says, "You learn quickly."

I feel my shoulders slump a little and mumble, "I wish."

He smiles and says, "That is not so, Jason. You learned to fix engines with ease and efficiency at an early age. You will use that ability in other areas as well."

Will I bring something back with me from this place that will make me smart? Is that what this is all about? Maybe this is how Albert Einstein got started. Egahi seems to know my thoughts and says, "Nothing to worry yourself about, Jason. You will see in time."

Time. What a funny thing it is. It reminds me of Dad's clock and how it stands as a reminder twenty-four times a day he is no longer with us. Maybe this old Indian knows where he is and what really happened to him that day.

"What about my dad?" the words literally leaping out of my mouth.

He pats me on the shoulder and says, "Your dad was called to the next life, Jason, but he didn't die alone, despite what you think." Edging closer he says, "Let me show you something."

Reaching down, he picks up a handful of sand and tosses it into the empty space between us. It hovers in the air, swirling in slow motion then begins to flatten out, and in the center, an image takes shape. Becoming clearer, I realize it is my dad's truck. He is driving down a deserted country road when something on the passenger seat gets his attention and he looks down. I can't tell what it is at first, but then the angle changes, and I see something nestled in the palm of his hand. He rolls them around then opens his palm and there lies two polished green arrowheads. I wonder where he got them.

A shot rings out and suddenly Dad's attention is drawn back to the road. The green arrowheads fall from his hand, bouncing off the steering wheel and disappear out the open window. A deer darts from the nearby trees, right in front of the truck. I wince as the animal collides with the bumper, then I hear the sickening sound of metal against bone reverberating through the cab. Dad tries to control the truck as it swerves this way and that. Glass shatters as the deer vaults onto the windshield, thrashing wildly, eyes wide with terror, then the truck leaves the road. I jump, feeling what Dad felt. Egahi's hand steadies me.

The view changes again. This time I see Dad's truck flipping over and over from high above, but this view looks different from the video on Uncle Vince's laptop. As I watch, four large beings of light swoop down and pull a glowing image of my dad out of the vehicle before it ever reaches the ravine. They let him watch from above as his truck finally comes to rest at the muddy bottom.

Egahi points at one of the glowing figures and says, "Jason, this is your real dad, the light he carried inside of him. As you can see, he was released before his truck ever crashed. The father you know and love is fine. Only the earthly body that housed it is gone. His spirit is in a wonderful place, doing things he needs to do. You will see him again at the appointed time."

I watch as six glowing figures rise into the air then, in the blink of an eye, they rocket into the clouds. I want so much to reach out and grab him, to stop the deer from running into the road, to put him on a different road, anything to change the outcome.

Wait a minute. There should have only been five points of light, not six. I start to ask, but Egahi says, "Not even a sparrow falls that He doesn't notice. The deer will find quiet pastures with more of his kind."

I raise my eyebrows and say, "So animals go to heaven, too?"

"But of course, heaven is filled with them."

I look back as the image fades away, the dirt raining back down to the ground again. I sit there in silence, not sure how to feel; my emotions are all mixed up.

After a moment I manage to pull a few words together and ask, "What kinds of things is he doing? Why couldn't he do them on Earth?"

"I can't share that with you Jason, I'm sorry, but you will find out at the appointed time."

The appointed this, the appointed that. I'm about appointed to death here. Frustrated, I realize this isn't going anywhere and try from a different angle, "What were those two green stones in his hand?"

"They were jade arrowhead heirlooms he found in his grandparents' attic. They have been in the family for generations and he wanted you and Mary to have them. Many years ago, these stones were chosen because of their significance. The arrowhead is a symbol of man's resourcefulness, and jade represents divine unconditional love. They are a reminder of God's good and faithful ways."

I remember Mom and Dad talking about those stones, but I never actually saw them. Anger wells up again as I think about how they were part of the reason Dad wasn't here anymore and say, "If he hadn't been fooling with those stones, he would've seen that deer."

Egahi shakes his head and says, "Not so, Jason. His truck would still have collided with that deer and lost control. It was your father's time. Jeremy, Jesse's stepdad, shot the deer, which caused the deer to run into the path of your dad's truck. Certain forces made sure that the deer and your dad's path crossed that afternoon with exact precision."

My face grows cold as the realization of what he said sinks in. "Wait a minute. You're saying God made sure my dad died that day? Is that what you're saying?"

Calmly, he says, "As I said before, your dad was needed elsewhere, so his departure from Earth had been planned for that exact moment, before he was even born."

I had been taught there was a God out there and that He was on the side of the good guys. They said He loved and cared about us, even though I had my doubts. Yet, here I'm learning today that He is not what they tried to drill into us. What kind of a God makes sure good men die in their prime, leaving behind children to raise? Now I know I was right all along.

Angrily I say, "So, God made sure my father was killed on that old highway so my mom would be a widow and my sister and I would have to grow up without our dad. Is that what you're telling me?" I ask, every word laced with venom.

He sighs deeply, closes his eyes and says softly, "I realize this is a very difficult situation for you, son. You must understand that man's time on earth is designed for him to accomplish his mission. Your father's spirit has been preparing itself for this day since before he was born."

He reaches over and gently places his hand on my chest and says, "Everything that your father was still remains inside of you. Love is the most powerful force in the universe and never goes away. In fact, all of the love he shared with you will continue to be shared with everyone you touch. A single drop in a pond sends out many ripples and all of those ripples multiply in size as they travel, affecting everything in their path.

"God, the Father of all creation, designed this from the very beginning. The tremendous love He has for all of His children transcends throughout eternity. The love you and your dad shared is only a tiny drop of paint on the canvas of your life that will bleed into every part of it. The life God designed for each of us is so much more than you can fathom."

He hesitates a moment, allowing what he said to sink in, then folds his hands onto his lap and says, "It is perfectly natural to be angry and bitter right now, son. These emotions are most certainly justified. Time and maturity will help bring about a better understanding. Difficult times like these come into everyone's life from time to time. They help to shape the kind of person you are to become. Will you collapse and give up, or will you learn to cope and become a stronger, better man?"

He already knows the answer, like he knows everything else about me. I think about what he said, and although I'm still angry, I am forced to acknowledge that the situation is so much bigger than me. He's right: it's my choice whether or not it will ruin me. It's my choice. Just like it's Papa's and Jake's.

More calmly I say, "What about Mr. Hylitt? Why was it important for him to shoot the deer that day instead of doing something else?"

He clears his throat, and with a somber expression says, "Jeremy has not followed his path; instead, he went down one of his own choosing. This event is intended to help him find the right one again, but in order for that to happen, you must find a way to forgive him, Jason. Without forgiveness, he will fail to find his way. We are all connected, like individual strands in an enormous elaborate web. Our lives intersect for a reason. Nothing is by chance."

He pauses a moment and says, "Son, without forgiveness, seeds of bitterness, resentment, and hostility find fertile ground to thrive and become a noxious weed. If they are not rooted out, they will destroy not only you, but also all those around you, including the ones you love the most. They can even affect children many generations down the road by altering the structure of their DNA."

"You mean someone can cause their great grandkids to be sick because they didn't forgive someone?" I ask incredulously.

"Exactly. That is how powerful and dangerous this is, Jason. They have very real and profound consequences. Forgiveness is a most powerful force."

Memories of standing over Mr. Hylitt with a bat ready to smash his skull flash through my mind. Anger once again bubbles in my chest at the terrible memory.

"I know this is much for a fourteen-year-old boy to grasp. Just promise me you will try," he says with a deep sigh.

I look at him for a long time, but say nothing. Right now I can't even begin to know how I feel.

"Maybe when I'm older, but right now I can't make any promises," I say, not disrespectfully or with malice, just honestly.

"You will work on this, Jason, okay?"

Another long silence. "I promise I will try, all right?"

A pleasant smile returns to his face as he says, "I know you will." Then suddenly he changes the subject again and says, "You were also wondering how your grandfather remains so calm and steady after your dad's death." I learned by now not to even bother asking how he knows these things.

"Yeah, that's right."

"Make no mistake, your grandpa misses your dad deeply, but he knows his son is in a wonderful place doing what he needs to do, and that he will see him again one day."

"Remember when your parents told you how your grandpa was injured during the war when he was a young man?" I nod. "Well, he had an experience that changed him. When his heart stopped, he left his body for a period of time. I met him as his spirit wandered."

My head shoots up and I almost shout, "You met my grandpa in Heaven?"

"It wasn't quite Heaven, but yes, I met your grandfather when he was not much older than you."

I remember my parents talking about that, how different he was after he returned home. How much more sensitive and kind he was. Then I say, "Why didn't he ever tell me about that?"

"He was probably waiting until you were a little older."

"Well, what happened? I need to know."

He places a hand on my shoulder and says, "Son, that needs to come from your grandpa. He will share all of this with you soon."

Disappointed, I close my eyes and feel them burn behind my eyelids. From head to toe, exhaustion rolls through me like a steam engine and all I want to do is sleep.

"Son, why don't you lie back and rest a while, you look totally spent." I really want to get back home, but if I could rest for just a few minutes.

He calls Chester to his side with a pat of his hand. The little fox jumps up and vaults beside Egahi, circles a few times then curls up into a tight ball.

The next thing I know, I awake with a start. I don't recognize the cave at first, feeling disoriented and confused. It takes me a minute to get my bearings again. The fire is still burning inside the cave and then it all comes flooding back. A few feet away, Egahi is looking at me with a satisfied, peaceful expression.

"How long have I been asleep?" I say groggily.

"We don't keep track of time here, but it was probably close to three hours where you come from."

Shaking my head, I say, "Mom is really going to be upset. I promised her I wouldn't take off without telling her first."

"Don't worry yourself about it, Jason, I think you are in for a few surprises when you return."

That depends on what kind of surprise he's talking about. I stand up to stretch and walk to the closest bookshelf and scan some of the titles. One on the lower shelf catches my attention. It's not the title, but the author that I notice. It's called *A Time Remembered* by Samuel T. Roberson, Ph.D. That's funny: he has the same name as Sam, including the middle initial. I pull the book off the shelf and open it. The words don't dance around or turn upside down and I feel a smile tug at my lips. I carry the thick book back to the fire and sit down.

Turning to the first chapter, I read a few words at the top of the page. "*And now these three remain: faith, hope and love, but the greatest of these is love.*"

There's no way this is my cousin I chuckle; he would never write a book about love. Love is one of the worst four-letter words in his vocabulary.

Flipping a few pages ahead, names appear: Jesse, Beth, Trey, Jake, and ... *Jason.* A little further, I see Riverview, Nonnie, and Papa. What kind of book is this? I turn a few more pages and see things written down that have already happened. Astonished, I look at Egahi. How could this be? A cold chill trickles up my spine.

Quickly I turn to the page that contains the publishing information. Blood drains from my face as the year 2049 appears. That's ... forty-six years into the future! Egahi places a hand on my shoulder. All I can manage is, "How?"

Gently he says, "Yes, that is your cousin Sam. One day he will write a book about his unusual childhood. If you are wondering why it is here, you should know that all sources of inspiration and enlightenment begin in Heaven and are sent here until their appointed time. Mozart, Beethoven, Bach, Hemingway, and Da Vinci are but a few that received their inspiration from here. Remember from your studies of the scripture, 'on earth as it is in Heaven?'"

Most of my time in church has been spent napping, but that much I remember, although I had no idea what it actually meant.

"It originates in Heaven, and then it comes here until it is manifested on Earth by those who are willing to listen. God speaks often, but not everyone listens."

I look at the book lying in my hands and wonder how much of the future is contained here. My future. Do I really want to know?

Could I flip through and see what will happen? Will my destiny be revealed in these pages? Could I avert some future tragedy with just a brief look?

I gaze into Egahi's face and his eyes tell me he understands my dilemma. Without a word, he places a hand on my shoulder. Slowly I close the book and lay it down between us. He smiles at me and says, "You have chosen wisely."

Then he says, "You are a most fortunate young man to have been blessed with such a large, loving family. Not everyone has the benefit of having so many caring souls to turn to in time of need."

I know he's right. Our family may have its fair share of weirdoes and a mean streak here and there, but for the most part, we are a kind and considerate bunch.

Jumping into my thoughts again, he says, "All of your family members are blessings, son, not just the ones you hold in high esteem. Each one is sent for a specific purpose, for reasons that will become clearer over time."

He sees the smile disappear from my face as he shares this latest newsflash and adds, "One day you will understand this wisdom, Jason, just give it time."

The insatiable need to see my family leaves me famished for their company. Before I say the words, he already knows them.

"It won't be long before you join them."

A strange mixture of emotions floods my mind, wanting to stay here and return home at the same time.

"Will I ever get to come back here again?"

"Of course, Jason, you've already done so many times before, just not so dramatically."

I nod my head, knowing exactly what he is talking about, but it happened on its own. I have no idea how to *make* it happen.

"Your visits will open the way for you to read just like you did here. When you meditate on this place, focus on the spring. The pathway that has been blocked will unlock a channel through a different part of your brain, allowing you to read effortlessly like you do here. Many others have done the same thing. You will become accustomed to this kind of travel, so do not become concerned or worried about how it will happen.

"As you become better at it, you will teach others to do the same. We never tire of those seeking their greatness. I look forward to our visits, Jason." He stands up and motions for me to follow. We walk back down the path that leads to the spring, Chester leading the way. Most of it is downhill, so we travel quickly.

The rich fragrance of flowers greets us along the path before we actually see the spring. The surface of the water is calm, reflecting the beauty all around. It's hard to imagine a more peaceful place. Could Heaven really be better than this?

We walk to the edge as Chester leans in for a quick drink. I peer into the crystal clear water and see a small tunnel forming about five feet down.

Motioning toward it he says, "This will take you back to your world, Jason. A heart-song will lead the way to expedite your trip."

He pats me on the shoulder and says, "Don't be anxious about the future. Remember, God did not give you a spirit of fear, but of power, love, and self-discipline. You will find many helpers along the way to facilitate your life's work as a healer."

He shifts to the other foot and continues, "I know forgiving Jesse's stepdad is going to take some time and work. But be sure to make it a priority in your life, okay, Jason? Forgiveness is a healer for both the giver and the receiver."

I look him in the eye, knowing what he says is true, but actually making it happen is going to be tough. I no longer want to injure Mr. Hylitt, but I'm still a long way from forgiveness.

"I'll work on it, Egahi, okay?" I concede.

Chester dances around our feet with the excitement only an animal can have. I sense he knows I'm about to leave and wants to say good-bye. Kneeling down, I give the little fox a hug as he desperately tries to lick my face. Pulling back, I allow a few of his kisses to touch my cheek, which delights him even more. I can't help but laugh as he begins springing up and down as I get back up.

I say, "Hey, little buddy, take care of the place, okay?" He gives a quick yip and wags his tail even harder.

Standing by Egahi again, I see a flutter of glittery colors rise from behind the tall trees. There, descending between us is the lunar moth from my dream! Its bright colors ripple through the air as it passes from the shadows into the sunlight. Egahi has the most satisfied look on his face as the amazing creature dances around our heads. I hold out my hand and watch as it hovers above for a brief moment, then comes to rest on my wrist. It slowly flexes its wings as it turns round and round. The more I look, the more beautiful it becomes.

Keeping my attention fixed on the moth, I say in amazement, "Its wings aren't damaged. In my dream they were destroyed."

"If you had remained on the path you were on, Jason, they would have become like the moth in your dream. It was sent as a warning, a wake-up call."

A moment later, the moth lifts into the air and flies away in an upward flight of pure delight. We stand there and watch as it disappears back to where it came from. We stare in silence for a moment longer, neither of us saying anything. Then, at the edge of the woods, something begins to stir. I look at Egahi, but he says nothing.

I start to speak, but a voice interrupts me. Every cell in my body reacts. Blood drains from my face as I see my dad step from the woods and walk toward us. The gap shrinks as I stand speechless. I open my mouth, but nothing comes out. I reach for Egahi, but he is no longer there.

"Son, it's okay, it's me. There's no need for you to be anxious or afraid." He's now standing only a few feet away, staring at me with overwhelming pride. I have not blinked once since he appeared, and suddenly my eyes are on fire. I blink several times, expecting the mirage to disappear, but he's still there, smiling at me.

"Jason, son, it's okay." Slowly he reaches his hand up and very deliberately places it on my shoulder. As soon as his skin touches mine, something inside of me snaps. That touch unlocks all the emotion I've kept locked up inside ever since he died. In an instant, the pain, heartache, loneliness, all of it comes out like a tsunami, obliterating everything around it. Hurling myself forward, I feel our bodies collide as I fall into him. His strong arms wrap around my bare back, keeping me from falling to the ground.

Great heaves of anguish rush out as painful sobs force the very last wisps of air from my lungs. His arms stay snug and firm around me, whispering things he used to say to me when I was a little boy. I feel so vulnerable and weak as all my thoughts run together in a mixed-up jumble.

His scent fills my nostrils when I am finally able to breathe again, invading those closed-off places I no longer visit.

Struggling to regain a measure of composure, I force myself to focus. I feel like I'm going to liquefy right where I'm standing.

Dad slowly lowers his arms and steadies me. After all the snot slinging and waterworks, I must be a sight. I have no shirt to wipe my face on, so using my arms and hands I do the best I can. Dad lets out a little laugh and reaches into his pocket and pulls out a cloth hanky. I just stare at it for a moment. He motions for me to take it, but I can't seem to get my arm to move. Without a word, he gently wipes my face like he did when I was a little kid. My body is so numb with shock I hardly feel the cloth on my face.

Dad clears his throat and steps back for a better look. Through puffy eyes, I just stand there and stare. Every detail, down to the little freckles that sprinkle the bridge of his nose are just as they were. One eye is just a hair lower than the other and the thin scar above his left eye when he cut it playing football as a kid is still there. The mix of copper, auburn, and gold in his hair is complete to the very last strand. If this is a replica, then they've done an incredible job.

"Sorry to give you such a scare. I know this must be quite a shock. I'm sure I'd feel the same way if the situation was reversed," he says with a little shrug.

Even his voice is exactly the same, the way he lilted his vowels like no one else I know. Finally, as the last of the muck from my face is wiped away, I try to say something. At first nothing comes out, but I try again and manage to croak one word. "Dad," and feel the tears building again. He rubs my shoulders and says, "It's okay, son, it really is me and I'm fine." He gently takes my hand, places it on his chest and says, "Here, feel my body; it's solid, just like it always was."

I move my fingers around on his bare chest and onto his shoulder, squeezing a little.

He takes my hand and says, "Come with me, Jason, I haven't much time and there are things I need to share with you."

We walk side by side together just like we did when I was little. My eyes are so completely on him that I am oblivious to our surroundings. If he walks off a cliff I wouldn't even know it until we begin falling.

He reaches his arm around my shoulder and smiles at me again and says, "There is a great big wonderful place out there waiting for you, son, and all you have to do is reach out and take it.

"When the time comes and you finish your journey on Earth, you will become a being of light, just like me."

"But you don't look like you are made of light, Dad. You look just like you always did."

He pats his chest with his open palms and says, "I look and feel exactly as I did when I was on Earth. The body you are seeing is precisely like the one I lived in for 39 years, down to the last detail. When we are in Heaven, the only bodies we take with us are the light contained inside, but once we get there we are given new ones."

"Oh, okay, I see," even though I really don't.

He continues, "Those who chose to follow the light, Christ's light, during their time on Earth, will follow it when they leave. Anywhere in the universe we want to go, all we have to do is think of it and instantly we are there.

"Those, on the other hand, who choose to remain in darkness, will find that is their path in the afterlife as well. They will not have a choice where they will go. It is a horrible place, completely devoid of God and none are able to leave. Do you understand what I am saying, son?"

I nod my head.

He nods his head approvingly then his voice takes on a serious tone as he says, "As long as you follow the light, all of the love you shared and the knowledge you acquired are taken with you, but it also remains inside those with whom it was shared. What a phenomenal and powerful thing love is. Don't ever forget that, son."

I nod my head and say, "I won't."

Anxious to know more, I say, "Tell me about what you've been doing since you left us, Dad."

His smile fades a little as he says, "There are things I'm not able to share with you right now and that is one of them. Even if I could, you wouldn't understand. The human mind cannot comprehend these things. I'm sorry, son, but it has to be that way for now."

I shake my head, not from disagreement, just trying to find a place for all of this to sink in. Automatically, I say, "Okay."

He pats me on the shoulder and says, "Nothing to worry yourself over, you will see it all in time."

Then a question pops into my mind, one I have wondered about for a long time, actually for a year now, but never had anyone who could really answer it.

"Dad, you know I can … see things that other people can't."

He nods his head and says, "Yes, son, you've been able to do that ever since you were a little boy."

I stop walking and just stare at him. He knows my next question before it is even asked.

Gently he takes my hands in his and says, "Son, I had to stay away because you needed to know what it's like to grieve. In order to help others, you must first know the kind of special hurt that only comes from losing someone who is dear to you."

Frustrated, I pull my hands away and let them fall to my legs where they slap down hard and say, "More pain? Haven't I suffered enough already? Just how much more of this do I have to take?"

He smiles with that crooked grin and says, "And look how far you've come. I haven't heard a single stutter."

"Yeah, I know, Dad, Mrs. Prainer has been helping me on the weekends," I say without enthusiasm.

He nods his head and says, "Yeah, I know, son. You two make quite a team. No one would ever even know you had a stutter."

I try to suppress a smile but it sneaks out anyway. "I guess I just needed the right motivation is all."

He laughs and says, "I guess so." Then he looks serious again and says, "Remember the night on the boat with Aunt Moe, Uncle Wyatt, and the kids?" I nod my head and recall vividly the dream of him and me sitting together at Grandma and Grandpa's house. "That night I just couldn't stay away any longer. The pull of the ocean and our special times took over and before I knew it, I had invaded your dreams."

I don't even try to hide my surprise and say, "You mean you were really there that night? It wasn't just a dream?" Smiling, he says, "No, son, that wasn't a dream, I paid you a visit. Seeing you growing into a man so fast and watching you having the kind of fun we had when I was still there, I stepped over the threshold and came to sit with my favorite son for a few moments."

"Uh, I'm your only son, Dad."

"Very true, but even if I had fifty sons, you would still be my favorite," he says, gently rubbing my head.

He gets quiet and looks at me a long moment, not saying anything, as if he wants to remember every last detail.

Finally he looks down at the ground, and as he brings his eyes up to meet mine he says, "Son, I understand from your vantage point you feel unjustly punished for crimes you never committed. What you fail to understand is, until someone has endured hardships and struggled with things that come so easily for others, you cannot attain the necessary perspective to help others. By enduring painful and frustrating situations and finding your way through them, you will progress past yourself and see the desperate situation of the world, a world that needs your special talents and abilities. Pain and frustration are the catalysts that hurl us past ourselves and into the place God prepared us to be, helping to ease the suffering of a hurting and dying world. Without these lessons, we would remain self-absorbed, missing our greatest calling. It has been said that if a person succeeds in life without suffering, it is only because someone else suffered without succeeding."

I wonder if this is the reason I feel such a kinship with Jake. I can relate so well with his afflictions because of the ones I've had to endure. Without these challenges, would I fail to see the real struggles he's had to overcome? What if the reason he is so tuned into those around him is because of his condition. Maybe that's what all of this is about.

Dad smiles as though he's read my mind.

"Besides," he says suddenly with a serious look, like he's caught me doing something wrong. Without warning, he slaps me on the shoulder and says, "You're it!" He jumps to his feet and runs fast as a cheetah through the woods, laughing at the top of his lungs.

I stand there stunned, unable to move at first. Without a conscious thought, my feet take flight and I give chase.

Dad has already cleared the first bend by the time I catch up so I have to slow down to make the turn. Up ahead, I see him running flat out, giving a quick glance over his shoulder.

Gunning it for every ounce of speed I can muster, I feel like Beth's horse, Stardust, racing through the pasture. Sweat begins to run down my back and chest as I force my legs to move faster. Man is he quick, dodging trees and jumping over large rocks as he gobbles up the ground in front of him.

I dodge the same trees and hurdle the same rocks, and actually begin to close the gap between us. Encouraged, I push even harder. Dad suddenly disappears and I start to panic, but realize he's only jumped down into a gulley just ahead. I drop down behind him and sprint through the maze of flowers and shrubs.

Up ahead I see the waterfall come into view and hear the thunderous roar of water as it crashes into the calm river below. Dad is slowing down now as he approaches the edge of the canyon and turns around as I close the gap. In the next few steps, I am beside him, both of us bent over, hands on our knees, panting.

As our breathing comes under control again, he says, "You sure have gotten fast since I've been gone."

I smile back and say, "I can do a lot of things faster since you've been gone, Dad."

He laughs and says, "You are more like a man every day, son—a good man, one your mom and I can be proud of."

At that moment, I've never felt more humbled and gratified in my whole life.

He reaches over and swallows me in a tight hug as we struggle to remain calm.

He says, "Jason, I've looked forward to this day for a long time, ever since I left. I've missed you and your mom and Mary so much, but I also know our time apart is for a good reason, and we won't be separated any longer than necessary."

I feel a "good-bye for now" speech coming and try to think of some way to stop it from happening. He quietly pulls away, keeping his hands on my shoulders.

I open my mouth to say something but Dad places a finger to my lips and says, "Son, it has to be this way for right now. I have to return from where I came. Tell Mary I think about her every single day and not a moment goes by that I don't miss her."

I raise my hands to protest, but he ignores them and says, "Tell your mom she is the most wonderful wife a man could ever have and to not close her heart to love. She will find it again one day soon."

I blink as my chest tightens and queasiness grows in my belly. Mom loves another man? That can't be. Dad was her one and only sweetheart. She said so herself. Bile rises in my throat at the thought of another man kissing her, his arms around her where only Dad's are supposed to be.

Then he reaches inside his pocket where he pulls something out and takes my hand. Very gently, he places two green arrowheads in the middle of my palm. I turn them over in my hand and look back up at him in disbelief.

"These are what I went to North Carolina to get. I wanted you and Mary to have them," as he closes my fingers around them.

Opening my hand again, I stare at the pretty pale green stones and ask, "How did you get these? I thought they flew out the window."

He smiles and says, "They did, but I went back and got them. Let them serve as a reminder that you can achieve anything you put your mind to. God has given you a fearless spirit that can conquer anything. He wants to be in every part of your life, son. He will never abandon you. Don't you ever forget that."

I look at him, the stones laying quietly in my hand and say, "I won't, Dad."

Tears brimming in his eyes, he says, "I know, son, I know."

He clears his throat and looks around and says, "Son, listen to Egahi. He is wise beyond the ages. It is time for you to return to him, Jason; he will help you find your way back home."

He places his hand on my head then gives it a short rub and I know what is about to happen. Stifling a sob, I say, "Please don't leave me again."

Tenderly he says, "Son, as long as you know how to love, I will be right there with you. Pay attention and you will see signs of me everywhere. It has to be this way for now. Give my love to Mom and Mary."

Numbly, I nod my head like a good boy. Then, with a quick turn, he disappears into the canyon and is gone. Hot tears spill down my cheeks as I yell, "I will, Dad. I love you!"

I stare at the spot where Dad was standing just a moment before. I close my eyes and try to burn every last detail into my mind.

From behind, Egahi calls my name and I jump. Lifting my wet face to his, I notice we are no longer by the canyon where the waterfall is. Instead, we are in the same spot by the spring where we were before Dad arrived. My mind is a blur.

Egahi places both hands on my shoulders, looks me solidly in the eye and says, "Jason, God has given you some magnificent wings. Stretch them out with confidence and let them catch the current of God's love. They will take you to the most amazing and glorious places."

I am unable to speak for a moment, the emotion of everything catching up with me. Finally I pull it together enough to say, "Thanks for showing me all this stuff today, especially letting me be with my dad again. It was incredible, all of it. I'll never forget this day as long as I live."

With a mischievous grin he says, "You're welcome, Jason. Not too shabby for a *Twilight Zone* guru, huh?" he says with a chuckle.

I feel the tops of my ears turn warm and look at him sideways. "Just a little joke."

He laughs and says, "I thought it was pretty good! I just love a good sense of humor."

He pats me on the shoulder and says, "I look forward to seeing you again soon. Just close your eyes and let your mind come back here. We'll have some more wonderful moments, I promise."

"I can only imagine."

As we wander closer to the spring, I say, "Egahi, just how far did I travel to get here?"

"Oh, you have gone a tremendous distance, but not in the way in which you think. You have traveled not out, but inward, deep inside to the place where many realms overlap. This is where the Kingdom of God resides," placing a hand on my bare chest.

Stunned, I say, "You're kidding! How can that be?"

"With God, all things are possible. Nothing is outside of His ability."

I just shake my head in amazement and say, "I always thought Heaven was a real place, like at the end of the universe or something."

His dark eyes twinkle as he leans closer and says, "Actually, Jason, it is in both places. It is a real place beyond the stars and also deep inside of you."

Now I'm really confused.

"How can that be?"

He places a hand on my shoulder and says, "How do I explain a handful of fish and a few loaves of bread feeding thousands with basketfuls left over? How do I explain a man four days dead being brought back to life? Or sight restored to the blind and the cripple able to walk again? These are but a few of His deep and mysterious ways. We just have to understand it as best we can, and let our faith fill in the rest."

I guess God wouldn't be much of a God if He could be so easily explained, and let it go at that.

"It gives me a lot to think about, that's for sure." I squeeze the arrowheads and say, "Thanks, Egahi, for everything."

"You are most welcome, my dear boy."

Then he takes a step back, squares his shoulders and says, "God wants you to be fearless, Jason, because He has redeemed you; He has summoned you by name and made you His. Now go and share this wonderful gift of yours with the world."

I look at him confidently and say, "Yes sir."

He shakes my hand again, says goodbye and walks back down the path. I look at the arrowheads one more time and shove them deep into my pocket where they will be safe.

As I turn to go, a nagging thought stops me. Looking back at Egahi as he walks away, I wonder where he really came from. What are his other names? He never told me what they were, and I wonder ... is it possible? Mom says The Holy Ghost is the voice that speaks to us. Without stopping, he turns and smiles at me, and I hear his familiar voice whisper, "Very good, my boy, I always knew you were smart."

With a little wave, he disappears down the path and is gone. I feel my face flush as the realization of what happened sinks in. Mom was right after all.

The air around me vibrates as a heart-song drifts in and hovers above then moves toward the water. It drops in dramatically as blue and gold hues shimmer just below the surface. Taking one more look around, I draw in a deep breath and jump in. The water is colder than I remember and I shiver as it envelops me. The heart-song drifts close and instantly the water warms up. It circles me two or three times then darts into the tunnel. I kick hard and feel a powerful flow of water draw me in.

The tunnel is wide and well lit by the heart-song, and surprisingly, I feel no fear, only elation. Ripples of jagged stone line the sides, but the strong current keeps me centered and moving forward. The bug stays just in front of me, careful not to get too far ahead. I try not to think about running out of air, but the thought nibbles at the edges of my consciousness, yet I am not afraid. Ahead, I see a trickle of light just as my lungs begin to ache.

I swim harder as the heart-song makes a sharp bend to the left, then straight up. Light filters through brightly now as it bounces off the sides and floor of the tunnel. I surge forward, ready to be out of here and back home. Blurry trees take shape as I angle upward. Now I can see blue sky beyond the trees as my arms and legs begin to grow weak. My chest feels like it is on fire as I concentrate on the light above. When my arms feel like they can't move any more, I break through the surface and suck in the delicious sweet air of home. I let out a shout, so elated to be breathing again, that I didn't give a thought to where I have arrived. Clearing the water from my face, I look around and realize I am in the spring—my spring back home! The canopy of flowering vines, the small circle of sky above, all of it exactly as it was. How can this be? I just shake my head and think *Jesse was right, this place is holy.*

I look around for the heart-song but it's not here, nor is the tunnel.

My mind tries to make sense of it all as the questions begin to mount. Did I come here after I left Jesse's place? Maybe I wandered here in the dark after I banged my head and don't remember. The line between reality and fantasy is so skewed, I can't be sure of anything.

There's one thing I know for sure. Jumping to my feet, I race toward home as fast as I can. I don't even know what day it is or how long I've been gone, but I have to see my mom.

When I left here earlier it was storming. The sky looks angry now, but the ground is still dry. Weird.

Rounding the corner, I see my house, and man, what a glorious sight! I can't remember ever being so glad to be home. I open the gate and run through the yard as Trixie jumps from the porch and pounces up on my chest.

"Hey there, ole girl, I'm so glad to see you!" as I get down and hug her tight. She tries to lick my face, wagging her tail so hard we almost fall over.

I stand up and finish the walk to the back door with her by my side. I look around for Uncle Vince's truck but don't see it. Walking into the kitchen, I bask in all that is familiar.

I never really noticed the little everyday things that make our house a home, like the clicking of the icemaker as it dumps ice, the fragrant cinnamon candles Mom keeps out, or even the broken clock on the stove that blinks the same time over and over. Every last detail is seared into my mind, each one attached to a special memory. Then Mom walks into the room and suddenly everything else falls away.

I want to wrap myself around her and never let go. For a brief moment I wonder if she's angry about what I did, but right now I don't even care.

Quickly I move across the room and pull her into me in the kind of hug we haven't shared in years. The kind where there are no pretenses, nothing held back, completely and totally vulnerable. At first she is a little stunned and hesitates a moment before returning the hug. Once she does, it's the most wonderful feeling in the world. We stand like that for a while, the warmth from our bodies moving together as one, just like when I was little. Then I feel her arms move across the cuts and scrapes on my bare back.

She pulls back quickly and looks at me with a startled expression and says, "Honey, are you okay? What is that all over your back?" Then she looks at my legs and notices more scrapes. The smile on her face disappears as she says, "Jason, what's happened to you?"

She turns me around to get a better look and I feel her hands move around like she's connecting the dots.

To be honest, I had forgotten all about them. None of them are serious, only superficial stuff kids living in the country get all the time. I look down at my legs and say, "I fell down."

She comes around in front of me again, puts her hands on the top of her head and says, "How many times, honey? You look like you've been drug behind Beth's horse, for crying out loud!"

A suspicious look crosses her face, and then very seriously she says, "Is something wrong, Jason?"

I smile broadly and say, "No, Mom, really, I'm okay."

She looks at me for a long time studying me and then starts to relax.

"You're sure?" she asks again.

"Really, Mom, I'm okay, it's just been a crazy day, one you wouldn't believe. I guess it's all just catching up with me."

Does she know what happened at Jesse's house? Maybe word hasn't made it yet. Surely she found the laptop and pictures scattered all over the couch. Why hasn't she mentioned it? I thought she would be furious.

She lets out a snort and says, "We've had lots of those crazy days lately."

I think to myself, *not even close.*

Suddenly I feel the need to tell her everything. I lead her to the dining room table where we sit down. She looks at me expectantly as I begin to talk.

"I think I had another weird dream, Mom. It was like I went to another dimension or something. I must've fallen asleep when I was lying down by the spring. This old Indian told me I was meant to be a healer and explained a lot of things I've always wondered about."

"Sounds like an interesting dream, honey. Sometimes dreams seem so real don't they?"

I nod.

"You've always had unusual dreams, ever since you were old enough to tell me about them," she says with a soft smile.

Looking into her eyes, pleading for her to understand, I simply say, "He also showed me …things … like how Dad died." The blood drains from her face as she tries to swallow. Instinctively I reach over and squeeze her hand.

"If this is too much ..."

Shaking her head, she brushes the hair out of her face and looks at me intently and says, "It's okay, Jason, I want you to tell me all about it. I need to know."

Nodding my head, understanding just how she feels, I say, "I dreamed I landed in this giant spring and found my way to a cave where this old Indian named Egahi lived," my hands trying to paint a visual picture as I speak. "It had huge deposits of rubies and emeralds and other stuff all over the ceiling and it was filled with this beautiful music. It had an enormous library in it and Egahi showed me what happened … that day." She stares at me like nothing could drag her away.

"Like we already know, a deer ran out in front of his truck." She nods her head. "After they collided, he lost control of his truck and crashed into a ravine." She nods her head again. I leave out the part about Jesse's stepdad.

"Right before the truck crashed, four angels pulled Dad's spirit out and they all floated in the air. Then, like a lightning bolt, they shot off into the sky," clapping my hands together then shooting one up high.

Mom looks kind of queasy, but hangs in there.

Rubbing her arm, I say, "And Mom, right before I left, Dad showed up." A blank stare is all that registers. Her body goes into autopilot as her eyes mechanically blink a couple of times. Then she seems to get upset when I don't say anything more.

With irritation she says, "And?"

"Are you sure you want to hear about all this at once, Mom?"

Sitting up straighter now, in a calmer tone, she says, "No, I mean yes, son, it's okay, I need to do this. Please, keep going."

I nod my head and say, "Dad looked exactly like he did right before, you know. Everything about him was just like we remember, his hair, skin, teeth, everything. Even the way he lilted his vowels, remember?"

A small smile creases her lips.

I continue, "We talked and even played a game of tag just like we used to." Looking down at my lap, I look back up at her and say, "Mom, Dad is in a great place and he's happy. He wants all of us to be happy, too, and not worry about him." Not quite sure how to say the next part, I just do the best I can. "And Mom, he doesn't want you to be alone. He says there's another man out there waiting for you, and to not be afraid to love again."

The tears that have been threatening to burst through the dam flow down her pretty face in torrents. She doesn't even try to hold them back. She leans into me and I just hold her until the river runs dry.

When she finds her voice again, she sits back up in her seat, straightens her shirt a little self-consciously and gives me a sheepish grin. She pushes away the shower of hair that fell into her face and says, "Son, you have always had the most amazing dreams, but this one I believe is the granddaddy of them all."

"Yeah, I know," I say, glad to get it over with.

She falls back into her chair, rifling her hand through her hair and looks up at the ceiling, letting out a long breath of air. Then she looks at me with teary eyes and says, "That's just amazing, Jason."

She sits back up straight in the chair, brushes her hand through her hair again and says, "I suppose stranger things have happened, but it certainly sounds like this dream of yours tapped into something incredibly profound. Thanks again for sharing it with me." I squeeze her hand and say, "Sure, Mom."

Both of us are spent, emotionally and physically. Sliding my chair back, I stand up straight, careful not to pull too hard on the scrapes beginning to thicken on my back.

"You sure you're okay?" she asks again, a frown tugging at the corners of her mouth.

"Yeah, Mom, I'm fine, just really tired. How about you, are you going to be okay?"

She looks at me for a moment and with a sad smile says, "I think so. I feel better after hearing about your dream. I think it will go a long way in helping us deal with this. I'm really glad you shared it with me. In so many ways you remind me of your dad. Like you, he was wise beyond his years, too."

"Thanks, Mom," I say, rubbing her shoulder, then turn to walk down the hallway, feeling her eyes on me as I go. Then from across the room I hear the familiar tone of Dad's clock ringing in the new hour. Glancing at it, I see it is six o'clock, a ripple distorting the image for just an instant. My mind reels as I hear a truck pull into the driveway and know instinctively who it is. Blood runs cold through my veins as I suddenly realize no time has passed since I left the house this afternoon.

Rushing into the living room, I look where I left the scattered papers, but see no sign of them anywhere. No laptop, no pictures, nothing but our stuff that's been here just as it was.

Running my hands through my hair, I shake my head and wonder what on earth could have happened. The more I think about it, the less I understand, and decide to just leave it at that. I suppose one day we'll figure it all out, but it probably won't be any time soon.

I hear Uncle Vince come into the house and know what's about to happen. My knees grow weak as I make my way to the kitchen to greet them.

After going back upstairs, I enter the bathroom and look at my reflection in the mirror. My blond streaked hair is starting to dry and the cinnamon eyes staring back at me glisten so intensely, they startle me. I close my eyes and shake my head in amazement. That dream seemed so *real.* The cuts and scrapes can be explained when I dove out of the window, so I guess that actually happened, but how do I justify the rest of it?

I reach to the back of my head and feel a knot, probably from hitting the ground so hard. One thing's for sure, I'm too tired to deal with any of this now.

A nice hot shower will feel good and then I'll hit the sack. Everything will look better in the morning.

Peeling out of my shorts, I drop them and watch as they float to the hard tile floor. An unfamiliar tinkling sound rises when they land. Perplexed, I retrieve my damp shorts, wondering what made that sound. Reaching into one of the pockets, I feel nothing. Turning them around, I plunge my hand into the other side and feel two cold hard objects bump against my hand. Wrapping my fingers around them, I carefully draw them out. Swallowing hard, I slowly open my hand and there, nestled in my palm, are two pale-green jade arrowheads. I stare at them in utter disbelief. Looking back at my reflection in the mirror, the face I see staring back at me is almost as white as the ghosts who occasionally drop in for a visit.

CREDITS: FACT AND FICTION

Many of the scenarios in *The Healer Saga—The Gift of Suffering* and *Wings of Redemption*—were developed from real experiences.

~Our Papa suffered from severe rheumatoid arthritis, yet was one of the most joyful people I have ever known. He was deeply passionate about his faith in Jesus Christ and shared his great love of God with people at every opportunity. All four of our grandparents were depicted true to their nature; however, Grandpa Leo's war injury and near-death experience were fictitious.

~My sisters, cousins and I were raised on a large piece of property our grandparents owned. We camped, rode horses, and fished nearly year round. The land encompassed about 140 acres, and actually had two ponds we swam and fished in. One had a diving board, and much of our growing-up years revolved around that one, which later became the foundation of a shopping center. This special land we enjoyed so much as children will remain a vital part of who we are, no matter who stakes ownership.

~I am 49 minutes older than my twin cousin Joy. We were born in the same hospital on the same day and made news in the local paper. They got the pictures reversed, so I was Joy and she was me and, like Jason and Sam, we share the same soul.

~The spring is based on a real one my dad found hidden in the woods.

~I jumped on the back of my uncle's notoriously mean bull as he innocently napped under a tree. Thank God it terrified him so utterly, all he could think to do was run as fast and far away as possible.

~Teenagers lounging naked in the river, except it was the other way around. According to a story my dad shared with us, the teenagers rolled in close to a dad and his young son, staying for an extended chat. The father thought the teenagers were quite friendly, unaware of his predicament. After the kids paddled away, his little boy said he could see his dad's toes. You can figure out the rest.

~I painted my stepbrother Kenny's fingernails bright red while he slept one Saturday night for no particular reason. Waking up late, he rushed getting ready and didn't discover my contribution until he bowed his head in church to pray.

~Sadly, both my stepfather and brother have been gone for quite some time. I loved and admired both of these good men, and I hope they knew that.

~Papa really brought a dead toad to church in his shoe.

~Everything inside the movie theater as Vivian tells off the obnoxious woman is how it actually occurred. The confrontation outside in the parking lot I made up.

~I touched a dolphin as it sped by while diving in the Keys. All accounts of the stories related to diving in the Florida Keys are based on actual events. Watching tailless live lobster heads plunge into the ocean from above, hopelessly trying to reach the safety of the ocean floor. I will never forget this atrocious act of cruelty as long as I live. Thank you, Mom and Dad, for teaching us better.

~The near drowning of a young girl in our dive party after passing out in forty feet of water. Divers from our group beneath saw her motionless shadow drifting on the ocean floor and rescued her.

~I lost control of a moped on a rocky patch of limestone, skinning my face and hands. My companions wanted to rinse my bloodied body at a nearby beach, but I refused for obvious reasons. They called me Shark Bait for the remainder of the trip.

~My Aunt Marianne actually hit dead center bull's-eye with a weapon she never fired until that moment. She proved her point, put the weapon down, and refused to shoot another round.

~I rescued an uninjured baby mocking bird from the jaws of our cat that was later adopted by a wild female cardinal.

~My sister Wendi got her name shortly after her birth from the suggestion of a sweet African-American cleaning lady at the hospital.

~Our cousin Keith's cheek was permanently christened with a smiling dimple after an angry cow rammed him with her horn.

~An uncle that vanished for twenty years, miraculously returning to his brother's house (my grandfather) with his family.

~Our church's live Nativity wasn't nearly as big as the one in the *Wings of Redemption*, but was just as much fun. Miss Kitty, our sweet lovable donkey, cut loose with a "bray" exactly at 7:00 p.m., just as we were set to go. We had no idea how she knew, but she got it right every single time. The only memorable mishap we experienced during my years in the program was the angel's gown taking flight, revealing the big company logo on the lift bucket. I was in a group of angels above the manger scene that learned to sign one of the songs for the deaf members of the audience. They did not know about it beforehand and I will never forget their reaction.

~A visit from a small bird, tracing the initials in flight of a friend who died the night before. Her husband called later that afternoon to inform me of her passing. She had been ill and bedridden for seven years. After my last visit with them at their house, I left in tears. On my way back home I kept saying out loud, "Girl, you are going to be like a little birdie set free from a cage when you leave here." Someone was obviously listening.

~All of Jason's dreams are based on actual ones I've experienced. The only alteration involves the dream on his aunt and uncle's sailboat in the Keys. My grandfather came to visit instead of my father.

~Bryce's father's condition interfering with achieving deep sleep. Brain surgery was recommended, but a chiropractic adjustment resolved the issue.

~The Kapok Tree was a real restaurant located in Clearwater, Florida, that closed its doors for good in 1991. It was a sad day to see this unique landmark disappear, so I pay homage to this special place by keeping the memory of it alive in *Wings of Redemption*.

~Jake walking across the stage to receive his diploma. We witnessed this happen not just once, but twice on the same night. During my cousin Scott's high school graduation, two girls with a condition similar to Jake's did the exact same thing.

~I have had some very unusual experiences with butterflies. The most impressive one involved my healing of rheumatoid arthritis. Shortly after the tragic death of one of our students, a butterfly the same auburn color as the child's gorgeous hair appeared. I placed some nectar beside her in a bottle cap, which she happily drank while I snapped her picture. The butterfly came back a second time on October 5, 2013, quietly announcing my gift of healing. I have been off all medication since December 31, 2013. Lab work performed on October 13, 2015, revealed the arthritis is in remission, without the use of medication. The necklace I am wearing in the picture in the back of the book and on my website was a Christmas gift this child gave me when she was 6 years old. It was broken, and probably found in the trash, but she fixed it good as new with a bright blue barrette. The butterfly perched on my shoulder is the image of the actual one that visited me.

A wild Monarch butterfly climbed up my nephew's face and perched on top of his head. I have photographs chronicling the special visit.

~All animals are based on actual ones we shared our lives with. None of our dogs were very good at herding cows, but were world-class companions. Their love was unconditional and I wouldn't change a thing about any of them. Stardust, Beth's beloved buckskin, came to us in the same way she did in the story. This beautiful young filly was tragically killed in a bizarre accident at a young age, leaving a great void in her absence. By keeping her memory alive in my books, she brings joy and purpose to the lives of the characters, just like she did with us all those years ago. She was a good friend and beautiful spirit and I feel privileged to have shared part of my life with her.

White Socks was a young calf when my cousin "adopted" her. Even from an early age, she honestly had no idea she was a cow and had no desire to hang out with anything that had more than two legs. We always had to be on the lookout for her when crossing the pasture, otherwise she would chase us down and try to crawl onto our laps. This bold and pushy bovine had more personality than most people you will ever meet.

Chester was the name I gave the small wild fox that visited our yard on a regular basis to sample the old bread I threw out for the backyard birds. He joyfully ate that dry old bread with such delight, I instantly fell in love with him. When I began writing my books, I knew he would be Egahi's sweet little companion.

~Egahi means "Light" in the Cherokee language. May God's light shine brightly in our souls, it spills onto everyone around us.

According to my family history, our grandfather, Papa, was part Cherokee Indian, and a major influence in my life. This played heavily in the development of Egahi's character. Ever since a young child, I've envisioned the Holy Spirit as He is depicted in my books. The use of Egahi, and other Indian references, is not intended to be disrespectful or offensive in any manner toward our Native American brothers and sisters.

ACKNOWLEDGEMENTS

The special needs children I have worked with since 2001, including one I met years before I ever considered going into this line of work, inspired this story.

After finding a young teenager riding in the middle of the road in his manual wheelchair, I invited him into my backyard. Thus began a unique and sweet friendship. He dropped in on a regular basis, never accompanied and almost always filthy. Some kids fall through the cracks in the system, and he was one of them. He could have done so much more if given the opportunity. I wish I had been in a better position to help, but I was young and had absolutely no experience with special needs children. I offered what little I had—friendship, an occasional lunch, and a shoulder to lean on. I hope you are in a good place, my friend.

My older cousin Gary was foremost in my mind with the development of Trey. He was one of the most compassionate people I have ever known and would be the first to offer his big beautiful wings to those who had none.

Jason's dad and Uncle Wyatt were primarily drawn from my dad, Bill Giles, and Uncles Phillip VenDitto and Ronnie Frazier. Besides my grandfathers, they are some of the finest men I've ever known.

Dad, you have a special knack for making learning new things so much fun. I didn't fully appreciate how patiently you answered the zillion questions every new adventure brought until I had children of my own. Thank you for your time, energy, and enthusiasm. Those grand adventures we shared instilled in us a lifelong love of learning.

Shortly before our Uncle Ronnie passed away, I wrote a letter to him thanking him for all he had done for us and the great memories he helped to create. My cousins told me how much he appreciated the "book" as he called it, reading it many times. If there is someone in your life you need to thank, do it today, not tomorrow. The love and appreciation we share with each other is one of the most precious gifts we can offer.

Mr. Collins is also based on a combination of real people, as well: Russ Amerling, Howard Ledbetter, Celestino Miranda, Seth Porter, David Phillips, and Keith Luoma. These extraordinary men work diligently in the most creative ways to make a difference in the lives of others every day.

Jason's mom, Aunt Moe, and Aunt Jean were influenced by my own mother, my aunts, and some very special ladies who were always there when we needed them. Thank you, Aunt Norma McInnis, Aunt Effie, and (Aunt) Trudy. The world is such a better place because of you.

Mom, your unshakable faith has been a source of inspiration to anyone lucky enough to know you. Through all the trials and tribulations in life, you never questioned God's love or faithfulness.

Thank you, Clifford and Alicia Thomas and Pat and Bo Exum for your friendship and the awesome mountain getaways we shared in your cabins. I couldn't imagine a better motorcycle gang to hang with. Those mountains gave me important insight into God's great and mysterious ways that enhanced the writing of my books.

Thank you to all of my aunts and uncles for keeping us straight.

Thank you to all of my cousins; I could not imagine my life without you. Each one of you holds a special place in my heart.

Thank you to the incredible folks at Boutwell Chiropractic: Randall and Darrell Boutwell, Beau Thigpen, Debbie See, Triva Duncan, and the rest of the staff. Thanks for keeping us healthy and well adjusted—in more ways than one.

Thanks to my husband Reggie for your weapons expertise in choosing the right equipment for Jeremy.

Thank you to my wonderful stepdad, Ronald Davis, for putting the smile back on Mom's face and graciously providing some hilarious hard-of-hearing stories. We appreciate your good energy and great sense of humor. Thank you to your daughters, my stepsisters Debbie and Donna, for accepting Mom with open arms and embracing my healing story with such conviction.

Thanks to Loretta Healy and The Claffey Printing Company for joyfully making copies of my initial drafts. You are the best!

A special thanks to my editor, Jack Minor, for your timely and much needed advice. Your helpful suggestions made my story flow like it should.

A big thank you to Barbara Tapp for scrutinizing and polishing the final manuscript until it sparkled. We are indebted to our good friend Tommy Gonter for introducing us to this marvelous lady. Thank you Tommy for also designing and building my website; you are a truly a jack of all trades!

Thank you to my great proofreaders: my mom, Sue Davis; my dad, Bill Giles; and good friends Mark and Monica Tikunoff, Steve Kloman, Karin Heise, Teresa Tatum and Dean & Kim Pfennig. I appreciate your time, energy, and friendship more than you know. If any errors slipped through, I bear full responsibility.

Thank you to our accountant Bob Harkrider and your awesome staff: John Demyan, Chris Rodwell, Cathie Goodenough, and Wendy Wiggins, for taking such good care of us.

A big thank-you to Benny Silva, the amazing father of my grandchildren, for your unique artistic talent in designing and preparing the covers of my books for publication. You are one of the most patient people I have ever known. We appreciate all you do.

Thank you, Janice Rehder, for providing the paintings that inspired the finished artwork. You are a rare gem.

Thank you, Byron Williams, for the professional photography you make look so easy. Thank you for your friendship. You and Becky make a great team.

To my grandparents: I thank God every day for you. I will never forget where I came from and the important lessons you instilled in us. You will always be the best part of me.

Thank you to my cousin John for sharing the fascinating stories of your friendship with the Seminole Indians. How fortunate you were to have those great experiences.

Many thanks to our fabulous school nurse at EES, Bobby Sue Schiffhauer, for the medical/technical advice that lends reality to the story. The world has never met a happier nurse.

Thank you, Mrs. Debra Roberts, our lovely and talented speech pathologist at EES. Thank you also to the gifted and beautiful Ms. Marissa Kryger for sharing your knowledge, expertise, and friendship, as well.

Thank you to my co-workers and good friends, Celia Burns and Karin Heise, who threatened to kick my butt if I didn't write a book. I loved our time together and appreciate your guidance and support over the years. Thanks for proofreading the initial and final drafts. I love you like sisters.

Thanks to my sisters Staci and Wendi for your unwavering support. The three of us could not be more different from each other, but God knew what he was doing. He certainly has a sense of humor!

Thank you to a world-class technical adviser, who will remain anonymous. Thanks, also, to our neighbor and good friend for many years, Deputy Mike Barrett and his lovely wife Corinne. Mike was a great help in the scenes involving legal/law enforcement issues. Thank you for allowing me to interrupt your yard work to answer my host of questions.

Thank you to my holistic doctor, Robert Pendergrast, for guiding me down the path that led to true healing.

Thank you to Dr. Ahmed for supporting me even when you thought I was grasping at straws.

Thank you to our lawyer, Frank Allan, and his secretary, Wanda G. Smith, for the helpful and timely legal assistance—you two are lifesavers. Thanks also to Frank's wife, Suzanne, for finding the humorous side to everything.

Thanks to our brilliant tech guy, Jacob Harms, for bailing me out on a number of occasions when my laptop had a mind of its own. You are brilliant.

Thanks to the irrepressible Mrs. Monica Lewis for sharing your hilarious twin pregnancy surprise with us. Your great stories always keep us in stitches. You and all the phenomenal teachers at Blue Ridge, Martinez, and Evans Elementary, along with the great teachers at Evans Middle School, give Mrs. Langston and Mrs. Lovensby their solid character and great love of children.

Thank you to all the extraordinary children I've worked with over the years. You inspire and motivate the rest of us in quiet and gentle ways. You teach us far more about ourselves than we ever imagined.

To the greatest blessings in my life, Emma and Andrew; you are the reason I wrote these books. Until I had children of my own, I had no idea what true love was all about. You both have learned to overcome so much and make us proud every day.

To Matreya, Luca, and Willow: you are my passion and joy. When you came along, I discovered the sweetest part of life had just arrived.

Note: Although the characters of Jake and Jason were inspired by real children, their family situations, personal experiences, medical conditions, and physical qualities were uniquely and wholly their own. All scenarios and situations regarding Jake and Jason are fictitious, constructed entirely from my imagination, bearing no similarities to the children in my care, other than broad generalities. Strict adherence to confidentiality was observed throughout this project.

Many of the scenarios in The Healer Saga: The Gift of Suffering *and* Wings of Redemption, *contain elements of real experiences; however, these books are works of fiction. The characters not specified in the acknowledgement section of these books were derived from fictional sources. None of the remaining characters or personalities were devised from actual people or situations. These are entirely fictitious, and any similarity, implied or otherwise, to persons living or deceased, is purely coincidental.*

Since biblical times, or even before, the role of tax collector has not been popular. The scenarios taking place in The Healer Saga: The Gift of Suffering *and* Wings of Redemption, *involving Federal Tax Agents in any capacity, are entirely fictitious and not intended as a reflection or suggestion of any actual situations or persons working in this field in any regard. Thank you for your hard work and dedication performing a necessary and, oftentimes, tough, thankless job.*

RESOURCES

The wisdom of *The Holy Bible, International Version,* with special consideration of Luke 12:7, Psalms 27:4, 139:14, 16; Jeremiah 33:3; Matthew 25:40; John 3:8, 4:23, 24, Hebrews 3:13; Isaiah 43:1; 1 Corinthians 6:19–20; 2 Corinthians 12:9; Romans 8:28, 10:20; Ephesians 2:13, 4:31,32, 5:8, 5:14–21; Philippians 2:13; The Gospels of Matthew, Mark, Luke and John.

www.irenasendler.org/in-memoriam/ Life in a Jar: The Irena Sendler Project. In memory of Irena Sendlerowa, 1910–2008.

Smithsonian Birds of North America, Fred J Alsop III, copyright DK Publishing 2001.

Please visit my website for more information or to leave a message. I would love to hear from you.

www.thehealersaga.com

God bless you!

Made in the USA
Monee, IL
22 May 2022